PRAISE FOR THE BOOKS BY THE BAY MYSTERIES

"Not only a great read, but a visceral experience. Olivia Limoges's investigation into a friend's murder will have you hearing the waves crash on the North Carolina shore. You might even feel the ocean winds stinging your cheeks. Visit Oyster Bay and you'll long to return again and again."

—Lorna Barrett, *New York Times* bestselling author of the Booktown Mysteries

"Adams's plot is indeed killer, her writing would make her the star of any support group, and her characters . . . are a diverse, intelligent bunch." —*Richmond Times Dispatch*

"I could actually feel the wind on my face, taste the salt of the ocean on my lips, and hear the waves crash upon the beach. *The Last Word* made me laugh, made me think, made me smile, and made me cry. *The Last Word*—in one word—AMAZING!" —*The Best Reviews*

"A very well-written mystery with interesting and surprising characters and a great setting. Readers will feel as if they are in Oyster Bay." —*The Mystery Reader*

"This series is one I hope to follow for a long time, full of fast-paced mysteries, budding romances, and good friends. An excellent combination!"

—*aders Connection*

D0950932

MURDER *in the* MYSTERY SUITE

❧

Ellery Adams

BERKLEY PRIME CRIME
New York

BERKLEY PRIME CRIME
Published by Berkley
An imprint of Penguin Random House LLC
375 Hudson Street, New York, New York 10014

ISBN: 9780425265598

First Edition: August 2014

Printed in the United States of America
9   11   13   15   17   16   14   12   10

Cover illustration by Shane Rebenshied
Cover design by Diana Kolsky
Book design by Tiffany Estreicher

*The Three Graces of Greek Mythology, goddesses
of beauty, mirth, and good cheer, endeavored to
spread joy wherever they went. My Three Graces
are three Loris. This book is for you, ladies:*

*Lori Caswell
Lori Cimino
Lori Gondelman*

A room without books is like a body without a soul.
　　　　　　　　　　　　　　—MARCUS TULLIUS CICERO

WELCOME TO STORYTON HALL

Our staff is here to serve you

Resort Manager—Jane Steward
Butler—Mr. Butterworth
Head Librarian—Mr. Sinclair
Head Chauffeur—Mr. Sterling
Head of Recreation—Mr. Gavin
Head of Housekeeping—Mrs. Pimpernel
Head Chef—Mrs. Hubbard

Select Merchants of Storyton Village

Run for Cover Bookshop—Eloise Alcott
Cheshire Cat Pub—Bob and Betty Carmichael
The Canvas Creamery—Phoebe Doyle
La Grande Dame Clothing Boutique—Mabel Wimberly
Tresses Hair Salon—Violet Osborne
The Pickled Pig Market—the Hogg brothers
Geppetto's Toy Shop—Barnaby Nicholas
The Potter's Shed—Tom Green

ONE

There were books everywhere. Hundreds of books.
Thousands of books. There were books of every size, shape, and color. They lined the walls from floor to ceiling, standing straight and rigid as soldiers on the polished mahogany shelves, the gilt lettering on their worn spines glinting in the soft light, the scent of supple leather and aging paper filling the air.

To Jane Steward, there was no sweeter perfume on earth. Of all the libraries in Storyton Hall, this was her favorite. Unlike the other libraries, which were open to the hotel's paying guests, this was the personal reading room of her great-uncle Aloysius and great-aunt Octavia.

"Are you ready, Sinclair?" Jane mounted the rolling book ladder and looked back over her shoulder.

A small, portly man with a cloud of white hair and ruddy cheeks wrung his hands in agitation. "Oh, Miss Jane. I wish you wouldn't ask me to do this. It doesn't seem prudent."

Jane shrugged. "You heard what Gavin said at our last staff meeting. The greenhouse is in disrepair, the orchard needs pruning, the hedge maze is overgrown, the folly is hidden in brambles, and the roof above the staff quarters is rotting away. I have to come up with funds somehow. Lots of funds. What I need, Sinclair, is inspiration." She held out her arms as if she could embrace every book in the room. "What better place to find it than here?"

"Can't you just shut your eyes, reach out your hand, and choose a volume from the closest shelf?" Sinclair stuck a finger under his collar, loosening his bow tie. Unlike Storyton's other staff members, he didn't wear the hotel's royal blue and gold livery. As the resort's head librarian, he distinguished himself by dressing in tweed suits every day of the year. The only spot of color that appeared on his person came in the form of a striped, spotted, floral, or checkered bow tie. Today's was canary yellow with prim little brown dots.

Jane shook her head at the older gentleman she'd known since childhood. "You know that doesn't work, Sinclair. I have to lose all sense of where I am in the room. The book must choose me, not me, it." She smiled down at him. "Mrs. Pimpernel tells me that the rails have recently been oiled, so you should be able to push me around in circles with ease."

"In squares, you mean." Sinclair sighed in defeat. "Very well, Miss Jane. Kindly hold on."

Grinning like a little girl, Jane gripped the sides of the ladder and closed her eyes. Sinclair pushed on the ladder, hesitantly at first, until Jane encouraged him to go faster, faster.

"Are you quite muddled yet?" he asked after a minute or so.

Jane descended by two rungs but didn't open her eyes. "I think I'm still in the Twentieth-Century American Authors section. If I'm right, we need to keep going."

Sinclair grunted. "It's getting harder and harder to confuse you, Miss Jane. You know where every book in this library is shelved."

"Just a few more spins around the room. Please?"

The ladder began to move again. This time, however, Sinclair stopped and started without warning and changed direction more than once. Eventually, he succeeded in disorientating her.

"Excellent!" Jane exclaimed and reached out her right hand. Her fingertips touched cloth and leather. They traced the embossed letters marching up and down the spines for a few brief seconds before traveling to the next book. "Inspire me," she whispered.

But nothing spoke to her, so she shifted to the left side of the ladder, stretching her arm overhead until her hand brushed against a book that was smaller and shorter than its neighbors. "I believe you have something to tell me," she said and pulled it from the shelf.

Sinclair craned his neck as if he might be able to read the title from his vantage point on the ground. "Which one chose you, Miss Jane?"

"A British mystery," she said, frowning. "But I don't see how—"

At that moment, two boys burst into the room, infusing the air with screams, scuffles, and shouts. The first, who had transformed himself into a knight using a stainless steel salad bowl as a helm and a gray T-shirt covered with silver duct tape as armor, brandished a wooden yardstick. The second boy, who was identical to the first in every way except for his costume, wore a green raincoat. He had the hood pulled up and tied under his chin and he carried two hand rakes. His lips were closed around a New Year's Eve party favor, and every time he exhaled, its multicolored paper tongue would uncurl with a shrill squeak.

"Boys!" Jane called out to no effect. Her sons dashed around chairs and side tables, nearly overturning the coffee table and its collection of paperweights and framed family photos.

Sinclair tried to get between the knight and the dragon.

"Saint George," he said in a voice that rang with authority, though it was no more than a whisper. "Might I suggest that you conquer this terrifying serpent outdoors? Things are likely to get broken in the fierce struggle between man and beast."

The first boy bowed gallantly and pointed his sword at Jane. "Fair maid, I've come to rescue you from your tower."

Jane giggled. "Thank you, Sir Fitz, but I am quite happy up here."

Refusing to be upstaged by his twin brother, the other boy growled and circled around a leather chair and ottoman, a writing desk, and a globe on a stand in order to position himself directly under the ladder. "If you don't give me all of your gold, then I'll eat you!" he snarled and held out his hand rakes.

Doing her best to appear frightened, Jane clutched at her chest. "Please, oh fearsome and powerful dragon. I have no gold. In fact, my castle is falling apart around me. I was just wishing for a fairy godmother to float down and—"

"There aren't any fairies in this story!" the dragon interrupted crossly. "Fairies are for *girls*."

"Yeah," the knight echoed indignantly.

Jane knew she had offended her six-year-old sons, but before she could make amends, her eye fell on the ruler in Fitz's hands and an idea struck her.

"Fitz, Hem, you are my heroes!" she cried, hurrying down the ladder.

The boys exchanged befuddled glances. "We are?" They spoke in unison, as they so often did.

"But I'm supposed to be a monster," Hem objected.

Jane touched his cheek. "And you've both been so convincing that you can go straight to the kitchen and tell Mrs. Hubbard that I've given my permission for you both to have an extra piece of chocolate-dipped shortbread at tea this afternoon."

Their gray eyes grew round with delight, but then Fitz

whispered something in Hem's ear. Pushing back his salad bowl helm, he gave his mother a mournful look. "Mrs. Hubbard won't believe us. She'll tell us that story about the boy who cried wolf again."

"I'll write a note," Jane said. The boys exchanged high fives as she scribbled a few lines on an index card.

"Shall I tuck this under one of your scales, Mr. Dragon?" She shoved the note into the pocket of Hem's raincoat. "Now run along. Sinclair and I have a party to plan."

Sinclair waited for the boys to leave before seating himself at his desk chair. He uncapped a fountain pen and held it over a clean notepad. "A party, Miss Jane?"

Jane flounced in the chair across from him and rubbed her palm over the cover of the small book in her hands. "This is Agatha Christie's *Death on the Nile*."

"Are we having a Halloween party then?" Sinclair asked. "With pharaohs and mummies and such?" He furrowed his shaggy brows. "Did the boys' getups influence your decision?"

"Not just a costume party. Think bigger." Jane hugged the book to her chest with one hand and gestured theatrically with the other. "An entire week of murder and mayhem. We'll have a fancy dress ball and award prizes to those who most closely emulate their favorite fictional detective. Just think," she continued, warming to her idea. "We'll have Hercule Poirot, Sherlock Holmes, Sam Spade, Lord Peter Wimsey, Nick and Nora Charles, Brother Cadfael, Miss Marple, and so on. We'll have readings and skits and teas and banquets. We'll have mystery scavenger hunts and trivia games! Imagine it, Sinclair."

He grimaced. "I'm trying, Miss Jane, but it sounds like an awful lot of hubbub and work. And for what purpose?"

"Money," Jane said simply. "Storyton Hall will be bursting at the seams with paying guests. They'll have the time of their lives and will go home and tell all of their friends how wonderful it was to stay at the nation's only resort catering specifically to readers. We need to let the world know that while we're a place of peace and tranquility, we also offer excitement and adventure."

Sinclair fidgeted with his bow tie again. "Miss Jane, forgive me for saying so, but I believe our guests are interested in three things: comfort, quiet, and good food. I'm not certain they're interested in adventure."

"Our readers aren't sedentary," Jane argued. "I've seen them playing croquet and lawn tennis. I've met them on the hiking and horseback riding trails. I've watched them row across the lake in our little skiffs and walk into Storyton Village. Why wouldn't they enjoy a weekend filled with mystery, glamor, and entertainment?"

The carriage clock on Sinclair's desk chimed three times. "Perhaps you should mention the proposal to your great-aunt and -uncle over tea?"

Jane nodded in agreement. "Brilliant idea. Aunt Octavia is most malleable when she has a plate piled high with scones and lemon cakes. Thank you, Sinclair!" She stood up, walked around the desk, and kissed him lightly on the cheek.

He touched the spot where his skin had turned a rosy shade of pink. "You're welcome, Miss Jane, though I don't think I was of much help."

"You're a librarian," she said on her way out. "To me, that makes you a bigger hero than Saint George, Sir William Wallace, and all of the Knights of the Round Table put together."

"I love my job," Jane heard Sinclair say before she closed the door.

Jane turned in the opposite direction of the main elevator and headed for the staircase at the other end of a long corridor carpeted in a lush crimson. She was accustomed to traveling a different route than the paying guests of Storyton

Hall. Like the rest of the staff, Jane moved noiselessly through a maze of narrow passageways, underground tunnels, dim stairways, attic accesses, and hidden doors in order to be as unobtrusive as possible.

Storyton had fifty bedrooms, eleven of which were on the main floor. And even though Jane's great-aunt and -uncle were in their late seventies, they preferred to remain in their third-story suite of apartments, which included their private library and cozy sitting room, where her aunt liked to spend her evenings reading.

Trotting down a flight of stairs, Jane paused to straighten her skirt before entering the main hallway. Along the wood-paneled walls hung gilt-framed mirrors, brass sconces, and valuable oil paintings in ornate frames. Massive oak doors stood open, inviting guests to while away the hours reading in the Jane Austen Parlor, the Ian Fleming Lounge, the Isak Dinesen Safari Room, the Daphne du Maurier Morning Room, and so on. There was also a Beatrix Potter Playroom for children, but that was located on the basement level as most of the guests preferred not to hear the shrieks and squeals of children when they were trying to lose themselves in a riveting story.

Jane greeted every guest with a hello and a smile though her mind was focused on other things. She made a mental checklist as she walked. *The door handles need polishing. A lightbulb's gone out by the entrance to Shakespeare's Theater. Eliza needs to stop putting goldenrod in the flower vases. There's pollen on all the tables and half the guests are sneezing.*

She'd almost reached the sunporch when the tiny speakers mounted along the crown molding in the main hallway began to play a recording of bells chiming. Jane glanced at her watch. It was exactly three o'clock.

"Oh, it's teatime!" a woman examining an attractive still life of cherry blossoms exclaimed. Taking the book from a man sitting in one of the dozens of wing chairs lining the hall, she gestured for him to get to his feet. "Come on, Bernard! I want to be the first one in today."

Jane knew there was slim chance of that happening. Guests began congregating at the door of the Agatha Christie Tearoom at half past two. Bobbing her head at the eager pair, she walked past the chattering men, women, and children heading to tea and arrived at the back terrace to find her great-aunt and -uncle seated at a round table with the twins. The table was covered with a snowy white cloth, a vase stuffed with pink peonies, and her aunt's Wedgwood tea set.

"There you are, dear!" Aunt Octavia lifted one of her massive arms and waved regally. Octavia was a very large, very formidable woman. She adored food and loathed exercise. As a result, she'd steadily grown in circumference over the decades and showed no predisposition toward changing her habits, much to her doctor's consternation.

As Jane drew closer, she noticed a rotund tuxedo cat nestled on Aunt Octavia's expansive lap. The feline, who often took tea with the family, had arrived at Storyton Hall during a thunderstorm the previous spring. The twins had discovered the tiny, shivering, half-starved kitten in a corner of the garage, and assuming it was female because of its long eyelashes and stunning gold eyes, named the pathetic creature Miss Muffet. The local veterinarian later informed them that not only was Miss Muffet a male, but judging from the size of his paws, was likely to grow into a very large cat. By this time, everyone had gotten used to calling the cat Miss Muffet. The twins insisted the name be altered to preserve the cat's dignity and so Miss Muffet became Muffet Cat.

Muffet Cat had the run of the resort. He came and went as he pleased, darting through doorways between the feet of startled guests and indulgent staff members. During the day, he vacillated between hunting, napping on the sunporch, and begging for treats, but he spent every night with

Aunt Octavia. For half a year, the twins complained that Muffet Cat was a traitor. They claimed they'd rescued him from certain death and he owed them his allegiance, but Muffet Cat merely tolerated them. Aunt Octavia was the center of his feline universe.

"You can't command a cat's affections," Aunt Octavia had explained to the boys. "Muffet Cat prefers the gentler sex. He's a very intelligent animal and knows that he only has to gaze up at a lady with those big yellow eyes and she feels compelled to feed him a tasty morsel or two."

It was true. Muffet Cat had so perfected this plaintive look that he'd gone from an emaciated kitten to a portly cat within a matter of months.

As Jane took a seat at the table, Muffet Cat opened his eyes into slits, licked a dot of cream from his whiskers, and went back to sleep.

"Hello, everyone," Jane said as she put her napkin on her lap. This was the only time during the day in which she would sit in view of the guests. Very few people noticed the Steward family gathering for tea, being far too busy filling their own plates with sandwiches, scones, cookies, and cakes inside the main house.

Fitz plucked her sleeve. "Mom, can I have another lemon cake?" He glanced at his brother. "Hem too?"

"Fitzgerald Steward," Aunt Octavia said in a low growl. "You've already had enough for six boys. So has Hemingway. Let your mother pour herself some tea before you start demanding seconds. And you should say 'may I' not 'can I.'"

Nodding solemnly, Fitz sat up straight in his chair and cleared his throat. Doing his best to sound like an English aristocrat, he said, "Madam, may we please have another cake?"

This time, the question was directed at Aunt Octavia. Before she could answer, Hem piped up in a Cockney accent, "Please, mum. We're ever so 'ungry."

Aunt Octavia burst out laughing and passed the platter

of sweets. "Incorrigible," she said and put a wrinkled hand over Jane's. "Are you going to the village after tea? Mabel called to say that my new dress is ready and I can't wait to see it. Bright fuchsia with sequins and brown leopard spots. Can you imagine?"

Jane could. Her great-aunt wore voluminous house-dresses fashioned from the most exotic prints and the boldest colors available. She ordered bolts of cloth from an assort-ment of catalogs and had Mabel Wimberly, a talented seam-stress who lived in Storyton Village, sew the fabric into a garment she could slip over her head. Each dress had to come complete with several pockets as Aunt Octavia walked with the aid of a rhinestone-studded cane and liked to load her pockets with gum, hard candy, pens, a notepad, book-marks, a nail file, treats for Muffet Cat, and other miscel-lanea. Today, she wore a black and lime zebra-stripe dress and a black sunhat decorated with ostrich feathers.

In marked contrast to Aunt Octavia's flamboyant attire, Uncle Aloysius dressed like the country gentleman he was. His slacks and shirt were perfectly pressed, and he always had a handkerchief peeking from the pocket of his suit. The only deviation from this conservative ensemble was his hat. Aloysius wore his fishing hat, complete with hooks, baits, and flies, all day long. He even wore it to church, and Aunt Octavia was forever reminding him to remove it before the service got under way. Some of the staff whispered that he wore the hat to bed as well, but Jane didn't believe it. After all, several of the hooks looked rather sharp.

"What sandwiches did Mrs. Hubbard make today?" she asked her great-uncle.

He patted his flat stomach. Uncle Aloysius was as tall and slender as his wife was squat and round. He was all points and angles to her curves and rolls. Despite their phys-ical dissimilarities and the passage of multiple decades, the two were still very much in love. Jane's great-uncle liked to tell people that he was on a fifty-five-year honeymoon. "My darling wife will tell you that the egg salad and chive is the best," he said. "I started with the brie, watercress, and walnut." He handed Jane the plate of sandwiches and a pair of silver tongs. "That was lovely, but not as good as the fig and goat cheese."

"In that case, I'll have one of each." Jane helped herself to the diminutive sandwiches. "And a raisin scone." Her gaze alighted on the jar of preserves near Aunt Octavia's elbow. "Is that Mrs. Hubbard's blackberry jam?"

"Yes, and it's magnificent. But don't go looking for the Devonshire cream. Muffet Cat and I ate every last dollop." Her great-aunt sat back in her chair, stroked Muffet Cat's glossy fur, and studied Jane. "You've got a spark about you, my girl. Care to enlighten us as to why you have a skip in your step and a twinkle in your eye?"

Jane told her great-aunt and -uncle about her Murder and Mayhem Week idea.

Uncle Aloysius leaned forward and listened without interruption, nodding from time to time. Instantly bored by the topic, Fitz and Hem scooted back their chairs and resumed their knight and dragon personas by skirmishing a few feet from the table until Aunt Octavia shooed them off.

"Go paint some seashells green," she told Hem. "You can't be a decent dragon without scales. We have an entire bucket of shells in the craft closet."

"What about me?" Fitz asked. "What else do I need to be a knight?"

Aunt Octavia examined him closely. "A proper knight needs a horse. Get a mop and paint a pair of eyes on the handle."

Without another word, the twins sprinted for the basement stairs. Jane saw their sandy heads disappear and grinned. Her aunt had encouraged her to play similar games when she was a child, and it gave her a great deal of satisfaction to see her sons following in her footsteps.

"Imagination is more important than knowledge," was

Aunt Octavia's favorite quote, and she repeated it often. She said it again now and then waved for Jane to continue.

Throughout the interruption, Uncle Aloysius hadn't taken his eyes off Jane. When she'd finished outlining her plan, he rubbed the white whiskers on his chin and gazed out across the wide lawn. "I like your idea, my dear. I like it very much. We can charge our guests a special weekly rate. And by special, I mean higher. We'd have to ask a pretty penny for the additional events because I expect we'll need to hire extra help."

"But do you think it will work?"

"I do indeed. It's quite splendid." He smiled. "In fact, it could be the start of a new tradition. Mystery buffs in October, Western readers in July, fantasy fans for May Day."

"A celebration of romance novels for Valentine's!" Aunt Octavia finished with a sweep of her arm.

Uncle Aloysius grabbed hold of his wife's hand and planted a kiss on her palm. "It's Valentine's Day all year long with you, my love."

Watching her great-aunt and -uncle exchange tender looks, Jane felt a familiar stab of pain. It was during moments like this that she missed her husband most. She'd been a widow for six years and had never been able to think of William Elliot without a pang of sorrow and agony. While her great-uncle and -aunt exchanged whispered endearments, Jane wondered if ten years would be enough time to completely heal the hole in her heart left by her husband's passing.

"Jane? Are you gathering wool?" Aunt Octavia asked.

Shaking off her melancholy, Jane reached for the teapot and poured herself a nice cup of Earl Grey. "I'm afraid I was. Sorry."

"No time for drifting off," Uncle Aloysius said. "There's much to be done to prepare for this Murder and Mayhem Week of yours. And might I say . . ." He paused to collect himself, and Jane knew that he was about to pay her a compliment. Her uncle was always very deliberate when it came to words of praise or criticism. "Your dedication to Storyton Hall does the Steward name proud. I couldn't have asked for a more devoted heir."

Jane thanked him, drank some of her tea, and went into the manor house through the kitchen. She tarried for a moment to tell the staff how delicious the tea service was and then walked down the former servants' passage to her small, cozy office.

Sitting behind her desk, Jane flexed her fingers over her computer keyboard and began to type a list of possible events, meals, and decorating ideas for the Murder and Mayhem Week. Satisfied that Storyton Hall's future guests would have a wide range of activities and dining choices during the mystery week, she set about composing a newsletter announcing the dates and room rates. She made the special events appear even more enticing by inserting colorful stock photos of bubbling champagne glasses, people laughing, and couples dancing at a costume ball. She also included the book covers of popular mystery novels from the past century as well as tantalizing photographs of Storyton's most mouthwatering dinner and dessert buffets.

"They'll come in droves," she said to herself, absurdly pleased by the end result of the newsletter. "Uncle Aloysius is right. If this event is a resounding success, we can add more and more themed events over the course of the year. Then we'll be able to fix this old pile of stones until it's just like it was when crazy Walter Egerton Steward had it dismantled, brick by brick, and shipped across the Atlantic. We'll restore the folly and the hedge maze and the orchards." Her eyes grew glassy and she gazed off into the middle distance. "It'll be as he dreamed it would be. An English estate hidden away in the wilds of the Virginia mountains. An oasis for book lovers. A reader's paradise amid the pines."

She reread the newsletter once more, searching for typos

or grammatical errors and, finding none, saved the document. She then opened a new e-mail message and typed "newsletter recipients" in the address line. It gave her a little thrill to know that thousands of people would soon read about Storyton Hall's first annual Murder and Mayhem Week.

After composing a short e-mail, Jane hit send, releasing her invitation into the world. Within seconds, former guests, future guests, and her newspaper and magazine contacts would catch a glimpse of what promised to be an unforgettable seven days. Tomorrow, she'd order print brochures to be mailed to the people on her contact list who preferred a more old-fashioned form of communication.

I'll have contacted thousands of people by the end of the week, Jane thought happily. *Thousands of potential guests. Thousands of lovely readers.*

Closing the open windows on her screen, Jane found herself staring at one of the book covers she'd used for the newsletter. It was Agatha Christie's *The Body in the Library,* and this version from 1960 featured the silhouette of a woman standing in front of shelves of colorful books. Her hands were raised in an effort to fend off an attacker, but the assailant's hands were almost at her throat. The woman's demise was clearly imminent.

"Yes, I'm sure they're lovely people. Each and every one," Jane murmured firmly. "We'll have no scenes bearing any resemblance to this cover. After all, this is a work of fiction."

TWO

Before riding her bike to the village of Storyton,
Jane stopped by her cottage to change into jeans and a
T-shirt. Most of the ancillary buildings on the resort's property had been built within the last two decades to house the
department heads, but Jane's cottage, which was once the
estate's hunting lodge, was much older. Like the rest of Storyton Hall, it had been dismantled in the 1830s and transported
from its original seat in the English countryside to an isolated valley in western Virginia.

When Jane moved in, the house hadn't been used as a
hunting lodge for years, but there had still been enough
animal heads mounted to the walls to give her the creeps.
Following her husband's death and her acceptance of her
great-aunt and -uncle's offer to take over as resort manager,
Jane had done much to lighten up the lodge's dark, masculine décor. The house was markedly different from what it
had been the day she'd shown up at Storyton Hall, newly
widowed and pregnant. Aunt Octavia and Uncle Aloysius
had welcomed her with open arms and immediately began
grooming her to inherit Mr. Blake's position. Mr. Blake had

run the resort for thirty years and was ready to retire to Florida.

"Fitz! Hem!" Jane called as she opened the door and stepped into the kitchen. She and the boys lived in the back half of the house. Mr. Sterling, the head chauffer, occupied the front half. He had the main entrance and the garages while the Steward family shared three bedrooms, two baths, a kitchen with breakfast nook, and a cozy living room with a fireplace, lots of bookshelves, and a window seat overlooking the orchard. Jane loved their house. Her favorite room in any home was the kitchen, and hers was large, sunlit, merry, and constantly filled with wildflowers, delicious aromas, and commotion.

"We're upstairs!" Hem yelled after such a long pause that Jane knew he and Fitz were up to no good. This was hardly a surprise, seeing as the twins spent most of their time getting into mischief.

"I'm going into the village," she said. "And it's Saturday, which means I owe a certain pair of boys their allowance."

A resounding cheer arose from the top of the stairs and the boys barreled down, leaping from the fourth step from the bottom and landing with loud thuds on the hardwood floor. "Can we go to Geppetto's?" Fitz asked, holding out a dirt-encrusted palm for his earnings.

The twins' hands had been spotless at teatime, but the boys were hopelessly attracted to all things muddy, sticky, gooey, slimy, and grime covered. Jane spent a small fortune on laundry detergent and stain-fighting products each week and had given up trying to keep her sons clean until it was time for baths and bed.

"Yes, we can go to Geppetto's. I also have to pop into La Grand Dame and pick up Aunt Octavia's new dress."

The twins let out a unified groan. "Not clothes *again*!"

"Oh, please." Jane cuffed the closer boy lightly on the head. "You only have to go clothes shopping twice a year."

Fitz grimaced. "That's two times too much. We should

wear ours until we look like characters from *Robinson Crusoe*."

Jane glanced at his tattered army shorts and soiled T-shirt. "Mission complete. Come on, get your bikes."

The three of them took their bikes from the shed and started for the village. This was a regular outing for the family and one of Jane's favorite pastimes. She never grew tired of the quiet country lane that wound its way through tree-covered hills, rolling cow pastures, and cornfields. The grassy shoulders were dotted with wildflowers and, just before they reached the little bridge straddling the Red Fox River, a chestnut pony would be waiting at the fence, hoping for an apple or a lump of sugar.

The last bend was a sharp one, so Jane and the boys would squawk the horns affixed to their handlebars to alert other cyclists or motorists of their presence. Many a tourist had driven off the road at that curve, plunging into thickets of blackberry bushes and poison ivy if they were lucky or slamming into a tree if they weren't. Dubbed Broken Arm Bend by the locals, that bit of road had the village's only doctor stocking fiberglass for casts all year long.

"Last one to the Cheshire Cat is a rotten egg!" Hem taunted and shot off like a loosed arrow.

Fitz reacted to the challenge, pumping his thin legs—speckled with bruises and scrapes—as fast as he could.

"That's how boys should look," Aunt Octavia would say. "Let them wear themselves to the bone during the day and, at night, fall asleep with a book and flashlight in hand."

Jane smiled. She loved that the twins would have a hard time deciding whether to spend their allowance on a toy or puzzle from Geppetto's or a comic from Run for Cover Book Shop. Either purchase would do more to foster their burgeoning imaginations than the majority of the items at the sprawling shopping mall over the mountain.

Storyton Village looked like it belonged to another era. The buildings were made of brick or stone and had leaded windows with diamond-shaped panes and thick oak doors polished to a high gloss. Each cottage had its own small, but spectacular, garden. Herbs, roses, perennials, flowering vines, and vegetables vied for space and sunlight in front of every shop, office, and eatery. All the business owners tried to outshine their neighbors by crowding their gardens with benches, birdbaths, statuary, and gazing balls. This friendly competition lent the village an eclectic air.

For example, Storyton's pub, the Cheshire Cat, had an enormous sculpture of a smiling feline in its garden. The cat's famous toothy grin was made out of chipped dinner plates, which glimmered eerily in the dark. Betty, the publican's wife, had planted five varieties of catnip around the base of the statue. As a result, most of Storyton's tomcats crept to the pub after sundown to nibble the fragrant leaves. Jane had heard tales of inebriated men stumbling out of the pub to encounter a herd of felines high on catnip. According to local legend, the two species would sometimes join together in yowling at the moon. Their high-pitched keening often resulted in the sheriff being roused from his bed.

"I'm first!" Fitz shouted upon reaching the pub's gate.

Without slowing, Jane pedaled past her son and called back over her shoulder, "Last one to touch Pinocchio's nose is a rotten egg!"

She didn't maintain the lead for long. Hem whizzed by her, his sandy brown hair forming two wings above his ears.

"Maybe we should stop at the barber's!" she shouted at him, knowing the remark would only spur him into increasing his pace.

"No way!" Fitz protested as he drew up alongside her. "We had a haircut last month!"

Jane laughed. "You two truly belong in Neverland."

"Yeah, then Hem could kiss a mermaid," Fitz goaded his brother as he and Jane came to a stop in front of the toy shop.

Hem, who'd already dismounted and parked his bike against Geppetto's picket fence, ran into the garden to touch the metal statue of Pinocchio. Standing on his tiptoes, he grabbed hold of the puppet's steel nose and stuck his tongue out at his brother. "And *you* could kiss Wendy. I know you love her and want to marry her." He began to blow raspberries against his palm.

Knowing this conversation would likely escalate into a full-blown fight, Jane held out a warning finger. "One more word, and I will revoke your allowances."

Hem gave her a guileless stare. "What does revoke mean?"

"It means that I'll take your money back," she said.

The boys exchanged horrified glances.

"You can't do that!" Fitz declared indignantly.

Jane smiled. "I'm your mother. I can do anything I want."

Grumbling about the imbalance of power in the family, Fitz and Hem entered the shop. Barnaby Nicholas looked up from the pirate marionette he was painting and beamed.

"Ah, Ms. Steward! Master Fitz! Master Hem! How are we on this fine day?"

Hem brandished his leather wallet, which he'd sewn using a kit the toymaker had sold him. "We have money."

Grinning at the boy over his half-moon reading glasses, Mr. Nicholas worked the strings on the marionette so that the wooden pirate bowed. "A man with gold coins in his pocket is me favorite kind of customer, to be sure," he growled in his best swashbuckler voice.

"Can I leave them here for a bit?" Jane asked. "It always takes them forever to decide what to buy."

"Certainly, my fair lady." It was the pirate who replied. "And if they give me so much as a spot of trouble, I'll make them walk the plank."

Hem was unimpressed. "We're not on a boat, so there's nothing for us to be afraid of."

"No?" Mr. Nicholas pivoted the pirate until the marionette faced the twins. "Come, me mateys, and I will tell you a tale of sharks and sirens, treasure and tragedy. And when I'm done, you will know much about fear." His eyes sparkling, he nodded at Jane and led her captivated sons over to a display of wooden swords.

Jane left him to it and headed across the street to pick up Octavia's dress. Mabel Wimberly's shop, La Grande Dame, was located down a narrow lane between Merry Poppets Day Care and Spokes, the village's center for bike rentals and sales. La Grande Dame's first floor was dedicated to Mabel's business. Her living space was divided between the second story, the kitchen, and a tiny backyard. Of all the shop gardens in Storyton, Mabel's was the wildest. Throughout the growing season, her plants flourished in an untamed tangle of color and scent. Sunflowers towered above gladiolas while purple clematis wound its tendrils around stalks of bamboo. Jane gently pushed aside a cluster of hollyhocks obscuring the front path and stepped over the limb of a butterfly bush.

"Did you make it through the jungle?" Mabel asked when Jane entered the shop.

Jane glanced around at the orderly baskets of yarn, the neat shelves of fabric bolts, and the meticulous displays of needles, pins, thread, scissors, and patterns lining the walls and said, "I think you've got a Jekyll and Hyde complex."

Mabel let out a hearty laugh. She was a large woman with a mop of auburn hair going to gray, which she wore in an elaborate twist high on the top of her head. The twins called her hairstyle "the cinnamon bun." Jane found the image quite accurate, especially since the blend of reds, browns, and grays gave the arrangement a striated appearance, reminding Jane of a sweet pastry dough drizzled with white icing.

"I have your aunt's dress all wrapped and ready." Mabel motioned for Jane to follow her into the sewing room. Tailor mannequins draped in a variety of incomplete outfits stood like stuffed sentries before a pair of sewing machines and a large worktable. The room was a riot of colors and prints. Fabrics were draped over every surface, and sunlight glinted off mounds of straight pins, safety pins, and needles stuck into velvet pincushions. Mabel handed Jane a gold La Grande Dame shopping bag.

"Aunt Octavia will be thrilled to add this to her wardrobe," Jane said.

"One of these days, you'll let me make you something." Mabel wriggled her long fingers. "These are finely tuned instruments, my girl. I could craft you a gown that would have people swooning in the lobby or a cocktail dress as chic as any you'd see on a Paris runway."

Jane shrugged. "There's no call for me to own custom gowns or cocktail dresses. I wear work suits during the day and jeans and T-shirts when I'm off duty. I'm a waste of your talent, Mabel."

"A beautiful woman should wear beautiful things. You have the perfect figure for finely tailored clothes. You're tall and slim with a decent amount of cleavage and a long and lovely neck. You should pull all of that strawberry blond hair up and show it off."

"I am wearing a ponytail," Jane said, pivoting her head. "If I don't, I can't see a thing when I'm riding my bike."

Mabel frowned. "I'm being serious. You should dress for you. No one else. All women deserve to look and feel beautiful. Take me, for instance." She spread her plump arms wide and spun in a circle. Her dress, which was flamingo pink with a box pleat skirt and a bodice fastened with rhinestone buttons, flared as she twirled.

Jane smiled. "Fantastic."

Mabel touched her on the arm. "I know you've tried to hide your freckles since you were a girl. Your aunt told me. But they're a part of you, just like your gorgeous green eyes and those legs that go on for miles. Let people see a bit more skin."

"I've gotten used to my freckles," Jane assured her. "And I will order a dress from you. It's probably not the kind of project you had in mind, but I need a late-1920s-style flapper dress. I'm trying to emulate Agatha Christie's Tuppence, the feisty half of Christie's famed Tommy and Tuppence detective partnership. I'm envisioning something tubular with a drop waist. But not fancy. A classy day dress. With a hat and gloves too, of course. I don't need it now, but can you work your magic by mid-October?"

Mabel gazed into the middle distance, and Jane could tell she was already envisioning the cut and color of the fabric. "That's appropriate attire for the daytime, but any lady worth her salt would have changed for dinner. I can see you in a sleek, backless number with fringes and frills. Garnet silk perhaps? Or gold with a bias cut?" She rubbed her hands together with glee. "When can I take your measurements?"

"As soon as the reservations start rolling in," Jane said. "If this event is to be a success, then the whole village will have to be involved in some way or another." Picking up the shopping bag, she thanked Mabel and headed back into the sunshine.

The moment she closed the door, she heard shouting coming from the main road. Quickening her pace, Jane silently prayed that her boys hadn't gotten into too much mischief.

When she reached the end of the lane, she saw a bay mare galloping down the center of the street, a woman clinging to the saddle pommel. Her feet had come out of the stirrups and her face was a mask of terror. Jane heard someone shout *"Stop!"* but the mare flattened her ears and ran even faster, causing pedestrians and cyclists to rush for the sidewalk as the horse shot by.

Jane had barely taken in the scene before the sound of another set of hooves striking against the pavement caught her attention. A man riding a dapple gray was in pursuit of the spooked mare, crouched over the gray's shoulders like a jockey. The man's dark hair whipped off his forehead and his eyes were fixed on the bay horse ahead of him. Jane only saw him for a second before he flew past, but every fiber of his being was clearly focused on halting the mare and saving her rider from a dangerous fall.

In that brief flash of time in which Jane had seen the

man's face, she'd instantly recognized him. Not him per se, but his familiar features.

She moved toward Run for Cover, her best friend's bookshop, but kept her gaze locked on the two riders. It was impossible not to be riveted by the mad dash of the horses, and Jane could practically feel the thundering of their hooves reverberating all the way up her spine. The people of Storyton were frozen. They stood with eyes wide and hands clenched, completely absorbed by the drama. No one made a sound.

After a few breathless seconds, the mare seemed to be tiring. The gray was closing fast and his rider stretched out an arm, reaching for the bay's reins. In two more heartbeats, he had them in his grasp and quickly forced the sweat-covered horse to slow to a trot and then, finally, mercifully, to a walk.

The onlookers cheered and applauded the nimble horseman. Jane put her fingers in her mouth and whistled with relief and admiration. She then hurried down the bookstore's front path, her feet treading on the familiar word stones her friend Eloise had placed throughout the garden. The twins loved to hop from one word to another, making up nonsense poems or silly songs as they leapt. Jane was in too much of a rush to pay attention to where her feet landed. She stepped on "hope" and "dream" but absently skipped over "wish" and "believe" to pause on "imagine" before pushing the heavy door open.

Eloise was bent over a coffee-table book on the Appalachian Mountains. The woman standing beside her pointed to a photograph of a bald eagle and then gesticulated with both arms, her expression one of awe and delight. Jane assumed she was a guest at Storyton Hall and had just returned from a memorable nature hike. Eloise glanced up from the page and winked at Jane. It was her way of saying "Give me a minute. I need to close this sale."

Jane wandered over to the cookbook section, where she was easily distracted by a collection of bound recipes from *The Storyton Sewing Circle*, 1951. She turned to the table of contents, intrigued by recipes like lemonade fried chicken, sardine and bacon rolls, Mexican corn sauté, and Pepsi-Cola Cake.

"Are you going to make the boys a rainbow Jell-O delight?" Eloise asked after her customer left with a bag in hand and a satisfied expression on her face.

Jane closed the book. "You didn't tell me your brother was coming to town."

Eloise looked stunned. "How did you—"

"He tore past me on the street a few seconds ago on a gray horse. He just rescued some woman on a runaway mare."

"That's Edwin for you. Full of surprises." Eloise moved to the window. "Like the way he showed up at my house last night. No phone call, no e-mail, nothing. Just rings the doorbell at half past ten. He's forgotten that we country folks don't take well to unexpected guests. I had one hand on the knob and the other on my rifle."

"I can't believe I'm finally going to meet the mysterious Edwin Alcott," Jane said in a dreamy voice, fluttering her lashes like a lovesick teen. "He's become like a book character in my mind. A young Radcliffe Emerson or Dirk Pitt."

"He's a food writer, Jane. Check your Indiana Jones fantasies at the door," Eloise said. "Seriously, don't envision him as some dashing hero, even if he did rescue that woman. Edwin's moody, self-centered, and secretive. He doesn't have good manners, rarely bothers with pleasantries, refuses to participate in small talk, and always looks like he disapproves of whatever it is you're doing. If he weren't my brother and didn't send me the most amazing gifts from the most amazing places, then I'd probably hate him."

At that moment, Fitz and Hem burst into the shop, their cheeks flushed and their chests rising and falling rapidly.

"Mom!" Fitz rushed over to Jane. "Did you see those people on the horses?"

"I did," she said. "Exciting, right? And a little scary too. Ms. Alcott's brother was the rider on the gray horse. He saved the lady on the bay mare."

The twins shot a curious glance at Eloise and then turned back to their mother. "He didn't save her," Hem said. "He tried, but he couldn't."

Both women stared at the little boy. Jane put a hand on his shoulder. "Catch your breath, Hem, and then tell us what you mean."

Fitz didn't wait for his brother to speak. "She slid right off the horse. *Plop!*" He pulled a blue and green hacky sack from his pocket and dropped it on the floor. "Like that. She didn't move after she hit the ground either." He gestured at the footbag he'd probably just purchased at Geppetto's.

"It's true," Hem said in case the women doubted his twin. "Someone ran to get Doc Lydgate. He told the man who stopped her horse to carry her into his office."

Nodding gravely, Fitz picked up his new toy and returned it to his pocket. "Your brother is really strong, Miss Alcott. He looked like Superman carrying Lois Lane."

"The lady probably fainted," Eloise said airily. "I wouldn't worry about it too much."

The boys looked disappointed by the notion and immediately drifted over to the spinner rack of comic books and graphic novels.

However, the next customer through the door was quick to dispel Eloise's theory. It was Mrs. Eugenia Pratt, the biggest gossip in Storyton. She was so puffed up with news that she looked like an overinflated balloon. Her round cheeks were flushed, and her beady eyes glimmered with delight.

"Oh, Eloise!" she exclaimed. "Did you hear?"

Eloise put on a patient smile. Mrs. Pratt was forever trying to set her up with every single man in Storyton. The older woman was also fond of cautioning Eloise about the hazards of becoming an old maid. Like Jane, Eloise was in her mid-thirties and resented being told that her beauty, charm, and the likelihood of her producing a brood of healthy children were swiftly diminishing. Still, Mrs. Pratt was a regular customer and a member of Jane's book club. She faithfully purchased half a dozen romance novels each week, so Eloise did her best to be friendly to the cantankerous gossipmonger.

"About the asphalt steeplechase?" Jane asked.

"Yes." Mrs. Pratt's enthusiasm waned in the face of Jane's reply, but then she brightened. "But do you know how it ended?"

Eloise shrugged, trying to appear disinterested. "Judging by what the twins said, the woman fainted and had to be carried into Doc Lydgate's office."

"Fainted?" Mrs. Pratt took out the Japanese fan she kept in her purse, opened it with a practiced flick of her wrist, and began to wave it in front of her face. "No, no, my dear. Well, she *might* have fainted at one point, but by the time your brother"—she stopped her narrative and cocked her head like an inquisitive bird—"Edwin, is it? He's very handsome. Why hasn't he visited before? And what brings him to our sleepy little village now? You two certainly look alike, but he got all the height while you got all that curly hair. I'd say there's about three years separating you. Maybe four. Am I right?"

"The woman?" Jane prompted. "What happened to the woman?"

"Oh, yes!" Mrs. Pratt's eyes twinkled with relish before she hastily adopted an expression of woe. "Well . . ." She paused theatrically and lowered her fan. Casting a surreptitious glance at the twins, she leaned closer to Eloise and Jane and whispered, "Your brother carried her into Doc Lydgate's office, but the good doctor couldn't do her much for her, the poor thing. He's a fine physician, but he's not a miracle worker."

Jane was confused. "He wasn't able to wake her up?"

Mrs. Pratt shook her head. "No, dear, he wasn't. After all, there's no rousing the dead."

THREE

"She's dead?" Jane whispered. "Just like that?"

"It's quite the mystery," Mrs. Pratt confirmed. "After all, she was younger than both of you, and though she was clearly terrified when we saw her charging down the street, she didn't look to be on the brink of death." She paused, pulling at the loose skin under her chin as she often did when she was turning over a thought. "If her horse had pitched her into a wall or trampled her, then this would make more sense."

Jane glanced at Hem and Fitz, who were too busy ogling the cover of the new Green Lantern comic book to eavesdrop, and took Mrs. Pratt by the elbow. "Perhaps we should move away from the door. We wouldn't want to frighten any of Eloise's customers."

Pleased by the results of her macabre imagery, Mrs. Pratt continued to describe how the rider could have met with a violent ending. She didn't resist when Jane, followed closely by Eloise, steered her deep into the stacks of the romance section. Instead, she grabbed several paperbacks and clutched them to her ample chest. Turning to Eloise, she said, "Your brother was magnificent." She caressed the cover of a romantic suspense novel. "He was just like one of these heroes. Tall, dark, and handsome with an animal magnetism that crackles like lightning during a summer storm." Mrs. Pratt was nearly panting. "The way he lifted that woman in his muscular arms and carried her into the doc's office like she weighed no more than a throw pillow—strong as a bull, he was! It's enough to make a woman swoon. Oh, my, my, my."

Exchanging a nervous look with Eloise, Jane took a firmer hold of Mrs. Pratt's elbow. "You're not going to faint are you, Mrs. Pratt?"

"No, no, no. I'm quite all right," the older woman said. "I'm simply not accustomed to this much excitement, that's all. Not in real life anyway. These books provide me with the thrills I crave, but every once in a while I dream of a moment in which reality could mirror fiction. And this afternoon, it *did*." Her gaze grew distant. "A wild ride through the center of town, people scrambling to get out of the way, a damsel in distress, a young stallion—I mean man—who happens to be the brother of our own Miss Alcott . . . This sort of thing doesn't happen every day, my dear. I can't help but be caught up by it all."

"I only wish her story had had a different ending," Jane said glumly. "The poor woman."

"Indeed." Mrs. Pratt didn't appear very distressed by the rider's fate. "I should dash. Can you ring me up, Eloise?" She gathered three more books and then hurried off to the checkout counter.

"She can't wait to get next door and tell everyone what happened," Eloise said. "I'd better see to her before she starts talking to the twins."

Luckily, Fitz and Hem showed no interest in anything but the rack of comic books. "Do you have any money left?" Jane asked the boys.

"I do," Hem boasted. "Fitz spent all of his at Geppetto's."

"Yeah, but we're supposed to share the stuff we buy."

Fitz glared at his brother and then gave Jane a plaintive look. "Only I don't want him to pick the Green Lantern. See this?" He pointed at a cover showing a group of masked characters poised for battle. "It has a whole bunch of superheroes. Hem's only has one."

Mrs. Pratt passed by in time to catch Fitz's remark. "It only takes one hero to set an entire town aflutter, young sir. Just ask Edwin Alcott!"

The boys turned to Jane with inquisitive eyes, but she merely tapped the face of her watch and said, "We'll barely make it home for supper at this point. Choose a comic book and meet me at the Pickled Pig."

Jane turned to wave at Eloise, but her friend was busy with a customer, so she signaled once more for the twins to hurry up with their decision and headed outside. She'd just cleared the garden gate when a man barreled into her hard enough to drive the breath out of her lungs.

"Oh!" she cried, startled, and grabbed on to the gatepost to keep her balance. Her handbag fell to the ground and her change purse, which hadn't been closing properly for several weeks, popped open and disgorged her coins into the grass.

"Do you live here or are you a tourist?" the man demanded while Jane was still trying to steady herself.

Scowling angrily, she glanced up, fully prepared to lecture the cad on his lack of courtesy. But when she looked into his eyes, she forgot all about the scolding. His dark gaze was so fierce, so incredibly intense, that she immediately answered, "I'm a local. I live—"

"Come to the doctor's office," he interrupted. "Someone needs to identify the body and I can't." He started off in the direction from which he'd come without waiting to see whether Jane was following.

"Hey!" Jane called, but he didn't slow his pace. Annoyed, Jane shouted, "Edwin Alcott. You stop right there!"

He froze and swung around, his piercing stare fixed on her. "How do you know my name?"

"I'm your sister's best friend," Jane explained once she'd drawn alongside him. "You look alike. Even on horseback, I knew who you were." She put her hands on her hips. "And though you clearly share DNA with Eloise, you lack her impeccable manners. I need to get my purse, which fell on the ground when you rammed into me like a jousting knight, and then I'm going to the food market. There's no need to take me to the doc's because I wouldn't be able to help."

Edwin raked his fingers through his thick hair, seemingly at a loss. "Are you squeamish? Because if you are—"

"I most certainly am not." Jane was quick to dispel the notion. "I am mother to six-year-old twin boys. I've seen every manner of cut, burn, scrape, and bruise in addition to several cases of broken fingers and toes." Edwin looked unconvinced, and Jane felt her irritation growing. She had an inkling that she was being manipulated, but she was unable to extricate herself. "Fine. Let's go. *After* I get my purse."

"Allow me." He ran back to the gate, as nimble and fleet-footed as his horse, collected her bag, and returned it to her with an exaggerated flourish.

Jane almost pointed out that he'd failed to pick up her change purse but decided that would be churlish. Someone would turn it in to Eloise who'd recognize it as Jane's and return it to her later. "Thank you," Jane said.

If she'd expected Edwin to respond by apologizing for nearly knocking her over, she was to be disappointed. He walked away without speaking, and his stride was so swift that she had trouble keeping pace.

"Jane! Good, good, good," Doc Lydgate said when she entered his office. "Would you come on through?"

Jane hesitated. She'd never seen a dead body, and despite her boast to Edwin, she was, just at that moment, feeling a little squeamish.

She darted a sidelong look at Eloise's brother, and he raised his brows as if to question her resolve. "Of course," she told the doctor firmly. "Though I doubt I can identify her."

"You know everyone at the Hall and in the village by sight. If this woman was a guest at Storyton, I suspect you'll recognize her." Doc Lydgate led Jane into his examination room. He drew back the blue curtain obscuring a stainless steel table before Jane had a chance to prepare herself. Suddenly, she was staring down at a figure covered from feet to shoulders by a crisp, white sheet. Her first impression was that the woman was unnaturally still and had a face as pale as milk.

This is what death looks like up close, Jane thought.

She took a step toward the table, inexplicably drawn to the lifeless stranger, and studied the blue tint of the woman's lips, her high cheekbones, dimpled chin, and smooth brow. Then Jane's gaze traveled over the length of honey blond hair, which cascaded off the side of the table and pooled onto the floor like a puddle of spun gold.

"Rapunzel," Jane whispered inaudibly and then turned to the doctor. "Was her hair hanging loose? I don't remember seeing so much hair when she was on horseback."

"No," Doc Lydgate replied. "It was fastened in a complex knot at the nape of her neck. I had to undo the arrangement in order to check her scalp for lacerations or signs of swelling. When I heard that she'd fallen from her horse, I assumed she'd been concussed."

Jane couldn't tear her gaze away from the woman's face. The delicate curve of her brows, the soft bow of her upper lip, her unblemished skin. "She's certainly not from around here, and I doubt she's a guest at the resort either. Look at her, Doc. A woman like this couldn't walk through a room without being noticed by everyone. It'd be like ignoring a shooting star." She thought for a moment. "What about the mare? Where'd she come from?"

"She's one of Sam's," Edwin said.

The doc was clearly taken aback. "A horse from Hilltop

Stables ran wild through the center of town? Why'd she leave the mountain path? What spooked her?"

Edwin didn't answer.

Jane scrutinized him closely. "You were on horseback too. Did you rent that gray from Sam?" She then gestured at the woman without turning to look at her lovely, but lifeless, features again. "Someone might be waiting for this woman at Hilltop as we speak. Did you see her on the trail? Sam never lets strangers ride on their own. He always serves as a guide to people he doesn't know."

"Sam doesn't play nanny to me," Edwin said blandly. "We went to school together and he knows I'm practically a centaur. So no, I wasn't riding with the lady, but Sam must have her name. I should have thought of that earlier, but I figured if I just found someone to identify her, then I could . . ."

"Leave that person to deal with this?" Jane guessed and Edwin looked away. Whether he was angry or embarrassed, Jane couldn't tell.

Doc Lydgate cleared his throat and held out his hand, indicating Jane should step away from the table. He drew the curtain closed, giving the dead woman privacy once more, but her image was imprinted in Jane's mind. It was as if the barrier of blue cloth didn't exist.

"Well, I'm glad you chose Jane to assist," the doc told Edwin. "She's got a sensible head on her shoulders and is perfectly capable of handling delicate situations. Even so, I think you should remount your horse and return to the stables. Get Sam to examine this woman's paperwork. I'm going to call Sheriff Evans and have him drive up there." He laid a hand on Edwin's arm. "This woman has family somewhere and they should be notified as soon as possible. It's the only kindness we can offer them now. That and the knowledge that the brother of one of our own showed true courage in trying to save her. Well done, sir."

Little spots of color appeared on Edwin's cheeks. "If only

I'd caught hold of the reins sooner. Maybe she . . ." Without finishing his thought, he abruptly pivoted and strode from the room.

Speechless, Jane and the doctor stared after him.

"Interesting fellow." Doc Lydgate collected a patient folder from the counter and cleared his throat officiously. "I believe the lady suffered from heart failure and, if that's the case, there's nothing Mr. Alcott could have done to prevent this woman's demise. Of course, that's only an opinion. Because we're dealing with a patient who's young and fit, it's hard to determine what happened based on a preliminary examination." Doc Lydgate seemed to have forgotten about Jane. Stroking the whiskers of his neat white beard, he murmured, "She needs to be taken to the coroner. I'll have to call an ambulance to carry her over the mountain." Releasing a heavy sigh, he seemed to suddenly remember that he wasn't alone. "Ah, Jane. I'm sorry to have troubled you with this business. How are my favorite patients? It seems like ages since I've sutured one of them or administered a tetanus shot. At least three months by my calculations."

"The boys are fine, thank you. Their summer injuries have been superficial thus far, though I'm not foolish enough to believe my luck will hold." She smiled. "If there's anything I can do for the woman or her family, please let me know."

"Certainly. Thank you, Jane." The doctor led her into the waiting room, where his receptionist, who also served as his nurse, was whispering excitedly into the phone. Pippa Pendleton had fiery red hair and a propensity for ignoring doctor-patient confidentiality. It was obvious to both Jane and Doc Lyndgate that Pippa had been busy discussing the dead woman with a girlfriend. Jane had known Pippa since she wore her vibrant hair in pigtail braids and was the village's most notorious kleptomaniac. Years after Jane had moved away and married, Pippa had also left to attend nursing school where she cut off all her hair and had a leprechaun tattooed on her calf. She was also promptly fired from her first and only nursing job for breaking into a hospital vending machine.

"I really wanted a bag of chips," Pippa complained to anyone who would listen upon her return to Storyton. "I forgot my purse. Honestly! And it was, like, a twelve-hour shift!" Somehow, she managed to convince Doc Lydgate to give her the job Nurse Collins had vacated when she ran off with Mrs. Simpkin's husband.

Doc Lydgate was a good man and agreed to take Pippa on a trial basis. It was common knowledge that right after hiring her, he walked straight to the hardware store and bought a dozen padlocks.

Now, the doc stood directly in front of Pippa and coughed loudly into his hand. She glanced at him and, without the slightest hint of shame, told her friend she'd fill her in on all the juicy details at the pub and hung up the phone.

"Do you need a cough drop or some cold medicine?" she asked while unwrapping one of the lollipops set aside for the doctor's pediatric patients.

Doc Lydgate frowned and gestured at the phone. "Please call an ambulance, Pippa. Tell them our patient has expired and needs to be transported to the coroner for a thorough examination as soon as possible."

Pippa opened her mouth and shoved the candy inside her right cheek. "Expired?" she asked, her words a wet garble.

"Just repeat exactly what I said." He reached forward and tapped on the lollipop stick. "This interferes with your pronunciation, so please refrain from eating while you're on the phone. It's no wonder my patients are showing up for appointments on the wrong day of the week."

Glowering, Pippa removed the lollipop and dialed while Doc Lydgate disappeared into his office down the hall.

On her way out the door, Jane heard Pippa connect with the EMT operator. Glancing back at the rebellious redhead, Jane was unsurprised to see the young woman pause in the middle of her conversation and pop the candy into her mouth once more. She caught Jane staring, grinned, and gave a saucy wriggle of her fingers in farewell.

Shaking her head as if to shuck off the experience of the past few minutes, Jane made her way to the Pickled Pig. The boys were waiting for her in the market's herb garden. To her relief, they'd yet to flatten any of the Hogg brothers' plants. She bought them each a gumball as a reward along with the items she needed to prepare a supper of garlic bread, Caesar salad, and spaghetti Bolognese. After placing their purchases in their bike baskets, the trio rode home.

While the boys watched TV in the living room, Jane sipped red wine and stared at the spaghetti noodles rolling around in a pot of boiling water. Gazing into the steam, she considered how different Edwin was from his sister.

"Eloise was right," she murmured to herself as she gave the meat sauce a quick stir. "Her brother isn't like a hero from a thriller novel. He's got more of Mr. Rochester about him. Maybe a little brooding Hamlet mixed in as well. In any case, I doubt he'll stay in Storyton long. There's nothing to capture his interest here."

"Edwin has no intention of leaving anytime soon," Eloise announced several weeks later during the bimonthly meeting of the Cover Girls, the ladies' book club Jane hosted. "In fact, he wants to take over Loafing Around. Claims he's always had aspirations of elevating the sandwich to new heights."

"It wouldn't be hard to improve on Gertrude's selections," said Violet Osborne, the owner of Tresses Hair Salon. "She's a sweet woman, mind you, but her club sandwiches are drier than dust."

Phoebe Doyle, who ran the Canvas Creamery, an art gallery combined with a frozen custard shop, nodded in agreement. "The ham's the worst. There's a slimy film around the edges of every slice. I tried to tell Gertrude to buy her meat from the Hogg brothers, but she wouldn't listen. She gets all her supplies from one of those big warehouse stores over the mountain."

Mrs. Pratt curled her lip in distaste. "Over the mountain" referred to the closest big town. The locals frequented the town's businesses or medical facilities only when absolutely necessary. They were fiercely loyal to their little village and had adopted a host of prejudices, many of which were unjustified, about other towns. "It's no wonder the tourists won't eat at Loafing Around twice," Mrs. Pratt said. "At Storyton Hall, they're served the finest cuisine within a hundred miles. Then, they take an excursion into the village, shop for a spell, and eventually build up an appetite. They enter our only café where, to the embarrassment of us all, they're presented with stringy roast beef and soggy lettuce on bread hard enough to chip a tooth." She took a deep breath. "Though I'm not surprised Gertrude is unable to made a decent sandwich. Why, just the other day I heard that her—"

"Pickles are limp," interrupted Anna Shaw before Mrs. Pratt could circulate a fresh piece of gossip. "And there's no excuse for that. The Hogg brothers have the best pickles in the world. Have you ladies tried their Packing Heat pickles? Wow, what a kick." She fanned herself with a copy of *The Great Gatsby*.

Jane smiled. "It's a good thing you work at the pharmacy. Plenty of antacids handy."

Anna rolled her eyes. "And I definitely need them after spending eight hours a day with Randall."

The women laughed. Randall, the town pharmacist, was constantly lecturing his customers on how to improve their health. He seemed to have no interests or hobbies beyond this subject, and no one could stand to speak with him for more than a few moments at a time.

"Insufferable man," Betty Carmichael muttered. "He gave me a pamphlet on alcoholism the other day. My husband and I run a pub, but that doesn't mean I'm a lush."

"Speaking of booze, let's have a toast!" Mabel declared and raised her glass. "Jane, which quote from this month's book selection have you chosen to recite to kick off our meeting?"

" 'So we beat on, boats against the current, borne back ceaselessly into the past.' " Jane's voice resonated in the roomy kitchen. She liked the idea of F. Scott Fitzgerald's words floating up to the rafters to roost like birds. She loved his writing so much that she'd named one of her sons after him. Lifting her glass, she continued, "And to Gatsby, Daisy, that green light in the distance, and all the dreams we refuse to stop chasing."

"Hear! Hear!" The women enthused and took sips of their cocktails. This was followed by a collection of appreciative sounds.

"What's in this, Jane?" Violet poked the lime half floating on the top of her highball glass with a lavender nail. Her clothes, nails, and eye shadow were always a shade of purple.

"It's a gin rickey, a drink F. Scott Fitzgerald enjoyed very much—among many others." Jane held her glass out to the light. "There's not much to it. Two ounces dry gin, half an ounce of lime juice, club soda, a lime half, and ice."

Mabel took a healthy swallow. "Very refreshing."

"I hope you made a few pitchers of these," Eloise said, clinking the rim of her glass against Jane's. "After living alone for so long, it's quite a challenge to have Edwin sharing my house. He's such a moody creature."

"I have a charming guest room. Tell him to pack his suitcase and come over to my place," Mrs. Pratt said with a licentious gleam in her eyes. "He can be as temperamental as he likes if he promises to walk around without a shirt."

Anna swatted her on the arm. "He's half your age!"

"That means she could probably teach him a thing or two," Mabel said and sat down at the kitchen table. Mrs. Pratt giggled like a schoolgirl and joined her.

"I'd gladly send him your way." Eloise sighed. "I love my brother, and you'd think with all his worldly sophistication that he'd have more refined social skills, but he's impatient, demanding, and taciturn."

Betty tapped the cover of her paperback. "Is he a modern Jay Gatsby?"

"No, Gatsby's far too suave, too polished. Edwin's more like Heathcliff," Eloise said. "Or that prickly dapple gray of Sam Neely's. That horse won't let anyone ride him except for Edwin."

"Lucky horse." Mrs. Pratt mumbled.

Violet leaned forward. "Did anyone hear what actually happened to that woman who died? It's been weeks since it happened and there hasn't been any mention of it in the paper."

The group of women looked to Mrs. Pratt to supply the answer. There was nothing she liked better than being the center of attention. Her face glowed as she sucked in a great lungful of air. "Well . . ." She then raised a finger and took a delicate sip of her gin rickey, as if she couldn't possibly begin without first moisturizing her throat. "They never did discover her real name, you know."

While the rest of the women exchanged perplexed glances, Jane recalled an image of a motionless body covered by a white sheet. She thought of a pale, lovely face and waves of golden hair and felt a prick of guilt.

How could I have put her from my mind so quickly? It was true that she'd been overwhelmed with preparations for the Murder and Mayhem Week, but it was no excuse for forgetting that a stranger had recently lost her life in the middle of Storyton Village.

"I thought she rented a horse from Hilltop Stables," Anna said.

"So she did," Mrs. Pratt agreed. "But under a false name."

This statement was met with several shocked gasps.

Delighted, Mrs. Pratt fed her captivated audience another

tidbit. "She used a fake name and address on both the information form and liability waiver. Claimed she was staying here at the Hall. She even wrote down a room number. Paid in cash, mounted that mare, and, well, you know how her tale ended, poor girl."

"But what spooked her horse?"

Mrs. Pratt shrugged. "No one knows. But I think it's quite peculiar that her horse was frightened near the wooden bridge leading into the village. It's as if someone wanted the mare to leave the path and come racing down Main Street."

Betty made a dismissive noise. "That's rather fanciful. The mare probably saw a snake or was bitten by one of those giant horseflies."

"Big as hummingbirds," Phoebe said with a shudder. "That's why the garden's full of lavender, bay leaves, and tansy. Keeps the flies away."

"Is that also why you have so many pinwheels?" Eloise asked.

Phoebe nodded. "The art I display out front features types of kinetic sculptures. You know I keep the naughty stuff behind the shop."

A wave of laughter swept through the kitchen. Phoebe's "back garden" statues were well known throughout Storyton and beloved by all the Cover Girls. Crafted by Phoebe, these sculptures were made of everyday objects such as bottle caps, tin cans, vinyl records, road signs, wire, buttons, and cooking utensils. Each one featured a woman reading. The ladies were as big as giantesses and more voluptuous than Peter Paul Rubens's Venus. Jane loved their auras of repose. One woman lay on her belly with a book propped open on her palms. Another was sprawled sideways in a chair, a book resting against her ample thighs, while a third was flat on her back, asleep, a hardcover splayed across her mountainous breasts. Like her bibliophile sisters, the dozing reader was completely nude.

There were seven altogether, forming their own little

book club behind the Canvas Creamery. Phoebe's "Book Junkie" sculptures had been photographed by most of Storyton's guests, and occasionally, she sold one for a ridiculous sum of money to a besotted tourist. Whenever that happened, Phoebe would round up the Cover Girls and they'd all take a ride to a salvage yard to help her choose treasures for the next sculpture. Phoebe was a superstitious woman who felt that the number seven was truly lucky. There had to be seven women in her garden and seven flavors of frozen custard in the shop. Even the toppings she offered were multiples of seven. The last time Fitz and Hem counted, there'd been twenty-one types of candy and thirty-five charcoal sketches hanging on the wall.

"What about Doc Lydgate?" Anna asked Mrs. Pratt. "Didn't the coroner get back to him? Enlighten him as to the cause of death? Or mention that she wasn't claimed by anyone?"

A cloud passed over Mrs. Pratt's round face. "Oh, that Pippa Pendleton won't tell me a thing. I even tried to offer her a fair trade for the information, but she refused to deal."

Mabel raised her hand. "Let me guess. Pippa tried to swipe something at the Pickled Pig and you saw her."

"Correct!" Mrs. Pratt replied. "You're a clever woman, Mabel Wimberly. Yes, Pippa was pocketing two tins of mints when I caught her in the act. And did she show an ounce of shame? None. When I promised not to inform the Hogg brothers of her crime in exchange for news on the dead woman, she stuck her chin in the air, called me a nosy female dog, and marched out the front door."

Jane and the others tried not to laugh. Mrs. Pratt's indignation was nearly palpable, but it was amusing to picture Pippa telling her off. After all, Pippa was certain to become Mrs. Pratt in thirty years' time.

Eloise made a sympathetic noise. "I'm surprised she didn't accept your offer. I wouldn't want to face any of the Hogg brothers if I'd been caught pilfering. But Pippa's young. At that age, I thought I was invincible too."

"You're a baby," Mabel scoffed. "When you get to be my age—"

"Or mine," Mrs. Pratt and Betty chimed in simultaneously.

Mabel nodded at her contemporaries. "Given a few more decades, Pippa will learn that life is fragile. When I'm done with my sewing and my supper, I go out into the garden every evening at twilight and just sit there, wondering about the woman who died in the middle of our village. The rest of you are far too busy for such musings, but I wish I knew her whole story."

"I bet the unanswered questions have been bothering Edwin too." Eloise looked stricken. "I think he blames himself for her death, though the doc has since assured him that he couldn't have done anything more to help her. I never stopped to consider how what happened might be affecting him."

Mrs. Pratt grinned. "If he needs a nursemaid, you know where to find me. Tell him I am quite adept at sponge baths."

Once again, the room filled with laughter. Hearty, shrill, and musical notes intertwined, the sounds as different as the women who produced them.

Violet waved her copy of *The Great Gatsby*. "Shall we talk about this then?"

"We should," Jane said. "And remember that we're moving to the *F*'s next month as we continue to work backward through the alphabet. Eloise gets to pick first, but start thinking about which *F* title you want us to read after hers."

"I've chosen *The Forgotten Garden* by Kate Morton," Eloise announced.

Anna clapped her hands together. "Thank goodness. After *Gilead*, *The Grapes of Wrath*, *Ghosts*, *The Glass Menagerie*, *The Giver*, and *The Great Gatsby*, I'm ready to delve into some women's fiction."

Jane murmured in agreement, but the title of their next selection served only to remind her of the dead stranger again. Instead of Rapunzel, she now pictured the woman as

Sleeping Beauty, lying in Mabel's wild garden, her golden hair entangled with vines and flowers.

In that tale, however, a prince eventually showed up to rescue the slumbering princess, but the woman who'd slipped off a runaway horse in Storyton Village hadn't been saved. She'd fallen in the middle of the street, never to rise again.

"Jane? Are you listening?" Eloise's voice called her back from her maudlin thoughts.

"Sorry," she told the rest of the Cover Girls. "What were we discussing?"

Mabel pointed at her empty glass. "Refills."

FOUR

Jane could scarcely remember the last time she'd felt such a delicious blend of anticipation and fear. Today was the first day of Storyton Hall's Murder and Mayhem Week, and she expected the initial round of guests to begin checking in any moment now.

She tried to imagine what it would feel like to be guests coming to Storyton Hall for the first time, to alight from the train and find a smiling gentleman in livery holding up a sign bearing one's surname written in splendid calligraphy. The gentleman would introduce himself as their chauffeur, offer to take the luggage, and lead them to a magnificent vintage Rolls-Royce Silver Shadow.

After making sure that his passengers were comfortable in the back of the luxurious car, he'd steer the majestic sedan over the winding roads leading to Storyton Hall. During the scenic drive, he'd gently and courteously remind the guests of the resort's restrictions on technology.

"Storyton aims to be a place of peace and tranquility, a place conducive to reading. Therefore, all electronic devices may only be used in the privacy of one's room. No computers, cell phones, handheld games, or e-reading devices will be allowed in the public areas. Ignoring this request could lead to an early termination of one's stay."

Occasionally, a guest protested, saying that he or she was expecting an urgent call. "May I suggest using room service until your call comes through?" the chauffer would respond pleasantly.

Other guests would insist that they needed their e-readers to increase the font size of the books they wished to read, but their driver would have a solution for that conundrum as well.

"I recommend you acquaint yourself with Storyton's vast library. Sinclair, the head librarian, can direct you to an impressive selection of large-print books."

And so, feeling slightly anxious about separating from the gadgets, the guests would fall silent. But as the trip continued, they'd begin to let go of their fears and would suddenly notice the stunning vistas beyond their windows. They'd comment on the blue mountains, stretching on and on like the waves of a great ocean, or gasp as a hawk flew into view, circling high above the treetops in search of prey. As the miles passed, they'd forget about their BlackBerries and iPhones. They'd start to relax, sinking into the oiled leather seats and dreaming of hours of uninterrupted reading, cups of strong tea, and plates filled with delicate sandwiches, scones with clotted cream, and sweet fairy cakes.

"At last, the Rolls will crest the final rise and the guests will be treated to their first glimpse of the resort," Jane murmured to herself. "They won't be able to stop from gasping over the splendor that is Storyton Hall. They'll gape at the central tower with its enormous clock in the middle, the tall windows, and the dignified gray stones." Smiling, she heard the crunch of tires on gravel. "Ah, here you are now, your body tingling with impatience to come inside, to explore every inch of this big, rambling place as if you were Alice and this, Wonderland."

Butterworth interrupted Jane's musings. The dignified butler carried a silver tray holding four champagne flutes.

Standing as straight and rigid as a soldier, he took his place just inside the front doors. A bellhop sprang forward to open them, and two couples entered the lobby. Jane watched their eyes widen in delight. Butterworth gave them a few moments to take in the sparkling chandeliers, the groupings of soft chairs and inviting love seats, the polished sideboards and end tables, and the stunning floral arrangements.

"Welcome to Storyton Hall," he announced in his deep, eloquent voice.

"Oh, thank you!" The first woman accepted a glass of champagne and then stepped aside to let Butterworth serve her husband. That's when Jane caught a glimpse of the little man waiting patiently behind her. He was the spitting image of Umberto Ferrari, the Italian detective made famous by the late Adela Dundee, the most popular authoress of traditional mysteries since Agatha Christie.

In the brochure she'd created for the Murder and Mayhem Week, Jane had encouraged attendees to dress in costume for "particular occasions." There were several events requiring a costume, but the guests were encouraged to remain in character whenever they chose.

Now, as Jane listened to the Umberto Ferrari look-alike thank Butterworth in a honeyed voice with an elegant Italian accent, she felt a thrill of pleasure. Here was someone clearly devoted to the Adela Dundee character. Jane was amazed by how closely he resembled Ferrari. He was short for a man—she put him at five feet five inches—and like Dundee's famed detective, he was completely bald. His brown eyes darted about the lobby, observing everything. But the pièce de résistance of his costume was not his magnificent custom three-piece wool suit complete with wing collar, hat, gloves, and walking stick. It was his pencil mustache.

"Magnificent," Jane exclaimed softly. It was hard to look away from the dapper little man.

The Umberto Ferrari doppelgänger accepted his champagne flute and moved forward in small, brisk steps. As he drew closer, Jane noted that he even wore a lapel pin fashioned into a *tussie mussie*—a vase made to hold a nosegay of flowers or herbs. This Ferrari had chosen to fill his *tussie mussie*, a delicate silver amphora, with sprigs of fresh lavender.

"Welcome to Storyton Hall, *Signor* Ferrari," Jane said when he drew near. "I'm Jane Steward, the resort manager."

The man took her hand and bowed over it. "I am most charmed to make your acquaintance," he said in his melodious Italian-accented voice. Utterly charmed, Jane led him to the check-in desk and then returned to the front entrance to greet her other guests.

"It was such a treat to be in the car with that man," one of the women told Jane.

"He never broke character," a second woman agreed. "If more people like him are headed to Storyton Hall, this week will be truly memorable!"

Her husband nodded. "We'll have to make an effort to breathe life into our fictional selves. We brought enough clothes to maintain our characters, so I say we do this thing properly."

"Jolly good," the two women answered in unison. Giggling like schoolgirls, they scurried to the registration desk and got in line behind Ferrari.

Jane was about to return to her office when she saw Ferrari's face redden in anger. Spluttering with indignation, he jabbed the tip of his walking stick into the floor and said, "It is I, Umberto Ferrari. Men are in awe of my intellectual prowess. When I am near, women feel faint and criminals cower. Do you truly not recognize me? Is it possible?"

Looking flustered, the desk clerk stammered in confusion until Jane swept over and put a comforting hand on the young woman's arm. "I'm sure *Signor* Ferrari is very particular when it comes to his personal documents. After all, there are so many dangers afoot these days. Perhaps I might borrow your billfold for just a moment, *signor*? I'll copy the necessary facts and return it to you directly."

"That will be satisfactory. *Grazie.*" Bobbing his perfectly round head in gratitude, he handed Jane a vintage wallet.

I'm going to have to print out a Who's Who cheat sheet for the staff, Jane thought. *If the rest of our guests are like this gentleman, we'll have to take care not to spoil the fantasy.*

Withdrawing into the back room where the resort's copiers, fax machine, and computers were housed, Jane photocopied Umberto Ferrari's aka Felix Hampden's driver's license and swiped his Visa card in case he incurred additional charges over the course of his stay, which Jane certainly hoped he would.

"Lots of additional charges," she said and selected a brass room key from the key case. Hampden had booked the Mystery Suite, a corner suite with heavy wooden furniture and framed prints of mystery novel book jackets lining the walls. The red and gold color scheme lent it a Gothic air, and Jane found it rather dark, but it was one of Storyton's most coveted rooms.

The afternoon passed quickly as more and more guests arrived. Many of them had taken great care with their costumes and, because detective characters spanned the centuries, the clothing varied dramatically between one person and the next. According to an unofficial poll being run by the front desk staff, there were more Miss Marples than any other character.

"Makes sense, don't you think?" a clerk asked Jane while running another credit card through the machine. "It's an easy disguise. Slap on a hat, some spectacles, a wig, and a cardigan or a tweed coat, and you're all set. Not much to being Miss Marple."

"Don't let Sinclair hear you say that," Jane cautioned. "He's very fond of Jane Marple. He refers to her as one of the 'shrewdest gentlewoman detectives of all time.' "

A second clerk entered the tiny office and began to copy a pair of driver's licenses. "I'm checking in James Bond and his fiancée, Grace, aka Fred Stevens and Joyce Little.

Doesn't the guy realize this isn't a spy-themed event? Secret Service agents aren't detectives."

Jane laughed. "Believe it or not, Agatha Christie created a character named James Bond. He showed up in one of her short stories. What was it called?" She tapped her finger against her temple. "Ah! It was 'The Rajah's Emerald.' Bond found a priceless emerald accidentally putting on the wrong pair of pants while changing out of his swim trunks in a seaside cabana. So you see, Christie came up with the name James Bond before Fleming."

The clerk shrugged. "All I know is that I've read Ian Fleming and he's good. Never tried any of the classic mystery writers like Sayers or Christie or Conan Doyle. No offense, but their books seem kind of stuffy. Manor houses and old ladies. Boring. I'll stick to thrillers."

Jane was tempted to fly to the defense of the authors he'd mentioned, but she wanted to influence the clerk's opinion, not get into an argument. "There are lords and ladies in many of the books, that's true. But some of the most fascinating characters are the maids and chauffeurs, doctors and movie stars, athletes and soldiers. Wait until you see our guests at the costume ball. The variety of characters will astound you."

"But they'll all drink tea and dance the waltz, right? Those mystery detectives weren't nearly as flawed as one of the cops in a contemporary police procedural."

Jane knew her employee was egging her on, so she smiled. "They're no prudes. Did you know that Sherlock Holmes used cocaine on occasion?"

The young man's eyes went wide. "No way." Then he shrugged. "But the bad guys aren't as scary. Modern crimes are creepier."

"What if I told you that Agatha Christie wrote a novel about a serial killer? One of the most brilliant villains I've ever come across, in fact."

"I'd be willing to give that book a try."

Scribbling the title, *The ABC Murders*, on a piece of scrap paper, Jane handed it to him. "Visit Sinclair on your lunch break. He'd be delighted to introduce you to some new authors."

Inspired by their conversation, Jane returned to the lobby to greet a seemingly unending flow of guests. Chauffeurs escorted their passengers up the front steps before having to jump back into their cars and set out for the train station again. Soon, Storyton Hall was filled with the melodious cacophony of a sold-out hotel. Guests were everywhere—sitting, standing, chatting, exploring, admiring—while the staff buzzed around them like worker bees. Glancing at her watch, Jane decided to stop by the tearoom just to make sure that today's spread was as impressive as the one pictured in the brochure.

She needn't have feared. Storyton Hall's cream china plates were stacked in neat columns on the end of the buffet table. Hundreds of diminutive sandwiches had been artfully arranged on silver platters, and Jane felt her mouth water as she recited the handwritten placards identifying each sandwich. "Smoked salmon and dill crème fraîche, Virginia ham and Dijon mustard, curried chicken salad, truffled egg salad with watercress, and salted cucumber with minted yogurt. Yum."

"That's nothing. Wait until you see the sweets," a server said while setting a mammoth tray of assorted scones on the table. Jane inhaled the scent of warm, sugary dough and sighed in contentment. "Our guests are already lining up. Are we on schedule?"

The woman grinned. "We're running behind, Ms. Jane. We always are. You know what Mrs. Hubbard says whenever we try to get her to pick up the pace."

Together, the two women recited the cook's declaration, " 'Perfection cannot be rushed. It must be coaxed forth.' "

"This spread is pure perfection." Jane ogled the lemon madeleines with a raspberry ganache, two Victoria sponge cakes, cream puffs drizzled in chocolate, strawberries Romanoff, shortbread, mini poppy seed cakes, and dark Belgian chocolate cakes. "All of this plus scones with clotted cream and three kinds of jam? Mrs. Hubbard's outdone herself."

Jane paused to examine the flatware, water cups, and napkin fans placed on the empty tables. Everything was polished to a high shine and precisely arranged. The centerpieces, blush-colored roses bursting from silver vases, added the final touch of elegance to the scene.

"This is going to be a wonderful week," she declared and then turned back to the server. "Gather the troops, Ginny. We're about to open the door and invite our guests to enjoy a taste of paradise."

Paradise didn't last long. At least not for Storyton Hall's staff. Jane had to field an unusual number of complaints regarding luggage and room mix-ups, and she soon realized that having a resort full of people using fictional names created a unique set of challenges. She did her best to mollify ruffled guests by giving them complimentary cocktail vouchers.

"The bartenders in the Ian Fleming Lounge have come up with an array of special drinks honoring our fictional detectives. They include the Thin Man Manhattan, Sam Spade Sidecar, Jacques Clouseau Cosmo, and Hercule Poirot champagne punch," she said, offering a voucher to a displeased lady guest. "And if you'd prefer a nonalcoholic beverage, we'll be serving Nancy Drew Virgin Daiquiris."

"I'm going to try at least two," the woman said happily and Jane smiled with relief. She'd turned another disgruntled guest's mood around.

That had better be the last one or we'll lose money at the bar tonight, she thought.

Jane hoped to type the cheat sheet for the staff in order to help them recognize the various detective characters, but decided to put if off until the morning. She was certain that none of the guests would be in costume for the evening's events because she'd created a detailed itinerary for the week and mailed it to the registered guests weeks ago. Along with the times and locations, Jane had provided dress code suggestions for each activity. For the first event, a "Find the Clues" scavenger hunt, she'd recommended casual dress, citing that the game would take guests all over the hotel and its grounds.

"Hem! Fitz! Are you ready?" Jane entered the back office to find her boys bent over the copier with their tongues pressed to the glass. "Stop that this instant!" she commanded in her sternest voice.

Her sons, dressed in matching safari outfits, slammed the copier lid shut and saluted her. The trio then marched into the lobby, where the twins raised kazoos to their lips and hummed a boisterous reveille. The guests, who'd been chatting excitedly among themselves, immediately fell silent.

"Hear ye! Hear ye!" Hem shouted theatrically. "The hunt is about to begin."

Jane fought to keep a straight face, but it was difficult. Her boys were impetuous, mischievous, and bullheaded, but they were also clever, imaginative, and fearless. Watching them now, she longed to throw her arms around them and kiss their cheeks, where the icing from dozens of stolen tea cakes still clung to their skin, but she restrained herself.

Once the guests had fallen silent, Butterworth stepped forward and gave the lapels of his uniform coat a firm tug and explained the rules of the hunt clearly and succinctly. Each guest would receive an envelope with a literary clue. Their task was to work out which Storyton Hall location the clue directed them to. If they guessed correctly, the next clue would be waiting for them in that particular spot. The person who found their clues the quickest would win the prize. When Butterworth was done, he told his rapt audience to direct their attention to the grandfather clock. The guests stared fixedly at the second hand, their fingers clutching the white envelopes the staff had distributed during Butterworth's speech.

You could hear a pin drop, Jane thought, reveling in the air of suspense.

When the second hand reached the twelve, Butterworth gave a slow nod. "You may now open your envelopes."

Every envelope contained a line of dialogue spoken by a famous fictional detective. The quotes were meant to have people scurrying all over the estate, thus helping the guests become familiar with the buildings and grounds. If guests couldn't figure out their clue, they were allowed to ask certain staff members for help. Fitz and Hem, who'd helped the housekeepers, bellhops, and groundskeepers hide the clues, wore their "Ask Me!" badges with pride.

"I read this book in June!" a woman told her male companion after seeing her clue. "It's from Adela Dundee's *The Hollow in the Heart of the World*. In this scene, Umberto Ferrari finds a rare Padparadscha sapphire hidden inside an old globe. I saw a globe in the library." She bounced up and down in excitement. "This is such fun! Where are you going?"

"In the opposite direction from you, my dear," the man replied cheerfully. He pointed to a map of the resort. "I'm off to the rose garden. Apparently, there's a pink rose with my name on it."

Jane smiled. Hercule Poirot had had a rose named after him in *How Does Your Garden Grow?* She was pleased to see that most of the guests were enjoying a successful start to the scavenger hunt. However, a few were obviously stumped.

"I must win that prize," Jane overheard a woman muttering to herself. She caught a glimpse of white hair streaked with silver and a periwinkle blouse before the woman hurried down the hall.

The twins were assisting a flustered man in his early thirties. "I only came to this thing to impress my girlfriend," he moaned. "I'm an investment banker, for Pete's sake. Never read a mystery novel in my life."

Fitz murmured something to the agitated guest. The man nodded enthusiastically, pressed several bills into Fitz's hand, and then dashed off. Looking supremely satisfied. Fitz counted the money and handed Hem several dollars, and the two boys exchanged one of their many secret handshakes.

Jane was about to chastise her sons for accepting bribes

when they wriggled their way through a knot of giddy women and abruptly vanished.

At that moment, Felix Hampden, the Umberto Ferrari look-alike, appeared from behind a potted ficus tree. He glanced about in desperation and then, seeing Jane, made his way to her side with that quick, funny little gait of his. He was the only guest in costume. "Beautiful *signora*. Would you be so kind?" He stroked his pencil mustache in agitation. "I, the most dashing and intrepid inspector in all of Europe, am confounded by this clue."

Examining the slip of paper, Jane read the line out loud. "'Hemlock in the cocktails, wasn't it?'" She tapped her chin and tried to remember which book the quote came from. "I believe this is from *The Mirror Crack'd from Side to Side*."

When the little man gave her a baffled frown, Jane tried again. "You didn't investigate this case, *signor*. Miss Marple, the British lady sleuth, was the investigator. However, I believe the key word here is 'cocktail.'"

Hampden's eyes darkened. "*Signorina* Marple? She is no detective! A woman cannot detect. It is a man's job!" And with that, he spun on his patent leather heels and waddled off in the direction of the Ian Fleming Lounge.

Butterworth sidled up to Jane. "The gentleman seems rather upset."

"Mr. Hampden seems to take his role as Ferrari very seriously," Jane said. "I hope he isn't nasty to the Miss Marples, Nancy Drews, or Harriet Vanes over the next six days, or things could get unpleasant."

The butler nodded in agreement. "I heard several individuals express a keen interest in winning the hunt. If I might ask, what prize has them so motivated?"

They both watched a young woman run into the lobby, stop in the middle of the floor to examine her map, give a small cry of dismay, and then leave again the way she'd come.

"It's a book," Jane said. "A lovely book, to be sure, but I hadn't expected it to create such zealous reactions. The collection of letters written by Adela Dundee to her husband before he died in the war supposedly reveals how she came up with Umberto Ferrari among other writing secrets. Aunt Octavia donated the first edition copy from her personal library. She's been looking forward to this event ever since I mentioned it."

"So I gather," Butterworth said with the barest hint of a smile. "A bellhop told me that your great-aunt has had a wing chair and footstool moved from the Daphne du Maurier Morning Room to the back porch. She is presently holding court at the top of the stairs. She has that ridiculously coddled cat on her lap and is feeding him tidbits while he casts superior glances at all the guests."

Jane laughed. "She must be loving the attention. And if Muffet Cat is getting treats, then I can only assume Aunt Octavia is gulping down shortbread cookies and tea cakes as fast as she can."

"Indeed." Butterworth cleared his throat, a sure sign of disapproval.

"She eats as though she had the metabolism of an Olympic gymnast, which, unfortunately, she doesn't, but none of us can do a thing with her," Jane said helplessly. "Aunt Octavia is the queen of Storyton Hall. Unfortunately, our monarch won't even acknowledge that she's diabetic."

Butterworth opened his mouth to reply when the woman with the cloud of white hair returned to the lobby. Gripping a clue in her closed fist, she marched up to Jane and said, "I don't have time to play silly games. What's the answer to this?"

What a poor sport, Jane thought but pasted on a smile. "May I?" She gestured at the crumpled scrap of paper.

The woman issued a snort of impatience and peeled the clue from her damp palm. Her forehead was also glistening with perspiration and her eyes were wild.

"Are you feeling all right?" Jane asked in concern.

"I'll feel better after I've won," the woman replied tersely. Ignoring the guest's rudeness, Jane scanned the quote.

"You need to proceed to the Isak Dinesen Safari Room. It's down the lobby, through the—"

"I know where it is!" The woman snatched the paper from Jane and jogged away.

Butterworth cleared his throat again. "Perhaps we should have retained Dr. Lydgate for the evening. If the other guests are as desperate to achieve victory as that one, they might very well come to blows."

"Don't be silly," Jane said, giving the butler an affectionate pat on the arm. "These people are mystery fans. Readers. Bibliophiles. They're far too refined to resort to violence."

In the end, it was Felix Hampden, aka Umberto Ferrari, who claimed the prize. Jane presented him with Aunt Octavia's gift-wrapped book in the Ian Fleming Lounge. Most of the guests applauded the little bald man with the pencil mustache and then rushed to the bar to alleviate the thirst brought on by physical and mental exertion. However, several people hung back, obviously interested in sharing a private word with Felix Hampden.

Jane noticed that the woman with the white hair was the first to approach him. Brandishing a checkbook, she took out a pen and held it over a blank check. When Hampden shook his head and politely excused himself, her face grew purple with fury.

He didn't get far when his path was blocked by a man who looked remarkably like Hugh Fraser, the actor who'd played Captain Arthur Hastings opposite David Suchet's Poirot in several film adaptations of Agatha Christie's novels. The man clapped Felix Hampden on the back and gestured for him to take a seat. Jane couldn't hear Hampden's response, but she saw him stiffen, execute a dismissive bow, and walk away. She didn't care for the manner in which the Hastings doppelgänger glared at the smaller man as he departed.

If the Hastings look-alike's angry expression had Jane concerned, it was nothing compared to the unease she felt when she saw a man step from the shadows in the corner of the room to follow Felix into the hall. The man's black clothing and the stealth with which he moved unnerved Jane. She also didn't care for the way his baseball cap, emblazoned with a green sea serpent, was pulled down over his brow. She was about to go after both men when Fitz and Hem came barreling through the doorway.

One glance and Jane knew that her sons were scared. They were so rarely frightened that the sight of their pale faces and wide eyes filled her with dread.

Jane signaled to them, and within seconds, Fitz was tugging on her arm. "Aunt Octavia's sick!"

Hem nodded frantically. "Come quick!"

"Show me," she said in a steady voice that belied her anxiety.

The boys led her to the Jane Austen Parlor. Four male staff members had managed to move Aunt Octavia onto the rose-colored fainting couch. A housekeeper was removing her shoes while another dabbed at her forehead with a wet cloth. Muffet Cat was under the couch, his yellow eyes wide as moons. Upon seeing Jane, he released a frightened mewl that was so out of character that everyone in the room exchanged startled glances.

Crossing the floral rug, Jane maneuvered around groupings of Victorian furniture and side tables crowded with knickknacks. She could feel the portraits of her Steward ancestors watching her from within their gilt frames as she dropped to her great-aunt's side.

Jane lifted her aunt's hand and gave it a gentle squeeze. "Aunt Octavia? Can you hear me?"

Her aunt's closed eyelids fluttered and she moaned. Jane fought back tears. Her indomitable aunt seemed deflated. Diminished. And when she spoke, her voice was thin and weak. "The book. The one you gave as a prize. Two copies.

I gave you . . . wrong book." Octavia opened her eyes. "It cannot leave Storyton. Get our copy back before . . ." She trailed off. Her eyes fell shut and she lay utterly still.

"Aunt Octavia!" Jane shook her aunt's shoulder. "Call the doctor!" she shouted while her fingers searched for a pulse in her aunt's fleshy neck. She found it. Thready and faint, but there all the same. "Thank God." Jane allowed herself a single sob and then looked up, taking in the pinched and worried faces gathered around the couch. "Anyone have a mirror?"

"I do." A desk clerk rushed forward and placed a silver lipstick case in Jane's hand. Jane opened the case and held the narrow mirror beneath her aunt's nose. When it turned cloudy, she nearly sobbed again.

"Is she going to be all right?" Fitz whispered and knelt beside Jane.

"I think so," she whispered back.

Hem got on his knees on her other side and put his small hand on her arm. He didn't say a word, but the presence of her two sons gave Jane the strength she needed to regain her composure.

"Lizzy, would you go to my aunt's rooms and fetch her insulin kit? And tell my uncle what's happened." A pretty young woman nodded and hurried from the room. "Ned, would you wait by the entrance for Doc Lydgate?" The bellhop snapped his heels together and departed. "Thank you, everyone. Thank you for staying calm and acting so quickly. Well done. I think we should clear the room now. Give my aunt a little space."

The statement was absurd, considering that only a handful of people were in the spacious room. However, the combination of the ornate furniture, busy wallpaper, curios, and shock had Jane feeling claustrophobic.

After murmuring words of encouragement, the staff withdrew, all except for Mrs. Hubbard. She refused to budge. "I've known Ms. Octavia my whole life and I won't abandon her now," the head chef declared, and Jane had no choice but to demur.

"What book was Aunt Octavia talking about?" Fitz asked, reaching under the couch to stroke Muffet Cat's head. But the cat didn't want to be touched. He retreated deeper into the shadows, his yellow eyes shining with agitation.

"I'm not sure," Jane said. "She might have been referring to the book we awarded the victor of the scavenger hunt."

Hem's fingers tightened on her arm. "Did the man with the funny mustache win?"

Jane studied her son. "Yes, he did. Why? What is it, Hem?"

The boys exchanged guilty looks. "He only won because of us," Fitz said. "We helped him every time he got stuck."

"And he got stuck a lot," Hem added.

Jane opened her mouth to chastise her sons when Fitz suddenly cried, "We had to! He said he had to win—that he'd die if he didn't win! He wasn't kidding, Mom. Really."

"Why would he say such a thing?" Jane felt the stirrings of alarm. Was Aunt Octavia's book that valuable?"

"I don't know." Fitz shrugged innocently. "But he was a really good tipper."

Just then, Jane heard Doc Lydgate's voice echoing down the hallway. She prodded each boy in the chest with her index finger. "Off to bed. No arguments. I'll send Ned to watch you, and we'll talk in the morning."

When the boys were gone, Jane reached up and brushed a strand of damp hair from her aunt's cheek. "We'll get the book back. I promise."

It was a promise Jane sincerely hoped she could keep.

FIVE

An hour later, Jane stood with Doc Lydgate in the hospital waiting room. A physician in green scrubs had just informed her that Aunt Octavia had suffered a stroke.

"May I see her?" Jane asked. "My great-uncle is on his way, but I'd like to wait with her until he arrives."

Glancing down at a patient chart, the man shook his head. "Not just yet, but we'll come get you as soon as she's resting comfortably." His voice was kind and Jane tried to be reassured by his words.

Nodding absently, she sank into a chair.

Doc Lydgate sat beside her. "I'm sorry, my dear. I wish I could say that I'm surprised, but I warned your aunt a hundred times about her diet. I've repeatedly given her brochures outlining the risks of Type 2 diabetes and have advised her to exercise, but whenever I pay her a home visit, she dismisses all of my recommendations. For the past year, she's refused to step onto a scale. In the end, there's only so much a local GP can do."

"She's impossible. And you've been devoted to her, I know." Jane patted his hand. "We've all chided, nagged, and pleaded for her to pay more attention to her health, but it's no use. She simply won't change her ways."

Doc Lydgate gestured around the waiting room. "If she doesn't, we'll be here again."

Jane didn't like that thought at all. "That might be the one arguing point that will finally convince her to heed your advice. She abhors having to come over the mountain for any reason and she hates being away from Storyton Hall. She hasn't left the grounds or village in years."

"I hope she can return home soon," the doc said. "And if she requires occupational therapy or a full-time nurse, we'll find the most highly skilled and trustworthy individual."

"She has to come home! I can't imagine Storyton Hall without her." Jane interlaced her fingers to keep them from trembling. "Oh, why won't they let me see her?"

Doc Lydgate gave Jane's arm a paternal squeeze. "What you need is a strong cup of coffee and something to eat. You look quite peaked. I'll fetch something from the cafeteria." He held out a finger to stave off her protests. "Doctor's orders."

"Thank you. It's such a comfort to have you here." Jane gave him a grateful smile.

Five minutes after the doc left, a nurse approached Jane. "Are you with Octavia Steward?" When Jane nodded, the woman waved toward the double doors leading to the hospital's inner passages. "You can come on back."

Jane got to her feet just as Uncle Aloysius and Sterling, Storyton Hall's head chauffeur, rushed into the waiting room.

"Where's my sweet? Where's my wife?" her uncle asked. His fishing hat was crumpled between his hands, and Jane saw a spot of blood collect near his wrist and fall onto the tiled floor.

"You're bleeding!" Jane carefully pried his fingers away from the hat. Fishhooks protruded from his middle and pinkie fingers.

The nurse peered over Jane's shoulder. "You need to register, sir, and let someone take care of that before—"

"Stuff and nonsense," Uncle Aloysius interjected. "Take me to my wife."

The nurse frowned in response to his patrician tone.

"Wrap this around your hand, sir," Sterling said, offering Jane's uncle a handkerchief. "It'll keep the floor clean until these fine people can fix you up."

Jane shot the nurse a plaintive look. After a moment's pause, she dipped her chin and gestured for them to follow her down a brightly lit corridor.

"She's sleeping right now," the nurse said as she entered a room containing a bed, an upholstered recliner, and a wall-mounted television set.

Aunt Octavia was tucked under a pale blue blanket. Her arms were stretched out, and lines ran from both wrists to IV and medicine bags on stands next to the bed. Monitors flanked the headboard like sentinels, humming and beeping without pause. A second nurse bustled about, making notes on Octavia's chart and conferring with the nurse who'd led them to the room, but Jane's aunt didn't move.

Uncle Aloysius lifted his wife's hand, kissed her palm, and then pressed it to his cheek. "Darling."

Sterling's eyes grew moist. Swallowing hard, he leaned over to Jane and murmured, "I'll be out in the hall if you need me, Ms. Steward."

Jane nodded and approached the nurse holding the chart. "We were told she had a stroke. How serious was it?"

"The doctor will go over everything with you," the nurse said. "We don't know the full effects of the stroke at this time. When she wakes up, we'll run more tests."

Jane wished Doc Lydgate would appear. She had no idea which questions to ask. "Did she say anything? Is she . . ." Casting an anxious glance at her uncle, Jane lowered her voice. "Was there brain damage?"

"She was talking right up until we gave her something to help her rest. We had no trouble understanding her, which is a good sign. She kept saying, 'Get the book back. The prize book. Wrong copy. Get it back.' The nurse hugged the chart against her chest. "She became so agitated that we were concerned she might harm herself. But you don't have to worry about that now. She'll sleep until morning, and we'll be checking on her all night long."

"Oh, Aunt Octavia." Jane covered her mouth with her hand and stifled the sob welling up in her throat. "Please. If she wakes up, will you tell her that we're getting the book back? Will you tell her that Jane said everything is fine?" She touched the nurse on the wrist. "And please don't let my uncle know that she was so upset she needed sedation. He's stressed enough as it is."

The nurse smiled. "Sure thing, honey."

Doc Lydgate arrived carrying a beverage tray filled with four cups of coffee. He distributed coffee to Jane, Sterling, and Uncle Aloysius, who put his cup on the table next to the bed and let it sit there, untouched. The only thing he could focus on at that moment was his wife.

"I'll hunt down the attending physician," Doc Lydgate said, leaving Jane standing there with nothing to do but listen to the machines and watch the steady rise and fall of her aunt's chest.

Jane remained in that position for what seemed like a long time. Eventually, Doc Lydgate reappeared and offered to drive her home.

"You might as well save your strength for tomorrow," he said kindly. "We already know who'll be sleeping in that recliner tonight."

They both looked at Uncle Aloysius.

Jane nodded. "Sterling can take me back to Storyton Hall. You've done more than enough for us already."

Sterling had had the foresight to grab one of the resort's extra toiletry kits and a blanket in case Uncle Aloysius should need to spend the night. When he offered them to Jane, she praised him for being so thoughtful and then laid them on the seat of the recliner.

"I'll be back in the morning," she told her uncle and

kissed him on the cheek. His skin felt cold and paper-thin, so Jane wrapped the blanket around his shoulders. "You need to take care of yourself in order to take care of her," she whispered and rubbed his back.

He gazed up at her with frightened eyes. "I might be the one with Steward blood in my veins, but it's Octavia who has the true heart of a Steward. She loves every brick and piece of timber that is Storyton Hall. It cannot endure without her. *I* cannot endure without her."

"You won't have to," Jane promised. "We just need to be as stubborn and determined as she is. We have to monitor what she eats and get her to exercise more often."

Uncle Aloysius raised his shaggy eyebrows. "Easier said than done, my dear. I haven't won an argument with your aunt for nearly thirty years."

"It won't be you against her. Everyone at Storyton Hall will unite in this common cause. We all want her to live for a long, long time, and if that means incurring her displeasure and having a few bowls of sugar-free pudding thrown at our heads, so be it."

"Best warn the housekeepers now." Her uncle managed a small smile. "You're a good girl, Janie. Go home. Your aunt will rest easier knowing you're holding down the fort, and the boys will be wondering what's happened."

Kissing him once more, Jane left.

At Storyton Hall, the gazes of a dozen concerned staff members followed her through the employee entrance. Sterling had offered to tell the staff about Aunt Octavia and Jane had gratefully accepted. She didn't want to let another second pass until she'd gotten her aunt's book from Felix Hampden.

Because she'd given Hampden his key, Jane knew that he was in room 316. The Mystery Suite. Heading for the servant's staircase, Jane pushed on the door marked STAFF ONLY and nearly collided with Mrs. Hubbard.

"I've been waiting up for you!" she cried. "Don't spare me. Tell me quickly! Is she . . ."

"Sleeping," Jane said.

"Thank the Lord!" Mrs. Hubbard exclaimed and pulled Jane into a fervent embrace. As comforting as Mrs. Hubbard's warm arms were, Jane hastened to free herself. She thought she'd succeeded until the head cook's hand closed around her wrist. "I'm to blame, aren't I? I've killed her with my rich food, haven't I?"

Jane shook her head, moved by the stricken look on Mrs. Hubbard's face. "We're all at fault for indulging her every whim. But that's over and done with now. As soon as Aunt Octavia is well enough to return to Storyton, she'll be on a strict diet. Anyone who sneaks her sweets will answer to me."

Putting hands on hips, Mrs. Hubbard puffed up her generous bosom. "And to me as well."

"With your help, I'm confident that Aunt Octavia will not only recover, but add a decade or two to her life."

Mrs. Hubbard lifted her eyes to the heavens. "God willing."

"I need to see a guest." Jane said gently but firmly. "There's no sense in worrying any more tonight. I'll come to the kitchen in the morning if there are any updates. But for now, go home and put your feet up."

"Yes. That's a good idea. The feet will go up and the nightcap will go down," Mrs. Hubbard murmured as she headed down the corridor toward the kitchen.

Jane sighed. She'd love nothing better than to follow her own advice. She longed to put on her pajamas and flop onto her bed, but she had to tell Felix Hampden about the prize mix-up and assure him that she'd have another copy of the book in his hands first thing tomorrow.

When she reached his room, however, she found a DO NOT DISTURB sign hanging from the doorknob.

"This is a fresh quandary," Jane muttered. She glanced up and down the hall, making sure there were no other guests around before putting her ear to the door. Not a sound came from within.

Stepping back a pace, Jane stared at the sign. She was at a total loss. Aunt Octavia needed her to recover the book, but Jane had been taught to adhere to a strict code when it came to Storyton Hall's guests. It was so ingrained in her that she never questioned it. Guests were to be treated with courtesy and respect at all times, even when they were behaving badly. Even though Felix Hampden had bribed the twins in order to win the scavenger hunt, his actions still did not give Jane permission to disturb him. He was a guest. The very word created an automatic response deep within Jane's psyche.

Defeated, she turned away from the door. But as she did so, an image of Aunt Octavia's anguished face entered her mind, and before her determination could falter, she raised her fist and wrapped softly on the thick, polished wood. She waited. Listened. And lightly knocked again. There was no answer. Taking a deep breath, Jane knocked with more force and then snapped her hand down to her side as if she'd been caught stealing cookies from Mrs. Hubbard's special jar in the butler's pantry.

"He might be wearing earplugs," she whispered to herself. Down the hall, the elevator pinged, causing Jane to start. It would be unseemly for her to be seen standing in front of an occupied guest room, especially one with a DO NOT DISTURB sign hanging from its doorknob, so she fled.

Descending the staircase to the second floor, Jane found Muffet Cat waiting to be let inside her aunt and uncle's apartment.

"Oh, you poor thing," Jane said, scooping the big cat into her arms. Muffet Cat pressed his face against her chest and purred while she unlocked the door. After turning on the lights, Jane set Muffet Cat on a chair in the sitting room and assured him that Aunt Octavia would be home soon.

She then entered her aunt and uncle's private library and immediately spotted a familiar roll of wrapping paper. Felix Hampden's prize had been packaged in the same paper. "If there are two copies of the same book, this might be where Aunt Octavia wrapped the wrong book." Feeling a thrill of hope, Jane sifted through a large box of bows, ribbon, tape, and tags, but came up empty-handed. She then spied a rectangular lump under her aunt's copy of the *New York Times*, which was spread open on the club chair by the fireplace. When she peeked underneath the Arts section, she found the missing book.

The hardback had a dark blue cover featuring a photograph of an old-fashioned typewriter. There was nothing remarkable about the image and Jane didn't recognize the name of the editor, one Alice Hart, so she flipped to the copyright page. "A first edition. And it's in pristine condition. Mr. Hampden shouldn't be disappointed." She fanned the pages to dislodge any loose papers, but the book didn't seem to be keeping any secrets. "No surprise there," she murmured. "It's my aunt's copy that's special. I just wish I knew why."

Tucking the book under her arm, Jane turned off the lights, locked the apartment, and walked home.

She thanked Ned and tried to pay him, but as usual, he refused. Though Ned was in his early twenties and had plenty of friends his own age, he genuinely enjoyed spending time with Fitz and Hem.

"I have five sisters," he'd once explained to Jane. "I grew up in a house filled with dolls, dresses, and the color pink. Do you know how much I would have loved a little brother? When I hang out with Fitz and Hem, I feel like I have two of them."

"One of these days, I'm going to find a way to thank you properly," she told him now.

Ned smiled shyly and wished Jane a good night. As she moved through the house, Jane saw signs of what Ned and the twins had gotten into during her absence. They'd had hot chocolate with half a bag's worth of marshmallows in the kitchen, made a tent of blankets in the living room, and judging from the wet spots on the walls, had waged a bubble war on the way to bed. Ned did a fabulous job entertaining the boys, but he rarely tidied up afterward.

"Oh well. At least nothing's broken or burned," Jane said, collecting the plastic bubble bottles off the floor. They were covered with a sticky film and the soapy liquid had leaked all over the hall runner.

Too worn out to scrub the rug, Jane tossed the bottles into the trash, rinsed her hands, and opened the door to the boys' room to make sure they were truly asleep. Fitz and Hem had perfected the art of fake slumber years ago, so she stood in place until she was convinced that they were actually asleep.

Satisfied that the twins were slumbering peacefully, Jane washed her face and put on her favorite pajamas, which were covered with designs of reading glasses, coffee cups, and books. She'd had them for so many years that they were quite threadbare at the knees and elbows, but she refused to discard them.

"You look like an orphan from our comic," Fitz had told her several months ago while brandishing a graphic novel version of *Great Expectations*. The adaptation of Dickens's famous tale had been geared toward a younger audience, and the twins had reread it a dozen times. In fact, they'd spoken in a Cockney accent for weeks and had only given it up when Eloise showed them a beautifully illustrated nonfiction book about Blackbeard the pirate. From then on out, Jane heard phrases like "shiver me timbers" and "walk the plank, ye dirty hornswaggle" until she thought she'd go mad.

Jane climbed into bed, smiling at the sudden memory of Hem helping himself to a butterscotch candy from the crystal bowl in Aunt Octavia's sitting room. When she caught him in the act, he'd swaggered up to her and growled, "I give no quarter to wenches." Aunt Octavia had responded by thwacking him on the bottom with her cane. The blow was feather-light, but Hem had been so shocked that he nearly burst into tears. Fitz came forward to defend his brother, threatening to make Aunt Octavia walk the plank. She'd squinted her eyes, curled her lip, and snarled, "Touch my plunder and I'll send you straight to Davy Jones's locker." Seconds later, all three of them were doubled over in laughter.

"We have loads more memories to make together, Aunt Octavia," Jane whispered as she settled back against her pillow. Picking up the book of Dundee's letters, she decided to examine it a final time before calling it a night.

Jane was so groggy that she barely made it to the end of the introduction. She was about to set the book on her nightstand when, on a whim, she decided to see if there was a photo of the editor on the inside of the dust jacket. The moment she laid eyes on the image of a lovely young woman with long, wavy blond hair, Jane let out a gasp.

"It's her!" she cried softly. "The woman who fell from her horse. The woman who died in the village."

With her heart thudding against her rib cage, Jane grabbed the phone and willed her shaky fingers to dial Eloise's number. It never occurred to her to call the sheriff. Jane was scared, shocked, and emotionally drained. She didn't want to speak with the sheriff. She wanted to hear the familiar voice of her best friend.

Eloise managed to say hello before a tumult of words poured forth from Jane. She spoke clearly at first, describing Aunt Octavia's collapse and how she'd been rushed to the hospital, but by the time Jane reached the part about discovering the identity of the dead woman, her speech had turned into an incoherent jumble.

"You can tell me the rest in person. I'm coming over," Eloise said and hung up.

Jane dissolved into tears for several minutes and then went into the bathroom to splash water on her face. By the time she'd donned a robe, turned on a few lights, and cleaned up the mess Ned and her sons had made in the kitchen, Eloise was tapping on the back door.

As soon as she stepped into the house, Eloise threw her arms around Jane. "You poor thing! I brought an overnight bag, so go on and tell me everything from the beginning."

Moved by her friend's devotion, Jane squeezed Eloise's arm and led her to the living room. She showed her the photograph of Alice Hart and said, "Now that you're here, I should call Sheriff Evans. The last time I ran into him, I asked him about this woman. Alice. He told me that no one had come forward to claim her and that she'd finally been cremated. No final words were spoken for her. No prayers. Isn't that terribly sad?"

Eloise studied Alice's photograph and then met Jane's eyes. "She's so young. You told me that Doc Lydgate believed her death had something to do with her heart. Did Sheriff Evans confirm that theory?"

"He didn't come right out and say it, but I got the impression that the doc was right." She grasped Eloise by the hand. "We need to get in touch with the sheriff. Alice's family must be in agony. All this time, they had no idea that she visited Storyton. That she died here. *I* may forgotten about her, but there must be someone who's been waiting for her to come home."

Nodding, Eloise said, "I'll take care of the phone call, but only if you promise to go to bed. You're as pale as a wraith and I could pack the contents of La Grande Dame in the bags under your eyes." She tapped the face of her watch. "You'll be in high demand tomorrow morning. With your aunt in the hospital, a resort full of guests, and a lineup of special events, you can't afford to stay awake another minute longer. And don't set your alarm either. I'll get you up by serving you a steaming cup of coffee."

"That sounds really nice," Jane said and gave Eloise a fierce hug. "You're the best."

"So my customers tell me. But I'd really like to hear those words spoken by a gorgeous single man. One who reads, has impeccable manners, and can watch *Masterpiece Theater* without dozing off. I'm setting the bar ridiculously high, I know." Eloise grinned and shooed Jane up the stairs.

Jane awoke the next morning feeling surprisingly well rested. It was only when she looked at the clock on her nightstand that she understood why.

"It's so late!" she croaked and flung the covers aside. Pulling on her slippers, she opened her bedroom door, hurried to the end of the hallway, and paused. The twins' laughter floated up from downstairs, but she also heard the timbre of a deep and unfamiliar voice intermingling with their high, excited tones. The strange voice was mistakably male.

It can only be Sheriff Evans. It must be urgent if he's here at this time in the morning. He might need my help.

She was so focused on this possibility that she forgot she was dressed in slippers and ratty pajamas and had yet to brush her hair, let alone her teeth. Flying down the stairs, she hastened through the living room into the kitchen to find a tall man wearing black jeans and a slate gray T-shirt standing at her stove.

Sheriff Evans was in his late fifties. He was fair-haired, stocky, and had a slight paunch. This man was as sinewy as a panther and moved about Jane's kitchen with a cat's fluid grace. To Jane, the entire scene was surreal. There were Fitz and Hem, perched on their stools at the counter, casually drinking orange juice and exchanging knock-knock jokes with Edwin Alcott.

Why is Eloise's brother in my house? What is he doing cooking eggs for my sons?

"Good morning," she said, her voice hoarse. "What's going on?"

When he glanced at her, Edwin's eyebrows shot up his forehead, but he didn't say a word about her appearance. He simply turned, picked up the frying pan, and slid a picture-perfect tomato and basil omelet onto a plate. "Breakfast is served," he said, a glint of amusement in his dark eyes.

Jane didn't react. She just stood there staring until Fitz said, "Mom's a total zombie without her coffee."

"Yeah," Hem added. "You'd better get her some or she might start eating our brains."

"If she tries, I'll tell her I need to cook them first. They're much better that way." Edwin winked at the twins and reached for the coffeepot while Jane wondered when she'd awaken from what could only be a very peculiar dream.

SIX

Fitz jumped off his stool and tugged on Jane's hand.
His fingers were sticky and dotted with flecks of pulp from
the orange he'd been eating. Jane knew then that she wasn't
dreaming.

"Your eggs are getting cold," Edwin said.

Still confused, she took a seat at the counter. After a few
fortifying sips of coffee, her mind was able to function
coherently. "Clean up your plates," she told the boys. "And
then get dressed and brush your teeth. It's a school day."

"Prison day, you mean," Hem grumbled, but did as he
was told. Fitz followed suit, murmuring something about
jailbreaks under his breath.

After the twins thundered up the stairs, Jane turned to
Edwin. "Thank you for making breakfast." She indicated
the empty stools the boys had vacated. "It looks like Fitz
and Hem enjoyed every bite, and I don't mean to sound rude,
but why are you here? Where's Eloise?"

"She went to the registration desk to find someone to
cover for you." Again, he looked amused. "You must sleep
very soundly. Your sons don't seem to have indoor voices."

Even though it was accurate, the comment annoyed Jane. "So Eloise asked you to drive in from the village to babysit?"

"Actually, she tricked me into coming by suggesting that I practice my culinary skills on you. She thought I should get a second opinion and a third and a fourth before investing in a café." He gestured at her untouched omelet. "Fitz and Hem ate while their food was still warm. If that tastes like tire rubber, it has nothing to do with my cooking."

Taking the hint, Jane picked up her fork and popped a bite of omelet in her mouth. A medley of flavors—balsamic tomatoes, warm goat cheese, fresh basil, and fluffy eggs—washed over her tongue. "Delicious," she pronounced after she'd swallowed.

It didn't take her long to devour the rest of the omelet, and she realized that she'd eaten very little since tea the day before. And although Jane could feel the weight of Edwin's gaze on her, she didn't take dainty bites or pause to chitchat. Most women would probably be mortified over the idea of inhaling their food while such a handsome man watched their every move, but Jane didn't care. She had too much on her mind to be concerned about being ladylike.

When she was done, Edwin removed her empty plate and served her a bowl of sliced strawberries garnished with a dollop of cinnamon sour cream. "No time to savor this, I'm afraid. You're supposed to meet the sheriff in the lobby in fifteen minutes."

"What?" Jane nearly overturned her coffee cup.

Edwin nodded, his expression turning somber. "It's about the woman who lost control of her horse." Suddenly, he was leaning over the counter, his face inches away from Jane's. His dark eyes were piercing, hawklike. "Tell me how she died. No one seems to know and I can't stop thinking about her. A dozen times each day I wonder if I could have done more. Maybe if I'd reacted sooner or caught up to her faster . . ."

Jane shook her head. "You did everything you could. I

saw you. You rode like the wind. You were intent on catching her. I could see it in every muscle in your body." She was strangely tempted to reach out and touch his strong jaw. Shaking her head again, this time to clear it, she went on. "Doc Lydgate believed that she had some kind of preexisting heart condition. No one could have saved her, but at least you tried. I think that will mean a great deal to her family."

Edwin didn't respond, and Jane could see that he was deeply troubled by Alice Hart's death. Jane recalled the fury with which he had pursued Alice's spooked mare, the look of intensity in his eyes as he flew past the bookstore, his hand stretched out, grabbing desperately for the mare's reins. She could easily imagine him scooping Alice off the ground, her long hair brushing against his shin as he rushed her into Doc Lydgate's office.

Jane looked at Edwin now, but his face might as well have been made of stone so she abandoned the idea of trying to comfort him further. She didn't know what else to say, and she didn't have the time to search for the right words.

"I'd better get dressed," Jane said, and he dipped his chin in silent agreement.

Upstairs, she showered and put on a wrap dress the color of fresh persimmons and a pair of brown leather boots. Hollering at the boys to make their beds and meet her at the front door, she gathered her hair into a loose knot at the nape of her neck and spent another precious two minutes applying lipstick and mascara.

When Jane got downstairs, Edwin was gone and Fitz and Hem were engaged in a wooden sword duel.

"We're way tardy, Mom," Hem pointed out, sounding quite happy.

"We've already missed first period," Fitz said, chiming in. "And we don't have any lunch."

Jane grabbed her purse and the book of Adela Dundee letters. "If you don't hurry, you'll miss second period too. Run straight to the kitchen and ask Mrs. Hubbard to pack you something to eat. Make sure to use your best manners because she's very busy today. Then track down Mr. Sterling and see if he'll give you a ride to school. I'll write a note to your teacher. With Aunt Octavia in the hospital, she's sure to excuse your lateness."

The twins abruptly stopped their swordplay.

"Eloise said that she might not come home for a while," Fitz said.

"And she'll have to wear a paper hospital dress," Hem added soberly. "Aunt Octavia won't like that, so we thought we could bring her a dress. A new one from Miss Mabel's shop."

Fitz gestured at the mound of crumpled dollar bills on the kitchen table. "That's our tip money from yesterday. We want to get her something nice."

Jane gave them a tender smile. "That's very sweet, boys, but I don't want you worrying about Aunt Octavia. She's going to be just fine. It might take a while, but she will be. We'll see about having a new dress made for her before she comes home. Okay?"

"Okay," they said in unison.

"Now get going or you'll be so late that you won't need a lunch." She gave each boy a gentle push and watched them race down the gravel path leading to Storyton Hall. Her pace was a trifle slower. Even though she was also late, the resort manager could hardly be seen hiking up her skirts and running across the back lawn, but she walked as fast as she could and arrived in the lobby breathless and flushed.

Sheriff Evans was pouring himself a cup of coffee from one of the large urns set up on a table near the grandfather clock. Jane would have loved another jolt of caffeine too, but she decided to wait until she'd spoken with the sheriff about Alice Hart.

"Good morning," she said with forced cheer. "Sorry to keep you waiting. Should we go into my office?"

The sheriff nodded. "I heard about your aunt. I hope she

recovers quickly." He held up his mug. "Excellent coffee, by the way. We only have Folgers at the station. Nothing wrong with the instant stuff, but it can't hold a candle to this."

"We like our guests to start their day with a zing. Shall we?" Jane led him behind the registration desk and into her office. The moment she'd closed the door and Sheriff Evans had settled into a chair, she opened the book of Adela Dundee letters and pointed at the photograph on the dust jacket. "Is it her? The woman who died in the village?"

"Yes, it is."

Jane took a seat and clasped her hands together. "Goodness. How did her family take the news? Had they reported her missing?"

The sheriff frowned. "Miss Hart's parents weren't aware that she was missing. They admitted to not being close with their daughter. For instance, they had no idea that she'd left her job as a faculty member at a school for the arts in Vermont or that she'd broken her engagement with a fellow teacher at the same school right before coming to Storyton. Miss Hart didn't even tell them she had a boyfriend. They had to hear about him from one of Alice's high school friends."

"Are her parents coming here?"

"No. Mr. Hart isn't well enough to travel from their Nebraska farm. That's where Alice was from originally."

Jane looked down at the splayed book on her desk. "This gets sadder and sadder. What about her fiancé?"

The sheriff made a helpless gesture. "Can't get hold of the fellow. He's on sabbatical this semester in some town in England. I left him a voice mail message. Not with specifics, mind you, but I made it clear that I needed to speak with him about Miss Hart immediately."

"The poor man. I can't imagine—" Jane began when the door to her office was suddenly flung open by a housekeeper named Lizzie.

"Ms. Steward!" Lizzie's voice was hushed but agitated.

"We have a Rip Van Winkle on the third floor." Spotting the sheriff, she added, "Sorry to interrupt, sir, but this is urgent."

The sheriff gave Jane a quizzical look. "What's a Rip Van Winkle?"

"It's code among our staff," Jane replied, getting to her feet. "It's only supposed to be used when one of our guests has gone to sleep. Permanently." She turned to Lizzie. "What room? Is our Van Winkle traveling with someone or are they alone?"

Lizzie looked dismayed. "I don't know. I came straight here. This is my first Rip Van Winkle. I've never seen a . . ." The middle-aged woman trailed off. "I heard about the guest who met his Maker on the tennis court five years ago, but I've only been here for a few months. To be honest"—she prattled on, clearly flustered—"I never thought it would happen in one of my rooms. It's awful."

Jane had never set eyes on a dead body before Alice Hart's, so she completely understood the housekeeper's distress. She'd been away at a hotel management convention when an elderly man had expired on the tennis courts. He'd been playing against his wife, who was twenty years his junior and extremely fit. Apparently, the heat and exertion had proved too much for him and he'd slumped to the ground in the service box, clutching the tennis ball in his left hand. "You did the right thing, Lizzie," Jane said soothingly. "We'll take it from here."

"I'll call an ambulance," the sheriff said. "Which room is your Rip Van Winkle in?"

"The Mystery Suite, sir. It's that funny little man who kept pretending to be a fictional Italian detective. That Umberto Ferrari character."

Jane flinched as if she'd been struck. "Our Van Winkle is Felix Hampden?"

"Yes, that's his real name! I remember writing it on my welcome letter." Each member of the housekeeping staff left a personal note in the guest rooms they serviced in order to let their guests know how to reach them should they require extra linens, pillows, a cot, or anything else.

Jane picked up the book of Adela Dundee's letters and showed it to the sheriff. "He won a book just like this one last night. My great-aunt donated it, but she wrapped up her personal copy by mistake, so I went to his room last night to see if I could make a trade. For some reason, my aunt's copy was very special to her." Jane sighed. "Unfortunately, Mr. Hampden didn't respond to my knock. Because it was late, I didn't feel I had the right to disturb him. And yet, what if he'd been ill at that moment? What if I could have helped him?" Jane knew her words echoed those Edwin had spoken back in her kitchen.

"Well, whenever his end came, I don't think it was a peaceful one," Lizzie whispered theatrically.

Sheriff Evans paused in the middle of dialing the paramedics. "What makes you say that?"

"He looks like he was in terrible pain. His eyes are bulging out and his hands are like claws. He fell in a heap with his arms and legs twisted this way and that." She shuddered. "I don't mean to sound disrespectful, but it was really scary. I don't want to go in there again."

The sheriff stood. "Don't worry, Ms. Steward can show me the way. In the meantime, it would be best to keep the news about the Rip Van Winkle between the three of us. Could you do that for me Mrs. . . ."

"Benton," Lizzie said. "*Miss* Benton." She blushed prettily; obviously not as upset as she'd been several minutes ago.

"Why don't you take a break?" Jane suggested to Lizzie while the sheriff made his call to emergency services. "Have a cup of strong tea and something to eat. After you've taken a moment to recover, would you keep an eye out for the ambulance? I'd like its arrival and the removal of our Rip Van Winkle to be witnessed by as few guests as possible." Lizzie promptly agreed, and Jane ushered the housekeeper from the room.

Jane led Sheriff Evans to the third floor where she unlocked the door to room 316. Gathering her nerves, she was about to step inside when the sheriff said, "I should go in first."

Jane felt a tightening in her throat. Keeping her hand on the knob, she glanced back at the sheriff. "I don't understand."

"Based on Miss Benton's description, I should assess the scene before anyone else enters the room. Would you please remain in the hall? Just for the moment?"

Though he'd asked politely, Jane knew she was being given a command. She moved aside, but held her foot against the inside of the door so it wouldn't close all the way.

I am the manager of Storyton Hall, she thought. *I have every right to see what's in that room.*

Peering around the door, Jane caught a glimpse of Felix Hampden. He was lying on the carpet, his arms and legs bent at odd angles. Jane took in his chalk white face and unblinking gaze. She noted that Hampden wore blue pin-striped pajamas and that his feet were bare. His fingers were curled into rigid claws.

No wonder Lizzie was frightened.

Jane stood in the threshold and watched Sheriff Evans circle around the body. Jane had never seen him work before, but she'd read enough books to recognize that he was examining the room for signs of foul play. When he disappeared into the bathroom, her attention was once again drawn to Felix Hampden's face. His pale skin was etched with agony, and his eyes, which had been so lively the last time she'd seen him, were frozen orbs of pain and surprise. Jane hadn't expected to see such emotion on the dead man's face. Alice Hart certainly hadn't worn such a tortured expression.

Without even realizing she'd done so, Jane was suddenly in the room and was standing an arm's length from the dead man.

"Do heart attack victims look like this?" she asked the sheriff in a hushed voice. The man who pretended to be Umberto Ferrari might be gone, but his death filled the space with a formidable presence that he could never have commanded in life. To Jane, there was a heaviness throughout the room. It was as if the shadows of night refused to depart with the dawn. They'd stayed with Felix Hampden, hovering around him like a black fog, turning the air inordinately cold.

Crypt cold, Jane thought and rubbed her arms.

Sheriff Evans came out of the bathroom, his brow creased into a trio of deep furrows, and beckoned to her.

"I see that you decided not to wait, Ms. Steward." His voice was full of reproach. "Now that you're in, please don't touch anything."

Jane narrowed her eyes. "I have a responsibility to my guests, including this man. If something suspicious has occurred, I need to know about it."

The sheriff returned her stare and then relented. Dipping his chin, he said, "I'm trying to get a sense of what happened. Can you look around and see if anything strikes you as out of place?"

Nodding, Jane moved deeper into the room. She eyed the capsized floor lamp and mahogany table and saw shards of broken glass on the floor. "Every room has a reading nook like this one," she told the sheriff. "A soft club chair, a side table large enough to hold a drink and a dessert plate, and an adjustable lamp. The glass on the floor looks like it came from the carafe we put alongside the ice bucket." She pointed at the desk. "We provide four tumblers as well. One of them is missing."

"It's next to the body," the sheriff said, and Jane pivoted until she saw the tumbler resting close to Felix Hampden's thigh. It appeared undamaged. "Anything else?"

Jane squatted near the broken carafe and sniffed. "I don't smell liquor or soda. The stain on the carpet looks clear. Mr. Hampden must have poured himself a glass of water at some point before he knocked over the table and lamp." She glanced at the bed. The snowy white top sheet had been turned down, and a chocolate truffle wrapped in gold foil rested in the center of each plump pillow. A floral arrangement had been placed on one nightstand, and a stack of Adela Dundee novels was on the other. Jane noticed that the books been arranged in order of publication, with her first novel, *Hall of Broken Mirrors*, on top.

Jane frowned.

"What is it?" Sheriff Evans asked.

Jane gestured at the matching nightstand. "It's probably nothing, but I'm surprised that the book Mr. Hampden won last night isn't in plain view. He was so eager to claim it and leave the celebration in the Ian Fleming Lounge that I expected him to read every page before bed. It's not on the desk either."

"Hmm," the sheriff grunted and opened the closet door. "His clothes are old-fashioned. Right down to his shoes. Take a look at this. I haven't seen this kind of suitcase since we sold my grandmother's at the church rummage sale. Mr. Hampden didn't dress like he belonged to this century. That seems strange to me."

"Not as strange as you'd think." Jane joined him in front of the closet, relieved to turn her back on the little man's body. As her gaze roamed over Felix's Hampden exquisite suits, ties, hats, smoking jacket, and overcoat, she told Sheriff Evans about the Murder and Mayhem theme. "Mr. Hampden must have *really* wanted to be Umberto Ferrari for a few days. Even his pajamas are monogrammed with the famous inspector's initials. It takes a true Adela Dundee fan to know that Umberto's middle name was Benito."

The sheriff ran his hands over the suits and then flipped open the suitcase lid and prodded the silky lining with his fingertips. "The book Mr. Hampden won. Is it valuable?"

Jane recalled her aunt's extreme agitation over accidentally giving away her copy of *Lost Letters*. She couldn't tell the sheriff why Aunt Octavia's copy was special because she didn't know. "A handful of people were determined to win that book. It's a first edition and is probably worth several hundred dollars. Two guests tried to buy it from Mr. Hampden right after I presented it to him. I believe he refused both offers and seemed to be in a great hurry to get it away from everyone."

The sheriff asked another question, but Jane's mind had returned to the previous night. Once again, she was standing in the Ian Fleming Lounge as Felix Hampden maneuvered first around the man who looked like Colonel Hastings followed by the woman with the white hair. With a chill, Jane remembered the man who'd been skulking in the dark corner near the door. The man who'd left close on Mr. Hampden's heels. But then the twins had dashed in to tell her about Aunt Octavia's collapse and Jane had put aside all thoughts of Storyton Hall's guests.

Jane glanced around the closet. "Except for the suitcase, there's no place to hide a hardcover in here. Should we check the rest of the room?"

Sheriff Evans opened his mouth to answer when they heard a trio of sharp knocks. "That must be the paramedics," Jane said.

The sheriff opened the door and gestured for the EMTs to enter. After they rolled in the gurney and knelt next to Felix Hampden's body, Jane closed the door partway and stared at Lizzie through the crack. "Did they attract any attention?"

"None whatsoever," Lizzie said. "The ambulance is parked at the delivery dock and the men came up in the staff elevator. I wouldn't have let them out if there'd been guests in the hallway. Most of them are on the Lewis Carroll Croquet Lawn participating in today's tournament."

Jane sighed in relief. "Well done. I know you've already gone above and beyond for Storyton Hall today, but can you stand guard until our Rip Van Winkle has been moved downstairs?"

Lizzie stood arrow straight. "I'll do whatever needs to

be done, Ms. Steward. You gave me a job when no one else would. I spent half of my life raising children or caring for my ailing mother. You're the only one who believed I had anything to offer an employer." Suddenly, she cocked her head. "Hurry, Ms. Steward! Close the door!"

Jane did, but not before she caught a flash of white tennis shoes from across the hall.

"We took such a long nature walk that we're afraid we've missed the whole croquet tournament," Jane heard a woman say in response to Lizzie's greeting.

"I think you can still participate, ma'am. It's so beautiful outside that most of the guests showed up to play."

"We'd better hurry," a man said and then his voice faded as the couple headed to the elevator. Because Storyton Hall was built of thick plaster, stout beams, and the finest quality timber, guests rarely lodged noise complaints. So when Jane shut the heavy wooden door, the only sounds she could hear came from inside the room.

". . . looks like a cardiac arrest," a paramedic was saying to Sheriff Evans.

The two young men loaded Mr. Hampden onto the gurney and covered him from feet to crown with a sheet. Jane crept closer as they strapped his body into place, thankful that their movements were both deft and gentle.

"Will someone be following us?" one of EMTs asked Jane.

She shook her head. "He was by himself, I'm afraid. We should have emergency contact information on his registration form. We'll need to retrieve that immediately and inform his family of his passing."

"I can place that phone call for you," the sheriff was kind enough to offer. "You've been through quite enough already."

While the paramedics packed their kits, Jane pulled the sheriff aside. "What about the book?"

He brandished a pair of gloves. "I plan to search for it as soon as the room is clear."

Jane drew herself up. "And I plan to join you. This room, the missing book, and the gentleman who had it in his possession are my responsibility." Without waiting for a reply, she moved to the door and peeked out. The hallway was empty of guests so she turned to the paramedics and waved for them to wheel the gurney across the hall and into the staff elevator.

After touching Felix Hampden's arm through the thin, white sheet in a gesture of farewell, Jane stepped out of the cab. When the elevator doors slid shut with a mournful sigh, she collected a pair of gloves from the housekeeping supply closet and returned to the Mystery Suite to examine Felix Hampden's belongings.

At first, Jane was uneasy about rummaging through a guest's drawers, but her discomfort was soon displaced by amazement. She'd never seen such a marvelous collection of vintage clothing.

"Every item conforms to Adela Dundee's descriptions of her detective," she told Sheriff Evans. "The reading glasses, white undershirts, suspenders, short ties, leather gloves, and a rolled umbrella are exactly like those Umberto Ferrari owned. Mr. Hampden traveled with a whole drawer of silk handkerchiefs. He must have spent a small fortune on these items."

The sheriff pointed at the bathroom. "His toiletry kit looks old, and as far as I can tell, his grooming tools are too. However, Mr. Hampden had to resort to a few modern amenities like a toothbrush and nasal spray. Those were hidden inside one of the hand towels next to the sink."

Curious, Jane walked into the bathroom. Her eyes swept over a Bakelite comb, wooden lint brush, gold-plated razor, silver travel soap and toothbrush container, tweezers, scissors, and a nail file. There was also a jar of Morgan's Pomade, which Umberto Ferrari used to keep his neatly trimmed mustache and goatee from turning gray. "Unreal," she whispered and then spied the plastic bottle of nasal spray and tiny tube of toothpaste tucked into the fold of a towel.

"It's as if he were ashamed of them," she murmured to herself.

She found Sheriff Evans running his hand between mattress and box spring, but after another fifteen minutes of searching, he sighed and said, "The book isn't here."

Jane had to agree. "Maybe he sold it last night after all."

The sheriff stared at her. "You don't really believe that, do you?"

"No" she admitted. "He bribed my twins to make sure that he'd win that book. He wanted it very, very badly. I could see the triumph in his eyes when I handed it to him. There was a look of joy there. Greed too. A sort of crazy zeal."

"Now he's dead and the book is gone."

Jane hated to voice her fears, but she had no choice. "Is it possible that the two things are related?"

"I hope not," the sheriff said, stooping over to pick up a shard of broken glass. He pivoted it to the light, and tiny rainbows speckled the carpet. "But until we find out how Mr. Hampden died, this room should remain off limits."

"I'll inform the staff." Though she sounded cool and professional, Jane was filled with a quiet dread. After telling Sheriff Evans that she'd meet him downstairs, Jane locked the door to the Mystery Suite and glanced at the brass key nestled in her palm. Like all of Storyton Hall's guest room keys, its tag was engraved with the image of an open book and the Steward family motto. Written in Latin, the motto, *De Nobis Fabula Narratur*, roughly translated to *Their Story is Our Story*.

Jane ran her fingertips over the letters. "Heaven help me," she whispered. "What am I going to say to Aunt Octavia?"

SEVEN

By the time the croquet tournament was over, Jane had assigned a front desk clerk to provide Sheriff Evans with Felix Hampden's personal information. That being done, she'd retreated to her office and called the hospital. Her uncle told her that her aunt was still sleeping peacefully, and when Jane offered to take a turn watching over Aunt Octavia, Uncle Aloysius politely declined. Unsurprised by his response, Jane promised to bring him a change of clothes and a nourishing lunch as soon as she made sure that everything was running smoothly throughout Storyton Hall.

It was clear that spending the morning on the back lawns had given the Murder and Mayhem guests a healthy appetite. The Kipling Café, Storyton Hall's al fresco eatery, was packed. Guests savored the October sunshine while the waiters bustled about serving Julius Caesar salads, Herman Melville chowder, Homer's pulled pork sandwiches, or Mark Twain chicken biscuits along with iced tea and lemonade. Guests in search of a more refined meal bustled inside the manor house, hoping to find a vacant table in the Madame Bovary Dining Room.

To call forth the atmosphere of the wedding feast in Flaubert's novel, Storyton Hall's dining room had been decorated in shades of white and pale blue. Louis XVI–style dining chairs painted a snowy white were gathered around tables draped in blue cloth. William Morris's Brer Rabbit wallpaper brought the room's high walls to life, and the wood paneling had been painted the color of fresh cream. The centerpieces were filled with roses, lavender, freesia, and fern leaves, and the linen napkins were rolled into tight scrolls and secured by a piece of ribbon. At the end of each ribbon was a strip of paper bearing a quote about food. Jane was examining the reservation book when a nearby guest read his quote out loud.

"Mine's by Oscar Wilde," the young man told his three dining companions. "It says 'After a good dinner, one can forgive anybody, even one's own relations.' "

"Then I might forgive *you* for thumping me and Dad in croquet," said the girl seated to his left. "At breakfast, Dad was totally bragging about how easy it was going to be to beat you and Mom."

"I was off my game," admitted the older gentleman across from her. "But I promise to make it up to you when we play pickleball tomorrow."

"Hear that, Mom? You'd better not party too hard at tonight's costume ball. You need to bring your A game so we can crush these two tomorrow." The young man gave his sister a playful nudge.

"I don't get to be a tomboy named George every day," the mother replied. "I plan to take full advantage of being thirty-something years younger. And if that means I'm moving a little slow during pickleball, then too bad. I've been looking forward to this ball for weeks. Do you know how rare it is to meet other people who've heard of Enid Blyton? Let alone The Famous Five? I am in literary heaven!"

The family entered into a good-natured debate over whether Georgina would attend any event that required fancy dress. Jane would have liked to listen in some more, but she didn't have the time. As she moved through the dining room toward the kitchen, she realized that she was envious of the family of four. Her family was meant to have four members instead of three. But now Jane had to raise the twins by herself.

"That's not true. There's also Aunt Octavia and Uncle Aloysius," she murmured. "And Eloise. The Cover Girls. Sinclair, Sterling, Butterworth, Ned, and Mrs. Hubbard." She silently listed names until her heart felt full enough to burst. In the kitchen, Mrs. Hubbard's warm and floury embrace chased away the remnants of Jane's temporary melancholia.

"I called the hospital a few minutes ago," Mrs. Hubbard said after releasing her. "Your aunt's awake and showing signs of her glorious, feisty self. I didn't tell your uncle about the Rip Van Winkle—figured he had enough on his mind. But I think he's wondering why you haven't left Storyton Hall yet. I couldn't come up with a good enough excuse except to tell him that you were taking care of some important tasks and would be on your way shortly."

Jane frowned. "You know about the Rip Van Winkle? I thought we'd been so discreet."

"You were, honey. One of my assistants stepped outside for a cigarette break while the men were loading the Van Winkle into the ambulance. Was the gentleman old? Did he depart in his sleep?"

This was precisely the type of conversation Jane wanted to avoid. "I'm not sure what caused him to pass, but we must protect his privacy. Can you ask your assistant to refrain from discussing this with anyone?"

Mrs. Hubbard crossed her heart. "On my honor, I won't let her breathe a word!"

Now that the cook had been made aware of the choicest bit of gossip to grace Storyton Hall in years, Jane doubted that Mr. Hampden's death would remain a secret for long, but there was nothing she could do about that. The kitchen was the epicenter of the resort. Sooner or later, all news of import was shared here. "I need to fill a hamper with fresh fruit and sandwiches for my uncle," Jane said, hoping to change the subject. "Any suggestions?"

Beaming, Mrs. Hubbard gestured at the picnic basket sitting on a nearby counter. "There's enough there to keep Mr. Steward going for two days. Butterworth took the liberty of packing a bag for him as well. Sterling has it in the car, and he's waiting for you out back. Is there anything else I can do for you besides look after Muffet Cat?"

Jane had to fight back tears. Giving Mrs. Hubbard a quick hug, she said, "You're like a mother to me. Thank you."

Mrs. Hubbard dabbed at her eyes with the corner of her apron. "Go on now before I cry in the au jus, and the guests complain that I've been too heavy-handed with the salt."

Picking up the laden wicker basket, Jane found Sterling polishing the "Spirit of Ecstasy" hood ornament on his favorite Rolls-Royce. When he heard Jane approach, he stuffed the chamois cloth into his pocket and opened the passenger side door with a flourish.

Sterling didn't talk much during the drive, preferring to hum along with a Mozart piano concerto instead. Both the music and Sterling's low humming were relaxing and Jane let the stirring notes of the piece wash over her as the sleek sedan climbed up and down the mountain roads.

Jane got out at the hospital's main entrance. Sterling handed her the picnic basket and promised to bring in her uncle's suitcase after he found an acceptable parking place. Smiling, Jane wished him luck. She knew that he was extremely particular about parking spots and that he kept a stack of orange cones in the trunk of every Rolls. She had no trouble visualizing him building a barrier of cones around the car in, say, the newly paved lot reserved for physicians.

As she approached her aunt's room, Jane's smile broadened. She could hear Aunt Octavia complaining. Her voice was loud and determined. She sounded strong. "I most certainly will *not* eat that!" she declared heatedly.

Quickening her pace, Jane entered the room to find her aunt glaring at a bowl of soup broth. "Oh, Jane!" she cried upon seeing her great-niece. "Would you please explain that I am not an infant? That I require solid food if I'm to get better? I want to be discharged from this prison as soon as possible."

Jane gave the nurse an apologetic shrug. "You've been through an ordeal, Aunt Octavia. Why don't you eat this just to make sure your system can handle it, and then later on, we'll see if your doctor thinks you can partake of the picnic Mrs. Hubbard prepared."

Her aunt's eyes darted to the basket. "What did you bring me, my sweet girl?"

"This is really for Uncle Aloysius," Jane said. "He needs to keep his strength up if he plans to spend his days and nights in that recliner."

Aunt Octavia dropped back against her pillows and crossed her arms over her chest. "Mark my words. We are going back to Storyton Hall before sundown."

The nurse shook her head. "Tomorrow is the earliest you can expect to be discharged, Mrs. Steward. The doctor wants you to try to stand again after lunch, and we still need a complete assessment from the physical therapy department."

Jane shot a concerned glance at her uncle and then turned to the nurse. "After a meal and a short rest, she'll give it another go. In the meantime, could I speak with you in private?"

Handing Uncle Aloysius the picnic basket, Jane ignored her aunt's splutters of indignation and followed the nurse into the hall. "Is my aunt having trouble with balance? Is that a result of the stroke?"

The nurse nodded. "It's not uncommon. Her muscles are weak. It'll take time and hard work before she can stand without assistance, let alone walk." She put a hand on Jane's arm. "I've seen lots of stroke patients. A stroke can affect one person in a totally different way from the next person, but what I've noticed is the patients with the strongest personalities—those with the most passionate resolve to get back to normal—have the best recovery. And your aunt seems like the type of person who won't accept life in a wheelchair. She's a fighter and that's really good."

"A wheelchair?" Jane was horrified. "She'll hate that. She doesn't mind her cane because she thinks it lends her an air of elegance and authority. But a wheelchair? She'll see that as a total loss of independence. Does she know yet?"

"Like I said, we need a full eval from a physical therapist before the doctor can come up with a cohesive prognosis. She's got a tough road ahead of her, but I can tell that she also has a great support system."

The nurse gave Jane a comforting smile and headed into the room across the hall.

"Jane!" Aunt Octavia called out. "Stop talking about me this instant. I might be in the hospital, but it's not a mental hospital. Therefore, I have a right to know what's going on!"

"I'm sorry." Jane stepped back into the room. "I was just trying to get caught up on the situation. Last night, you were sleeping peacefully and I had a million questions no one could answer. I still feel like the world's turned upside down and I need to understand exactly what happened. Storyton Hall feels empty without you and Uncle Aloysius."

Jane sensed she'd chosen her words well because the stormy expression vanished from her aunt's face. "Tell me, Jane. Were you able to get the book back without too much trouble?"

Uncle Aloysius, who'd been happily consuming a roast beef sandwich, stopped chewing and gave his wife an anxious look. "My dear, you should focus on your recovery. I'm sure Jane has everything under control."

Jane shrank under her aunt's penetrating gaze. "All is well at home," she said. "I don't have the book, but I will. I paid a visit to the gentleman's room last night but he was indisposed." Pulling a chair up next to the bed, Jane laid her hand on her aunt's. "What makes your copy special? Why were you so upset when you realized you'd given away the wrong book? I've examined the version of Adela Dundee's *Lost Letters* we were supposed to award as the prize, and though it looks like a fascinating read, I can't see why the mix-up has caused you such distress."

"You wouldn't spot the difference unless you removed the dust jackets from both copies. There is a letter hidden inside my copy," her aunt said.

"A letter? From whom? Is it important?"

Aunt Octavia gave a little shrug. "I haven't read it, but I believe it contains a secret about Adela Dundee. It's her handwriting on the envelope, of that I have no doubt.

Jane was flabbergasted. "Why didn't you read it?"

"Because both the letter and the book belong to Storyton Hall, not to me. I was tempted to read it, I can assure you, but the envelope is sealed and I've learned over the course of my tenure at Storyton Hall that it's best to leave such things undisturbed." Aunt Octavia released a heavy sigh and turned to her husband. "I believe the time has come, Aloysius."

He closed his eyes for a long moment, as though reluctant to agree. When he opened them again, he seemed to have aged ten years. "The burden should have fallen on our son's shoulders. Or on your father's shoulders. Jane, you will be the only female and the youngest Steward to bear its weight."

"And its honor," Aunt Octavia said, looking at her husband. "Remember how you fretted that I'd leave after I learned your secret? Instead, I shared in your pain and your pride. It brought us closer together. Being married to a Steward has made my life rich and colorful. And it gave me meaning—something to hold on to after we lost Cedric." With a tender smile, Aunt Octavia reached under her hospital gown and pulled a long, gold chain from the depths of her décolletage.

Jane had seen the chain against the skin of her aunt's neck since childhood, but had never known that a large gold locket decorated with intricate scrollwork was attached to its end.

"How beautiful," she said, her fingers reaching out of their own accord. "Is it old?"

"Very," her aunt replied. "Far older than what's inside. Here. See if you can open it." She laid the locket in Jane's palm.

Turning the heavy oval locket over, Jane saw that the motto written on the key tags of Storyton Hall had also been engraved into the gold. She ran her fingertips around the locket's smooth sides, marveling at the lack of visible hinges. Jane had always loved puzzles, and though a dozen different tasks awaited her at Storyton Hall, she was too enthralled to pass up the chance to solve a riddle. Bringing the locket closer, she inspected the scrollwork on the front. At the very center was a plain rectangle that immediately reminded Jane of a closed book. On each side of the rectangle was a cluster of arrows.

Acting more on impulse than anything else, she laid the locket on its back in the palm of her left hand and pressed down on the arrows with her thumb and the next three fingers of her right hand. Nothing happened, so she readjusted her fingers, leaving the thumb free to put gentle pressure on the book-shaped rectangle. The locket opened with a soft click. Inside was a key.

Her aunt and uncle were smiling at her as if she'd just performed a heroic feat. Jane was shocked to see tears in her uncle's eyes. "What does this open?" she asked, pointing at the key. "What burden? What secret?"

"The symbols on that locket represent the ancient and venerable role of the Steward family," Uncle Aloysius said. "Do you see the arrows surrounding the book?" When Jane nodded, he continued, "Before the locket was made, my great-great-grandmother kept a key inside the hidden compartment of a gold, diamond, and opal bracelet. The key was hidden behind the largest opal. Prior to that, there was another vessel and another key. Our family's mission is, and always has been, to protect knowledge."

Jane gestured at the locket. "What does this key open? A vault with a Gutenberg Bible? A lost Shakespeare play?"

"Those and more," Aunt Octavia said. Jane was about to laugh when she realized that her aunt wasn't kidding.

"We've worked for a host of sovereigns, but we answer to no man," Uncle Aloysius explained. "We live by a code written by the Greek scholars Socrates, Plato, and Aristotle. Centuries ago, they penned a detailed set of rules and guidelines for us to follow. We have abided by this code ever since. One of the rules clearly states that a guardian who can no longer fulfill his duties must pass the responsibility to his heir. That, my dear, is you."

Plucking the key from the heart of the locket, Jane held it to the light. It didn't look particularly special. "I've read too many Gothic novels, Uncle, so right now I'm imagining you using this to open a door hidden behind a bookcase. It creaks on rusty hinges as you push it inward. You travel down a worn spiral staircase that leads into a cold underground cave filled with vacuum-sealed chests of rare books."

Uncle Aloysius gave a wry chuckle. "Not bad, my dear. But in this case, your winding staircase leads up. The secret room isn't a cave or an attic strewn with cobwebs. It's a library. A soundproof, fireproof, bulletproof library."

"Oh," Jane said in a small voice.

"When you return to Storyton Hall, find Sinclair," her uncle commanded. "Tell him I have named you the new guardian. He will know what to do next. He has been waiting for this day for many years."

Jane's head was spinning. "I don't understand."

"You will," Aunt Octavia said. "And then you'll realize why you must recover our copy of Adela Dundee's *Lost Letters* at all costs."

At that moment, the nurse returned to see if Aunt Octavia had eaten her lunch. "Mrs. Steward, you need to get your strength back," the nurse remonstrated her gently. "You have to finish that soup."

"You're right. I've been talking so much that I've let it go cold. Would you be a love and heat it up for me? I promise to swallow every distasteful mouthful if it's hot." When the nurse left carrying the soup bowl, Aunt Octavia gave Jane a weary smile. "You'd better get on home. I'm feeling quite tired and you have so much to do."

Jane was about to argue when she noticed the wan look to her aunt's face. After giving her a soft kiss on the cheek, she put the long chain over her head and tucked the locket inside the fold of her wrap dress. Aunt Octavia stared at the bulge the pendant made with a critical eye. "You need to gain at least fifty pounds. There's no place for that locket to hide. I suppose a breast augmentation is out of the question. We just don't have the funds for cosmetic surgery."

"Octavia." Uncle Aloysius wagged a finger at her, his eyes shining with affection.

"I'll call you two later," Jane said and left.

She found Sterling waiting some distance down the hall, suitcase in hand. He quickly delivered the case to Uncle Aloysius and then asked Jane to wait by the hospital's front entrance while he fetched the car. On the ride back to Story-ton Hall, he asked after Aunt Octavia. Jane explained that, although her aunt still needed a complete physical therapy assessment, she was likely to need a wheelchair.

Sterling's brows rose when Jane mentioned Aunt Octavia's inability to stand on her own. "I can't begin to picture that, Miss Jane. Even with a cane, Mrs. Steward has a knack of popping up around the house or grounds with no notice. She's quite stealthy for a woman her age."

"She adores those surprise inspections," Jane said with a wistful smile. "But I'm afraid those will cease for the time being, as will her late-night visits to the kitchen. Right now, that's the only bright side I can see to this whole mess."

Sterling looked thoughtful. "It's none of my business,

Miss Jane, but I don't think Mr. Steward can manage on his own. With the lifting and all that."

Jane shook her head. "No, he can't. Aunt Octavia is as solid as the Hall's foundation stone. She doesn't like to be touched by strangers either. Did you ever hear the tale of what she did when a little girl sat on her lap uninvited?"

Grinning, Sterling nodded. "It happened during afternoon tea. The girl, who was terribly behaved according to the waitstaff, wanted the tea cakes from Mrs. Steward's plate, and when your aunt told her she couldn't have them, she decided to help herself."

"Yes. The precocious child climbed onto Aunt Octavia's lap as if she were telling Santa Claus what she wanted for Christmas. That's when my aunt upended the pitcher of pink lemonade over the child's head." Jane chuckled at the memory, though at the time, she'd been aghast. "Her parents were furious that their daughter's new party dress had been ruined, but Aunt Octavia didn't give them the chance to vent their anger. Instead, she gave them such a long-winded lecture about the importance of manners and how they were failing their daughter by not exercising their right to discipline that they checked out of Storyton Hall before suppertime."

It felt good to remember that Aunt Octavia wasn't easily intimidated. If, as her nurse said, fighters made the best progress after suffering a stroke, then Jane's aunt wouldn't be cowed by muscle weakness or balance problems. She'd battle against her own body to get out of her wheelchair, but she'd need plenty of help along the way. Professional help.

"I'll need to hire a nurse," she told Sterling. "Someone who can assist with Aunt Octavia's physical therapy and monitor her diet. Someone with sturdy arms and a strong back who isn't easily bullied." Jane sighed. "Where am I going to find this strapping saint?" *And how much will his or her services cost?*

Jane's fingers touched the chain on her neck. She hadn't worn such a heavy necklace in years, but she found the locket's weight a comfort. The last twenty-four hours had been replete with unpleasant surprises, and she hoped that whatever Sinclair would tell her would be more positive. And yet she was fearful. What did it mean to be a guardian? And how could she serve in this age-old role in addition to her other responsibilities? She had her boys and Storyton Hall and its staff to look after. And now she also had Aunt Octavia to worry about. That was enough, as far as Jane was concerned, but before she knew it, she was saying good-bye to Sterling and heading for the main library.

She found Sinclair standing by the large-print section. He gestured at the shelves and asked a pair of elderly ladies if he could locate a particular author or genre for them.

"I want something steamy," the first woman announced. "A rugged Scottish Highlander kidnapping a naïve and ravishing noblewoman. I'd rather the Scot were bare-chested through most of the book. And by the end, I'd like to know exactly what he has under his kilt."

"Madge!" Her companion turned away in embarrassment.

"Don't pay attention to her," Madge said, unabashed. "She'll read it the second I'm done."

Sinclair's gaze traveled over the shelves. "I believe the perfect book awaits you right . . ." He paused, frowned, and then whispered a triumphant "A-ha!" He presented Madge with a book. Its spine was covered by gold lettering and a blue and green tartan design. She clutched it to her chest in delight while Sinclair inquired after her friend's reading tastes.

"She likes ghost stories," Madge said. "The old-fashioned kind—not these new ones where the spirits are friendly or act like glorified house pets. Something like *Rebecca* or *The Tell-Tale Heart*."

"Has she read *The Haunting of Hill House*? I think Shirley Jackson pens a deliciously creepy psychological tale." Sinclair pulled the book from the stacks and held it out.

Madge's friend wandered over, shot a curious glance at the cover, and lit up from the inside. Jane had seen the same look on the faces of so many of Storyton Hall's guests, but she never grew tired of it. Sinclair was born to match readers with books.

"Well done," she told him after the two women rushed off to read in the Isak Dinesen Safari Room.

Sinclair was about to answer when he spied the outline of the locket beneath the thin fabric of Jane's dress. His expression turned grave. "Is your aunt's condition that serious?"

In a hushed voice, Jane gave him a brief update and then put her palm over the locket. "Can someone take over here? I won't be able to get anything else done today until I understand what secrets my great-aunt and -uncle have been keeping and precisely what it is to be the guardian of Storyton Hall."

"This is a life-changing moment for you, Miss Jane. Most of us who've been called to serve have already lived a full life. We've married, had children, worked a host of jobs, and traveled the world. You are very young to wear this mantle, but with the loss of your parents and Mr. Cedric . . ." He released a mournful sigh and then squared his shoulders. "We cannot always choose our fate, I'm afraid, so we shall face it head-on. Therefore, if you'd accompany me to your aunt and uncle's apartments, I will humbly introduce you to the Eighth Wonder of the World."

More confused than ever, Jane unlocked the door to her aunt and uncle's rooms and followed Sinclair inside. He walked to the center of the sitting room and put his finger to his lips. Jane realized that he was listening, but for what, she had no idea. He then beckoned for her to join him in the bedroom. "This way, please," he said, walking straight into Aunt Octavia's spacious closet. Uncle Aloysius used a closet half the size, but his suits, sweaters, and fishing hats were nowhere as numerous as Aunt Octavia's custom-made dresses. And though Jane reveled in the bright colors and wild patterns her aunt favored, she couldn't fathom how being among her zebra-stripe or leopard-print garments would help unravel her family's secret.

At the back of the closet, Sinclair squatted and pushed a metal shoe rack away from the wall, revealing an air vent. After removing four small screws, he pried the vent cover off and laid it on the floor. Jane expected to see a yawning hole, but when Sinclair moved aside, she saw only a small keyhole and a metal lever.

"Turn your key clockwise as you move the lever handle counterclockwise. You must perform these actions in unison."

Dumbfounded, Jane bent down to follow his instructions. The key turned easily, but she had to use all her strength to get the handle to budge. When it did, she heard wheels turning behind the wall. It sounded like something was moving to her right, which was the east wall of the sitting room. "This was the first time I've had an advantage because I'm a lefty."

"The majority of your relatives are left-handed. To access a Steward vault, your forbearers have always needed to use both hands, and the locking mechanisms have favored lefties for generations." Sinclair offered Jane his hand. "And now the entrance to the greatest treasure trove in human history has been opened. You need only return to the sitting room to see it for yourself."

"Please come with me," Jane said. "For some reason, I'm a little frightened."

"It would be my honor."

In the sitting room, the bookcase containing Aunt Octavia's prized collection of Meissen porcelain teapots had swung away from the wall, creating a gap of about two feet through which a person could pass sideways. "Why didn't the teapots break?" she asked Sinclair. "Aunt Octavia warned me a million times not to go anywhere near her fragile collection."

"They're held in place with pieces of wax," he said. "It's a brilliant ruse. You see, most people would assume that a secret panel would be concealed behind a bookcase. After all, it's not practical to have a priceless collection of antique porcelain jolted and jarred each time one wants to enter a hidden room. Therefore, it's unlikely that the opening would be discovered by all but the shrewdest of thieves." He gestured at the floor. "There's a battery-powered lantern just inside the passage."

Jane reached into the blackness and made contact with the lantern. She turned it on and took a hesitant step into the shadows. And another. And another. She then came to the base of a staircase. Raising the lantern, she saw that rough stairs had been hewn into the stone. They curled up and up. Too intrigued to hesitate, Jane climbed to the top and paused before a small metal door.

"This is just like one of my favorite childhood stories," she said in a hushed voice. "It's *Through the Looking Glass* and *The Chronicles of Narnia* and Nancy Drew's *The Hidden Staircase* all mixed together."

"Miss Jane," Sinclair whispered behind her. "If you did not believe in magic before, that is about to change."

EIGHT

Hand trembling in anticipation, Jane pushed down
on the handle and entered a cool, dark chamber. Sinclair
reached around her and flicked a switch on the wall. Instantly, the room was illuminated with a soft light.

The first thing Jane noticed was the gleam of metal. From
floor to ceiling, the walls were lined with metal drawers.
They reminded Jane of the safety-deposit boxes inside a
bank. Passing the lantern to Sinclair, she approached the
first row of drawers and read the label out loud. " 'Shakespeare, William. Three unpublished plays.' " After glancing
back at Sinclair, she read the label directly to the right.
" 'Dickens, Charles. *The Mystery of Edwin Drood (Complete
Manuscript).*' " She shook her head. "Impossible. Dickens
didn't finish that novel."

"He most certainly did. Unfortunately, the final scenes
were written from Edwin Drood's point of view as he lan-
guished in a prison cell. The passages were more of a harsh
social commentary on the need for reform in Britain's peni-
tentiary system than a resolution of the murder mystery.
This wasn't the first time Dickens wrote about prisons. After

all, his father was sent to debtors' prison. But in *The Mystery of Edwin Drood*, Dickens basically accuses the Parliament of encouraging corruption in prisons. He even named names, though he scrambles a few of the letters. A high-standing member of Parliament hired a thief to steal the final chapters. I've heard several rumors that this villain helped Dickens to his grave, but that's neither here nor there. A guardian recovered the original *Edwin Drood* and it's now in Storyton Hall, safe and sound."

Jane stared at him. "The Shakespeare plays?" She tried to catch her breath. "Are you telling me that the public doesn't know about the three plays in that drawer? They've never been read? Or performed?"

"That is correct. Only a handful of people have laid eyes on them."

"For the first time in my life, I may swoon," Jane whispered, feeling genuinely light-headed.

Sinclair put his palm on the small of her back. "That is why I'm standing so close to you, Miss Jane. However, I expect your wonder and curiosity will overcome your astonishment."

He was right. Jane moved from drawer to drawer, gasping and exclaiming as the labels revealed Storyton Hall's secret collection. The vacuum-sealed drawers contained volumes of poetry, illuminated manuscripts, ancient scrolls, history books, a Gutenberg Bible, Leonardo da Vinci's journal, *The Canterbury Tales*—Part Two, the scientific notes of Galileo, and on and on.

Eventually, Jane couldn't absorb any more. She stopped where she was and leaned against the wall. "All of these treasures and I've only been around half of the room. This library . . . it's absolutely priceless." She smiled at Sinclair. "You were right to call it the Eighth Wonder of the World. Who would have guessed that these gems were hidden on the other side of Aunt Octavia's feather boas and leopard-print shoes?"

Sinclair grinned. "Indeed."

Jane released a heavy sigh. "What now, Sinclair? We should have armed guards on staff. How am *I* supposed to protect *this*?"

"First, you must train. Your body and mind must be honed like a sword. We'll begin with fencing and martial arts classes. Sterling will teach you weaponry, and when Gavin recovers from his knee surgery, he and his successor will work with you on hunting, tracking, and survival techniques."

Jane nearly laughed, but then she saw that Sinclair was deadly serious. "I'm a hotel manager. And a mom. I host book clubs and ride around on a bicycle. I can't turn into a ninja warrior overnight! It's not as if my great-uncle had these kinds of skills." She paused to consider the possibility. "Did he?"

"Mr. Steward is quite deft with a knife, even at his present age. And in his prime, no one could outshoot him. He was a fencing master. With his long limbs, he could lunge from across the room and strike with the deadly accuracy of a cobra. He had the hearing of a bat, the eyesight of an owl, and the quickness of antelope. And yet he carefully masked those abilities beneath a veneer."

Jane was beginning to understand. "The tweed suits. The worn leather boots and the fishing hat. His appearance as a country gentleman from a bygone era was nothing but a costume?"

Sinclair touched her arm. "No, Miss Jane. Aloysius Steward is the epitome of a country gentleman. Everything you know about him is true. He just never revealed his special talents to you. In turn, yours must also be kept secret. If you are bruised during Tae Kwon Do practice, you'll say you fell off your bike. If you're cut juggling daggers, you'll tell people that you were distracted in the act of chopping onions."

Jane gaped. "Did you actually say 'juggling daggers'?"

"Don't concern yourself with that now, my dear. We have a missing book to recover."

The childish delight Jane had felt upon entering the secret library instantly vanished. Despite the wonders held in this room, she still had to find Storyton Hall's copy of Adela Dundee's *Lost Letters* and find out exactly what happened to Felix Hampden.

"And here I thought my to-do list was quite long enough," Jane mumbled to herself as she and Sinclair left the small tower room. "After overseeing tonight's fancy dress ball and the rest of the Murder and Mayhem events, I'm to become a ninja assassin. Nothing to it."

Stepping into the brightness of her aunt and uncle's living room, Jane blinked a few times and glanced around. The familiar room should have been comforting, but she felt as if everything she'd known since childhood was suddenly strange and foreign. "Who else on Storyton Hall's staff is not what they seem?" she asked Sinclair.

"There are a few of us. The Stewards have always been very particular about their help. Sterling is former CIA, Gavin, a retired Navy Seal, and Butterworth was an analyst in Her Majesty's Secret Service."

"Holy sh—"

"Yes," Sinclair interrupted smoothly. "It is imperative that their pasts remain a secret. One of the advantages we have over those who wish to steal from our library is that the thieves assume they need only get past the guardian to gain access to Storyton Hall's treasures." He gave a smug chuckle. "Before they set foot in our lobby, every guest is screened. If our suspicions are aroused, they are then watched throughout their stay. No one escapes our scrutiny, Miss Jane."

Jane sank into her aunt's favorite reading chair. The wide cushion was no longer flat, but bowl-shaped. Aunt Octavia's rump had created such a deep depression in the fabric that Jane felt as if she were caught in a chintz quagmire. "So can my staff of trained spies tell me anything pertinent about Felix Hampden?"

"We have no proof that he came to steal our copy of *Lost Letters*. If that was his intention, he was clearly an amateur. The fact that he didn't have the hidden letter taped inside the dust jacket on his person at the time of his death tells me that he wasn't aware of its existence. However, there are others we're watching who've raised more serious red flags."

Jane nodded. "Yes, there's a woman with white hair and a man resembling Colonel Hastings. And I saw another man. Well, more of a shadow than a man, but he followed Mr. Hampden out of the Fleming Lounge after I awarded him the prize. The other two, the white-haired lady and the Hastings look-alike, were both keen to get the book away from Mr. Hampden."

Sinclair looked ridiculously pleased. "Your powers of observation are excellent, Miss Jane. Even as a child, you noticed particular details about Storyton Hall's guests."

Instead of acknowledging the compliment, Jane frowned. "With all these people after the book, I have to wonder about the significance of the letter. If it was truly written by Adela Dundee, it could be quite valuable. People would pay a great deal of money for a newly discovered piece of Dundee paraphernalia." She paused. "Yet, how could these potential thieves have known that Aunt Octavia gift-wrapped the wrong book by mistake? There's only one explanation and I hate to voice it."

"You must."

"Someone got into this apartment and examined the book. They saw a chance to make some money and contacted a potential buyer. Who else could it be but a Storyton Hall employee? Most of our staff is exceedingly well read and would recognize Adela Dundee's name. And if they found the letter and opened it . . . who knows what they could have learned?" She gestured at the ceiling. "Is there an easy way to know who entered here? Are there hidden cameras in every room?"

Sinclair shook his head. "We value our guests' privacy,

Miss Jane. We only intrude upon that privacy if we believe there's an imminent threat to our special collection. Messrs. Sterling, Gavin, and Butterworth aren't here to guard the books. Their main priority is to protect those bearing the Steward name. These men are devoted to your family and to Storyton Hall. Their service goes back several generations. Unfortunately, they haven't had any luck discovering who might have seen the book while it was in your aunt's possession."

Jane pursed her lips in thought. "I'll ask Aunt Octavia. She's very particular about the people she allows into her rooms. Now I know why! In the meantime, I need to know what you and—" She stopped. "What do you and the other undercover staff members call yourselves?"

Instead of replying, Sinclair removed his suit coat and folded it over the closest chair. He then unbuttoned his shirt and laid it over the coat, leaving him standing in a white T-shirt. Jane had expected the librarian's arms to be pale and doughy, but they were tan and muscular.

"You've got the forearms of Popeye the Sailor!" she exclaimed.

"No anchor tattoo, however." He shoved his sleeve higher up his arm, revealing a bicep that any twenty-year-old would envy. Inked into his skin was a cluster of arrows matching those on Jane's locket. "We call ourselves the Fins after the Finsbury Archers, England's most famous archery association. The Finsbury Archers existed for hundreds of years and have always served the Steward family. And while we don't exactly keep longbows under our desks, we're prepared to defend these walls at all times."

The tattoo was small and crudely drawn. To Jane, it seemed incongruent with Sinclair's penchant for bow ties and silk handkerchiefs. "Do all of Storyton Hall's Fins have this tattoo?"

"Yes." He put his dress shirt back on. "It has been a long-standing tradition for the current Steward guardian to mark himself as well. It's a symbol of commitment. Of courage and sacrifice."

Jane didn't think she could handle any more surprises. "Wait a minute. Uncle Aloysius has a tattoo?"

"He most certainly does." Sinclair buttoned his shirt, slipped his coat on, and straightened his bow tie. Shooting a quick glance at Jane, he said, "Perhaps we'll postpone your tattooing for a later date. We have more important things to do before tonight's costume ball."

"*My* tattoo? I think not." Jane had had enough. Pushing against the arms of the chair, she managed to extricate herself from the concave cushion. "I made it through college without a tattoo. I tagged along with my girlfriends when they got dolphins on their ankles or flowers on their shoulders, but I refrained. And now, all these years later, I'm supposed to be marked with a permanent image of what? A book? A sword? A quiver of arrows?" She snorted in a most unladylike fashion. "Yes, a deadly weapon inked onto my bicep really says 'I'm a hotel manager, a mother, and a respectable member of my community.'"

"I don't think you'll find the traditional tattoo objectionable, Miss Jane," Sinclair said. "It's an owl holding a scroll in its talons."

Jane thought of all the tales she'd read in which characters sought help from a wise owl. The idea of being compared to the astute bird appealed to Jane. She liked helping people. She liked being needed. The more she thought about it, the more she found all of Sinclair's proposals, from getting a tattoo to learning martial arts, rather appealing. "All right. I'll do my best to adjust to this strange new life. I don't think any of it will be smooth or easy, but a tattoo? That's a piece of cake. How much can it hurt when compared to giving birth to twins?"

Sinclair tried not to smile. The corners of his mouth twitched as if he were being tickled. "I am confident that you can tolerate the discomfort of the procedure. However, you might object to the customary location of the tattoo."

"I'm not even going to ask," Jane said. "You're enjoying this, aren't you?"

"Perhaps, but I won't be smiling later." He suddenly sobered. "After all, I've known you since you were a little girl in pigtails and it will be somewhat unsettling to tattoo your, ah . . ." He patted his chest, just above the heart.

"I'll be sure to wear my raciest bra," Jane teased, feeling more like herself. "Let's go downstairs so I can learn more about the current threats to Storyton Hall."

Sinclair, who'd obviously needed a moment to regain his composure following the bra comment, hustled forward to open the door.

Jane had been in Sinclair's small and exceedingly tidy office many times before, but she'd never seen him shut and lock the door and then flip his bulletin board around to reveal enlarged driver's license photographs. Each five-by-seven image was surrounded by a halo of yellow Post-it Notes listing brief biographical details. Jane realized that Sinclair had access to all of Storyton Hall's online files. Every guest presented a driver's license upon check-in and the licenses were scanned into an electronic guest file. Sinclair obviously examined those files every day.

Leaning closer to the board, Jane pointed at the photo of the woman with the cloud of white hair. "Moira McKee." Her eyes moved to the street address. "Another Vermont resident? That can't be a coincidence." Next, she examined the dignified visage of the Colonel Hastings look-alike. "Desmond Price, eh? From Cambridge, Mass. Harvard's town." Jane looked at Sinclair. "Is Mr. Price a professor?"

Sinclair nodded. "He is. As for Ms. McKee, she's the current president of the Broadleaf School of the Arts. Alice Hart was a faculty member at the same institution."

"And Felix Hampden? Was he affiliated with a college or university?"

"No. Mr. Hampden managed a small theater company in Boston. He had a police record involving several cases of fraud that he committed in his twenties. It would be my guess that he lived well above his means."

Jane touched the photograph of Alice Hart. It was the image from the *Lost Letters* dust jacket. "Felix, Moira, and Desmond wanted to get their hands on Aunt Octavia's book. But what about Alice's story? Why did she come to Storyton Hall?"

"I don't know," Sinclair admitted. "She must have presented a fake driver's license when she checked in. There is no record of payment under the name 'Alice Hart' either."

"She must have used cash while she was here and held the room using a borrowed credit card. Sheriff Evans said that she broke off an engagement shortly before coming to Storyton. Perhaps she used her fiancé's card."

Sinclair looked impressed. "I have a contact at the sheriff's department. I'll see what I can find out."

"In the meantime, I need to get better acquainted with Moira and Desmond. I'll ask the housekeeper from their floors to describe how they've disguised themselves for tonight's ball." She glanced at her watch. "Speaking of which, I have much to do before it begins. Can you keep researching the connections between these guests and Alice? And try to discover if any of them knew Felix, or if he was merely the victim of circumstance?" Seeing that Sinclair was beaming, she paused. "You haven't worn that expression since Uncle Aloysius told you of his plans to expand your library. What is it?"

"It's you, Miss Jane. You were born to do this. They say blood will tell. I can practically hear the Steward blood singing within you, and if I may be so bold, it fills me with pride."

Jane smiled. "Thank you, Sinclair. Unfortunately, the owl tattoo commemorating my new role will have to wait until tomorrow. I'm wearing a shockingly low-cut dress to the ball." Winking at the flustered librarian, she left the office and headed for home.

She'd barely made it halfway across the back lawn when her phone rang. It was Tom Green of the Potter's Shed, the garden center in Storyton Village.

"Miss Jane!" he cried. "My van won't start. I tried giving her battery a jump and even changed her oil, but she's refusing to budge."

Jane turned to face Storyton Hall. The costume ball would begin in two hours. That was plenty of time to send a few cars to the village to collect the floral arrangements. When she called Sterling, however, she was told that guests had rented every available car and driver.

"Can you blame them, Miss Jane?" Sterling said. "It's a perfect afternoon to spend wandering through the village."

Glancing at the sun-dappled grounds, Jane wished she could do the same. She'd love to hop on her bike and race the boys to the Canvas Creamery. She'd treat them to a scoop of frozen custard while she indulged in an iced latte. "I'm sure the merchants are thrilled, but the ballroom won't be very impressive without Tom's magnificent flowers." Suddenly, she had an idea. "I may have a solution. Thank you, Sterling."

"My pleasure, Miss Jane. And if you have a spare hour tomorrow, I'd like to begin your training."

Jane had to remind herself that Sterling was a Fin. "Remind me. What's your specialty?"

"Archery. We should meet at the Robin Hood range before the guests arrive. How does seven sound?"

Jane silently wondered where she'd find the energy to survive her indoctrination as guardian. "A few bruises on the forearm before church? Why not? But I'll have to bring the twins. I can't just leave them alone while I become Lady Robin Hood."

"Certainly," said Sterling. "It's never too soon for the boys to learn useful skills. After all, they're both Stewards."

After saying good-bye, Jane stood rooted to the ground for a moment. She pictured the twins clad in black ninja uniforms, shouting like banshees as they cartwheeled across the lobby, firing quarrels from miniature crossbows. "Archery? Tae Kwon Do? Fencing? Fitz and Hem are going to think I'm the coolest mom in the world!"

The ladies from the Cover Girls arrived at the loading dock behind Storyton Hall, their cars stuffed with flowers.

Mrs. Pratt was clearly put out. "There's pollen all over my dashboard! Why does Tom insist on using every variety of lily? I sneezed so hard that I almost drove into an oblivious pedestrian at Broken Arm Bend."

"It's a good thing you're such an excellent driver. We can't run over guests on their way home from spending money in the village. It wouldn't be polite." Jane gave Mrs. Pratt a grateful smile and gestured for the bellhops to unload her car.

The rest of the Cover Girls were more congenial over having their vehicles turned into floral delivery vans. "Look!" Violet exclaimed as she threw open her passenger door. "I transported all the purple and blue arrangements. Aren't these freesias exquisite? Tom gave me one to put in my hair. He's such a sweetheart."

"He has a crush on you," Eloise said, handing a centerpiece to one of the bellhops. "The Potter's Shed never carried so many shades of purple flowers until you moved here."

Violet waved off the notion. "Tom Green is ten years older than me and a solid twelve inches shorter." She hesitated and then added, "But I'll give him this: The man has *gorgeous* hair."

After helping to empty the last car, Anna asked, "Where's Betty?"

"She can't make it," Jane said. "The Cheshire Cat is slammed."

Mabel crossed her hands over her heart. "I was too! I sold things that have been gathering cobwebs for months. You're an angel for having a costume ball and nowhere else for folks to shop except for La Grande Dame. I had to tailor things on the spot. I swear there was smoke coming out of my sewing machine at one point." She laughed. "I'll be dancing to the bank come Monday."

"My shop was packed from the moment I opened until I hung the CLOSED sign," Phoebe said. "At first, I thought I'd be too tired to come tonight, but the sight of all that cash in my register perked me right up."

Anna sighed. "Not me. I was run ragged fetching this and restocking that. Randall barely moved a muscle. He filled some prescriptions but spent most of the day doing what he does best."

"Lecturing!" the women shouted in unison.

"You got it. Today's topic was seasonal allergies. If a guest from Storyton Hall made the mistake of sneezing or using a tissue in the pharmacy, Randall would immediately corner them. He'd give the poor soul a handful of pamphlets and then drone on and on until their eyes glazed over like ice on a pond. I swear, I think one man fell asleep on his feet."

Threading her arm through Anna's, Eloise said, "We won't let that happen to you. Time to make ourselves beautiful, girls!"

Giggling, the women piled into their cars and used the narrow lanes behind Storyton Hall to reach Jane's house. They swept inside, talking a mile a minute and clutching garment bags and totes filled with hair products and cosmetics.

"Maybe I'll meet a prince at this ball," Eloise said, dumping her things on the kitchen counter.

"Dressed as a detective? If your goal was to play the siren this evening, you've chosen the wrong costume." Mrs. Pratt said, examining her own dress with a satisfied grin. "I wouldn't mind a dance with your handsome brother. Is he coming?"

Eloise shook her head. "Edwin doesn't do parties. He prefers to spend his free time cooking exotic foods, reading obscure books, and tinkering. He'd be perfectly content living in a cave. He's like the Grinch."

"I'm quite fond of the Grinch," Mrs. Pratt murmured.

Phoebe and Violet lugged a cooler into the kitchen. "Stand back, ladies!" Phoebe called brightly. "We can't get ready without libation."

"I hope it's nothing fattening," Anna said warily. "My dress is already too tight. I'll have to yank my pantyhose up to my armpits if I ever hope to zip the thing."

Mabel snorted. "I told you I'd make you something with a little more give to it. I know you wanted an authentic ladies' suit from the forties, but you and I have more padding through the middle and far more junk in the trunk than most of the gals from that era."

Anna put her palm over her belly. "Once upon a time, I had a muffin top. Seems like I've got the whole bakery now."

The women laughed and Violet squeezed Anna around the waist. "You're gorgeous. We all are."

Phoebe helped herself to seven tumblers and began to pour a creamy white liquid into each one. "In honor of Jane's theme week, I invented a cocktail called the Lady Vanishes. It's one part spiced rum, one part butterscotch schnapps, one part chocolate liqueur, and two parts half and half. Shaken and poured over ice."

"Sounds delish." Eloise distributed the cocktails. "Shall we have a toast?"

"What are we drinking to?" Jane asked.

"Aunt Octavia's speedy recovery."

Mrs. Pratt's nose quivered. She'd caught the scent of a fresh piece of gossip. "Is she ill?"

"My aunt had a stroke," Jane said. "She's going to be

okay, but she'll need physical therapy and a new diet and exercise regime." She raised her glass. "To Aunt Octavia."

The women echoed her words, clinked rims, and drank.

"Oh, this is sweet!" Violet exclaimed.

"And smooth as butter," Mabel added.

Phoebe grinned. "Lovely, isn't it? That's why I call it the Lady Vanishes. She disappears right down your throat."

Mrs. Pratt hadn't touched her drink. Her eyes were glittering as she stared at Jane. "Tell us the details. Did your aunt suddenly collapse? Did the guests see her? Were you terrified?" She was practically salivating.

After a moment's hesitation, Jane waved her friends into the living room. "I know we need to get ready, but I want to tell you why my aunt became so upset that she literally made herself sick. That and all the sugary foods she loves but shouldn't eat."

Jane went on to explain how her aunt's copy of *Lost Letters* had accidentally been given to Felix Hampton. She didn't elaborate on what made the book so special. That had to remain a secret, as did the existence of Storyon Hall's hidden library. No one could know about her new role. Not Eloise. Not even Fitz and Hem. Jane's boys liked to gossip almost as much as Mrs. Pratt.

When Jane was done describing the missing book, Felix's demise, and her suspicions about Moira McKee and Desmond Price, her friends exchanged astonished looks.

"So there's a book thief staying at Storyton Hall?" Phoebe was aghast.

Eloise was furious. She slapped her right fist against the palm of her left hand. "How dare they! Your aunt values each and every title in Storyton Hall. I've heard about guests pilfering paperbacks or unintentionally walking off with a hardcover from a hotel library, but this is different."

"That's right. This is personal," Mabel declared heatedly. "It almost sounds like the crook came to this event just to get your aunt's book." She put her hands on her hips. "How can we show these people that they can't go messing with our friend or her family?"

Jane smiled over her friends' willingness to aid her. "I was hoping you'd engage in a reconnaissance mission this evening. Nothing too obvious. I'd just like you to chat with Moira or Desmond if the opportunity presents itself. Having a good time is your first priority, however. You paid to attend this ball, and I want you to enjoy every minute of it."

Mrs. Pratt raised her chin defiantly. "You gave us a discount, so the ticket price was a bargain. In this case, I'd gladly give you twice the amount. Not only do we get to dress in costume, dine like royalty, and dance, but now you've involved us in a mystery as well. What could be more splendid?" She shivered with delight.

The Cover Girls took turns staring at Mrs. Pratt and then they all started to laugh. Jane joined in, thankful that she'd had the foresight to send the twins to Mrs. Hubbard for an early supper. She raised her glass and polished off her cocktail in three swallows. "All right, ladies. Let's transform ourselves into detectives. And remember that tonight is about more than just putting on a costume and playing a role. It's about doing what real detectives do. Seeking justice."

NINE

Because Jane needed to make sure her staff was ready for the ball, she was dressed and ready to leave before her friends had finished their second round of cocktails. She descended the stairs with deliberate slowness while the Cover Girls clapped and whistled. At the bottom, Jane performed a little twirl. Her black flapper dress flared out and the sequins caught the light, twinkling like a hundred stars. Mabel had sewn the sequins in a fan pattern over four layers of silk georgette. The neckline was lower than the conservative Jane would have preferred, but Mabel insisted that the amount of skin she'd be showing was a reflection of the times.

"I've never seen someone wear a flapper dress with such elegance," Mabel said. "As for the design? Am I good or am I good?"

"You're amazing," Jane said. "I feel beautiful and delightfully comfortable."

"And your hair!" Phoebe exclaimed. "You look like a different woman with those glossy curls. I think you've lost four inches of length to hot rollers and hairspray."

"Here's to losing inches," Anna said, raising her glass.

Eloise held up a full tumbler. "One for the road, you gorgeous creature?"

Jane shook her strawberry blond curls. "I'd better not. I have to be razor-sharp tonight." She glanced at her watch. "My first task will be to identify Moira McKee and Desmond Price. It won't be easy with everyone in costume, but we need to chat those two up. Eloise, can you flirt with Desmond? He's a professor, so talk books with him. Get him plenty of punch. See if he'll let his guard down enough to reference *Lost Letters*."

Eloise nodded and then turned to Mrs. Pratt. "Will you be my lifeboat? If this Desmond guy starts creeping me out, I'll signal for you to rescue me."

"I'll watch him like a red-tailed hawk." Mrs. Pratt stood straight as a soldier. "What will the signal be?"

"How's this?" Eloise pinched her nose.

"You look like you're about to dive in a pool," said Violet. "Or just caught a whiff of a noxious odor."

All the women laughed.

"You two enjoy your intrigues. As for me, I plan to dance, flirt, and misbehave," said Anna. She hooked an arm through Phoebe's. "Come on, lovely. It's time to transform ourselves into goddesses of mystery."

Jane left the Cover Girls to their costumes, wigs, and makeup kits and crossed the lawn toward Storyton Hall. Even though she had much to do, she didn't rush. It was impossible not to savor the lavender twilight and the large, lustrous moon.

She took a seat on a garden bench facing Storyton Hall and stared at the rows of illuminated windows. A couple opened the back doors and the sound of trumpet music drifted out from within. Jane guessed that a member of the Storyton Band was warming up, and though that was a sign that the start of the ball was close at hand, Jane wanted to take a moment to collect her thoughts. She couldn't help but dwell on the terrible notion that a Storyton staff member had recognized the value of the letter in Aunt Octavia's copy of *Lost Letters* and had decided to betray her employer in exchange for a quick buck.

Storyton Hall had dozens of employees, most of whom were middle-aged. Younger staff members rarely stayed for more than a year. Many bright-eyed men and women came to Storyton Hall to gain experience, but oftentimes, the slow pace of both the resort and the village became intolerable and they'd leave. She understood, of course. There were no nightclubs or all-night coffee shops in this part of the world. There were thousands of books and miles of pristine countryside. There were glorious gardens and book clubs and neighbors who'd come running if someone needed help, but Storyton wasn't exciting.

"Until now," Jane muttered. She'd asked Mrs. Pimpernel for a list of the housekeepers who'd had access to her aunt and uncle's apartment over the past week, but she knew it was unlikely that those women were the only employees who'd gained entry. Bellhops delivering packages or any member of the Activities staff hoping to discuss fishing with Uncle Aloysius would be invited into the sitting area. Jane would need to ask her aunt and uncle to remember which staff members they'd seen the day the books had been switched and then Sinclair would have to conduct a thorough background search on each employee.

Jane didn't expect such a search to bear much fruit. After all, both Butterworth and Mrs. Pimpernel were involved in the staff's hiring process and they were far too discerning to permit anyone with an unsavory background to don a Storyton Hall uniform. However, Jane realized that even a decent person could be tempted by money. She paid her employees a fair wage and the cost of village living was relatively low, but for those who resided over the mountain and were struggling to raise a family in the midst of tough economic times, an offer of extra cash in exchange for information might prove difficult to resist.

Jane got to her feet. She'd have to tackle the employee list tomorrow. Tonight, she and Eloise needed to find out if Moira or Desmond had Aunt Octavia's book.

"And what of the man in black?" she murmured as she made her way to the rear entrance. "If he isn't skulking in a dark corner, I won't be able to recognize him."

She only had to enter the Great Gatsby ballroom to see that there was an abundance of shadowy nooks. Suddenly, she recalled discussing the ball's décor for this event several weeks ago. Her staff had suggested color palettes from funerary blacks and purples to opulent reds and golds. In the end, they'd voted to incorporate Halloween hues and create a sophisticated, yet spooky atmosphere. Two-dozen Victorian-era brass floor candelabras, polished and fitted with orange candles, lined the perimeter of the room, creating a sense of old-world grandeur. Small tables draped with black linen cloths occupied the spaces between the candelabras. Each table was empty save for a tall vase filled with roses the color of old amber. The effect was both elegant and mysterious.

With the ball beginning in ten minutes, Jane quickly examined the contents of the buffet table. She walked past four crystal bowls filled with blood orange champagne punch, two rows of dessert plates and disposable cups, napkins stamped with black-and-white skulls, vanilla cupcakes decorated with chocolate fondant fingerprints, platters of tuxedo strawberries, and sesame cheddar cookies shaped into magnifying glasses. Everything looked perfect. Jane made a mental note to praise Mrs. Hubbard for her culinary prowess.

The Storyton Band was onstage tuning their instruments. Most of the members wore different hats during the day, but Jane paid them extra to perform in the summer concert series, at weddings, and at other special events like the Murder and Mayhem costume ball. Butterworth served as conductor. He entered the ballroom through a side door, baton in hand. When he spied Jane, he abruptly stopped. "Heavens, Miss Jane. You're a vision."

Jane blushed. "Thank you, Butterworth. And you look very fetching in your tails."

Butterworth closed the distance between them and performed a stiff bow. "I understand the mantle has officially been passed. It is my great honor to serve you as I have served your uncle. I pledge all that I am and all that I have to you, Jane Steward, guardian of Storyton Hall."

Slightly flustered by Butterworth's formality, which was even more pronounced than usual, Jane searched for an appropriate response. However, all she could come up with was a stilted thank-you.

Butterworth inclined his head and made for the stage. He mouthed something to the musicians and the band struck up the first few notes of the butler's favorite waltz, "Tales from the Vienna Woods." For a splendid moment, Jane forgot about Aunt Octavia's missing book and Felix Hampden's death. She turned in a slow circle, delighting in the haunting beauty of the room. For a brief flash of time, the grand space and the graceful music belonged to her alone.

Closing her eyes, she swayed from side to side. Suddenly, someone caught her hand and spun her around so swiftly that she nearly lost her footing. And then a strong arm curled around her waist and a man's palm pressed into her lower back.

Jane's eyes flew open in surprise, and before she could utter a word of protest, Edwin Alcott began to waltz her over the gleaming dance floor.

"One cannot stand still when Strauss is being played," he said, a small smile softening the corners of his mouth. "Especially with such a beautiful woman waiting to be swept off her feet."

Jane's eyes flicked to Edwin's costume before meeting his dark gaze again. "Isn't it difficult to sweep someone off their feet in a toga?"

His smile grew wider. "Not for Marcus Didius Falco, the most intrepid investigator in all of first-century Rome."

"You make a dashing Roman, I admit," Jane said rather breathlessly as he whirled her around and around. "But I wasn't waiting for a partner. I was merely taking a moment to appreciate the Storyton Band."

Edwin didn't reply. His grip tightened and his pace quickened. Gathering her closer, he seemed lost in the melody and in the movement of their bodies. Jane didn't like to admit it, because she prided herself on being too preoccupied with her double roles of resort manager and mother to bother with attractive members of the opposite sex, but she enjoyed the feel of his arm around her waist. It was a rare delight to be able to let go for a few seconds, to follow Edwin's lead as he twirled her, lifted her, and then ended the dance by dipping her so low to the ground that her strawberry blond curls nearly kissed the polished floor.

When the song was over, Edwin gently raised her to her feet. He held her for a heartbeat, smiling that roguish smile, and then abruptly released her with a graceful bow. The musicians put down their instruments and applauded. The only person who didn't clap was Butterworth. He was far too busy casting his most disapproving glare in Edwin's direction.

"Thank you for the dance, Marco," Jane said, heat rushing to her cheeks. "I never introduced myself, but I'm Tuppence." At Edwin's blank look, she added, "She's an Agatha Christie heroine."

"Ah, and here I thought you were Jane Steward, heroine of Storyton Hall."

At that moment, there was a noise at the other end of the room and Jane saw several couples enter, their faces alight with pleasure and anticipation. Sam, the owner of Hilltop Stables, trailed behind the guests. Spotting Edwin, he raised his arm and waved.

Jane couldn't help but grin at Sam. He was dressed as G. K. Chesterton's Father Brown. Clad in black robes and hat, priest's collar, and silver spectacles, he looked very much the part.

He must have heard that Eloise would be here, Jane thought. Sam had had a crush on Eloise for years, but Eloise saw him as another brother and didn't feel an ounce of romantic inclination for him. She was always friendly, but never encouraged his advances. In fact, she'd gone out of her way to call attention to Violet's attributes whenever Sam was around. Eloise was certain that Sam and Violet would make a very happy couple. However, someone would need to convince Sam of that, and Jane guessed that he'd bought tickets to the ball in the hopes of dancing with Eloise.

Costumed guests continued to stream into the ballroom, and Jane knew she needed to take up her station near the door in order to spot Moira McKee and Desmond Price. She was about to excuse herself to Edwin when she realized he was no longer standing behind her.

"Stealthy as a cat," she reflected, and moved forward to greet a man who bore a striking resemblance to Raymond Burr as Perry Mason. She then shook hands with Nick and Nora Charles, Inspector Morse, Sam Spade, and Precious Ramotswe. A dead ringer for Lord Peter Wimsey eyed the buffet offerings through his monocle, and a lanky Hamish Macbeth, sporting a kilt and a shock of red hair, helped himself to punch.

"Let's get this party started," said a familiar voice behind Jane.

Jane turned to see the Cover Girls posing en masse.

Flaunting convention, Eloise had come as Sherlock Holmes and had convinced Phoebe to be her Dr. Watson. Mabel was Mrs. Pollifax, and Mrs. Pratt made for the perfect Miss Marple. Anna wanted to wear something contemporary, so she'd chosen to be Temperance Brennan while Violet was an adult-sized Nancy Drew. Mabel had done a wonderful job with everyone's costumes, but the Nancy Drew was Jane's favorite. It called to mind a vintage prom dress and was made of lavender tulle. Most women would have looked ridiculous in such a getup, but the dress showed off Violet's curves, turning the traditional schoolgirl sleuth image on its head.

"If the Hardy Boys are here, they'd better watch out," Jane told Violet and then opened her arms to include all of her friends. "You're amazing! All of you! Go enjoy yourselves." She leapt forward to stop Eloise from moving. "Not you, Sherlock."

Eloise removed a pipe from her mouth. "Unhand me, madam."

Ignoring the British accent and the fake scowl, Jane said, "I hadn't considered this before, but how can you flirt with Desmond dressed like that? Should I give Violet the assignment?"

Eloise shook her head. "Violet's reading repertoire isn't nearly as expansive as mine."

"No one knows more about books than you, but your costume isn't very . . . alluring." Jane gestured at Eloise's houndstooth coat and matching cape.

"The solution is elementary, dear Jane." Eloise unbuttoned the coat. "It's bound to get warm in here, leaving me no choice but to remove a layer or two. I'm only wearing a white tank top under this houndstooth. The top is rather tight and leaves little to the imagination. Observe." Eloise parted the lapels of the coat, allowing Jane an eyeful of impressive décolletage.

"Thy cup runneth over," Jane said and both women laughed. "Ah, here's your victim now. The one in the vintage suit and the fedora. Colonel Hastings in the flesh." She took Eloise by the elbow. "Try to get all the info you can on the classes he teaches, his interests, and what brought him to Storyton Hall. Once he's loosened up, work Adela Dundee's *Lost Letters* into the conversation. Perhaps you can say how disappointed you were that you didn't win the book. Watch him closely when you mention the title."

"Aye, aye, Captain." Eloise tipped her bowler hat and disappeared into the growing crowd.

The Storyton Band launched into a jaunty version of Sinatra's "It Happened in Monterey," and couples took the dance floor. Jane edged past an Alex Cross and fixed her gaze on the room's entrance again.

"Have I missed her?" she wondered aloud.

A Hercule Poirot led a Miss Marple into the room. The latter put her hand over her heart and exclaimed, "This is the best vacation we've ever had in all our twenty-five years, Bernie. I'll never forget it!"

Her husband smiled, kissed his happy wife, and led her to the refreshment table. Jane watched them. Though pleased by the woman's comment, she was also worried that most of the guests had arrived and that Moira was either not among them or was so well disguised that Jane couldn't recognize her.

She bought a ticket. She'll be here, Jane told herself. *I need to stop looking for a cloud of white hair.*

Moving closer to one of the floor candelabras, Jane unfolded a photocopy of Moira McKee's Vermont driver's license. She studied the shape of the woman's eyes and noted her angular chin and the deep parentheses framing her mouth. Tucking the paper back into her purse, she said hello to a man dressed as Nero Wolfe, smiled at a marvelously attired Tommy and Tuppence, and came face-to-face with an Umberto Ferrari.

The man wasn't Felix Hampden, of course. He wore a false mustache and goatee as well as a bald cap, and his outfit couldn't hold a candle to Hampden's custom-made pieces. However, he gave a gentlemanly bow that reminded her of Hampden. Her stomach twisted and for a moment, all she could see was Felix Hampden's lifeless body splayed on the carpet of the Mystery Suite. Remembering the image of Hampden's pain-ridden face and clawlike fingers, she felt a whisper of sepulchral air pass over her and shuddered.

"Ma'am? Are you all right?"

Jane nodded, clearing her head of the macabre visions. "Yes, thank you. A ghost walked over my grave."

The Umberto Ferrari smiled in understanding. "It's no wonder with all of these detectives in one room. The whole place is permeated by an aura of mystery. The only thing missing is a crime."

The song ended and the couples on the dance floor dispersed. Jane caught a glimpse of Eloise and Desmond Price heading for a vacant table in a quiet corner. "Oh, I think we'll have plenty of excitement without that," she told the Umberto Ferrari look-alike and wished him a pleasant evening.

Just as the band struck up Glen Miller's "Stardust," Jane saw Moira McKee enter the ballroom. At first, she wasn't sure that the brunette was Moira, but the more she stared at her, the more convinced she became. Moira was obviously wearing a wig and her conservative green dress didn't provide any clues about her sleuth's identity, but as Jane sidled closer, she was able to read the other woman's name tag.

"How lovely!" she declared merrily. "You're the only person who thought to come as Agatha Raisin. And she's one of my all-time favorite detectives. She's so genuine and so fallible that I can't help but empathize with her."

Moira seemed taken aback by Jane's enthusiasm, but she recovered quickly. "I find her relentless pursuit of every available bachelor rather endearing."

"I'm Tuppence," Jane said even though she suspected Moira knew her true identity. "Would you join me for a glass of punch?"

After a brief hesitation, in which Moira's eyes anxiously scanned the room, she politely accepted.

The waitstaff was doing a splendid job keeping the punchbowl filled and the food platters replenished. Jane had made arrangements for a specific waiter to be at the ready in case she needed a particularly potent glass of punch. Now, as the young man handed her two glasses, he winked conspiratorially and whispered, "I added a few splashes of vodka to the cup with the orange slice."

Jane gave Moira the punch and set a plate of cheddar cheese cookies on the table. It was her hope that the saltiness of the cookie would encourage Moira to gulp down her punch with alacrity.

"Delicious," Moira said, taking a bite of one of the cookies. "How did they ever shape them into magnifying glasses?"

"I have no clue," Jane admitted. "I believe that a great deal of magic goes on in the resort's kitchen when no one is looking."

Moira grinned. "Perhaps they have a fairy or a helpful sprite. I could use one myself."

"Me too. I'd make mine do the ironing. I hate ironing." She turned to watch the dancers. "What would you have your sprites do?"

"Keep an eye on certain people. Listen to their conversations." Her grin slipped. "That would prove most useful."

"A troop of tiny spies." Jane nodded as if this were a perfectly reasonable idea. "Do you need to keep track of people in your line of work?"

Moira took a large slug of punch. "You could say that. I serve as president at a very prestigious college."

Jane tried to look duly impressed. "Wow. What an enormous responsibility. It would be like running this place. Overseeing a large staff, maintaining the buildings and grounds, raising funds. Here's to you."

Lifting her glass in response to Jane's toast, Moira finished her punch and picked up a cookie. "It isn't an easy life, but I'd do anything for Broadleaf. Our school used to be the Juilliard of New England, you know." Her face shone with pride. "Once upon a time, we had so many applicants that we had to turn away over half of them. Now we're lucky if our classrooms have enough registered students to warrant a full-time faculty member." She nibbled on the cheddar cookie, her gaze distant and slightly morose.

"Let me get you a refill," Jane said and hurried to the waiter manning the punch bowl.

Moira was still wearing a faraway look when Jane returned with her drink. She absently raised the glass to her lips and drank while Jane wondered if it was too soon to work Alice Hart into the conversation. The memory of Felix Hampden had sharpened her resolve, however, so she decided it was time to see if Moira had anything to do with his death or the disappearance of Aunt Octavia's book.

"What of your faculty? Are they loyal?" Jane asked. "In this day and age, no one seems to stay in one place. They see something better and brighter and off they go."

"Loyalty? What a romantic notion." Moira snorted. "Not only has our endowment dried up, but no one seems to care about the arts at all. There's no value to music and dance and drama. Not when compared to technology. My faculty used to be the cream of the crop. These days, they'll run off at the drop of a hat if they have a chance to make more money. Recently, one of my teachers took an unscheduled leave in the middle of the semester! Can you imagine?" A malicious gleam entered her eyes. "She paid for her reckless behavior, I can assure you."

Gooseflesh arose on Jane's arms. Moira had to be referring to Alice Hart's death. "Oh? What happened?"

"She dropped dead. Just like that." Moira snapped her fingers. "A pretty, young thing too. When I called her parents to find out what had caused such a sudden demise, they told me that she had a condition called . . ." She trailed off. "Ah, I remember now. It was called hypertrophic cardiomyopathy. Alice had an enlarged heart with thick walls and something particular going on at the cellular level. Apparently, this condition kills young athletes with no warning. And by young, I mean people in their teens and twenties. It's very rare."

"Was Alice an athlete?"

"She was a runner. And though she was in her late twenties, she was fitter than most of our students." Moira was clearly warming to her subject. "That's why Alice's condition was so remarkable. There are no symptoms. No warning signs. One day, the heart is so stressed that it can't maintain a regular rhythm and the ventricles go haywire. They quiver, I believe. And then, the person often faints, never to come to." Again, Moira scanned the crowd, her gaze keen. When it was obvious that she couldn't find the person she was looking for, she leaned close to Jane and whispered, "It happened here, you know. In Storyton village."

She has no idea who I am, Jane thought and felt a surge of relief. "What did?"

"Alice's dramatic finale. She was riding a horse that got spooked and bounded off the woodland trail right onto Main Street. Word has it that Alice was able to hang on, but couldn't control her mount. I imagine her heart was racing far too fast." Moira clicked her tongue. "If she'd been at Broadleaf teaching her students, then she might not have suffered such a terrible fate."

Jane actually detected a small trace of sympathy in Moira's voice. A very small trace. "Why would she leave such a respectable position to come to Storyton? Was she a reader? Most people come here to escape the modern world."

"Alice Hart wasn't running *away* from anything. She was running *toward* something. Something that could change her life forever. Grant her fame and fortune. She believed it was here and that she was one of the few people in the world who realized that such a treasure even existed." A shadow passed over Moira's face. "Alice conducted her Adela Dundee research on the school's dime. I scrambled to find her grants and begged the alumni for donations, and when her book was published to rave reviews, how did she repay me? By quitting! By going off on some treasure hunt. Any fortune she unearthed rightfully belongs to Broadleaf." She was muttering now. Speaking so softly that Jane could barely make out her words over the music.

Of course, Jane knew exactly what treasure Moira was

referring to. Had Moira been able to acquire Aunt Octavia's book? To succeed where Alice Hart had failed? If so, then why would she still be at Storyton Hall? And who was she looking for in the crowd?

"I hope I'm not keeping you from your family or friends," Jane said as Moira polished off the rest of her punch. "You seem to be trying to find someone. Can I help?"

Moira nodded and her next words were slightly slurred. "A little man. He's the spitting image of Umberto Ferrari, and was the last to speak with Alice before her doomed ride. And then he won . . . well, that's not important."

Jane stared at Moira. Was it possible that she was innocent of any wrongdoing? If she'd come to the costume ball to find Felix Hampden and to perhaps make him another offer for his copy of *Lost Letters*, then she hadn't killed him.

If *he was murdered*, Jane reminded herself. Sheriff Evans obviously believed something suspicious had occurred, but without the medical examiner's report, no one could be certain how he'd died.

"I've only seen one Umberto Ferrari tonight," Jane said and began to search for him. "There he is! At that table to the right of the stage. Do you see him? He's waving his arms in time to the music. Maybe he has aspirations of becoming a conductor."

"He'll be a man of leisure if he realizes what he's won," Moira murmured darkly. "I must speak with him. Thank you for the company, uh, Tuppence."

Moira stumbled across the dance floor, forcing several couples to veer around her. Jane followed in her wake, though she was more careful not to disturb the dancers as they moved to the lively strains of "Voices of Spring."

She lost sight of Moira for a moment, but after scooting around a Kinsey Millhone in the arms of a dapper Alex Cross, Jane was able to see Moira drag a chair over to the Umberto Ferrari look-alike's table and begin to scrutinize him as if he were a slide under a microscope.

Eventually, the man felt her eyes on him. Turning, he smiled graciously, but Moira didn't smile back. Instead, she glowered fiercely and spoke a few words. The man shook his head. Once. Twice. Moira said something else, and this time, the man shrugged his shoulders and faced the band again, signaling the conversation was at an end.

Moira got to her feet and backed away. After casting a final, desperate glance around the room, she made a rather ungainly exit. Jane was still watching the doorway when Eloise appeared at her side.

"Desmond Price has some nerve posing as Colonel Hastings. Agatha Christie created the perfect gentlemen in Hastings, but Price has no idea what it means to be a gentleman." Fuming, Eloise shoved her pipe into her coat pocket.

"Come on, Sherlock. I think you need some air."

As the two women headed for the terrace, Jane spied Moira stepping into an elevator cab. Just as the doors were closing with a soft whisper, a man dressed in monk's robes thrust his arm between the doors, causing them to spring open again. He entered the elevator, his head bent low. With his hood pulled forward over his face, he looked every inch the penitent monk.

Perhaps he went to the ball as Brother Cadfael, Jane thought.

The doors started to slide shut again. At that moment, the monk raised his head and Jane immediately saw that the young man's face was nothing like the kind, earnest countenance of the monk in the Ellis Peters novels.

Jane only caught a glimpse of thin lips, a narrow nose, and a pair of penetrating eyes filled with a cold, black rage. But in the space of a single heartbeat, she detected such an overwhelming sense of menace that she nearly stumbled.

Eloise grabbed her by the arm. "Steady there, Tuppence. How much punch have you had?"

"Not nearly enough," Jane said breathlessly and led Eloise out into the October night.

TEN

"So Desmond Price is a creep?" Jane asked Eloise once they were settled in a pair of wicker rocking chairs on the terrace facing Milton's gardens.

"Totally. And it wasn't just his propensity for touching me in an overly familiar fashion, though that was distasteful enough." Eloise curled her lip at the memory. "He's one of those people who see themselves as being far superior to the rest of us, but for no obvious reason." She shot a glance at Jane. "Aren't you cold? It's October and you're in a glorified nightgown."

Jane rubbed the skin of her arms. "It's more of mental chill. Once you tell me about Desmond, I'll let myself into my aunt and uncle's apartments and grab a shawl. Uncle Aloysius gave Aunt Octavia a gorgeous silk and velvet number embroidered with peonies and peacock feathers that my aunt won't wear because it's black. It's neither garish nor colorful enough for her, but I've been coveting it for years. Not only that, but I have to check on Muffet Cat. The poor kitty must be terribly lonely and I'll need to soothe him with several treats or he's liable to yowl all night long."

"I'll be quick then." Eloise took her pipe out of her pocket and rubbed its smooth neck while she talked. "Desmond is a professor of literature at Harvard. He boasted about his many accomplishments in the academic arena, but it was only when he started in on his illustrious family history that things got interesting. You see, Desmond is related to Adela Dundee. He's a cousin—a second cousin once removed or something like that. His mother was a Brit."

"The British have such impeccable manners," Jane said, clicking her tongue. "And yet, Desmond sounds rude. In fact, he sounds like an utter cad."

"Well, his mom passed away when he was a child. I believe she meant a great deal to him—that it was she who introduced him to modern mystery stories and to Adela Dundee." Eloise frowned. "It's sad, really. Desmond's obsession with all things Dundee probably boils down to a boy who has never gotten over losing his mother."

Jane stared out over the dark lawn. She too knew of loss and how it could shape a person. How it could change a life in a heartbeat. Hers was forever altered following William's sudden death. She sighed. "I wish our suspects were less complex. It was easier to think of Desmond as a villain before I knew about his mother."

"Don't worry, you can continue to cast him in that role," Eloise said airily. "After his fourth glass of punch and the second time his elbow *accidentally* brushed against my buxom bosom, he started in on how the Dundees had snubbed him." She pulled her cell phone from her coat pocket. "Alice Hart wasn't the only Storyton guest who wrote a book on Adela Dundee. Desmond penned one too, though his was more of a memoir. Unfortunately for Professor Price, Adela's descendants publicly slammed the book, saying that Desmond's tales were nothing but fabrication and conjecture. He tried to make readers believe that he was part of the fold, when in truth, he'd met his Dundee relatives exactly once. And he was just a boy at the time."

She showed Jane a book cover featuring a photograph of a child in a sailor suit posing in front of Adela Dundee's London town house.

"He couldn't be much older than the twins," Jane said.

"Desmond didn't spend long inside the town house. According to a spokesman for the Dundee estate, Desmond's mother was invited to tea. It was the appropriate thing for the family to do, seeing as a cousin of theirs was visiting London with her son, but that was the extent of Desmond's contact."

Jane was confused. "He turned an afternoon of cakes and Darjeeling into a memoir?"

"*Tea with Adela Dundee* is a partial biography of Adela, though not nearly as thorough or well researched as Alice Hart's *Lost Letters*. For example, Alice found a packet of letters in some long-forgotten, dust-covered box belonging to a historical society in Cornwall. The letters had been misfiled by a senile archivist decades ago, and Alice only came upon them by chance."

"I never have that kind of luck."

Eloise smirked. "Me neither. Anyway, she copied every letter before replacing them in the same box. This way, no one would discover the letters before Alice's book was published. The sly fox. *Lost Letters* sold amazingly well because Alice had made a new discovery." Eloise tapped on her cell phone screen, enlarging Desmond's book cover. "Professor Price just rehashed old material and added a few stories about the tea and a family tree showing how he and his mother were connected to the Maven of Mystery. The book was a flop. A total embarrassment. I'm sure it hurt Desmond's academic reputation. He was up for tenure this year and it wasn't granted."

"He told you that?" Jane was surprised.

Eloise nodded. "He listed it as one of the many wrongs done to him and is clearly desperate to restore his good name." She began typing, and a few seconds later, Desmond's faculty member profile appeared on her phone screen. "This must be a recent photo. Look at him, Jane. The guy is like a pot of simmering water on the stovetop. He wants someone to pay for his own failures, and I think it's only a matter of time before he boils over. He told me that he'd get even with the Dundees for slighting him if it was the last thing he did." Eloise's expression was grim. "It wasn't an empty boast, Jane. Desmond Price has come to Storyton with a purpose. And if you ask me, it's a nefarious one."

Jane took the proffered phone and studied Desmond's taut lips, the haughty set of his jaw, and the angry defiance in his eyes. She shivered again, thinking of the monk who'd joined Moira McKee in the elevator cab. The look in his eyes had been very similar. "Were you able to insert Felix Hampden into the conversation?"

"Yes. I pretended to be disappointed that I hadn't won the scavenger hunt prize." Eloise pulled the lapels of her coat closed, as if protecting herself against a cold wind. "When I mentioned the book, a thunderstorm gathered on Desmond's face. I swear, Jane, lightning flashed in the man's eyes. It was scary."

"Did he try to buy *Lost Letters* from Felix?"

"All he said was that Hampden was a fool who possessed something that only a person with blood ties to the Dundee family should have." Eloise got to her feet. "Let's go back in. I'm almost done with my story anyway."

Jane readily agreed. The magic she'd felt gazing up at the stars before the ball had disappeared. The sky was ink-black and the day's mild air had been chased away by a damp, brisk wind. Jane knew that rain was in tomorrow's forecast, but she hoped it would hold off until after the pickleball tournament.

Inside, she and Eloise walked to the door leading to the staff staircase. "Desmond's last words had me so freaked out that I pinched my nose again and again, waiting for Mrs. Pratt to fly to the rescue." Eloise scowled. "Trust me, you do not want that woman beside you in battle. She's too easily distracted to be anyone's wingman."

"Oh, dear. I thought she'd leap at the opportunity to be in the middle of a drama."

"She was hell-bent on creating her own," Eloise said. "She started dancing with a nice-looking older gentleman and instantly forgot about me. Just when Desmond started talking like a serial killer, the wife of Mrs. Pratt's dance partner barreled onto the dance floor and gave her husband what for."

Jane couldn't help but grin. "I never took Eugenia Pratt for a home wrecker."

Eloise rolled her eyes. "I blame it on all the erotica she read this month. Over twenty novels, each steamier than the last."

Laughing, Jane made a hurry-up gesture. "Okay, enough about Mrs. Pratt's reading tastes. It seems reasonable to assume that Desmond Price could be the book thief, right?"

"That, and maybe more." The amusement in Eloise's eyes died and she spoke in a low, grave voice. "Desmond Price knew Felix Hampden *before* they both came to Storyton. He said Felix ran some third-rate theater in Boston, but was better known as a swindler and a charlatan. Seriously, he used those words. The man constantly borrows phrases from Adela Dundee's novels. Listen to me, Jane." Eloise touched Jane's arm. "The professor isn't right in the head. *Tea with Adela* was published less than a year ago, and his wounds are still raw. The false image he created for himself has suffered a serious blow. He's been humiliated and passed over for tenure. He can't move on until he feels vindicated."

"How can you be so sure?"

"Because he told me that he came to Storyton to get what rightfully belonged to him and that he'd stop at nothing to show the world the real Desmond Price." Eloise gave Jane an imploring look. "Doesn't that sound like a man on the edge? A dangerous, desperate man? Someone you need to be quite leery of?"

"Yes," Jane said. She silently considered the strange co-incidence that Desmond's words were identical to Moira's. They both believed that Aunt Octavia's copy of *Lost Letters* "rightfully belonged" to them.

Eloise studied her. "How did your sleuthing go?"

Jane quickly shared what she'd learned about Moira. When she was done, Eloise agreed that it was unlikely Moira had succeeded in acquiring the book.

"What's our next step?" Eloise asked.

Jane gave her friend a hug. "You go back to the ball and have a good time, but keep your Dr. Watson close by in case Desmond misbehaves. And if Watson doesn't work, there's always Sam."

At the mention of Sam's name, Eloise perked up. "When I left, he was dancing with Violet. I knew he wouldn't be able to resist her in that Nancy Drew-turned-vixen costume."

Suddenly, an idea came to Jane. "You know, Sheriff Evans spoke with Sam about what happened to Alice Hart on his trail ride, but I haven't. I wonder if Sam knows what spooked Alice's horse."

"I'll get Violet to ask him." Eloise's eyes twinkled with mischief. "Is the waiter still there? The one who had the *special* punch just for Moira and Desmond?"

"Shame on you!" Jane nudged Eloise in the side. "Violet wouldn't want any man who only showed interest because he was drunk. What kind of matchmaker are you anyway?"

"An impatient one," Eloise said. "Go upstairs and grab that shawl. I'm getting colder and colder just looking at you."

Jane pushed open the door to the stairwell and glanced back at Eloise. "Thank you for being such a good sport tonight."

Eloise smiled. "Are you kidding? I haven't felt this invigorated in ages. And thanks to you, balancing my books this month will be far less frightening. I know things have taken a strange and unwelcome turn, but hang in there, Jane. Having a theme week was a brilliant idea. Don't let a few cretins ruin it for you."

"I won't. It'll take more than murder and mayhem to stop my endeavor from being a success," Jane said. The door closed behind her, and she stood there for a moment, her palm on the wall as if feeling for the house's heartbeat. "It can't fail. Too much depends on it."

When Jane reached her aunt and uncle's apartments, she found Muffet Cat curled up against the polished oak door. Seeing her, he slowly unfolded himself, got to his feet, stretched, and released a pitiful meow.

Sweet boy!" Jane cooed and stroked the cat's glossy fur. Muffet Cat began to purr and rub himself against Jane's calf. He then raised his front paw and, using the tip of his claws, scratched at the door.

"Ready for bed, are you?" Jane unlocked the door and pushed it inward. "Come on, let's get you settled."

The apartment was silent. Too silent for Jane's tastes. Aunt Octavia was not a quiet person. She barked rather than spoke, guffawed rather than laughed, and filled the spaces she occupied with color and sound.

"You're larger than life," Jane said, picking up the framed photo of her aunt that had been on her uncle's nightstand for as long as she could remember. She sat on the edge of their bed and prayed that Aunt Octavia wouldn't be diminished by her physical disability. "Each of us has a tough battle to fight, but we can make it through."

Muffet Cat joined her on the bed. He sniffed Aunt Octavia's pillow and then glared at Jane, as if making it clear that she was not welcome to sleep in his favorite person's bed. Jane tried to pet him again, but he flattened his ears and squeezed into the space between the pillow and the headboard. From this position, his yellow eyes shone with displeasure.

"You have no poker face, Muffet Cat," Jane told him. "And I'm sorry that Aunt Octavia isn't here. I miss her too, believe me." Jane fetched a freeze-dried chicken treat from a powder jar on the dresser and placed it on the top sheet. Muffet Cat's paw shot out from under the pillow like a striking snake. Piercing the treat with his claws, he pulled it into his lair. Jane heard crunching sounds followed by a rumble. Muffet Cat was purring again. "See? Everything will be all right."

After taking the silk shawl from her aunt's closet, Jane retraced her steps through the apartment, locked the main door, and headed down the hall. Passing through another exit marked EMPLOYEES ONLY, she walked over the plush carpet leading to the third-floor guest rooms. Without planning to, she found herself standing at the door to Felix Hampden's room. Jane suddenly realized that this was the appropriate place to reflect on all the information she'd gathered tonight.

Unfortunately, Jane didn't have a key to room 316, so she crossed the hall and unlocked the housekeeper's closet. A set of room keys was stored on every floor in the event of an emergency and Jane was just about to help herself to the third-floor key ring when she heard sounds of a scuffle.

A woman's cry reverberated down the corridor. It wasn't loud, but it was filled with enough fear that Jane leapt into action. She grabbed the only weapon at hand—a mop—and rushed toward the source of the noise. Rounding a bend in the hallway, she heard a whimper coming from the small room where the vending and ice machines were located. Jane gave the door a rough push.

Lizzie, the housekeeper, was huddled in a recess between the wall and the ice machine. Her uniform was rumpled and her eyes glistened with tears. Her hands, which were balled into fists, shook violently.

Hovering over Lizzie in an undisguised pose of malice was the man in the monk's robes.

"Lizzie!" Jane yelled. She shifted her gaze from the terrified housekeeper to the monk, brandishing the mop as if it were a long sword. "What are you doing?" she demanded. Raising twin boys had taught her how to infuse her voice with steel, and the man in the Brother Cadfael costume immediately responded. He pivoted and glowered at Jane.

His hood had fallen away, revealing a tangle of unkempt chestnut hair and the same furious eyes that had peered out at her from inside the elevator cab. Though the beginnings of a dark beard covering his chin and the deep furrow of anger between his brows made him look older, Jane put him in his late twenties.

"I asked you a question, *sir.*" Jane stared down the stranger. She wasn't the least bit frightened. All she saw was a guest assaulting a Storyton Hall employee, and she wasn't about to stand by while someone abused one of her staff members.

The man's gaze flicked to the mop in Jane's hands and he seemed to come to a decision. Turning to Lizzie, he spoke in a low snarl. "This isn't over."

And before Jane had a chance to wonder what he meant, he barreled right into her, shoving her so hard that she dropped the mop and stumbled backward, pinwheeling her arms madly.

Jane thrust out her hand and her fingers found purchase on the door casing. "Stop!" she shouted after the man, but he was already a blur of black robes and patent leather loafers disappearing into the guest stairwell. Jane was tempted to pursue him, but in her dress and heels, she knew that she was ill equipped to overpower him. The mop wouldn't help much either.

"Lizzie! Are you all right?" She rushed to the older woman's side and put an arm around her. "What did he want from you?"

"Oh, Miss Jane!" Lizzie chocked back a sob. "He wanted me to open another guest's room for him. And when I said that I didn't have my keys on me, he went crazy."

Jane was stunned. "Which room?"

Lizzie took a tissue from her pocket and wiped her eyes

and cheeks. "He didn't say, Miss Jane. He must have guessed that I was lying about not having my keys because he started shaking me . . ."

Fearing that Lizzie might start crying again, Jane quickly told her that she'd shown remarkable courage.

"I'd do anything to protect the privacy of our guests," Lizzie said. She gave a firm tug to her uniform dress and straightened her crooked name tag. "I could see that that man was up to no good from the get-go. He told me a story about forgetting his key because his costume had no pockets, but there was something I didn't like about his face. I said that I'd be glad to get an extra key for him right after I called the front desk to verify that his name matched the room number." She snorted. "No one's going to bully me into unlocking another guest's room. No, ma'am!"

Seeing that Lizzie was well on the road to recovery, Jane said, "Let's go to my office. We need to report this incident to Butterworth right away so he can get word to the rest of the staff to be on the lookout for this monk. He'll soon be answering to Sheriff Evans for assaulting you."

Lizzie vigorously shook her head. "No, no, Miss Jane. I'm fine. Really. I don't want to bother the sheriff. I'd be happy if Mr. Butterworth told that horrible man to relocate to a hotel over the mountain. Someplace befitting a person of his . . . his . . ." She seemed unable to come up with an appropriate word.

"Ilk?" Jane suggested.

"Yes." Lizzie managed a thin smile. "His ilk."

Jane laced an arm through the housekeeper's arm. "Let me stow my weapon and then we'll get you a nice glass of . . ." Now Jane was at a loss.

"A shot of Jameson's would be lovely," Lizzie said in a charming Irish lilt.

Jane grinned. "Remind me to talk you into trying out for the next production of the Storyton Hall Players."

Lizzie's eyes widened in terror. "Oh, please don't, Miss

Jane. I really don't like the spotlight. I just want to care for our guests and live a quiet little life. In a way, this job is the most peaceful thing I've ever done. It's much easier than being at my mom's beck and call or raising kids."

Thinking of all the mischief Fitz and Hem got into on a daily basis, Jane had to agree. She put the mop away and then led Lizzie downstairs and into her office. After telling her to sit and relax, Jane ordered a whiskey from the Ian Fleming Lounge and then went in search of Butterworth.

Jane knew that Butterworth had been training one of the groundskeepers to serve as a second conductor. By this time of night, the understudy would have taken up the baton, leaving Butterworth free to enjoy a few hours of leisurely reading. Since the devoted butler was working his way through a list of novels with African themes, Jane headed for the Isak Dinesen Safari Room.

Of all the rooms in Storyton Hall, the Safari Room was Jane's least favorite. Due to her great grandfather's penchant for hunting game all over the globe, there were far too many animal heads mounted to the walls for Jane's taste. And though the souvenirs he'd placed throughout the room fascinated her—the African tribal masks, Aboriginal shields, and primitive weaponry—she could never relax in the zebra-print chairs or the leather settees covered by faux-fur throws. She couldn't shake the accusatory stare of the animals, and she was more than a little ashamed of the pair of elephant tusks flanking the fireplace. Once, she'd asked Uncle Aloysius to have the tusks and all the taxidermy trophies removed, but he refused.

"We should never try to conceal the mistakes of the past, my girl," he'd said in a firm but gentle tone. "Otherwise, how can we learn from them?"

So the tusks remained. And while lady guests typically avoided the Safari Room, men flocked to it. Dressed in seersucker or khaki pants, they'd enter the masculine space with beer or brandies in hand, and immediately feel at home. The room smelled pleasantly of cologne and wood smoke and was not as well lit as the other public reading spaces. It was by no means gloomy, and the men seemed to prefer reading or playing cards by lamplight.

Butterworth had the Safari Room all to himself. He sat in a club chair facing the fire, a glass of red wine on the side table and a hardback splayed on his right thigh. His gaze was fixed on the crackling flames, but when he heard footfalls, he glanced over to see who'd entered the room. Jane was unnerved by his troubled expression. Butterworth had always been the epitome of calm composure.

She gestured at the book. "Not a riveting read, I take it?"

Butterworth showed her the cover of Chinua Achebe's *Things Fall Apart*. "An excellent rendering of Nigerian tribal life, but I fear that certain events have me distracted." Closing the book, he got to his feet, his body as tense as a drawn bowstring. "What's wrong?"

Jane quickly told him about the man in monk's robes. The moment she was done, Butterworth pulled a cell phone from his pocket, pressed and held a single number, and then said, "Sterling? We have a rabbit. Male. Mid to late twenties. Brown hair. Five o'clock shadow. Attired in black monk's robes. Patent leather loafers. Assaulted a housekeeper. He may have teeth. Proceed with caution."

"A rabbit?" Jane asked.

Butterworth's gaze swept the room. Even though they were alone, he lowered his voice. "A rabbit is a type of intruder. An individual that must be tracked and captured."

Glancing nervously at the head of an antelope mounted on the opposite wall, Jane said, "And the part about the teeth?"

"The intruder might be armed." Butterworth tucked his book under his arm and collected his wineglass. "You will learn all of the codes, Miss Jane. However, now is not the time. Let us adjourn to Sterling's office. I want to see if he can find our man on the security cameras."

Sterling's small office was across the hall from Jane's,

and she'd grown used to the bank of small television screens displaying views of the front driveway, the back terrace, the lobby, and the hallways leading to guest rooms. Jane thought she knew where every hotel camera was located, but she was in for a surprise. The moment Sterling opened the door and ushered her into the office, she saw an entire wall of screens she'd never noticed before.

"I don't know how many more secrets I can take," she said, feeling tired and irritable.

Sterling looked a trifle abashed. "These are usually hidden behind my map of Virginia. I only check them a few times each day. Ever since Mr. Hampden's passing, however, I've done my best to track the movements of Moira McKee and Desmond Price. So far, I haven't noticed any suspicious activity. Neither has Sinclair. Of course, we might have missed something, seeing as we both have other responsibilities."

Sinclair cleared his throat. "Sterling and I take turns watching the screens, but this level of scrutiny is only employed when a person of questionable repute is at Storyton Hall. It is not our intention to invade the privacy of our guests, Miss Jane, but our duty, above all else, is to keep the guardian of Storyton safe."

"That's a mouthful," Jane said and smiled at Sinclair. "I didn't mean to be crabby. It's been a long and confusing day, and to have it culminate with someone putting their hands on a member of my staff? That's unacceptable."

"If you came upon that man a few months from now, you'd have had enough martial arts training to render him harmless," Sterling said.

Jane smirked. "Preferably with a well-aimed kick to the groin."

The three men in the room winced.

"An attack to that part of the body is rarely taught in the better-known martial arts disciplines, but certain street-fighting tactics may prove highly effective for you, Miss Jane," Butterworth said.

"Anything would be better than going after an assailant with a mop," she said.

"Not necessarily." Sinclair put a hand on Sterling's shoulder. "This man would have used the handle to deliver a debilitating blow to the monk's windpipe. The fight would have been over before it began."

Jane pointed at the television monitors. "Where is he now? Have you spotted him, Sterling?"

Sterling shook his head. "Not yet. He's still at the resort. Whether he's inside or somewhere on the grounds is unknown. Unless he's a complete imbecile, he's shed his costume and is, at this very moment, blending in with the other guests."

Jane didn't care for that idea at all. "How do you know that he hasn't left Storyton Hall?"

"Because I reviewed the feed coming from the front gate, main doors, and side and back terraces. There's been very little outdoor activity since the ball got under way."

"It's dark and cold out there." Jane barked out a half-crazed laugh. "I'm living such a double life that I'm worrying about a lunatic running loose in the resort and whether it will rain during tomorrow's pickleball tournament at the same time!"

Sinclair gave her a pat on the arm. "You're managing brilliantly, Miss Jane. You identified our possible suspects and came up with a plan to question them. For now, we're willing to let you adopt your, ah, more gentile techniques, but neither Ms. McKee nor Professor Price will be allowed to leave Storyton Hall until your aunt's book has been returned."

"What will you do to them?" Jane asked. Part of her feared the answer, but part of her looked forward to hearing it. After all, that book belonged to Storyton's secret library. How dare someone try to steal it? How dare someone attempt to gain fame and fortune from an object that belonged to another person?

"You're about to find out." Sterling tapped his finger against a screen.

Jane leaned closer to the monitor and saw a figure appear in the second-floor hallway. He wore jeans and a hooded sweatshirt. The hood obscured his hair and most of his forehead, and he walked with his gaze on the carpet.

"Is that our man?" Jane narrowed her eyes. "I can't tell."

"Look at his shoes," Butterworth commanded and told Sterling to reverse the feed several frames.

Jane stared at the patent leather loafers and then gasped. "It *is* him!"

And before she could utter another word, Sterling and Butterworth leapt up and dashed from the room. Sinclair closed the door behind them and took Sterling's vacant seat.

"If he enters a room and it's registered under his name, I'll be able to identify him." Jane continued to watch as the man stopped in front of a door. Jane counted silently in her head. "That must be room two twenty-seven."

Using Sterling's computer, Jane logged into the guest tracker program and typed the room number in the search box. When the results appeared, her breath caught in her throat.

"Who's our monk, then?" Sinclair asked.

"I have no idea, but I'm sure of one thing. That isn't his room."

Sinclair frowned. "Who's the registered guest?"

When Jane answered, her voice was tight with apprehension. "Moira McKee."

ELEVEN

The man in the sweatshirt raised his fist and knocked on the door. Jane watched, heart hammering in her chest, as he waited for Moira to answer. The man shifted impatiently, and then knocked again. This time, he used both fists.

Jane couldn't move. She didn't dare blink. The seconds stretched out and the rest of the world fell away. There was only the man on the screen. And then, there were three men. Jane saw a wink of metal as Sterling pressed something to the stranger's neck. An instant later, he and Butterworth each grabbed one of the man's arms and began pulling him toward the servants' stairs. He struggled at first, twisting violently in an attempt to break free from their grasp, and then he abruptly stopped and slumped forward.

"What happened?" Jane asked. "He looks drunk."

"That's precisely the image that we're trying to convey," Sinclair said. "Mr. Sterling injected our rabbit with an animal tranquilizer. It works in less than a minute and wears off without harmful or residual effects."

Jane hid her face in her hands. "I can't believe it. We're copying the *modus operandi* of a fictional serial killer."

"Are we?" Sinclair was nonplussed. "Which serial killer?"

"Dexter Morgan."

Sinclair nodded. "Ah, yes. Jeff Lindsay's disturbed vigilante. However, we were using this particular technique long before Mr. Lindsay's first novel was published, my dear."

The trio entered the stairwell and vanished from view.

"Where are they taking him?"

"To a room behind the bowling lanes."

Jane thought of the narrow corridor behind the lanes. She'd been back there countless times in search of the twins. It was one of their favorite places to hide, hatch mischievous plots, or eat the macaroons or lemon cakes they'd filched from the kitchens. Despite the fact they'd been told over and over not to stretch out on their stomachs behind the triangle of pins in order to watch a bowling ball come hurtling down the lane, Fitz and Hem continued to claim that the dim and dusty pit area was another "Boys Only" zone. They had a half dozen such places around Storyton's house and grounds, including a decrepit tree fort in the orchard, a cedar closet in the attic, a secret nook under the main stairs, an antique car on blocks in the garage, and so on.

"What room?" Jane asked. "The corridor behind the lanes?" She'd been back there most recently to examine the pin elevator on lane five, which kept jamming and was in need of repair.

"The mechanical closet at the end of that corridor leads to another space."

Jane tried to mask her irritation. First thing tomorrow, after her archery lesson, she was going to speak with Uncle Aloysius about obtaining a copy of the *real* blueprints for Storyton Hall. This was supposed to be her home. Her ancestor built this manor, and it galled her that others knew more about its secrets than she did.

Sinclair must have guessed her thoughts for he gave her another paternal pat on the arm and said, "I know these revelations irk you, but you'll be fully briefed tomorrow. For now, you should get some rest. Our monk will be out of commission for a while."

"What happens when he wakes up?" Picturing the supply closet with its lane and gutter mops, lane polish, cases of shoe sanitizer, cracked pins, and a motley assortment of steel levers, gears, and pulleys, she wondered exactly how the Fins planned to extract information from the monk. "Please tell me we don't have some sort of torture chamber behind the bowling pits."

"Its appearance *is* rather intimidating. Bare gray walls, hissing pipes, a workbench covered with rusty tools, and a metal chair bolted to the floor. There's a single lightbulb swinging from a frayed wire as well." Sinclair grinned. "Sterling and I agonized over every detail. We had a terrible row over whether to install a drain in the floor, but I felt that was overdoing things. After all, we were aiming for a particular style. Feng shui meets the Spanish Inquisition."

Jane gaped. "You're kidding, right? I really hope that you're kidding."

Sinclair shook his head. "I am not. The purpose of the room is to make it clear that any person entering Storyton Hall with the intention of committing a crime will face the consequences. We don't administer a physical punishment, Miss Jane. But we get the derelicts to talk. We must. We must know if they're working alone or are hired guns. We need to discover what they intended to steal from Storyton Hall and if they are motivated by money, fame, power, or a combination of temptations."

"If there's no physical torture, then how do you get them to confess? Read them long passages about the migratory patterns of North American insects?"

Sinclair cocked his head. "No, but I like how you think. Traditionally, we recite literary passages in which imprisonment is described in a thoroughly disagreeable light. We have selections from *Don Quixote*, Thoreau's *Civil Disobedience*, *Crime and Punishment*, *The Count of Monte Cristo*, and a Walt Whitman poem called 'The Singer in the Prison.' That's the one that usually breaks them."

Jane glanced at the monitors. She saw guests entering their rooms, standing in the elevator cab, ascending and descending the main staircase, and milling about the various reading rooms. How many guests had checked into Storyton Hall with evil intentions since it had become a resort? How many had been taken to the room behind the bowling alley? "I think I need to go to bed," Jane said. "I've reached my daily capacity for shocks and surprises."

Sinclair nodded. "I believe that's wise. Would you like me to walk you home?"

"No, thank you. I don't need a bodyguard just yet." She smiled to take the sting from her words. "After tomorrow's archery lesson, I'd like the two of us to examine the list of employees who've had access to my aunt and uncle's apartments within the past month. Unless the mysterious monk ends up telling you that he and Lizzie worked together to poison Felix Hampden and steal Aunt Octavia's book, then I still have a staff member to bring to justice."

"The scenario you presented is very unlikely," Sinclair said. "But if our stranger is in collusion with someone wearing a Storyton Hall uniform, then we'll find out soon enough." He reached into his suit jacket and removed a small book with a green leather cover. "After all, I'm armed with Whitman."

Things were becoming too surreal for Jane, so she wished Sinclair good night and headed back to the ballroom. She took a quick peek inside to make sure the Cover Girls were enjoying themselves and it certainly looked as though they were. Mabel and Phoebe were dancing the fox-trot while Mrs. Pratt, Eloise, and Violet were chatting with several female guests as if they were old friends. Anna sat at a table across the room, happily ensconced between Sam and Edwin. Jane paused for a moment, wondering why she hadn't seen Edwin again after he'd waltzed her around the empty dance floor.

As if sensing her gaze on him, Edwin glanced up. Their eyes met and Jane could almost feel his hand pressing against the small of her back. Cheeks burning at the memory, she quickly looked away.

He's Eloise's brother, she chided herself. *And you have more important things to think about.*

She hurried across the lawn and stepped into her blessedly silent house. Ned, who usually watched TV after the boys went to bed, was actually reading a book.

Jane plunked her handbag on the kitchen counter. "What do you have there?"

"It's called *Paper Towns*. Mr. Sinclair promised that it would be more entertaining than watching college football."

"And?"

Ned, who'd been stretched out on the sofa, shifted to a seated position. "I was only going to read during halftime, but I got sucked in. One of the characters is a girl who dresses like a ninja. She's cool. I told Mr. Sinclair that I don't like mysteries because I can never figure things out, but he said that the clues are right here, waiting to be found." He tapped on the open page. "To tell you the truth, I don't care if I solve the puzzle. I just want to know what happens in the end."

Jane smiled. "It sounds like that author has a new fan."

Ned nodded. "John Green? Yeah. Definitely."

As was customary, Jane tried to pay Ned, and as was customary, he refused to accept her offer. "Mrs. Hubbard left a dessert plate for me in the staff kitchen," he said. "Some cake, cookies, and this book are all I need."

When Ned was gone, Jane washed up and put her pajamas on. She was exhausted, but her mind refused to calm down and she knew sleep wouldn't come for a while yet. As she picked up her copy of Adela Dundee's *Lost Letters*, something Ned said struck her. "The clues are right here, waiting to be found," she repeated, turning to the photograph of Alice Hart. "The reason you came to Storyton in the first place is in one of these letters. You followed a clue left by Adela Dundee. But why would Adela mention Storyton at all?" Jane flipped to the title page. "At last, I can do my part to unravel this riddle. Alice used her brains and so shall I."

Jane plumped her pillows, took a sip of water from the glass she kept on her nightstand, and began to read.

The next morning, she was jarred awake by the sound of Fitz and Hem playing taps on their kazoos.

"Boys!" she croaked in protest and then rolled over, burying her face in her pillow. *Lost Letters* slid off the bed and hit the floor with a thud. A minute later, a small hand pushed against her shoulder.

"Mom, you have to get up. We have archery this morning." Hem's voice was shrill with excitement. "Fitz and I are ready!"

"I'm going to be the next Robin Hood," boasted Fitz. "Bet I can already shoot an apple off your head, Hem."

"Like Mom would ever let you. Anyway. I'll hit twice as many bull's-eyes as you," Hem said, and the two of them began to wrestle. They grappled on the empty side of the bed, and Jane ignored them until the jumping contest started.

"Try to touch the ceiling!" Hem shouted.

The twins bounced until Jane was certain her brain was the consistency of runny eggs.

"Okay," she rasped. "I'm up."

Letting out a triumphant whoop, the boys told Jane they'd meet her in the kitchen and thundered downstairs.

Peering at the clock, Jane groaned. She didn't have time

to make coffee. In fact, she'd be lucky to get out of her pajamas before the doorbell rang.

She was just pulling on a warm sweater when Hem yelled, "Sterling's here in the Gator!"

"I love beginning the day with a predawn ride in an ATV," Jane murmured as she put her hair in a ponytail. She hurriedly brushed her teeth and joined the twins at the front door.

"I haven't had any coffee," she told Sterling by way of greeting.

"There's a thermos in the front seat along with a basket filled with egg and cheese biscuits." Sterling gave the boys a once-over. "Grab your down vests, lads. Hats too. Until the sun climbs a little higher, it'll be cold on the range."

The boys rushed to obey, returning with Jane's pink down vest.

"I got you a hat too." Fitz handed her the knit sock monkey hat he and Hem bought her for Christmas. The monkey's smiling red mouth covered Jane's forehead and its googly eyes jiggled when she walked. The hat had small, floppy ears and a pair of brown, red, and white braids that framed Jane's face.

Jane put the hat on and climbed into the ATV's front seat. The sky was overcast and last night's wind had grown more persistent. Shivering, she reached for the thermos and turned to watch the boys clamber onto the Gator's bed. There were no seats in the cargo area, but the twins didn't mind. They stood up, clinging to the rail with one hand while beating their chests with the other. They alternated between bellowing like Tarzan or King Kong as Sterling drove over the uneven pathway leading to the archery range.

"I dare you to hold on with two fingers!"

"I dare you to only use your pinkie!"

"I dare you to stick a leg out like this!"

"I dare you to stick your butt out like *this*!"

Thrusting the basket of biscuits behind her, Jane said, "Eat up, boys."

At the sight of food, the dares were forgotten.

Sterling's mouth curved into a smile. "Motherhood provides a type of mental toughness that many a soldier fails to achieve."

Chewing a light, buttery biscuit, Jane returned the smile and then concentrated on the beauty of the autumnal woods. After a long stretch of silence, she whispered, "How's our monk?"

"Still sleeping. I'm afraid the dose was meant for a much heavier man. This fellow is rock-star thin." Sterling frowned. "Gavin used to prepare the syringes, but since he's been going over the mountain so often for physical therapy, the rest of us have had to perform his duties to the best of our abilities."

Jane was slightly disappointed to hear that the Fins hadn't made any useful discoveries since last night, but then again, neither had she. She'd read over half of *Lost Letters* without finding a single reference to Storyton Hall. Sterling stopped at the archery range and told the boys where to set up their targets. They raced toward the shed, bickering noisily over who'd get to open the padlock.

"Fitz and Hem have had lessons, so they're going to be much better than me," Jane said. "I haven't shot an arrow since I was a girl."

The boys returned carrying three bows and three quivers stuffed with arrows. They dumped these on the ground and darted away again.

Sterling handed Jane a black leather arm guard. "Not much of a fashion statement, but it'll protect your skin from the snap of the bowstring. Saves you from getting a huge bruise too." He fastened the Velcro straps around her forearm. "That's one less injury to worry about."

He'd barely spoken before Hem and Fitz started ramming into each other, using their archery targets as shields. Sterling's face darkened. He told the boys to set down their targets and then gave them a brief but stern speech about how to behave on the range.

"Do you want to be mice or men?" he asked them.

"Men, sir," the boys replied in perfect unison.

Sterling seemed satisfied. "Then respect yourself, your instructor, and your weapon."

Lecture concluded, Sterling demonstrated the proper stance and then showed Jane and the twins precisely where to place their hands and fingers when nocking an arrow.

"Your index feather—the one that has a different color than the rest—should face outward," he instructed.

Jane rotated her arrow so that her yellow feather pointed away from her cheek. The rest of the feathers were red. Fitz had chosen arrows with blue and white fletching, and Hem had gone for green and black. Like everything else at Storyton Hall, the arrows were a hodgepodge. There were quivers of new fiberglass arrows, old arrows with wooden shafts and tattered feathers, and sleek carbon arrows designed specifically for hunting. These were reserved for skilled archers, and Sterling was quick to mention that it would take months of training before he'd allow his three pupils to shoot using the elite arrows.

"For now, focus on your posture," he said, pushing Jane's shoulders back and barking at Hem to raise his elbow. "You are a straight, unbroken line. You. The bow. The nocked arrow. The line of sight to the center of the bull's-eye." Sterling moved around, making small adjustments. "Your pinkie doesn't make contact with the string. It just hangs out in space," he told Fitz. "Now. Everyone take a deep breath. Good. Let it out your nose. Relax. Release your arrow."

Jane heard a *thwack, thwack, thwack* as the arrows struck the straw targets.

"Hem got blue. That's five points. Fitz, you're in the black with three. Miss Jane, you got the outer circle of red. That's worth seven." Sterling seemed pleased. "For the next ten shots, we'll focus on your stance and aim. If you're able to hit all ten shots in the yellow and red zones, then I'll move your target back another five yards."

Jane and her sons concentrated on making improvements while Sterling walked behind them, pointing out errors and praising good shots. Jane was glad of her arm guard. Even with it on, she could feel the stinging snap of the bowstring against her skin.

After thirty minutes of straight shooting, her arms and shoulders were aching with fatigue. Luckily, Sterling announced their final round. "I'm moving the targets to fifty yards. I want to see how you adjust your aim at this distance. Believe me, it will require adjusting."

The twins, who weren't the slightest bit tired, each immediately nocked an arrow and took aim. They both missed the target altogether.

"Come on, Mom. Show us how it's done," Fitz said.

"Yeah. Pretend you're Maid Marian. She could hit that target," Hem added.

Jane nodded. "That's right. In the earliest versions of the Robin Hood legend, she was a crack archer."

The boys looked impressed, but couldn't help giggling when Jane's arrow sailed over the target to land somewhere in the grass beyond.

"At least we know you're capable of reaching that distance," Sterling said. He'd yet to say, "All clear," so none of them attempted to collect their arrows.

"Can we try again?" Fitz asked and Jane had to stifle a groan.

Instead of responding, Sterling reached into his quiver, nocked an arrow, and hit Jane's target in the bull's-eye. He'd taken them all by surprise with his quickness. The boys gasped and Jane applauded. "Speed. Accuracy. Distance," Sterling said. "We'll focus on those three skills during our next lesson."

"Before we go, can you show us how far you can shoot?"

Hem asked. "Can you hit that tree near the path? The one with the big knot?" He pointed at an old oak tree.

Jane expected Sterling to say that such a shot was impossible, but he fixed his gaze on the tree. In a seemingly effortless movement, he notched an arrow, pulled back the bowstring, and released a missile with blue fletching into the morning air.

As she followed the arrow's flight, Jane noticed a large, dark shape appear at the end of the path, right beside the oak tree target. She'd just processed the fact that the shape belonged to a horse when the arrow struck the tree.

The horse squealed in shock, reared, and then started galloping straight for them. Sterling notched another arrow.

"Boys. Get behind me," he commanded.

The twins were too riveted to move, so Jane stepped in front of them. She recognized the magnificent gray stallion flying across the field. "That's one of Sam's."

Sterling didn't lower his weapon. "I can't see the rider's face under that baseball cap."

As the rider struggled to gain control of his mount, Jane was transported back to that terrible day in Storyton Village when she'd watched in horror as a bay mare bolted down Main Street. She recalled the second rider. The man who'd tried to save Alice Hart. "It's Edwin," she told Sterling. "Edwin Alcott."

"Are you sure?"

"He's the only person who can handle that horse."

As if he'd heard Jane, Edwin forced the dapple gray to slow his gait. His full-out gallop eased to a relaxed canter. With the reins in his left hand, Edwin abruptly pitched himself to the right, leaning way over in the saddle so that his arm nearly brushed the ground. Scooping up Jane's arrow, he righted himself and trotted toward the archers.

"I think you can lower your bow," Jane said.

Sterling was staring at Edwin with the same look of distrust Jane had seen on Butterworth's face, but he let his weapon drop to his side. However, he kept the arrow notched, holding it in place with his index finger.

When Edwin was within speaking distance, he pulled back on the reins, reducing the stallion's pace to a brisk walk. He patted the gray on the neck and then removed his baseball cap. His hair was a mass of dark waves, and he looked as if he hadn't slept well.

"Are you a bandit?" Fitz demanded. Somehow, he was standing in front of Jane instead of behind her.

"Yeah. Are you?" Hem joined his brother, and together, the twins stood shoulder to shoulder and treated Edwin to their most threatening glares.

"I am not," Edwin said. "Which is a relief, seeing as the two of you are armed." His eyes met Jane's. "Hotel security training begins at an early age around here."

"We're just getting a little fresh air and exercise," Jane said.

Hem elbowed his brother and whispered, "How do we know he's not a bandit? Bandits are liars. Robbers too."

"I can assure you, young sir, that I'm no thief. In fact, I've come to return two arrows belonging to Storyton Hall."

After double-checking to make sure that Sterling's arrow was still stuck in the oak tree, Jane frowned in confusion. "Two?"

Edwin dismounted with his catlike grace and handed Jane the arrow with the yellow and red feathers. It was the last arrow she'd loosed, the one that had flown well past the target and landed in the grass. He then pulled a second arrow from inside his coat. It had a wooden shaft and striped fletching. Its PROPERTY OF STORYTON HALL stamp on the shaft was partially obscured by circles of black paint.

"It looks like a snake!" Fitz shouted.

Behind Edwin, the stallion snorted nervously.

"Try to speak softly," Edwin warned. "The smack of the arrow hitting the tree really scared him. He needs to calm down."

Fitz nodded obediently while Jane eyed the large gray warily.

"What's his name?" Hem whispered.

"My friend, Sam, named him Dorian Gray to impress a certain girl." He shot a knowing look at Jane, and she realized that he was referring to Eloise. "But I think that's a lousy name for a stallion, so I call him Samson because he's strong and willful."

Sterling took the arrow from Jane and examined it closely. "Boys, put away your equipment, please." Once the twins were out of earshot, he said, "Someone painted the shaft with these black stripes. Perhaps it *was* meant to resemble a snake. Then again, any bold pattern could startle a horse just as my arrow startled Samson." He peered at Edwin from under the brim of his cap. "Where did you find this arrow?"

"On the riding trail leading from Hilltop Stables to Broken Arm Bend. It was covered by leaves."

Jane felt cold dread creep up her spine. "Where on the trail?"

A shadow passed over Edwin's features. "Right where the path curves near the bridge. There's a break in the trees adjacent to the road."

"Exactly where a spooked horse would turn if an arrow struck a tree on the other side of the path," Jane murmured to herself. "Even the most skilled rider could be in danger of being hit by a car or thrown or, in Alice Hart's case, end up tearing down the middle of Main Street."

Sterling slid the arrow into his quiver. "And how did *you* happen to discover this arrow? It was my understanding that Sam and several deputies from the sheriff's department had combed that area for clues as to what could have startled Miss Hart's mount."

Edwin shrugged, seemingly unfazed by Sterling's brusque tone. "They used sticks and rakes. I had a metal detector."

Jane was impressed. "Clever."

"Yes, we're lucky to have such a concerned citizen," Sterling said. "Especially one who hasn't spent much time in these parts."

Now Edwin bristled. "I grew up here. And I feel partially responsible for what happened. If I'd seen the young lady's horse bolt sooner. If I'd ridden faster . . . but I sat in my saddle for a few seconds, trying to understand what I was seeing. I hesitated instead of acting."

Of all the people investigating the mystery of Alice Hart's death, Edwin was the only person who expressed guilt and remorse. He hadn't known her, but Jane could see that his failure to save her weighed heavily on him. He hadn't been able to put it behind him, and Jane suspected that it wasn't Alice's youth and beauty that haunted him, but the possibility that her heart might not have given out on her had Edwin been able to stop her horse and calm her down in time.

Jane laid a hand on Edwin's arm. "Miss Hart was never meant to reach old age. If her heart hadn't given out that day in the village, it would have when she was dancing or during a run. It was going to happen sooner or later. I didn't know her, of course, but she seemed like a woman who lived the time she was given to the fullest."

Edwin nodded. After a long pause, he said, "I should have gone straight to the sheriff, but I thought you should know where the arrow came from. After all, you were there. I watched you in the doc's office. I know what happened to her matters to you too."

"It does," she said softly. "Thank you. I'll call Sheriff Evans. I need to speak with him about another matter anyway," she said, feeling like a heel for acting so enigmatic when Edwin had been so open.

At that moment, the twins returned and asked Edwin if they could give Samson the apple left over from their breakfast. Edwin agreed, so the boys cut the apple into slices with their Swiss Army knives and then took turns showing him the different gadgets attached to each knife.

Seeing that the three of them were occupied, Jane turned to Sterling. "It's a good thing we have all of our employees' fingerprints on file. Maybe the sheriff can get something off the arrow shaft."

"I'll have a go at it first." Sterling motioned for her to walk with him to the Gator. He put the quiver on the passenger seat. "There's a small forensics lab in my apartment, and I have access to several law enforcement databases." He jerked a thumb in Edwin's direction. "I'd like to get to work on this immediately."

"A forensics lab in the garage? Of course. Why didn't I realize that?" Jane sighed. "So I won't call Sheriff Evans just yet. However, I *am* going to review my uncle's employee list with Sinclair. If your fingerprint analysis doesn't get us what we need, I want to have my own suspects lined up to interview."

Sterling glanced at his watch. "Speaking of interviews, our monk should be waking up now. It's suddenly become a very busy morning."

"Come on, boys! We need to go!" Jane shouted and hurried to put her bow and quiver in the archery shed.

"Awwww!" the twins protested in unison.

Hem said good-bye to Edwin and jumped in the Gator, but Fitz, who was stroking Samson's neck, didn't budge. There was a stubborn set to his jaw that always reminded Jane of her late husband.

"Fitzgerald Elliot. We are leaving. *Now.*" Jane put her hands on her hips and fixed her son with an impatient stare.

"Why can't we stay? It's Sunday! You don't have to work on Sundays."

Normally, that was true, and Jane wished she could spend the day reading, playing with the boys, and catching up on household chores. "Today is different, Fitz. There's something really important I have to do."

"Like superhero important?" Fitz asked, and Jane frowned. She didn't care for her son's sarcastic tone.

Gently, Edwin stepped between Fitz and Samson. He put a hand on Fitz's shoulder. "Isn't that why you're out here practicing when most people are just sitting down to breakfast? So all three of you can be top-notch crime fighters?"

Fitz's eyes grew round in wonder, and Jane sucked in a quick breath. Did Edwin know about the Steward legacy? But no, that was absurd. And when he winked at her, she relaxed. He was just coaxing her obstinate son to do as she asked.

Edwin mounted Samson with ease, dipped his chin in farewell, and trotted toward the woods.

"Lead on, Maid Marian," Fitz said cheerfully as he hopped in the Gator. "Let's find some villains."

"Yes," Jane agreed. "Let's."

TWELVE

Normally, Jane wouldn't walk around Storyton Hall looking like she'd just returned from a long and vigorous hike, but she didn't waste time thinking about her appearance. Instead, she sent the twins to Mrs. Hubbard for cups of hot cider and then followed Sterling into his office.

"Has he said anything?" Jane asked once they were alone. "The monk?"

Sterling handed over his cell phone and Jane read the two words on the screen. "'Kevin Collins.' That's his name?"

"Yes." Sterling turned to his computer. A few seconds later, he said, "Alice Hart's ex-fiancé. He's supposed to be in England on sabbatical."

"I remember Sheriff Evans saying that he tried to reach this man but was unable to. Once I knew that Evans had made contact with Alice's parents, I forgot about her former fiancé. I didn't think he mattered because he was no longer involved with Alice, and he was thousands of miles from Storyton when she died." She paused. "Or was he?"

Sterling grunted absently, too focused on the information

on his computer screen to give Jane his full attention. "The government tracks people using the radio frequency identification transponder in their passports. I'm accessing a database that— Ah, here we are. Looks like Mr. Collins entered the U.K. on August fifteenth and returned to the States . . ." He trailed off, searching for the exact date.

"Before or after someone shot an arrow at Alice Hart?"

"Three days before," Sterling said.

The phone in Jane's hand vibrated and she quickly read the text. "They want us to come down. Both of us."

Sterling frowned. "I don't think you should—"

"I am the guardian of Storyton Hall," Jane said, rising to her feet. "If that means I have to be present while Sinclair and Butterworth interrogate a young man, then so be it. I'm ready to do whatever it takes to protect our secret."

Jane managed to maintain an air of bravado until they entered the corridor behind the bowling pits. At that point she hesitated, wondering if she really had the backbone to carry on her family's legacy.

A bowling ball crashed into the pins and Jane jumped. She heard guests laughing and cheering at the other end of the lane and realized that her task was much bigger than protecting a hidden library. Storyton Hall's reputation was at stake as well. For decades, people had come to the resort seeking respite from the outside world. Now, one guest was dead and another had assaulted a housekeeper. And if it wasn't Jane's responsibility to protect the people who came to Storyton in search of a peaceful haven, then whose was it?

Sinclair led her into the maintenance closet and then showed her how to operate a pulley that caused the workbench to swing away from the wall. Jane stepped into the dark passage and then into a cold, damp room occupied by Butterworth, Sinclair, and Kevin Collins.

"Do you know why you're here?" Jane asked Kevin without waiting for direction from the Fins.

Kevin Collins twisted in his chair in time to see Sterling

close and lock the door. He turned to face Jane, his eyes wide and frightened. "Please," he said. "I know I was out of line with the maid, and I'm really sorry. But why am I here? What is this place?"

"We had two choices," Jane said calmly. "We could call the sheriff's department and have them take you away in cuffs, or we could handle this ourselves. You have a chance to leave without our filing an assault charge, but only if you're completely honest with us."

Jane handed Kevin a bottle of water. She was relieved to see that he wasn't wearing restraints. He drank thirstily and continued to stare at her with a mixture of confusion and fear. "Where am I?"

"That's not important right now. What's important is that you tell us why you attacked Lizzie and why you wanted to gain access to Moira McKee's room."

"I did both for the same reason," Kevin said quickly. "Because I want to know what happened to Alice. My fiancée. At least she *was* my fiancée until a few days before she came here."

Jane folded her arms over her chest. "We know who Alice is, and I'm sorry for your loss, Mr. Collins. However, I don't see how getting inside Ms. McKee's room has any connection to Miss Hart's unfortunate heart condition."

"I'm not trying to find out how Alice died. I want to know what she was doing here, and I thought that if I could look around Moira's room, I'd discover a clue. I tried talking to her in the elevator, but she said that she didn't know anything and told me she had no idea what motivated Alice to come to Storyton Hall. She was lying though. Moira was the only person Alice talked to besides me. And the fact that Moira is here now, just a few weeks after Alice's death, can't be a coincidence."

Jane studied Kevin. There were dark circles under his eyes, and his nails had been chewed down to the skin. His hands trembled slightly, and he looked pale and gaunt. Jane knew she was thinking like a mother, but she couldn't help it. The young man didn't look well, and she felt a pang of sympathy for him.

"Mr. Butterworth, could you arrange for a breakfast tray to be brought in? I could use some caffeine. Mr. Collins? Do you drink coffee?"

He nodded gratefully, and after Butterworth and Sinclair exchanged nearly imperceptible frowns, the butler left the room.

"Mr. Sterling? You have important business waiting in the garage, right?" When Sterling didn't move, she added, "I believe Mr. Collins has a story to tell, and it might be easier if there aren't too many people hovering over him during the telling. If he can just focus on me, it can be a conversation." She waved vaguely over her shoulder. "Mr. Sinclair will stay, of course." She smiled at Kevin. "He's a librarian and, therefore, an expert on stories."

Sinclair gave Sterling a brief nod and the chauffeur left. When he was gone, Jane saw Kevin relax a little. He took another sip of water and straightened in his chair. "Where should I start?"

"Tell me about how you and Alice ended up together."

Kevin examined his hands. "We met in college. It was a total 'opposites attract' kind of thing. She was into books, art, and music, and I was, and still am, a lab rat. I had this huge biochem exam coming up and I was pretty much living in the library. So was Alice. She was doing research on Adela Dundee for her senior paper. Eventually, we started talking. Before long, we were spending all our free time together."

"And you fell in love," Jane said.

"Yeah. We were committed to each other ever since that day in the library. I should have asked her to marry me ages ago, but I wanted to give her the best. A big wedding. A nice house. A new car. That was a mistake. If we'd been married sooner, maybe none of this would have happened." He shook his head. "But I'm getting ahead of myself. As I was saying, things were great until she decided to write a book on Adela Dundee."

Jane raised her brows. "*Lost Letters*?"

Kevin nodded. "Right from the beginning, I knew Alice was obsessed with Adela Dundee. She told me that the Dundee books were a way for her to mentally escape her life in Nebraska. Her folks are farmers, and Alice said she always felt like a changeling. Like she'd been stolen away from a smart, bookish couple and put in a house where the only reading material had to do with fertilizer or sewing patterns."

"She felt more at home with Adela Dundee's characters," Jane guessed.

"That's exactly what Alice said!" Kevin exclaimed. "At first, she wanted to write a book to honor Dundee, but then she became fixated on discovering something new about her. After Alice found those letters in Cornwall, she turned distant and secretive. She used to tell me everything about her research. Every detail." He looked pained. "All of sudden, she shut me out. I didn't even know about the letters until the book was published. By that time, any semblance of the Alice I'd fallen in love with was gone. She blew off her teaching responsibilities and canceled our engagement party. She didn't even visit her dad when he was undergoing chemotherapy."

There was a knock at the door, and Butterworth entered carrying a large rosewood tray. "Your breakfast, sir," he said, placing the tray on Kevin's lap. Jane nearly smiled over the absurdity of the scene. She doubted anyone had been served eggs, sausage, strawberries, croissants, and an assortment of jams in this horrid little room before.

"Thank you." Kevin took a bite of sausage and sighed. "I can't remember the last time I ate a meal. Over the last few weeks, I've become as obsessed as Alice was. I left my sabbatical at Oxford, I barely sleep, and I replay things over and over in my head until I feel like I'm going crazy."

Jane saw that a linen napkin was almost hidden under

Kevin's plate, so she pulled it out and handed it to him. "What were you trying to figure out?"

"Why Alice came to Storyton Hall," Kevin said through a mouthful of food. "She must have met someone. A guy who shared her mania for Adela Dundee. That must be why she left her job. Why she dumped me. I think she traveled here to meet him. So I followed her." The eggs seemed to stick in his throat, and he gulped down some coffee. His hand went to his lips, and Jane could practically feel the hot liquid burning his mouth. "I was hoping to stop her," he gasped. "To make her see that what we had was real."

Sinclair cleared his throat and Jane fell immediately silent. "You thought your fiancée was having an affair?" he asked. When Kevin nodded, Sinclair straightened his bow tie and looked pensive. "What makes you believe she came to Storyton for a tryst?"

"Because she broke up with me by leaving me a voice mail! That coldhearted bit—" He stopped himself. "There was an ocean between us, and she refused to call me back to explain. Not knowing why she ended it? That was killing me." He picked up the butter knife and ran the pad of his thumb along the dull blade. "I'm not proud of this, but I had a key to her apartment, so a few days before she died, I left England, flew back to Vermont, and let myself in. I found train tickets and a fake driver's license." He pushed the knife into the soft dough of the croissant. "I had to know. Nothing else mattered. Even though she'd changed, Alice was still my everything. So I followed her."

Sinclair's gaze was fixed on the butter knife. In a slow, casual movement, he took an awl from the workbench and twirled it idly in his hands. "Then you were in Storyton when Miss Hart's accident occurred."

"I stayed at a cheap motel in the next town over and rented a bike in the village so I could come to the resort every day. At first, I couldn't find Alice, but that's because she was wearing a brown wig and reading glasses."

"Costumes are the norm for this week's event, but why would Alice wear a disguise in September?" Jane murmured.

"Why would she use a fake ID?" Kevin asked by way of reply. "None of it made sense. I saw her stop by the front desk the morning she went on that ride. She was given a note. When she opened it, she looked like she'd been slapped. She quickly tossed it in the nearest bin, and after waiting for her to leave, I took it out and read it."

Jane was on tenterhooks. "What did it say?"

"I'll show you." Shifting carefully in his chair so as not to upset the food tray, Kevin reached into his back pocket. He then passed Jane a square of paper.

"This was written on one of our memo pads. We put them in every guest room." Jane showed Sinclair the telltale image of Storyton Hall's clock tower and then read the missive aloud. " 'I know what you're after and I know how to get it. I don't want anything except to hear how Ferrari's story ends. Adela's work means so much to me. I believe you understand. If I'm right, take the two o'clock trail ride at Hilltop Stables today. Nothing matters to the heart so much as the truth. Therefore, our hearts are linked.' "

"Clever," Sinclair said. "To end by paraphrasing two of Adela Dundee's most famous lines."

Jane examined the note. "The writer wanted Alice to view them as a kindred spirit. Not a Dundee fan, but a devotee. Someone more interested in Umberto Ferrari's last case than in acquiring fame or fortune."

"He said that their hearts were linked. That's a love note," Kevin said, a flash of rage in his eyes.

"I don't think Alice was interested in this person romantically. She was on an Adela Dundee quest of her own." Jane spoke very gently. "Did you follow her to the stables?"

Kevin's anger vanished. "Yes, but by the time I rode my bike there, her group of riders had already left. Instead of waiting for the next group, I just hung out by the bike racks near the stables. I never saw the man she'd gone to meet. And I never saw Alice again." He pressed his napkin over his face and released a gut-wrenching sob into the white cloth.

Jane found herself reaching out to comfort the anguished young man, but Sinclair caught her hand and mouthed a "No."

They waited until Kevin had regained control of his emotions.

Sinclair produced a flask from the inside pocket of his suit coat and unscrewed the top. Without a word, he poured a splash into Kevin's coffee cup.

The gesture seemed to reignite Kevin's ire. "First, you drag me to this creepy room. Then, you feed me breakfast and act like you care. Who are you people?"

"Forgive me. Where are my manners?" After formally introducing Sinclair and herself, Jane said, "We have a duty to protect both the guests and the employees of Storyton Hall. Your behavior marked you as a violent individual. You created this scenario when you assaulted Lizzie. You could be in a holding cell at the sheriff's station right now, and I can guarantee that you wouldn't have had such a nice breakfast."

"I'm sorry." Kevin held out both hands in a show of surrender. "I just haven't been myself since I lost Alice."

Jane proffered the note he'd given her. "Why didn't you show this to the authorities after Alice's death?"

Kevin looked surprised. "Because I'd been stalking her. Because I didn't want the head of my department to know that I skipped out on my sabbatical. Because I lied to my colleague at Oxford. I actually told the guy that I had to fly back to the States to attend a funeral. How ironic is that?" His voice cracked. "After Alice died, I called Oxford to say that I needed more time. Do you know what I've done since then? I've gone through every inch of Alice's apartment, read through her e-mails, computer files, and opened all of her mail. I've probably broken ten laws by now and I still don't know what happened to her."

Though Jane believed him, she couldn't let compassion cloud her judgment. Instead of speaking, she poured more coffee into his cup and warmed her own. As Kevin sipped his coffee, the whiskey Sinclair had added to his cup seemed to bring him a measure of calm. Sinclair asked if he knew Desmond Price or Felix Hampden, and Kevin insisted that he didn't. However, he'd met Moira McKee many times and suspected that she knew the identity of the note writer.

"Maybe Moira wrote the note," Jane suggested.

Kevin shook his head. "No way was she in Storyton that weekend. She was hosting a fund-raiser when Alice died. There are pictures of her with a bunch of alumni on Facebook."

At least we can eliminate Moira McKee as the archer, Jane thought.

At that moment, Jane heard a buzzing noise and Sinclair glanced at his cell phone screen. "Your aunt has returned," he said to Jane. "You should go. I believe we're finished here. I'll be sure to caution Mr. Collins not to leave the resort until the Murder and Mayhem Week reaches its conclusion and to be available for further questions if necessary."

Nodding, Jane tried to keep her hand steady as she set down her cup. The thought of having to tell her aunt about Felix's death and her failure to recover Storyton's copy of *Lost Letters* filled her with dread. She found herself hesitating for another reason as well. She wanted to ease Kevin's anguish before she left, but there wasn't much she could say without revealing what she and the Fins knew. "I can't get into specifics, but I believe Alice came to Storyton because of Adela Dundee. She then died from a rare heart abnormality. You couldn't have changed her fate. I know it's hard," she said. "But try to look ahead. When the week is over, go back to Oxford. Throw yourself into your work. Let time dull the pain."

"Do you know what this feels like? How much it hurts?" Kevin balled his hands into fists.

"Yes," Jane said very softly. "I do."

Kevin gave her a pleading look. "Will it ever go away?"

"No." She saw no reason to lie to him. "But it'll fade. Eventually, you'll laugh again. You'll feel joy again."

"It'd be easier to let go if I knew exactly what had happened."

"I know," Jane said. "But we don't always get to choose. Now, Sinclair will take you to Lizzie so you can apologize. As for Ms. McKee and the rest of our guests, keep your distance. I'd hate to see you back in this room."

Kevin swallowed hard. "Yes, ma'am."

Jane hurried back upstairs and wound her way through the knot of people heading outside to watch the pickleball tournament. She reached the front doors just in time to see Butterworth perform a low bow and to hear Aunt Octavia bellow, "I'm famished!"

Butterworth said something in a low voice, causing Aunt Octavia to slap the arms of her wheelchair. "This contraption? I won't be its prisoner for long. Mark my words, Butterworth."

Uncle Aloysius, who'd entered the lobby ahead of his wife, caught sight of Jane and waved. She rushed over to give him a hug. "How is she?" Jane whispered into her uncle's ear.

"Worried," he whispered back.

There was no sense delaying the inevitable, so she drew alongside Aunt Octavia's wheelchair, wrapped her arms around her aunt's shoulders, and kissed her warm cheek. "I'm so glad you're home. Let's get you to your rooms so we can talk."

"Only if you promise to order me some food! Pigs would turn away that hospital fare. Repulsive gelatins, oily soups,

and bread rolls that would make excellent catapult missiles."
She glanced around the lobby. "Speaking of catapults, where
are my two young knights?"

As if summoned from thin air, Fitz and Hem appeared
on the first-floor landing. Fitz was just about to slide down
the polished banister—an act that would cause him to lose
dessert for an entire week—when he spotted his family.

"Aunt Octavia!" Hem shouted, and the twins barreled
down the stairs and into their great-great-aunt's arms.

"My darlings!" she cried, kissing their faces.

The boys withstood the display of affection for several
seconds before squirming free. "Cool wheelchair!" Fitz said,
his eyes shining. "Can I try it?"

"Certainly. In fact, you can push me into the elevator and
I'll tell you all about the ogre assigned to handle my
rehabilitation."

"What's that?" Hem asked.

Aunt Octavia harrumphed. "It's when people refuse to
let you eat sweets and force you to do all sorts of uncomfortable things with your body."

Hem frowned. "We won't let the ogre touch you. Fitz and
I will shoot him with arrows."

"Yeah, we'll make him look like a hedgehog!" Fitz cried
in solidarity.

Aunt Octavia beamed. "Excellent. Come along, Jane. We
have much to discuss and I'm longing to see Muffet Cat."
She grabbed Butterworth's arm. "Please send word to the
kitchens immediately. I'm faint with hunger."

"Yes, ma'am." Butterworth gave Jane a conspiratorial
wink over Aunt Octavia's head.

Jane took the stairs in an attempt to reach her aunt and
uncle's apartments ahead of them. She was able to unlock
the door and push a few pieces of furniture aside to make
room for her aunt's wheelchair before she heard her twins'
chatter in the hallway.

"Dorothy was so right. There is no place like home."

Aunt Octavia told Hem to push her into the library and then told the twins where to find the model train set she'd been saving for their birthday.

"Awesome!" they shouted in delight and pulled the unwrapped gift out of the coat closet.

"You can assemble it in the office while we talk," Aunt Octavia said. The moment the boys were out of earshot, she looked at Jane. "Tell me everything."

Taking a seat, Jane said, "It all begins with Alice Hart."

She had just finished describing Felix Hampden's death when there was a knock at the door.

Aunt Octavia sighed. "Thank heaven! My food."

It was Mrs. Hubbard herself who wheeled the room service cart into the library, with Muffet Cat trotting along on her heels. The portly tuxedo made a beeline for Aunt Octavia and jumped onto her lap. The cat rubbed his chin against Aunt Octavia's cheeks and received a dozen kisses, coos, and scratches in return. Mrs. Hubbard waited for Muffet Cat to lie down before taking hold of Aunt Octavia's hand and giving it a fond squeeze. She then gestured to the silver dome on the cart.

"You're not going to be pleased, Ms. Octavia, but Doc Lydgate and I are in complete agreement as to what you can and cannot eat. Your dietary needs are my responsibility now. Any employee caught sneaking you contraband sweets will answer to me." She smiled warmly. "This is for your own good. And for mine. I want you to live to be a hundred."

Aunt Octavia scowled. "Whatever for? If I can't enjoy myself, why not die tomorrow?"

Mrs. Hubbard clicked her tongue. "There, there. It isn't all that bad. Look." She whipped off the dome with a flourish. "I've made a tasty tuna sandwich mixed with apples, walnuts, onions, celery, and a little pickle relish. To wash it down, you have a refreshing glass of sun tea sweetened with a few drops of agave nectar. And for dessert? Fresh peaches with honey vanilla yogurt."

Jane was impressed. "That's healthy?"

"Straight out of a diabetic cookbook." Mrs. Hubbard puffed up with pride. "I won't have it be said that I can't cook delicious, well-balanced meals. If she sticks to the plan, your aunt will drop two dress sizes and will be racing around the resort by Christmastime."

"Anything to escape the clutches of the PT ogre," Aunt Octavia mumbled disagreeably. She took a bite of her tuna sandwich and chewed. Slowly, a glimmer of pleasure appeared in her eyes.

Mrs. Hubbard was watching her closely. "See? You won't suffer a bit."

Uncle Aloysius thanked the head cook profusely and ushered her to the door. When he opened it, he found Sinclair and Sterling waiting in the hallway.

"Come in, gentlemen."

The librarian and chauffeur inquired after Aunt Octavia's health, but Uncle Aloysius waved off their questions. "No time for pleasantries. Sinclair, we need the board."

Sinclair nodded. He and Sterling removed a large landscape painting from the wall and turned it over. The reverse was covered by a piece of slate. Sterling took a tea caddy off the bookshelf and removed a piece of chalk from within.

"Jane's given us the background on Alice Hart and Felix Hampden," Uncle Aloysius told the two Fins. "Who else do we need to discuss?"

Sinclair wrote the names "Moira McKee," "Desmond Price," and "Kevin Collins" on the slate. He had Jane share what she knew about Moira and Desmond and then let Sterling summarize the morning's interview with Kevin Collins. While Jane and Sterling talked, Sinclair jotted notes next to the names. He also drew lines and added labels such as "ex-fiancé" or "employer/employee" between individuals to show how they were connected.

"So we have the president of a college, a faculty member of the same college, a Harvard professor, the owner of a small theater troupe, and—" Uncle Aloysius glanced at Sterling. "What does Mr. Collins do?"

"We don't know yet, sir," Sterling said. "But we will as soon as I get back to my lab."

The word "lab" triggered something Jane's in memory. "Kevin studied biology in college, so he might be some kind of scientist."

"What about the arrow?" Aunt Octavia asked, stroking Muffet Cat while he kneaded her poppy-colored sweater with his front paws. "Were you able to capture any prints?"

Sterling grimaced. "There's a fresh set, but those probably belong to Edwin Alcott. I'll check them against the automated fingerprint identification databases, of course, but I wouldn't be surprised if they weren't on file. After all, isn't he a food writer?"

Jane was about to respond when there was a knock on the apartment door. Sinclair moved through the living room and put his eye up to the peephole. He then opened the door to Butterworth.

"Pardon the interruption," Butterworth said, addressing Jane's aunt and uncle. "Could I borrow Miss Jane? She has a visitor."

"Can't it wait? We're not quite done here," Aunt Octavia said. Sensing her displeasure, Muffet Cat gave Butterworth his most scathing, yellow-eyed glare.

"I'm afraid she must go, ma'am." The butler turned to Jane. "The individual waiting in your office is very anxious to speak with you."

Jane didn't like the sound of that. "Who is it?"

Butterworth's jaw twitched, but his voice betrayed no emotion when he answered, "Sheriff Evans."

THIRTEEN

Though Butterworth had installed Sheriff Evans in Jane's office, the lawman had clearly not come to Storyton Hall for a casual chat. He stood in the threshold in the wide-legged stance of a cowboy, one hand clutching a file folder while the other drummed impatiently on the doorframe.

"I'm sorry to keep you waiting," Jane said and invited him inside. "My aunt just got home from the hospital, and things are a bit topsy-turvy now that she's wheelchair-bound."

For a moment, the intensity in the sheriff's face softened. "Your aunt's a fine woman. Please give her my regards and hopes for a speedy recovery."

"Thank you. Would you like something to drink? Coffee? Tea?"

Evans shook his head. He shut the door and asked Jane to make herself comfortable. "Ms. Steward, there's been an update in Felix Hampden's case."

Instead of sitting behind her desk, Jane took the vacant chair next to the sheriff's. "The word 'case' has my attention. Does this mean that Mr. Hampden's death wasn't accidental?"

"Not unless Hampden accidentally poisoned himself."

The sheriff opened the folder and slid on a pair of reading glasses. "The ME hasn't been able to identify the poison, but it's not a run-of-the-mill variety. He was able to explain that it's actually a toxin, and he believes this toxin has a biological origin. In other words, it came from a living organism."

Jane took a moment to process the information. "So we're not talking household cleaners here? Mr. Hampden was given . . ." She searched for an example. "Snake venom, for example?"

"It wasn't snake venom, but that's the idea. Something found in nature. A plant or animal toxin. The ME sent a sample to a colleague for a more complete analysis, and because he went to grad school with the guy, we can expect results in the next twenty-four hours. In the meantime, I'll need to interview your staff."

"Of course." Jane felt a churning in her belly. "Is this now an official murder investigation?"

"I am treating it as a suspicious death at the moment," Evans said. "I'd like to conduct my interviews discreetly. There's no need for your employees to come to the station, but I'd like to speak with anyone who came into contact with Hampden."

Jane laced her fingers together to keep them from trembling. "May I ask how he was poisoned? I remember that broken glass on the floor. Was the toxin in his water?"

"That's the other request I have to make. I need to collect evidence from Hampden's room. I trust you haven't allowed anyone to disturb it?"

"No, it's exactly as it was when you were last here."

The sheriff turned to a blank page of notebook paper. "It's now a crime scene. My deputies are parked near the loading dock because I assume you'd prefer that we use the service elevator."

"That would be best," Jane said and then frowned. "But what should I tell inquisitive guests?"

"I don't want to alarm your guests or tip off any possible suspects, so I've instructed my men to say nothing."

Jane sighed. "That won't help my front desk clerks. People are likely to ask them what's going on, and if I don't give them some information, they'll jump to conclusions. I don't want anyone to check out because they feel unsafe." An idea came to her. "What if I make it sound like it's Hampden who's under investigation? No one knows that he's dead—except for the poisoner and a few staff members— and it'll be less troubling for my guests to hear that he and his belongings have been removed from the premises because of petty theft or something of that nature."

The sheriff considered her suggestion. "In general, I try not to besmirch a man's character, but in doing background checks on Hampden, I discovered that he was quite a swindler. Therefore, it wouldn't be stretching the truth to call him a thief. We'll do it your way, Ms. Steward." He uncapped a pen and held it over the blank notebook paper. "Can you tell me the names of any guests Mr. Hampden interacted with? And it doesn't matter how briefly. If you saw him exchange a few words in the elevator or the buffet line, I'd like to know about it." He pointed his pen at Jane. "You mentioned two people trying to buy a book from Hampden the night he died. Can you identify them?"

Jane wondered how much she dared tell Sheriff Evans. She didn't want to hinder his investigation, but she couldn't let him know why the missing book was so important or that it had come from Storyton Hall's secret library. Still, it was his duty to uphold the law, and because she believed both Moira McKee and Desmond Price were after Felix's prize, she gave the sheriff their names.

Evans wrote notes on his paper and then looked at Jane again. "What do you know about these folks?"

Fibbing a little, Jane said that she'd had a chance encounter with Moira during last night's ball. She explained how surprised she'd been to learn that Moira was the president of the college where Alice Hart taught.

The sheriff's brows rose high on his forehead. "Interesting. Anything else?"

"Ms. McKee wanted Felix's book, but I don't think she has it or knows what happened to him. In fact, she came to the ball to find him. She was going to make him an offer on the book."

Evan grunted encouragingly and made another note. "And Desmond Price?"

Jane shrugged. "Since I haven't spoken with him, I can't be of much help. All I know is that he's a professor at Harvard."

Evans wrote this down. "And what about Hampden's book? Have you recovered it?"

"Unfortunately, no." Jane wanted to steer the conversation away from the missing book, so she leaned forward and said, "But I did find Alice Hart's fiancé. He also attended last night's ball."

That got the sheriff's attention. "He's here?"

"Yes." Jane hated to draw attention to Kevin Collins, but she had no choice. After all, she couldn't be sure if anything he'd told them had been the truth. Her instinct said that he'd been sincere when he claimed that he only came to Storyton Hall to find out why Alice had broken their engagement, but she couldn't risk the safety of her guests based on a gut feeling. And because she'd made a promise to Lizzie, Jane didn't explain how she first met the young man. She simply said, "Mr. Collins didn't return the voice mail you left him in Oxford after Alice passed away because he didn't hear it. He was in Storyton when she died and he hasn't been back to England since."

The sheriff barely moved. "He was here when she died?"

"Mr. Collins believed his fiancée was meeting her lover at the resort. He wanted to learn the man's identity." As Jane thought back on everything Kevin had told her, she suddenly felt chilled. "Oh, my," she whispered, rubbing her arms.

"Ms. Steward?" The sheriff's voice was surprisingly gentle. "Are you all right?"

"Kevin Collins was a bio major in college, and if I remember correctly, his work at Oxford University involved toxins."

The sheriff got to his feet. "I think I'll begin my inquiries with Mr. Collins. What's his room number?"

Jane told him and then gave him the key for the smallest conference room. She also unlocked her topmost desk drawer and handed him the key for room 316, the Mystery Suite. "Please keep me informed," she said.

Evans dipped his head in acknowledgment and strode off, tapping the folder against his gun holster.

"This is turning out to be a long day," Jane murmured and ran her hands through her hair. "There are way too many hours between now and cocktail time."

Thirty minutes later, Jane was at the pickleball courts. Gavin and the rest of the rec staff were in charge of the tournament, and from what Jane could see, things were proceeding splendidly. Despite the chill in the air, the chairs surrounding the tennis courts (which doubled as pickleball courts) were all occupied and the guests were enjoying themselves immensely. Waiters maneuvered in between the seats, serving hot chocolate, coffee, tea, and spiced cider, while the spectators waved tissue paper pom-poms that matched the T-shirt hue of their favorite team.

The teams had been divided into heats, and each had been assigned the name of a famous mystery novel. Now the tournament had come down to the final game: a match between The Maltese Falcons and The Ten Little Indians. The Falcons were in blue, and the Indians were in orange. Fans shouted, "Go Hammett!" or "Hurray for Christie!" as the team members shook hands with their opponents.

Gavin limped to center court and, using a handheld

microphone, reminded the spectators that not only would the winning team be treated to a complimentary fly-fishing excursion and receive gift certificates to Run for Cover and the Canvas Creamery, but it would also earn a remarkably unique trophy donated by the Hogg brothers, owners of the Pickled Pig Market.

When Gavin first showed the audience the trophy, they burst out in unified laughter. Jane caught a glimpse of the shiny object and joined in. The Hogg brothers had the trophy engraved with a net, Wiffle ball, a set of crossed paddles, and a plaque reading, PICKLEBALL CHAMPIONS, STORYTON HALL. But what had everyone in stitches was the trophy's shape. Instead of resembling a cup or an urn, the trophy was shaped like a giant pickle.

"I ran away," Jane told Sterling after the laughter had died down. "I needed a break and I knew they'd be having a grand time over here." She gazed around at the happy guests, wishing she could be as carefree, if only for a little while. "Felix Hampden was poisoned, and Sheriff Evans is collecting evidence from his room. I suppose you know that already."

"Yes. Butterworth sent me a text." Sterling waited until the Falcons had served before leaning closer to Jane. "I had no luck getting fingerprints off the arrow. There's only one set and those belong to Edwin Alcott."

"Are you sure?"

Sterling nodded. "Absolutely. Mr. Alcott's prints are on file."

Jane searched the head chauffeur's face. "Oh? Why?"

"He has a police record," Sterling said flatly.

The crowd roared as the Indians scored a point. Jane clapped her hands absently, but didn't take her eyes off Sterling. "Please don't tell me that he's some kind of book burglar."

Sterling shook his head. "His was an assault and battery arrest, and he was only eighteen at the time."

Relieved that she wouldn't have to add Edwin to her suspect list, Jane allowed herself a small smile. "I'm not surprised. Eloise always said that her brother was hotheaded."

Another cheer exploded around them as the Falcons scored. "We should turn the arrow over to the sheriff now," Sterling said, speaking into Jane's ear. "He'll be interviewing the staff anyway, and he might be able to use the arrow to elicit a reaction from the guilty party."

Jane stared out over the tennis courts to the dense woods and the blue hills beyond. She envisioned someone crouching in wait for the group of riders to make their way down the sloping forest trail. And then she pictured a man notching an arrow and taking aim the moment he spotted Alice Hart on her bay mare.

Jane turned back to Sterling. "Alice didn't wear her fake glasses or wig on that ride. She wanted to meet someone who was as influenced by Adela Dundee as she was. I bet she romanticized the whole thing, hoping to find that the note writer was a handsome young academic. Her ideal partner. A man who could share her obsession in a way Kevin never would."

Sterling grunted. "Little did Alice know that her Romeo only wanted to ambush her—to make sure that she would never get her hands on a certain book."

"I bet both the bow and the arrow came from Storyton Hall." Jane pulled a face. "I need to review that staff list with Uncle Aloysius ASAP." She glanced at the pickleball players once more. "It was nice to wear my resort manager hat for a few moments. I hadn't realized how much I enjoyed my day-to-day work until I was given my new position."

Taking in the merry crowd, Sterling nodded in understanding. "It won't always be like this, Miss Jane. More often than not, I'm a chauffeur. At times, I prefer that role. No car can hold a candle to a vintage Rolls-Royce Silver Shadow and I get to drive it around some of the most beautiful vistas in the world."

"Don't you ever want more than this?" Jane asked as she and Sterling headed back to the main house. "You, Sinclair, Butterworth, Gavin? You never married or had families of your own. Does being a Fin mean always having to be alone?"

"A Fin must be devoted to his task and to his brotherhood above all else. There aren't any rules requiring us to be bachelors, but most Fins step down if they want to start a family. Once Gavin's replacement arrives, I imagine our head of recreation will finally ask Mrs. Pratt to dinner."

Jane's mouth fell open. "Mrs. Pratt?"

Sterling grinned. "Cupid has a sense of humor, eh?"

Jane tried to imagine Gavin and Mrs. Pratt as a couple. "But he's so quiet."

"I only heard him talk about her once," Sterling said. "It was right after his surgery, and I think he was still under the influence of painkillers, but he waxed on about Eugenia's passionate nature and how he wanted to be loved by a woman like her. He then said that he planned to woo her just as soon as his successor takes the reins."

"I look forward to watching their courtship." Thinking of all the romance novels Mrs. Pratt devoured on a weekly basis, Jane smiled. "I just remembered that Gavin wears kilts on formal occasions."

"He's very proud of his Scottish heritage," Sterling said, opening the terrace door for Jane. "But what does that have to do with his courting Mrs. Pratt?"

Jane saw Uncle Aloysius at the other end of the hall and quickened her pace. "Because Eugenia Pratt thinks that a man in a kilt is undeniably sexy."

Sterling grimaced and, muttering something about turning over evidence to Sheriff Evans without delay, veered off for the staff staircase.

By this time, Uncle Aloysius had reached the front entrance and was shaking hands with a man dressed in maroon scrubs.

"Jane!" Her uncle beamed as if he hadn't seen her in days. "Good, good. I'd like you to meet Gordie Lowe. Mr. Lowe is your aunt's new physical therapist."

She took the man's proffered hand, which was as limp and slithery as an eel.

Gordie reclaimed his hand and tapped his watch face. "Okay, people. I'm a busy man. Can we get started?"

Unaccustomed to rudeness, Uncle Aloysius stiffened. He recovered immediately, however, and gestured to the staff elevator and said, "Of course. This way, please."

Jane fell into step next to her uncle. "Can we talk in your office while Aunt Octavia has her session with Mr. Lowe?"

Her uncle nodded. "It'd be better if we were in another country, but my office will have to suffice."

Stifling a grin, Jane pressed the button for the third floor while Gordie glanced around the elevator cab. As soon as the doors slid shut, Gordie began to whistle. He was far from being an adept whistler, and whatever tune he was trying to carry sounded jarringly off-key. Jane glanced at him out of the corner of her eye and saw that he was rocking back and forth on his heels.

Aunt Octavia is going to eat him alive, she thought with a small measure of satisfaction.

Uncle Aloysius unlocked the apartment door and invited Gordie into the living room, where Aunt Octavia was busy reading the newspaper. Muffet Cat was stretched out in the next chair, a felt catnip mouse nestled under one paw. Both Aunt Octavia and Muffet Cat looked at the man in scrubs with wary eyes. "Who the devil are you?" Aunt Octavia demanded.

Gordie put his hands on his hips and surveyed the room with a frown. "I suppose this will have to do." Instead of answering Aunt Octavia's question, he fixed a disapproving gaze on Muffet Cat. "I'm your new physical therapist. I heard that you and Max weren't a good fit."

"That's because Max is an ogre," Aunt Octavia replied, snapping her paper. "I hope you know how to treat a lady."

Gordie produced another fake smile. "I'm sure we'll manage. All you have to do is work hard and maintain a positive attitude. Negative energy will delay your healing."

Aunt Octavia stared at him with unmasked dislike. "You're not one of those yoga mat, New Age, incense-burning, mantra-spouting types, are you?"

Jane could tell that her aunt had struck a nerve. Gordie's jaw tensed, but then his humorless smile instantly returned. "One day, you might be open to trying a healthy activity like yoga. It has all kinds of benefits—even for someone your age."

"I'd rather have hot needles driven into my eyeballs," Aunt Octavia said. "Let's get started. The sooner we begin the torture, the sooner we can finish."

Gordie waved a warning finger. "*Tsk, tsk*. Where's that positive attitude?"

For some reason, Muffet Cat treated the finger wag as a threat. He leapt to his feet, his fur bristling like a Halloween cat's, and hissed.

Jane and Uncle Aloysius exchanged nervous glances. Jane hurried to open the front door and Muffet Cat shot into the hall in a blur of black-and-white fur. With Aunt Octavia's champion headed for the great outdoors, Jane and her uncle escaped to the office, where the twins were still happily occupied with the new train set.

"Look, Mom! I made a tunnel out of a tissue box." Hem pointed at his feat of engineering while attempting to hide the pile of unused tissues under his rump.

"And I'm almost done with my bridge," Fitz said. He had dozens of rubber bands spread out before him. "Can I borrow your rulers, Uncle Aloysius?"

"Certainly. Pedestrians must be able to cross over the railroad tracks in safety."

Hem turned to his brother. "Sweet! After that, we need—"

"People," Fitz said, finishing his twin's sentence. The boys did this all the time, but Jane never failed to marvel over how in synch they were.

While they debated the merits of Candyland figures, which they could poach from the game room in the basement, over LEGO figures, which were in their bedroom at home, Jane and her uncle sat in the Chippendale-style chairs overlooking the side lawn.

"Sheriff Evans is down the hall," Jane said. She wasn't concerned about the twins listening in. They were far too engrossed in their toys to pay attention to boring grown-up talk.

"I know. I've spoken with him." Her uncle took a piece of paper from the pocket of his tweed coat and laid it on the table between them. "These are the names of the staff members who've been to our rooms in the last month."

It was a short list and Jane read it aloud. "Ned, Gavin, Sterling, Butterworth, Sinclair, Mrs. Hubbard, and Mrs. Pimpernel." She sighed. "Hardly a suspicious lot. Four of them are Fins, and Mrs. Hubbard's been discussing menus with Aunt Octavia since time immemorial."

"Don't let *them* hear you say that," Uncle Aloysius cautioned.

"And Ned?" Jane continued. "We've known him since he was knee-high. Why did he come up? Package delivery?"

Her uncle made a noise of assent. "Indeed. Your aunt was a bit of a spendthrift last month. She's been engaged in early Christmas shopping and is always buying something to tuck away for the twins."

"I suppose this train set was among the items Ned delivered." When Uncle Aloysius nodded, Jane shook her head in amusement. "Aunt Octavia spoils those boys."

"She prefers the term 'doting' over 'spoiling.' "

Jane examined the list again. "The only name that seems out of place is Mrs. Pimpernel's. She hasn't cleaned a room since her promotion to head housekeeper last year. Why the sudden desire to care for your apartments herself?"

Uncle Aloysius furrowed his brow. "I'm not sure. Other than my office, I can't say that I pay much attention to the tidiness of our living space. While I can tell the papers on my desk blotter have been moved half an inch to the right or left, I wouldn't notice spots on the bathroom mirror or dust on the bookshelves. Octavia keeps an eye on that sort of thing."

At that moment, they heard a resounding crash from the direction of the sitting room. Jane bolted to her feet and rushed for the door, but the twins were faster. They raced into the next room in front of her and then came to an abrupt halt at the sight of broken glass.

Gordie was cowering behind a floral wing chair. Seeing Jane, he shouted, "She's crazy! She needs a psych eval, not a physical therapist!"

"How dare you?" Aunt Octavia bellowed. "Get out of here this instant. I never want to see that disingenuous smile or be subjected to another second of your patronizing banter for as long as I live."

"With that attitude, it won't be long!" Gordie hollered back and then ducked as a brass candlestick sailed over his head.

"Time out!" Jane waved her hands like a referee. "Aunt Octavia—"

"Tell him to take his bag of tricks and go!" her aunt cried. Jane caught a glimpse of the twins' startled faces and decided it was best to do as Aunt Octavia asked. Handing Gordie his duffle bag, she said, "I'm sorry things didn't work out. My sons will be glad to show you to your car."

The twins clearly didn't want to serve as guides. Jane could tell from the stubborn set of their mouths that they'd prefer to stay and hear what the man in maroon scrubs had done to make Aunt Octavia so angry. "Fitzgerald. Hemingway. *Now*," she said in a no-nonsense tone to which the boys mercifully responded.

Gordie left the apartment, muttering about "old hags" and "hopeless cases" on his way out.

When the door had closed behind him, Uncle Aloysius

moved forward to comfort his wife. Caressing her cheek, he murmured softly, "What happened, my sweet?"

"He treated me like an imbecile." Jane was surprised to see Aunt Octavia's eyes fill with tears. After all, her great-aunt cried only while reading particularly moving book passages. "I told him that I wanted to stand while holding a chair, but he insisted on grabbing me under my arms and hauling me to my feet without an ounce of decorum. And when I was finally upright, I said that I was feeling dizzy. He declared that my recovery would depend on mind over matter. As if I could simply walk again by sheer will and determination."

"We know you have an abundance of both, dear," Jane's uncle said.

"I do, but I feel weak and light-headed and frightened. And while I truly hate to admit to the latter, it's the truth. I don't want to be difficult, Aloysius, but I'm not strong enough to jump up and dance and I won't be forced into moving faster than I'm ready to move by some bumbling idiot." She gave Jane a look of appeal. "Can't someone I know help me? Ned or one of the chauffeurs?"

Jane considered the question for a long moment. "I think you need a professional, Aunt Octavia. But perhaps it would be better for you to meet a few therapists first. You can vet them the same way Butterworth would a new staff member."

Uncle Aloysius smiled. "That's an excellent idea. Now, why don't I order some tea and ask Mrs. Pimpernel if she could stop by with a dustpan? What object served as your projectile?"

Aunt Octavia waved her hand airily. "A plain flower vase. It was the only thing within reach besides that trout carving you're so fond of."

"Very considerate of you, my dear. I know you've never liked my trout. Perhaps I'll remove it to my office." Under his breath he added, "That way it'll be safe before your next PT appointment."

Jane was watching her uncle scurry off, wooden fish tucked under his arm, when the phone rang.

"Can you get that, Jane?" her aunt asked. "I'm simply too flustered."

The caller turned out to be Butterworth. "Sheriff Evans is looking for you," he said. "Shall I send him to your office, or would you like him to join you in your current location?"

"Have him come here, please. We'll have more privacy," Jane said. Her aunt and uncle's rooms were at the end of a long wing and were separated from the main hall by a door marked NO ADMITTANCE. It was unlikely that guests would be in the vicinity, and Jane felt more at ease meeting with the sheriff in the cozy sitting room with her family surrounding her.

She only had time to place an order with the kitchens for a tea service delivery when there was an authoritative rap on the door.

Jane opened it to find a grim-faced Sheriff Evans and a wide-eyed deputy standing in the hall. She invited them in, perturbed by the deputy's jittery behavior and the manner in which Sheriff Evans kept brushing his fingers against his gun holster as if to reassure himself that his side arm was within easy reach.

"Is there an update on the investigation?" Jane asked anxiously while Uncle Aloysius sat down next to his wife.

"Deputy Higgins was in the process of interviewing a Mrs. Pimpernell when she received an urgent call from a house-keeper on the fourth floor. Apparently, a staff member unlocked the door to a guest room and found another, what did you call them, a Van Winkle?"

Jane gasped. "No!"

"I've conducted an initial inspection and two deputies are guarding the room," Evans said. "I thought you'd want to know that we may now be facing two suspicious deaths. According to what you've told me, this Van Winkle has ties to Alice Hart and was also interested in acquiring Mr. Hampden's prize."

Jane pressed her fingertips to her temple where a headache had begun to bloom. Though she already knew the answer, she asked, "What's the room number?"

"Four twenty-six."

"Moira," Jane whispered sadly. "Moira McKee is dead."

Sheriff Evans nodded solemnly. "I'm afraid so. I'd like you to look at the deceased to determine if she resembles Mr. Hampden's body as it was *in situ*."

"*In situ*," Jane said dully, too stunned to react. "I need to see if she looks as if she was poisoned? Is that what you're saying?"

"It is. Can you come now?"

Aunt Octavia grabbed her husband's arm. "Aloysius, should you go with her?"

Jane's uncle shook his head. "My place is here. With you. Jane can handle this. I have complete faith in her."

Hoping to be worthy of her uncle's confidence, Jane squared her shoulders and told the sheriff that she was ready to view her second corpse of the Murder and Mayhem Week.

FOURTEEN

Jane walked to Moira's room as if she were wading through waist-high water. Her limbs felt heavy and unco-operative, and though she managed to greet passing guests with a smile and a friendly hello, her voice sounded alien and distant.

To Jane's relief, Sheriff Evans adopted a casual demeanor. Between his unhurried pace and pleasant grins, the guests would never guess that he was in the middle of a murder investigation. In fact, he and Jane strolled down the carpeted hallway looking like they'd just completed a routine inspec-tion of the carbon monoxide detectors.

When they reached Moira's room, Evans knocked on the door three times. It was opened only wide enough to reveal a sliver of freckled cheek and one suspicious brown eye.

"You can let us in now, Dawson," Evans said.

The face disappeared and Evans pushed the door open. As soon as he and Jane entered the room, and the freckle-faced deputy gestured at the bathroom. "No one's been inside, sir, and the ME's on his way. He'll be here in fifteen."

The medical examiner's office was over the mountain.

Jane wondered if he was surprised to discover that he was being called to examine yet another body from Storyton. Jane couldn't help but worry that a second poisoning victim might lead to an indiscretion. If the ME, whom Jane had never met, had loose lips, then everyone in the region would soon know about the horrors occurring at Storyton Hall.

That is, if *Moira was poisoned,* Jane reminded herself. *You have no idea what happened to her.*

"I must ask you not to touch anything," Sheriff Evans said, breaking into her thoughts. "And do not enter the bathroom. Just look inside, please."

Jane nodded and crossed the floor to the bathroom. She could feel the eyes of the sheriff and the two deputies on her, but a strong smell caught her attention, pulling her forward and making her forget about the other people in the room. The scent had heavy floral overtones—gardenia or magnolia—combined with a subtle hint of rot. It was both sweet and putrefying. Appealing and repellent. And it became more powerful the closer Jane drew to the bathroom. At the threshold, she stopped and peered in at the dead woman.

An involuntary cry escaped from Jane's throat, and she slapped a hand over her mouth, as if the subtle sound was disrespectful. It wasn't Moira's fault she'd been turned into something frightening, and Jane's initial repulsion quickly gave way to pity and remorse.

"Oh, no," she whispered. "You poor thing. I'm sorry. So sorry."

Moira McKee was sprawled on the floor in the small space between the sink and the commode. Jane glanced at the woman's plaid pajamas and wondered if Moira had been getting ready for bed before she fell. Jane steeled herself as her eyes slowly traveled from the dead woman's body to her face.

Moira's head was turned toward the door and her mouth was stretched wide as if she'd died in the middle of a yawn.

There was a smear of bright blood beneath her cheek marring the clean white tiles. Part of Moira's white hair was matted with dark, sticky blood, and there was another blotch on the edge of the commode. Jane guessed that the woman had lost her balance, struck her head on the porcelain, and then hit the floor. Her fingers were curled into tight claws, just as Felix Hampden's had been, but Moira's long nails had left little red half-moons in the skin of her palms.

"You were in pain," Jane murmured, staring at the marks. She looked at the dead woman's face again. The longer she stood utterly still, the more details she noticed. She didn't know how much time had passed when Sheriff Evans appeared at her elbow. "What do you see?" he asked.

"Her neck is arched at an uncomfortable angle. Her whole face seems stretched, with every muscle tensed to the max. Look at the veins in her neck. Look at her fingers. She must have been in incredible agony. The same agony Mr. Hampden experienced."

The sheriff said nothing, and Jane continued with her observations. The only way she could help the dead woman now was to stay sharp and calm. In an attempt to imprint the scene in her mind, she let her gaze roam all around the bathroom. There were other signs of disturbance. The water glass was on its side in the bowl of the sink, and Jane pictured Moira trying to fill the glass and then dropping it as she was battered by a wave of pain.

On the floor to the left of the counter was the source of the floral scent: a broken perfume bottle. Jane could tell from the torn label that the perfume was Flora by Gucci. An ounce of pink liquid still swam in the bottle's base, and Jane spied the words "Gorgeous Gardenia." She imagined Moira knocking the bottle off the counter at the same moment the glass tipped into the sink.

That pair of objects—one shattered and the other out of place and in the wrong position—showed how Moira must have panicked when she began to lose control of her muscles.

And then, she'd fallen. She'd smacked her head against the toilet and then collided with the cold, hard floor.

"Do you think she was still alive?" Jane asked. "After she hit her head?"

"I'm no expert, but I believe so. The ME will tell us more, but it'd be my guess that the blood made that pattern because she was moving. Arching her neck and back, just like you said. It would have been a gentler end had she been unconscious."

Jane's eyes filled with tears. She wasn't used to being near someone who'd died violently, and she felt grief overwhelm her. It grew in her like a cresting wave, and she fought to keep it from breaking.

Abruptly, she retreated from the threshold. She didn't want to look a moment longer at what had become of the woman she'd talked with at the ball. She didn't want the tortured, lifeless figure sprawled on the bathroom floor to replace the image of the woman who spoke with such emotion about the Broadleaf School of the Arts. Though Moira had acted a little overly desperate in trying to ensure a future for the college, her passion and devotion made her crackle with vitality. Jane could see the older woman now, her eyes shining as she talked about Broadleaf.

She's the kind of person who probably wasn't noticed much while she lived. But I bet she'll be deeply missed now that she's gone.

Jane was wondering what would become of the once-esteemed college when she backed right into Sheriff Evans. She turned to face him. "It looks like she died exactly as Mr. Hampden did. Do you think they were both given the same toxin?"

"It appears that way. The ME—" Evans was about to say more when a voice burst from the radio clipped to the front of Deputy Dawson's uniform shirt.

Jane couldn't understand the code-speak, but she recognized the names "Kevin Collins" and "William Faulkner."

"I'm going to interview Mr. Collins now," Evans said to

Jane. "My deputies will bring the ME up on the staff elevator." He waved vaguely toward the bathroom. "It would be best if you left now."

"Of course," Jane said. She had no desire to linger.

Back in the lobby, the sheriff veered toward the conference room wing and Jane headed for the Henry James Library. She found Sinclair filling out borrower's cards for a group of children. Unlike the traditional lined white rectangles with spaces for a title, due date, and date of return, Storyton Hall's borrower's cards were works of art. The cards were created on a hand press and featured beautiful script in the center and ornamental flowers and scrolls in each corner.

The cards were meant to remind borrowers of the value Storyton Hall placed on its library holdings. Guests who failed to return books before leaving the resort were charged a replacement fee (which, because many of the books were out of print, could be quite hefty), but those who followed the lending rules were rewarded. Whenever a guest returned a book, they were given a Storyton Hall bookmark. There were twelve designs in all, and the guests were always eager to acquire a complete set.

At this moment, Sinclair was presenting a young girl with a bookmark depicting an enormous moon rising over the roofline of Storyton Hall. A photograph of a barn owl occupied one corner and a partial quote by Byron ran along the bottom in gilt letters. It read, *The night of cloudless climes and starry skies.*

"This is my fifth one!" the girl whispered in excitement. "I want to finish twelve books while I'm here so I can collect them all."

"That's the idea, my dear," Sinclair said, smiling at the young reader. "And I think you'll be very entertained by the adventures of Ramona Quimby."

Jane tried to be patient as she waited for Sinclair to finish his duties. He spent another minute listening to an exuberant boy explain why he was so fond of the characters in Judy Blume's *Superfudge* before a Beatrix Potter Kids' Club staff member finally gathered her group together and led them out of the library. Jane watched the children leave, drinking in the twinkle in their eyes and the energetic bounce to their step. They were the polar opposite of what she'd just seen in Moira McKee's room.

When the kids were gone, Sinclair pressed a flask into her hand. "You'd better have a nip of this. I imagine what you saw was quite awful. Butterworth told me that Mr. Collins has been installed in the Faulkner Room. We need to listen in on that interview."

Jane waved off the flask. "That won't help. What I need is to find out who's targeting my guests. How can we overhear the conversation between the sheriff and Mr. Collins? Are the conference rooms bugged?"

"No. Ours is a far more antiquated system, but it's served us well for many years. Come. We must hurry."

Reentering the lobby, Sinclair led Jane through a doorway marked STAFF ONLY, and into one of the many cool and dimly lit service corridors. This one led to the west wing, which was where all the conference rooms were located.

Jane had walked the length of the corridor hundreds of times, so she couldn't understand why Sinclair suddenly stopped in front of a metal storage closet and pulled both doors open. Pushing aside several broken brooms and a discolored mop head, he reached inside the closet and rotated his entire arm to the left. Jane heard a click. Sinclair peered down the hallway to make sure they were alone and then gestured at the closet. "After you, Miss Jane. Go quickly and quietly. There will be a small ridge where the closet ends and a passageway begins, so be careful. It'll be dark, but I'll be right behind you."

Jane entered the closet. Feeling like one of the Pevensie children in *The Lion, the Witch and the Wardrobe*, she raised her hand and put one foot in front of the other. After three steps, her toe caught on the lip of metal dividing the closet from another concrete floor. She pressed herself against the bare drywall to her right until she heard Sinclair moving behind her. He shut the secret door and switched on a penlight.

"And from this point, we can't talk," he whispered in Jane's ear. "No coughing, sneezing, gasping, nothing. If you must make a sound, get inside this closet as fast as you can."

Perplexed, Jane followed Sinclair to the end of the narrow passage, where she saw an illuminated pattern on the floor. The rows of overlapping octagons were familiar, and Jane stared at them until she heard a man's voice. And then a second voice. They were coming from behind a rectangle of brass in the wall. With a start, Jane realized that she and Sinclair were standing on the other side of the air return screen attached to the wall of the William Faulkner conference room.

Light snuck through the vent to create the octagon pattern on the dusty ground, and when Jane shuffled closer, she could see the wood floor and the edge of the midnight blue rug inside the Faulkner room. She stopped, fearing that Sheriff Evans would notice the movement if she crept any closer.

"Mr. Collins—" Sheriff Evans was saying.

"That's what people call my dad. I'm just Kevin."

"All right, Kevin," the sheriff said. "Let's review what you've told me so far. You came to Storyton during the Murder and Mayhem Week to find out if Moira McKee knew why your fiancée, a Miss Alice Hart, called off your engagement."

"It wasn't just to talk to Moira. I could have gone to Broadleaf to do that. I was here in September because I was following Alice. Apparently, I wasn't the only one. When I read on Facebook that her boss planned to come to Storyton Hall in October, I knew something weird was going on. I wanted to see for myself who or what had drawn Alice here.

I didn't figure it out before Alice died, but I wasn't going to give up. I *had* to know." Kevin spoke so rapidly that his words ran together. "But I only talked to Moira once in the elevator. She kind of freaked out when she recognized me and refused to answer my questions unless I told her where the book was. The woman's gone nuts. Her train has derailed."

A brief silence. "Did you tell her about the book?"

Kevin laughed humorlessly. "I wish I knew what book she was talking about. In fact, after seeing how crazed Moira acted when she mentioned this mystery book, I'm beginning to think I was wrong about Alice. Maybe she didn't come here to meet a guy. Maybe she came here in search of a book. This place is loaded with them. There must be thousands. My university library doesn't have half as many." He released a derisive grunt. "But why would anyone get this worked up over a book, even one about Adela Dundee? A book is just wood pulp and glue with some text. How important could it really be?"

Feeling a rush of indignation on behalf of bibliophiles everywhere, Jane scowled. Beside her, Sinclair was practically radiating his disgust.

Sheriff Evans ignored the insult. "Are you absolutely sure that the only time you came in contact with Ms. McKee was in the elevator Saturday night?"

"Yeah, I'm sure. Wait. What's going on? Is this about Alice?" A note of fear crept into his voice. "It was an accident, you know. She had a heart condition. Look, I admit that I acted kind of like a stalker by following her in September and then coming back here to talk to her boss and find out who Alice's lover was, but I had nothing to do with what happened to her. Her heart gave out. Just like that." He snapped his fingers.

The sheriff wasn't about to be distracted from his initial question. "You saw her in the elevator. But did you also go to Ms. McKee's room Saturday night?"

"What?" Kevin was obviously stunned. "No. I mean, yes,

I went there, but I didn't go in. I knocked on her door, but she never answered."

"Why did you go to her room, Mr. Collins? You'd already spoken with her earlier."

"Because she didn't tell me *anything*!" Kevin shouted. "She only wanted to know about the book. She didn't care what *I* wanted! No one seems to realize that I lost the woman I loved! No one gives a crap about what I want or what I've gone through!"

His anger was almost palpable. It rolled off him in waves, and Jane imagined she felt the air grow a trifle warmer.

"If Ms. McKee had responded to your knock, how did you plan to convince her to talk when you'd already failed to do so in the elevator?"

There was a long silence. Jane guessed that Kevin was either composing himself or concocting a falsehood.

"I was going to offer her info about the book in exchange for info on Alice. I planned to lie, okay? Trust me, I've done worse than that since she dumped me, quit her job, and let her obsession with Adela Dundee ruin both of our lives."

Without skipping a beat, the sheriff asked Kevin where he was on the afternoon of Alice's death. Clearly flustered, Kevin haltingly repeated the story he'd told Jane about picking the letter out of the trashcan and waiting by the bike racks near the stables while Alice rode off on her horse to meet another Dundee fan.

Sterling had copied the letter and returned the original to Kevin, so he now had it on hand to show the sheriff.

"And when Alice didn't come back from her ride? What did you do?"

"I went into the village. I was hoping to catch her and her *special friend* having coffee or something. That's when I heard that she fell—that she was gone. All of these country bumpkins were gossiping about my Alice. About how she'd been taken away in an ambulance that didn't use its sirens. And I knew it was her because they mentioned Alice's hair.

She had such beautiful hair. Long and golden. It smelled like oranges and I loved to run my fingers through it." His voice grew hoarse. "I hung around the village for hours. I was too wrecked to move. But by the next day, I was back to wanting to know why she'd changed. If anything, my need to know was even more urgent. Because now she couldn't tell me. Only the guy who wrote that letter could. Him. Or Moira. I figured they'd both be here for this Murder and Mayhem thing. How could this other Dundee devotee miss out on something that was sure to include his *favorite author*?" He spoke the two words with venom.

"Did you believe that Felix Hampden wrote the letter?"

"Who the hell is Felix Hampden?" A chair creaked. "Wait. Was he Alice's lover? You have to tell me!"

Jane held her breath. Was Kevin lying? Did he really not know Felix?

Instead of replying, Sheriff Evans rustled some papers. "We'll get to Mr. Hampden, I assure you. First, I'd like to know about your work."

"My work? Why? What is this? What's going on?" Kevin was nervous again. Words burst from his mouth like bullets being fired from a gun.

"You were on sabbatical at Oxford University when Miss Hart ended your engagement, correct?"

Jane didn't hear Kevin speak, so she assumed that he responded with a nod.

"I don't know much about England," the sheriff said breezily. "My wife always wanted to vacation there, but I don't like to fly. So help me to understand. Why leave the States to study in another country?"

"I'm a biochem geek, and my main focus is pharmaceutical research. There's a professor at Oxford whose interests are similar to mine. We're both working on using frog toxins for medical purposes." Kevin quickly warmed to his subject, losing all traces of his former anxiety. "I didn't go to England for the equipment, but to work alongside Professor Tuckley.

He has amazing ideas on how to replicate toxins and produce a range of incredible new drugs."

The sheriff made a noise of encouragement. "Where do you get these frogs?"

"You can actually order them online," Kevin explained. "People like to keep poison dart frogs as pets so they can tell their friends that they own one of the most lethal creatures on the earth. They don't, of course. Most of them buy the *Colostethus* species. Very colorful and totally nontoxic. Even the ones I work with, the *Phyllobates terribilis* species, can't secrete the toxin in captivity. The only way we can get them to produce toxin is to import the beetles they like to munch on. It's the golden dart frog's special diet that makes it poisonous, and the food source is unique to the Pacific coast of Colombia. That's where we get the frogs, their food, and their fauna."

"Do you have any of these golden dart frogs at home?"

Kevin snorted. "No way, man. Our frogs aren't pets. They're objects of scientific study. We have a bunch at the lab, but that's not for public knowledge. These frogs are an endangered species, and even though we breed them, people don't like the idea of people using them for experiments. That is, until scientists like us stop the progression of their kid's MS or their dad's Alzheimer's."

"Can you tell me more about the toxin?" Evans maintained his airy tone. "How does it work?"

"It's really cool," Kevin said. "It's secreted through the frog's skin. All you have to do is touch it, and within minutes, you're a goner. It's that deadly. Each frog has enough poison to kill twenty thousand mice. Or ten humans. If you're unlucky enough to come into contact with the toxin, the first thing you'd feel would be a horrible burning sensation. We're talking sheer agony, and then the nerves and muscles would depolarize, which basically means you can't control your own body, and then your heart would go into arrhythmia. After that, you'd eventually have a cardiac arrest." Kevin talked about the killing power of the toxin with such glee that Jane felt sick. If he had poisoned Felix and Moira, he was a true devil.

"I don't get it," the sheriff said. "How could something so harmful help people?"

Though the dialogue between Sheriff Evans and Kevin fascinated Jane, she couldn't imagine why Evans was spending so much time discussing the nuances of the poison dart frog with a potential murderer.

"Because! We could use elements of the toxin as a muscle relaxant, a heart stimulant, and even as an anesthetic. Professor Tuckley and I are hoping to see it replace morphine in most hospitals. It's a far superior anesthetic to morphine for many reasons like—"

"Is it being used at all now?" Evan interrupted. "The toxin?"

"Not really, though some of the compounds found in the toxin are. Topical creams to relieve pain. Total over-the-counter stuff. Nothing as big as we're going for."

"Does it have a particular taste or smell? Is it clear?"

"Who knows? Who'd be crazy enough to taste it? You wouldn't live long enough to describe the flavor if it had one!" Kevin exclaimed loudly. "It really doesn't have an odor or color." There was a short silence. "I'm flattered that you're interested in my work, but I'd really like to get to the point of this interview."

"I'm almost there, Mr. Collins. Just one more question about the frogs."

"Okay."

"Did you bring the toxin to Storyton?"

Kevin spluttered. A series of incoherent sounds reverberated into the narrow space where Jane and Sinclair stood, waiting breathlessly for his answer. "Why would I do that?"

Jane heard a chair groan as the sheriff shifted his weight. Unable to restrain herself any longer, she bent over and peered through the gaps in the brass vent. From this vantage point, she found that she was gazing up at the men at the table. The angle made the sheriff's face appear fleshier, especially around the jowls, but somehow diminished Kevin Collins. He seemed younger and gaunter than he'd been in the gloomy space behind the bowling lanes. His skin was ashen, and his eyes were wild and haunted.

"Think carefully before answering, Mr. Collins. I already know the truth, so lying to me would be a terrible mistake."

Kevin chewed a fingernail and glanced furtively to his left and right. Jane wondered if he was searching for an escape route, but there was only one exit and it was behind Evans.

Or so I believe, Jane thought wryly. *For all I know, there could be a trapdoor under the rug.*

"I'll ask again. Did you bring toxin from the poison dart frog to Storyton?"

It was so quiet that Jane was certain someone would hear the thudding of her heart. Alongside her, she could feel Sinclair tense in anticipation.

"Yes," Kevin finally whispered.

"I didn't quite get that. Please repeat your answer," the sheriff said.

"Yes." The word was a mere tremble in the air.

There was an audible exhalation, and for a terrible moment, Jane thought it had come from her, but it was Sheriff Evans releasing his pent-up breath. "Why, son? What did you do with it?" His tone was surprisingly gentle.

A lump formed in Jane's throat, and she didn't know if the welling of sorrow was for Alice, Felix, Moira, or because of the tragic choice the young man sitting at the conference table had made. She was simultaneously afraid of him, repulsed by him, and furious with him, and yet, she pitied him too.

How twisted he must be inside. How full of darkness and despair.

She swallowed her emotions and watched as Kevin shook his head maniacally. "No, no, no!" he cried. "I didn't use it. I didn't!"

"Then why bring it?" the sheriff asked dubiously. "What were your intentions when you packed a deadly toxin in your bag?"

Kevin's face crumpled. He put his hands over his eyes and shouted, "When I came here in September, I was going to kill him. Alice's lover! I had this insane fantasy about squirting a few drops on his hand—to punish him for touching *her.*" He let loose a wrenched sob. "I couldn't have done it though. Not for real. I was just trying to convince myself that I was the better man. The bigger man. After all, I worked with some of the most lethal stuff on earth and I was trying to use it for good! *I* was the catch—not some loser booklover. Me!" He thumped his chest with his fist. *"Me."*

Sheriff Evans waited for Kevin to calm down. "Was the toxin in a test tube? How did you carry it?"

There was a lengthy pause and then Kevin mumbled, "In a syringe."

Jane thought of the broken perfume bottle. Had Kevin put drops of toxin on the stopper? Or in Felix Hampden's pomade? A syringe would have contained enough poison to kill a dozen people. If Kevin had brought the syringe in September, it was likely that he packed it when he returned to Storyton Hall for a second time for the Murder and Mayhem Week.

"Tell me how you used that syringe." The sheriff was still speaking gently.

Kevin swiped at his eyes as if embarrassed by his tears and then frowned. "What do you mean? I didn't use it. I never found out who the guy was, so I didn't even take the syringe out of my overnight kit."

"Alice died from a cardiac arrest," Evans said. "Isn't that how someone who'd come into contact with the golden dart frog's venom would die? Isn't that what you said?"

Kevin bolted to his feet, and both the sheriff's and his deputy's right hands flew to their gun holsters.

"I had nothing to do with what happened to Alice! I *loved* her!" Kevin's eyes were wide with fear, reminding Jane of Alice's spooked horse. "When she died, she took all the answers with her." He plunged his hands into his hair. "I. Want. Answers."

The sheriff produced a plastic evidence bag and slid it across the table. "What do you make of this?"

After darting wild glances between the sheriff and the deputy, Kevin reached for the bag. He leaned over it and then he gasped. "It's the same handwriting! It's *him*. The guy who told Alice to go riding." Staring at the sheriff with a look of utter desperation, he said, "Who is he? Who wrote this?" He slapped his palm on the bag, as if he could squash the evidence of his rival's existence. "What's his name?"

"It belongs to Felix Hampden. Unfortunately, Mr. Hampden is dead. He was poisoned."

"Good," The words came out as a snarl. "I wish I'd been there to see him die."

Sheriff Evans motioned to his deputy, and together, the men moved toward Kevin.

"Mr. Collins, I'm placing you under arrest."

"For what? I didn't do anything!" Kevin objected.

While Kevin was read his rights, Jane grabbed Sinclair's arm and gave him a little push. She felt terribly claustrophobic in the narrow, musty space and needed to get out of the passageway without delay. When Sinclair didn't respond quickly enough, she edged around him and groped along the wall until her palm met with the cool metal of the closet. She yanked on the recessed ring pull, stepped over the lip and into the closet, and then, without stopping to see if anyone was in the hallway, burst out into the warm and welcoming light.

FIFTEEN

Jane leaned against the wall and shut her eyes. It was all ruined now. The Murder and Mayhem Week would go down in the annals as the darkest time in Storyton Hall's history. The guests, seeing Kevin Collins led away in handcuffs, would grow alarmed. Searching for answers, they'd start making phone calls. Word would spread, and soon enough, a reporter from over the mountain would arrive. Alice Hart's death would be brought to the public's attention, and the murders of Felix Hampden and Moira McKee would become front-page news around the region.

"We'll be ruined," Jane murmured miserably.

At that moment, Sinclair stepped out of the storage closet. "We will not be ruined," he said firmly. "And this is far from being over. While the sheriff and his deputies were otherwise engaged, Sterling took the liberty of examining Mr. Collins's room."

"What did he find?"

"It's what he didn't find that's worth noting." Sinclair took Jane's elbow and steered her toward the lobby. "Aside from a collection of framed photographs of Miss Hart, Mr.

Collins brought few possessions to Storyton Hall. Other than his monk's costume and some jeans and shirts, he had a medicine kit. There was no syringe among his toothbrush, comb, razor, and deodorant."

Jane considered the implications of the missing syringe. "He must have gotten rid of it after our little chat in the room behind the bowling alley."

Sinclair paused. "I don't think the sheriff will be able to hold Mr. Collins for more than twenty-four hours. Not unless the lab results prove that the toxins found in Felix Hampden's body did, in fact, come from the golden dart frog. And even then, Evans will need our help. He doesn't have a shred of hard evidence against Mr. Collins. There are no witnesses to the crimes and no murder weapon. It's too circumstantial to hold up in court and Evans knows it. He must be hoping to buy time while his team sorts through the contents of Ms. McKee's and Mr. Collins's rooms."

"What can we do in the meantime? Empty the Dumpster and sift through the garbage?"

Sinclair nodded. "I'm afraid that's exactly what we must do. While most of the guests are occupied watching the Storyton Hall Players perform *Murder at the Vicarage* this evening, I'll recruit several discreet staff members to assist with the search."

Jane had a sudden vision of the scene from *Star Wars* film in which Luke, Leia, Han Solo, and Chewbacca are trapped in the trash compactor when the walls begin to close, threatening to squash them to death. That's how she felt right then. Like the walls were closing in and she had no way to stop them. "We still haven't found our copy of *Lost Letters*. If Kevin stole it from Felix, then where is it now? Could it be that he killed Felix out of jealousy and truly didn't care about the book? Maybe he sold it to Moira. Maybe he threw it out. Or maybe someone else helped themselves to it when Felix could no longer put up a fight." She sighed. "I fell for Kevin's whole story, you know. I saw him as a man who'd lost his way because of heartbreak and grief. I never believed him capable of murder."

"People are like book characters, Miss Jane," Sinclair said and started walking again. "In the beginning, they let us catch glimpses of their personality, but it takes time—a hundred pages or so—to really know them. Our challenge is that we don't always have the opportunity to learn the backstory of our villains."

"Well, if we're using book metaphors, then I didn't read him as a thief. He seemed intent on hurting the people he thought were involved with Alice, but he doesn't care about books and he seems to hate Adela Dundee." She stopped before the lobby door. "Alice was obsessed with Dundee. Kevin believes he was dumped because of Dundee. So what would he do if he came across a book about Dundee in Felix Hampden's room? He's just poisoned the man he believed to be Alice's lover and now he spies this book? What would he do?"

Sinclair grimaced. "Destroy it."

"Or bring it somewhere to study it. To try to learn what it was about this woman and her writing that so captivated Alice. He could have stuck it on a high shelf in any of the reading rooms."

"In other words, it could be anywhere," Sinclair said.

Steeling herself, Jane grasped the door handle. "I never thought I'd see a guest escorted from Storyton Hall in handcuffs, but I'd better take up a position in the lobby and assure our guests that there's nothing to worry about. If I can manage to look calm, perhaps I can assuage their fears."

Jane smoothed her hair and entered the lobby. She could tell by the excited tittering near the coffee stations that the sheriff had already come through. She and Sinclair had spent too much time talking. Anxiously, Jane started for her office. She moved slowly, expecting people to block her path and demand an explanation.

To her astonishment, no one paid her any mind. Even when

she tarried at the coffee station to make sure that it was fully stocked, the guests were too preoccupied to notice her.

"His uniform was *so* realistic," a woman said as she poured herself a cup of coffee. "I don't think that was a prop gun either!"

The man in front of her turned to pass her the cream jug. "And the young man was quite convincing too. The way he kept shouting that he was innocent. I was half tempted to fly to his aid."

The couple laughed and moved away, leaving Jane staring after them.

They think it's a charade—another element of the Murder and Mayhem Week!

Feeling hopeful, Jane strolled across the lobby. She heard similar remarks, but the guests quickly moved on to other topics such as when they should get in line for tea or what they planned to wear to dinner.

"I can't wait to see the play!" a woman exclaimed as she hooked her arm through her husband's. "Jerry, darling, this is the most wonderful vacation ever. I want to come back to Storyton every year."

"You'll get no argument from me," the man said, smiling at his wife indulgently. "The accommodations are excellent, the food is superior, and I enjoy the company of our fellow guests. I can't remember the last time that I felt so relaxed and yet so invigorated. I'm reading quite a bit, but who would ever have guessed that I, Gerald Houston, would go fly-fishing or sign up for a pickleball lesson?"

His wife laughed merrily. "And you look very fetching in your tennis whites, I might add."

"Really?" The man kissed his wife on the cheek. "Perhaps we should come twice a year. Do they have other theme weeks?"

"I don't know. We'll have to do some sleuthing and find out," the woman said before the couple moved out of earshot.

Jane felt like hugging the pair. She knew it was only a

matter of time before the guests learned the truth about the murders, but at least she'd been given a slight reprieve.

If only the scandal would break after this week is over, she thought. It was hard to say good-bye to the success they'd experienced thus far. The guests were happy and adventurous. They were booking excursions, sampling the offerings of the Activities Desk, and feasting like royalty. Their willingness to spend money on recreation, food, and alcohol meant an increase in revenue for Storyton Hall.

Jane had received jubilant notes from the managers of the Madame Bovary Dining Room, the Agatha Christie Tearoom, the Kipling Café, and the Ian Fleming Lounge. They all said basically the same thing: that they were experiencing their most lucrative weekend since Storyton Hall first opened its doors to paying guests.

Waving to the front desk clerk, Jane entered her office, sank into her chair, and gazed blankly at her desk calendar. Halloween was fast approaching, and the Beatrix Potter Kids' Club was always booked to capacity with children wanting to enter the pumpkin-carving competition, take a haunted hayride, and trick-or-treat around the resort while their parents enjoyed an autumn wine-tasting dinner. Later, the kids would reunite with their parents, settle on picnic blankets spread around a great bonfire, and be treated to a spine-tingling ghost story.

"Who'll bring children to Storyton Hall after two murders?" Jane asked the calendar.

As if on cue, she heard the sound of a child giggling. And then a second child began to laugh.

"I take it the two of you are tired of playing with your train set," Jane said as the twins entered the office.

"Yes, and we're starving." Fitz covered his stomach with both hands.

Hem groaned and copied the motion, adopting a pained expression to emphasize the gravity of their plight.

"How about a bike ride into the village? I'll get a coffee

and you can either have frozen custard from the Canvas Creamery or a donut from the Pickled Pig."

"Custard!" Hem shouted at the same time Fitz yelled, "Donut!"

Smiling, Jane waved at the door. "We'll go to both places and then drop in at Run for Cover on the way home."

Fitz rolled his eyes. "That means talking. Lots of talking."

"Yeah. You and Miss Alcott can go on for-ev-er." He stretched out the word as if it were made of taffy.

"That should give you plenty of time to check out the new comics. You know Miss Alcott often gets deliveries on Mondays."

The twins' faces lit up. "Maybe there's a new Superman!" Fitz said, pushing his brother out the door.

The physical prompt would have normally called for retaliation, but Hem was too excited to respond. Instead, he told Jane to hurry and the two of them sprinted through the lobby toward the terrace.

As much as Jane wanted to race out, she couldn't indulge in an hour-long escape without informing Butterworth first. He was stationed at his post by the main entrance, flipping through papers attached to a clipboard.

"It's been an eventful day, Miss Jane," he said, glancing up at her approach. "And we've yet to recover our missing book."

"Maybe the sheriff's men have found it by now."

Butterworth shook his head. "I insisted on seeing photographs of the evidence taken from Mr. Hampden's room and *Lost Letters* wasn't there. Mr. Sterling already went through Mr. Collins's effects, and he is currently watching over a pair of deputies as they bag items in Ms. McKee's room. The book is still unaccounted for." He studied Jane and frowned. "You look a bit peaked. Perhaps some fresh air would do you good."

"The boys and I were just heading into the village. But it feels wrong to leave, to enjoy the colors of the leaves and the scent of sun-warmed pine needles with all that's happened."

"We're at a temporary impasse," Butterworth said. "Investigations are about patience and vigilance. On those television crime shows, the facts are parceled out in tidy, sequential order and lab results are completed within hours. Our case won't fit into a sixty-minute time slot, so we must do our best to sort through the chaos and confusion."

Jane grimaced. "And a mountain of trash."

"Indeed."

"We should continue to keep an eye on Professor Price. He's the last man standing, so to speak. *Lost Letters* may very well have fallen into his hands. And if that's true, I doubt he came by it honestly."

Butterworth grunted and then excused himself in order to assist an elderly man descend the wheelchair ramp. The basket on the man's walker was so loaded with books that it threatened to overturn the entire support device. With a snap of his fingers, Butterworth signaled to the closest bellhop to accompany the gentleman to his final destination.

"Thank you, kindly," the man said, digging in his pocket for a tip.

"That's not necessary," Butterworth said. "It's our pleasure and privilege to help our guests enjoy an optimal reading experience. Where can Billy take you, sir?"

The man grinned. "To the lake, please. I grew up on the water, but I live in the concrete jungle now, and I miss hearing it whisper to me as I read." He turned to Billy. "Can you take me back fifty years, son?"

Billy considered the question. "I don't know if I can do that, but how does an Adirondack chair facing the lake, a wool blanket, and a thermos of hot cider sound?"

"Like heaven," the man said and allowed Billy to gather up his books.

Jane tried to hold fast to the warm feeling of pride she felt watching Billy and the elderly gentleman chat as they slowly made their way down the ramp. After giving Butterworth a quick salute, she left the main house and crossed the lawn. She wheeled her bicycle out of the garage and caught up to her sons, who were riding in circles on the gravel path. "What took you so long, Mom?" Hem cried. "We're wasting away!"

Laughing at his indignation, Jane followed the boys to the road. When they reached Broken Arm Bend, Fitz and Hem bellowed the poem someone had made up years ago to commemorate the danger of the infamous curve.

Broken Arm Bend,
Where rides come to an end,
In thistles and thorns.
Yes, our bones will mend,
But it would have been better
If you'd used your horn!

They made it to the village without incident, and Jane, who was feeling especially indulgent, treated the boys to jelly donuts followed by small frozen custard shakes. She also ordered two pumpkin lattes from Phoebe, who was thankfully too busy to chat. Jane wasn't ready to talk about the murders or Kevin's arrest to anyone but Eloise.

Luckily for Jane, Eloise had just finished ringing a sale and was free to lend Jane her ear while enjoying a latte and the afternoon sunshine in the shop's front garden. Jane settled down in a comfortable twig chair and tapped the nearest stepping-stone with her toe. It was engraved with the word *Persevere*. "I'm going to need a healthy dose of this," she said and then told Eloise everything that had occurred since the costume ball.

"If Professor Perv has the book, why wouldn't he just leave the resort?" Eloise asked when Jane was done.

"I don't think he'd be that foolish," Jane said. She turned toward the street, soaking in the bucolic scene. The gardens were a riot of sedum, chrysanthemum, and aster blooms, and the proprietors had arranged pumpkins and gourds of all shapes and sizes along the flagstone paths leading to the shop door. The Halloween decorations would be going up soon, and the merchants would expect guests from Storyton Hall to continue pouring into the village. Jane thought of how Barnaby liked to dress in a different costume for the entire week leading up to Halloween and how he'd transform Geppetto's Toy Shop into a haunted house every year. He would be crushed if there were no visiting children to wander, wide-eyed and deliciously frightened, through his displays of cob-webbed skeletons and rotting zombies. And his bottom line would suffer without a troop of kids dashing about Barnaby's store, begging their parents to buy one of his splendid toys.

A sorrowful sigh escaped through Jane's lips as she real-ized that the scandal at Storyton Hall would affect the live-lihood of each and every villager.

Eloise heard the sound and put an arm around her friend. "Buck up. Things will work out. Even if the news spreads around the country, it might not have the dire consequences you're imagining. In fact, if Storyton Hall gets loads of media coverage, you may have more guests than before. You could never afford that kind of advertising."

"But what about the murders?"

Eloise shrugged. "In this age of sensationalism, a violent crime could very well be a draw."

"We wouldn't be attracting our regular clientele, then," Jane said. "In general, our patrons are smart, cordial, and gentle."

"Oh, right!" Eloise snorted. "Look at your current batch. They spend all their free time reading about dead bodies. That's not to say that they aren't lovely. I've enjoyed getting to know every guest who's crossed my threshold over the last few days, but a pair of murders isn't going to scare them off. People won't leave. You'll see. If anything, you'll get loads of calls asking if there are vacancies."

Suddenly, a deafening mechanical whine pierced the si-lence. It sounded like it was coming from inside the bookstore.

Jane was about to leap to her feet when Eloise shouted, "Don't worry! That's just Edwin doing demolition."

"During business hours?" Jane yelled back.

"I told him he could only work when the shop was empty, so every time it clears out, I put in my earplugs and he starts using the tile saw or whatever it is he's got next door." Eloise smiled. "It never lasts long."

She was right. The noise stopped as quickly as it started, and then they heard the sound of a power drill. It was less unnerving than that of the saw, and Jane sank back into her seat. "Is he going to renovate the café himself?"

Eloise nodded. "He's really handy."

"Can he manage such a big project? I thought he was a food writer."

"He is, but he's picked up all sorts of skills during his travels," Eloise explained. "And he considers himself an anthropologist first and a writer second. In other words, he often stays in one place for several months to fully absorb the local culture. He finds temporary employment, and while researching the cuisine, he also learns a new trade and starts soaking in the language. At this point, he speaks six or seven, though I can't even remember which ones. He picks things up like that." She snapped her fingers. "It's so annoying. I'm no good at anything unless I practice like crazy. It took me years to learn how to play the piano. Not Edwin. He could perform Rachmaninoff's Third Piano Concerto from memory after just a few months. Do you know how tough it was to grow up in his shadow?"

"I bet." Jane turned toward the café. Edwin Alcott was becoming more interesting with each passing day. "So where did he learn his construction skills?"

"Italy. He was doing a series on Tuscan food and took a job as a day laborer. He was part of a crew working on a major museum renovation," Eloise said. "Unfortunately, the whole project was scrapped after one of the museum's priceless artifacts was stolen. A book, actually. By that point, Edwin had finished his series of articles and learned all about framing, dry wall, and laying tile, so he moved on to the next country."

Jane's throat had gone dry. "What kind of book was taken?"

"An illuminated manuscript," Eloise shook her head over the loss. "Edwin said it was a beauty too. A book of hours filled with gorgeous sixteenth-century illustrations done in tempera, gold, and ink on vellum." She sighed wistfully. "I hope the thief treated it with care. There aren't many books like that left in this world."

Except, perhaps, in the secret library of Storyton Hall, Jane thought and then felt a chill in her bones. Was it pure coincidence that Edwin had moved back to Storyton at the same time Alice Hart had appeared? Could he somehow have known of the existence of a rare and unusual copy of *Lost Letters*? A copy that had an unopened letter from Adela Dundee hidden under its dust jacket.

Jane furrowed her brow. She had yet to deduce how Alice Hart had tracked the book to Storyton Hall. It was time to finish reading the collection of Adela Dundee letters that had set the recent series of events in motion.

"I'd better get going," Jane said and finished her last sip of pumpkin latte. "I need to make sure everything's in order for tonight's performance."

" 'The play's the thing'!" Eloise exclaimed in a British accent.

"Please, no *Hamlet* references," Jane begged. "Things at Storyton Hall are far too close to a Shakespearean tragedy for my comfort."

After thanking Eloise for being such a good listener, Jane called for the boys and walked to where she'd left her bike leaning against the picket fence. When she gazed at the dirty window of what was once the Loafing Around Café, she thought she saw a face staring back at her. She looked down for a brief moment to release her kickstand, and when she glanced at the window again, the face was gone.

And then the twins appeared in a flurry of movement and

noise, shouting comic book quotes and pumping their fists in the air. Together, the trio mounted their bikes and headed for home.

With such dramatic goings-on at Storyton Hall, Jane knew that the chance of keeping her employees' tongues from wagging was unlikely. However, she deemed it necessary to send an e-mail to her staff explaining that Sheriff Evans was looking into the cases of the two Rip Van Winkles. She also asked that all inquiries concerning the subject should be directed to Butterworth or herself. Her in-box was full of unread messages, and she did her best to read and respond to the most pressing ones before shutting down the computer and heading to the Madame Bovary Dining Room.

Greeting the hostess on duty, Jane stood with her at the podium and watched as the last guest was seated for the special dinner theater performance of *Murder at the Vicarage*. Most of the guests, who were already tipsy after enjoying cocktails on the terrace, were about to be treated to a sumptuous meal of field greens with barley and red pear, creamy butternut squash soup, pomegranate roasted chicken, and mustard trout with capers. If the diners had any room left for dessert, they could choose between a warm apple-walnut cobbler with a scoop of maple-vanilla ice cream or a decadent chocolate-cranberry fudge cake.

Jane and the boys ate the same fare as the guests. They pulled stools up to a prep counter in the kitchen, ate their sumptuous meal, and lavished Mrs. Hubbard with compliments. Mrs. Hubbard glowed with pride when the twins told her that her soup didn't taste "like a yucky vegetable," and she let them sample both desserts. After supper, Jane saw that her boys were tucked away in her aunt and uncle's spare bedroom with a DVD of *The Jungle Book*, and then she stretched out on Aunt Octavia's living room sofa and resumed reading *Lost Letters*.

The apartment felt sleepy and tranquil. Uncle Aloysius was closeted in his office, and Aunt Octavia had fallen asleep on the sofa across from Jane's. Muffet Cat was snoozing on her belly and Jane tried not to laugh as the cat's body rose and fell with each of her aunt's breaths. Muffet Cat looked like a black-and-white buoy bobbing up and down in a gentle ocean. He also looked deeply content. Aunt Octavia's soft snores didn't bother Muffet Cat in the least, and Jane actually found that the rhythmic noises helped her concentrate on her reading. She was soon swept into Adela Dundee's past.

Adela had written most of the letters to her husband, George, but there were several short missives to her agent, Richard Cobb, as well. Cobb had been Adela's agent for her entire career, and Jane could tell from the easy and casual language in Adela's letters that she respected and trusted this man.

It was while reading the last of the letters meant for Richard Cobb that Jane believed she might have stumbled upon the clue that had led Alice Hart to Storyton Hall.

Clutching the book to her chest, Jane crossed the rug separating the two sofas and dropped to her knees next to her aunt's slumbering form.

"Aunt Octavia," she whispered. "Wake up. I need to ask you something." Jane put a hand on her aunt's fleshy arm and gave it a little shake.

Muffet Cat reached out a paw and laid it on the exposed skin of Jane's wrist. His claws were still retracted, but a slit of yellow eye warned her that she would be punished should she shake Aunt Octavia's arm again.

"Forgive me for interrupting your nap," Jane said, addressing both Muffet Cat and her aunt at once. "But this is important."

"What is it?" her aunt demanded without opening her eyes.

"A clue," Jane said. "At least, I hope so. One of the letters in this book was written to Adela Dundee's literary agent. Apparently, the letter was never mailed. It was still sealed when Alice found it in that historical society in Cornwall.

Here are the lines I want you to hear: '*After much thought, I have decided to heed your recommendation. Ferrari will not be retired just yet. He has more work to do, as do I. And I'm not certain that I've settled on the ending. In any case, I've sent a few scraps of paper to a storied knight for safekeeping. He will serve as its guardian. It was Richard who suggested I mail the package to America as a precaution. According to his friends at the War Office, not even the remotest corner of London will be safe once the bombing starts . . .*' "

Jane trailed off. Looking at her aunt, she said, "Wasn't there a Steward named after a knight?"

"Percival!" Aunt Octavia cried, startling Muffet Cat. He jumped off the sofa with an indignant meow and immediately leapt up onto Jane's. He flopped down on Jane's splayed book and blinked at her with a snide expression that Jane had learned was the feline equivalent of a human sticking out their tongue. Paying no attention to Muffet Cat, Aunt Octavia held out her hands. "Pull me up, Jane, dear. I can't catch my breath from this position."

Tugging her aunt upright, Jane waited expectantly while she readjusted the throw pillows. "Adela must be referring to Percy, my father-in-law. He was the guardian of Storyton Hall before Aloysius. Somehow, Miss Hart discovered that the knight Adela Dundee referred to in her letter was Percival Steward."

"Adela hints at the Steward surname by using the word 'guardian.' And she also says 'storied.' Alice must have researched well-known bibliophiles who were also named after a famous knight. From that point, it couldn't have been hard for her to realize that Percy Steward, a man who lived in a place called Storyton Hall, must have been the recipient of Adela Dundee's unpublished mystery. The last case of Umberto Ferrari." Jane had to pause for a moment. "She refers to it as 'a few scraps of paper,' but no matter its length, it's still an incredible treasure. And to think. It's here. Right above my head."

"As are many other wonders," her aunt agreed.

"Which we should share with the world!" Jane cried softly. "Stories are meant to be read—not stored in airtight containers until the end of time. Keeping them to ourselves— it's nearly as criminal as using poison dart frog toxin."

Aunt Octavia frowned. "Not true, my dear. Most of the holdings in our secret library were meant to remain secret. Either because they would have caused political unrest, were threats to the lives of an individual or to an entire group of people, or condoned intolerance, injustice, racism—the darker side of human nature."

"But surely the danger must pass eventually. The completed copy of *The Mystery of Edwin Drood*, for example. The men Dickens mentioned as having corrupted the prison system are all dead. We could sell the copy and secure our future while delighting Dickens fans the world over!"

"It is not ours to sell or share," Aunt Octavia said sharply. "We are but custodians of the treasures entrusted to us. Sometimes by the authors. Sometimes by people in positions of power. But more often, by good men and women merely trying to protect and preserve knowledge." She smiled tenderly at Jane. "I know it's hard to accept. But think of our special collection as you would a museum filled with artifacts."

"You can still look at things in a museum. No one gets to read or study or benefit from the most incredible library of all time."

Aunt Octavia released a little laugh. "We do let a few carefully screened individuals view certain materials. Sinclair will tell you more about that once our current crisis has passed. At the moment, I think it's more important that we talk to him about this Adela Dundee manuscript."

Jane knew that her aunt was right, but she silently vowed to resume the debate when things were less frantic. "He's probably rooting through trash."

"That is precisely what he's doing," said Uncle Aloysius from the doorway. "Sheriff Evans phoned about an hour ago to ask for our cooperation and assistance. I knew you were busy looking for clues in Miss Hart's book, so I fielded the call." He walked behind the sofa and planted a featherlight kiss on the crown of Aunt Octavia's head. Jane loved how her uncle always drew near to his wife when he was worried. It was as if her presence gave him an infusion of strength. "The results of the lab work were presented to Evans late this afternoon," her uncle continued. "It would appear that Mr. Hampden's death resulted from what turned out to be lethal contact with golden dart frog toxin. Mr. Evans informed me that the toxin was placed around the tip of Mr. Hampden's nasal spray. Ms. McKee's remains and effects are still being examined, but she also had nasal spray among her toiletries. The sheriff, who has sent every available deputy to search alongside our staff, said that the syringe Mr. Collins brought to Storyton Hall must be located tonight. It's of utmost importance."

"A genuine needle in a haystack," Aunt Octavia said, waving her hand dismissively. "Really, Aloysius. Do you think the killer would be dumb enough to toss the murder weapon in the rubbish bin? Because the Collins boy doesn't have it, just as he doesn't have our copy of *Lost Letters*, then I suspect the sheriff has yet to apprehend the real culprit."

Aunt Octavia had given voice to Jane's own fears. "Can the boys sleep here tonight?" she asked.

"Of course." Her uncle arched a brow. "Do you have a lead to follow?"

"I plan to shadow Professor Desmond Price. He's the only person with a motive who isn't behind bars or—"

"In the morgue," Aunt Octavia finished for her. And then she crossed her arms and added, "Give him time, dear. He may end up there yet."

SIXTEEN

Jane spent Monday morning in a state of agonized anticipation. She tried to work, but the feeling that her world was unraveling made it very difficult to concentrate. All she was really doing, in between reviewing next month's budget, bookings, and special events, was waiting. Waiting for the local newspaper to be delivered with its headline about the murders at Storyton Hall, waiting for panicked guests to rush the front desk, and waiting for reports from the Fins on Desmond Price's movements.

When she picked up a copy of the paper, she was infinitely relieved to see that it had gone to press before word of the shocking goings-on at Storyton Hall could reach the editor's ears.

"A stay of execution," Jane murmured, her gaze flitting over articles on football games and harvest festivals. She wasn't fooled into believing Tuesday morning's edition would feature such innocuous stories, however, and her supposition was proved right shortly after nine, when a reporter called to question Jane about Kevin Collins.

"I heard one of your guests is being held at the station," the woman said. "What did he do?"

"You'd better talk with Sheriff Evans. I don't want to divulge any information that might compromise his investigation."

"What investigation?" The reporter immediately perked up.

Gripping the phone, Jane wondered if she should have chosen her words more carefully, but she didn't want to act like she was concealing anything. Once the scandal broke, she planned to face it head-on, and to be as transparent as possible while still protecting Storyton Hall's greatest secret.

"I have no comment," Jane said and wished the woman a pleasant day. And though she expected the lady reporter to show up after she'd spoken with someone at the sheriff's department, that didn't happen. To Jane's relief, the guests remained clueless about the murders. They enjoyed Mrs. Hubbard's breakfast spread and then headed to their next activity in a state of blessed ignorance.

As for Desmond Price, he'd attended the dinner theater performance the night before and had gone to bed immediately afterward. And once the trash had been examined and neither the syringe nor the missing book found, Butterworth, Sterling, and Sinclair took shifts monitoring the corridor outside Price's guest room. There was nothing to see because Price didn't appear again until morning. Jane passed by him as he sat drinking coffee on the terrace, and she thought that his face looked pinched and haggard. However, there was an air of satisfaction about him too. Jane observed him for only a moment, but the impression she formed was of a man who'd been through a trial but now felt confident about his future.

"We can't lose track of him. Not for a second," Jane told Butterworth over a pot of strong tea and a midmorning snack of toast with jam. "He's like a cat waiting to be served a dish of cream."

"There's a restlessness to him as well," Butterworth said.

"He keeps glancing at his watch. I'm a fan of punctuality, but the professor seems to be acutely aware of the passage of time."

Jane's eyes involuntarily darted to the clock on her office wall. "Where is he now?"

"Participating in the Mystery Loves Company trivia contest. There are so many contestants involved that they should be tied up until lunch."

Jane frowned. "We're not giving books as prizes, are we?"

"No, Miss Jane," Butterworth assured her. Folding his napkin into a neat square and placing it on his empty plate, he got to his feet "We have some lovely items from the gift shop. Lap desks. Woven throws. Notecards. That sort of thing."

"All right. Keep me informed about Professor Price. I'm off to speak with Ned. I can't imagine that he'd behave inappropriately in exchange for money, but I need to be certain."

Butterworth, who'd been on the verge of leaving, turned to face Jane again. "Money is a powerful motive. With such a large staff, it's difficult to know the financial state of each employee, but if anyone had been especially vocal about their troubles, Mrs. Hubbard would surely know."

"Of course!" Jane exclaimed. "Why didn't we ask her sooner?"

"The answer to that is quite simple. Unlike Mrs. Pimpernel, who sees and hears every manner of impropriety and says nothing, Mrs. Hubbard is incapable of discretion. Grant you, she limits her gossip to staff members, but that is only because her role as head chef limits her exposure to the guests." Butterworth sniffed in disapproval. "Had anyone from *upstairs* questioned her about which staff members were strapped for cash, her finely tuned radar would have been set off and her tongue would start wagging double-time."

Jane pursed her lips. "And yet she's been uncharacteristically quiet about Aunt Octavia's illness."

"Mrs. Hubbard is fiercely loyal to your family," Butterworth conceded.

"That settles it. I'll drop by the kitchens when I'm done

with Ned," Jane said, and Butterworth left to take up his customary position by the front door.

Jane found Ned polishing the brass handrails outside the main entrance. The young man whistled as he worked and seemed the picture of contentment.

"Nice day, isn't it?" she asked him.

Ned sprung to attention. "Yes, ma'am. It sure is."

"You're in excellent spirits this morning."

He blushed. "Was I whistling again?"

Jane smiled knowingly. "What's her name?"

Ned's eyes widened and his blush deepened. "Sarah. From the gift shop."

Picturing the pretty girl who was hired over the summer, Jane said, "She's lovely. And very funny. I remember how she made me laugh the first time we met."

"She's the only girl who likes this place as much as I do. She's already planning to work up to a manager's position." Ned resumed his task. "We're going to the Canvas Creamery after our shifts are over." He shot Jane a worried glance. "Is that okay? I mean, we're just friends right now, but I know there are rules . . ." He trailed off, rubbing at the brass until it glowed in the October sunlight.

"Against staff members dating each other, you mean?" Jane said. "We tend to discourage it, but I trust your judgment, Ned."

Ned looked absurdly pleased. "Thank you, ma'am."

Jane chatted about the Murder and Mayhem Week and then came to the point of her visit. When she asked if any of the guests had sought special favors or made unusual requests, Ned's expression turned blank. Convinced that the young man had nothing to do with the disappearance of *Lost Letters* or the deaths of Felix Hampden or Moira McKee, Jane headed to the kitchens.

It wasn't the best time to have a word with Mrs. Hubbard as she was busy preparing for the lunch service, but Jane offered to keep an eye on the soups while they talked. Using wooden spoons, Jane stirred simmering pots of turkey noodle, pureed sweet potato, and creamy tomato and asked Mrs. Hubbard if any staff members had complained about financial woes.

"Well, none of us are rich," Mrs. Hubbard said, adding fresh parley to the turkey noodle. "I hear the usual complaints of 'I wish I could buy that flat-screen TV or that new car,' but most folks are satisfied with their lot. There are a few people who've been fretting about money lately."

Jane watched the parsley sprigs disappear as the spoon created eddies in the broth. "Such as?"

"The one who comes to mind first is Gavin. He wasn't planning on retiring this soon, you see, nor was he expecting to have a knee replacement. He doesn't know that he's put enough by."

Jane instantly crossed Gavin off her mental list. Following his recent surgery, he was still relying on crutches, and he could hardly sneak in and out of guest rooms without the rest of the staff noticing. Not only that, but he was a Fin. His entire life had been devoted to keeping the Stewards safe. "I'll have to talk with Gavin about his future," Jane said. "Such devoted service should be rewarded. Who else?"

"There's Ned, the bellhop."

Jane's heart was in her throat. "He talks about needing money?"

Mrs. Hubbard called for soup tureens. "Oh, sure," she said as she lifted one of the heavy stockpots and filled a tureen with tomato soup. "He's keen on Sarah Walter from the gift shop. And *she's* keen on men who ride motorcycles. He's been going on and on about saving up for a Harley. What's the boy thinking?" She snorted. "On these mountain roads? What with the ice and snow we get in the wintertime? He'd be better off buying an old Jeep and setting his cap on a different girl."

Jane thought Ned and Sarah would make a charming couple, but since she wanted Mrs. Hubbard to keep talking, she didn't argue. "Is there anyone else?"

"Lizzie from housekeeping is always going on about her mom's medical bills, and the cost of her monthly prescriptions."

Mrs. Hubbard clicked her tongue. "It's a shame really. The way old folks are treated these days. You have to mortgage your life away just for the privilege of spending a few more years on this earth. I thank the good Lord each day that I'm hail and hearty. I come from a long line of women who stayed able of body and mind right up to their hundredth birthdays."

"I'm glad to hear it," Jane said. "I can't imagine Storyton Hall without you. The heart of the whole house is in this kitchen. And you are its heartbeat."

"Oh, stop it." Mrs. Hubbard wiped a tear away with the corner of her apron, gave Jane a fierce hug, and then called for a second tureen. "I need to whip up the hollandaise sauce. Eat a bowl of soup before you go since you helped make it." She winked at Jane and then pulled something out of the nearest oven with her bare hands and set it on a salad plate. "Here's a warm and toasty grilled Gouda sandwich to go with it. I added a few slices of Granny Smith apples to give it a little crunch. The twins came up with the idea. The darling imps."

The meal was so delicious and comforting that Jane experienced a fresh injection of hope. "She might be overly fond of gossip, but Mrs. Hubbard is an angel in disguise," Jane said to herself as she finished her last bite of soup.

She was on her way back to her office when Sterling intercepted her in the stairwell. "A note was left for Professor Price at the front desk. No one saw who dropped it off and we couldn't spot the individual on the video feed. In any case, we know that Price will be meeting this person at approximately three o'clock."

"You read the note?"

Sterling seemed surprised by the question. "Naturally. Mr. Sinclair opened the envelope and sealed it in a plastic bag in case it needs to be dusted for prints. After sharing the contents with Mr. Butterworth and myself, he placed it in a fresh envelope and wrote the professor's name exactly as it appeared on the original envelope."

"What did the note say?"

"It contained instructions for Professor Price to make his way to where Mrs. Chater was caught with her lover by the start of the afternoon tea service. He was to bring the payment in a Storyton Hall gift shop bag. A postscript warned that if he did not come alone, he would meet the same fate as Laertes, Hamlet, and Claudius."

Jane drew in a sharp breath. "They all died from poison. Laertes and Hamlet received wounds from a sword with a poisoned blade, and King Claudius drank from a cup of poisoned wine. The letter writer must be the killer. The sheriff *does* have the wrong man!"

"Unless the person who wrote the note is strictly a blackmailer," Sterling countered. "Perhaps he or she possesses both the syringe and the book and is merely looking to profit from the demise of Mr. Hampden and Ms. McKee."

"We should call Sheriff Evans," Jane said.

Sterling shook his head. "We don't know the location yet. Mr. Sinclair believes that Mrs. Chater is a literary reference, but as he's now in the Jane Austen Parlor hosting a round-table discussion on the origin of the female detective character, he's asked that you research the clue in his stead."

"Of course. Right away." Jane was about to dash off when she paused. "Keep trailing Desmond Price. I don't care if we're short on drivers today. The guests can hitchhike into the village if necessary. Has the professor been told that there's a letter waiting for him at the front desk?"

Sterling shook his head. "No, he hasn't been to his room since this morning. He won't know about the note unless he listens to his voice mail."

"At least that gives me a chance to puzzle out the meeting place. I'll send word as soon as I know where he's supposed to be come teatime."

"Got it." Sterling walked off at a brisk clip and Jane did the same.

Back in her office, she typed "Mrs. Chater" into Google's search box and was rewarded with several hits. The first was a link to a website containing act-by-act summaries of a play called *Arcadia* by a British playwright named Tom Stoppard. Scanning the characters list, Jane read that Mrs. Chater was an unfaithful wife mentioned in Act One as having been caught in the carnal embrace of another man in the gazebo. "The gazebo." Jane's pulse quickened. "That must be it."

She pictured the white wooden structure with the green roof and railing at the end of one of the resort's secluded paths. Named the Green Gables Gazebo after the farmhouse in the books by Lucy Maud Montgomery, the gazebo faced the lake on one side and a copse of trees on two others. With most of the guests lining up for tea and treats, it was the perfect spot for a clandestine three o' clock meeting.

Just to be sure, Jane checked other references to Mrs. Chater, but nothing else stood out like the detail about the gazebo. After sending a text to the Fins explaining what she'd discovered, Jane looked at the clock on her computer screen and sighed. There were another two hours to go before Desmond Price was supposed to show up at the gazebo.

Jane decided to pass some time by seeing how Aunt Octavia was faring. She rang the apartment, only to be told that her aunt was attending Sinclair's roundtable. "She was quite eager to show the other mystery fans her edition of *The Adventures of Susan Hopley* by Catherine Crews," Uncle Aloysius said. "My darling wife has long been of the persuasion that Susan Hopley was one of the first female sleuths and—"

"I'm sorry to interrupt, Uncle Aloysius, but I need your advice on how to capture a murderer." She told her uncle about the note.

"The professor might be the real villain," her uncle pointed out. "He could have masterminded the entire plot. Just because he didn't carry out the murders doesn't mean he isn't involved. This situation is fraught with peril, Jane."

"How would you handle it?" Jane asked. "I don't have your knife-throwing skills, and I can't hang around the gazebo with a shotgun slung over my shoulder. I don't want to do anything that might endanger or alarm our guests."

"Quite right," her uncle said. "Have Butterworth retrieve the blowgun from the safari room. Mr. Sterling has special darts stored in his arsenal that will knock out the diabolical pair without causing permanent damage."

"I like the irony in your choice of weapon," Jane said. "That's how the poison dart frog got its name, you know. The natives used to dip their blowgun darts in the toxins secreted by the frogs. Their enemies stood no chance."

Uncle Aloysius made a low, guttural sound. "Neither will ours, my dear. Neither will ours."

According to Sterling, Desmond Price returned to his room shortly after two and immediately rushed to the front desk to collect his note. After reading it, he slid the envelope into his coat pocket, glanced at his watch, and hurried toward the gift shop. Sterling followed him at a safe distance.

Jane waited until both men were gone and then told Butterworth that she planned to hide behind a tree within earshot of the gazebo. "But I'm calling the sheriff first," she said. "I refuse to behave like a character in a horror novel—one of those ditzy women who race headlong into danger without considering the consequences. I have my boys to think about, and they'll be home from school by half past three."

Butterworth looked pensive. "I'd better have Ned take them straight to the kitchens. I'm certain Mrs. Hubbard can keep them occupied. Perhaps they can wash dishes in exchange for a cookie or two."

Jane laughed. "Knowing Mrs. Hubbard, she'll pinch their cheeks and then ply them with lemonade and ice cream." Seeing Butterworth peek at his pocket watch, she instantly sobered and shared her uncle's idea about using the blowgun.

Butterworth took out his phone and started texting as fast as a teenage girl. After receiving a reply, he gave a satisfied nod. "We're all set. I'm coming with you. Let me give Ned his instructions and hand my post over to Billy. Sinclair will join us as soon as he's able."

"I'll meet you on the terrace. I want to get in touch with the sheriff without delay so he can get here as soon as possible."

Butterworth agreed and Jane proceeded to the terrace to make the call. When Sheriff Evans got on the line, she hurriedly told him that she suspected the criminal activities at Storyton Hall had yet to come to an end.

"Your note writer could be Mr. Collins," Evans said when she was done.

Jane was stunned to hear this. "How?"

"He asked for legal representation, and due to our lack of evidence, we were forced to release him late this morning. When was the note delivered?"

"Just past noon." Jane glanced around, half expecting to see Kevin Collins skulking near the shrubbery at the edge of the lawn.

The sheriff's voice turned stern. "I'll be there as soon as I can. Do not approach Professor Price. Keep your distance."

"I will," Jane promised. She planned to have a dozen trees between herself and the gazebo, but nothing would stop her from learning the identity of the letter writer. She was immensely relieved when Butterworth appeared, the outline of the blowgun visible beneath his uniform coat. Sinclair was close on his heels.

"I'll hide within range after I've collected what I need from the garage," Butterworth said. He put a hand on Jane's shoulder. "Be vigilant and be careful."

Wordlessly, Jane and Sinclair struck out for the gazebo. Sinclair had a satchel in one hand and a pair of binoculars in the other. Jane noticed that the sleek viewing device doubled as a digital camera.

"Brilliant," she said. "Can it record voices too?"

"On the movie setting, yes."

The pair maneuvered around the gazebo and took up a

position between a maple tree with a wide trunk and the dense needles of a spruce. Sinclair opened his satchel and pulled out two thin jackets with a camouflage pattern. "Put this on," he said.

Jane complied, feeling ridiculous and excited and more than a little scared. Her body was producing so much adrenaline that she could barely force her trembling fingers to zip the jacket closed. After a few minutes of tormenting silence, Sinclair's phone buzzed. He examined the screen. "Mr. Butterworth is nearby and Professor Price is en route."

Tensing, Jane focused her gaze on the path leading to the gazebo. Sure enough, Price was heading their way, a plastic bag from the gift shop dangling from his right hand. However, he found his way blocked by a tall man with dark hair.

"Edwin," Jane said. She was confused. "Does he know Desmond?"

"It certainly appears that way," Sinclair said.

Because they were too far away, Jane couldn't hear the exchange between the two men but she could see that Desmond Price felt threatened. He held out his hands in supplication and shrank away from Edwin. Edwin loomed over the professor, his every movement channeling menace.

"Desmond still has the plastic bag," Jane said. "Is Edwin the letter writer?"

She didn't want him to be. Could her best friend's brother have plotted against Jane and everyone in Storyton Hall just to get his hands on their copy of *Lost Letters*? Recalling how the illuminated manuscript had disappeared from the Italian museum where Edwin had been working, Jane wondered if she'd been a fool for not trying to find out what he knew about rare books. She remembered the face staring out at her from behind the dirty glass of the café window. Assessing her. Watching her. Was Eloise's brother a killer?

She saw Edwin jab Desmond once in the chest, and then he strode off toward the path leading to the main road.

"He's not our man," Sinclair said, tapping his phone

screen. "He was threatening Desmond—telling him to stay away from Eloise. He also made Desmond promise to send her a note of apology." Sinclair raised his brows. "I guess Mr. Alcott heard about the professor's behavior at the costume ball and didn't care for it at all."

Jane sighed in relief. "Thank goodness. I really didn't want him to be involved."

Desmond was heading their way again. He'd barely stepped onto the gazebo's wooden platform when Jane spotted Ned running across the lawn. He was carrying something in his right hand. From a distance, it looked very much like a book.

"No," Jane whispered. "Not Ned."

Drawing closer to Desmond Price, Ned called out, "Sir! Sir!"

Desmond swung around. His legs were bent slightly at the knees, and his hands came up by his sides. He was coiled and ready to spring.

Not Ned, Jane thought miserably. She repeated the mantra over and over again in her mind as if she could change the scene unfolding before her. Ned had been one of her favorites since he started working at Storyton Hall. His fellow staff members liked him, guests found him charming, and the twins adored him. Would he really betray everyone who cared for him just to buy a motorcycle and impress a pretty girl?

"What do you want?" she heard Desmond say in a guarded tone.

"You left this in the gift shop," Ned said, breathing hard. He handed Desmond the book. Jane couldn't read the title, but she knew from the rose pink cover that it was one of three Storyton Hall cookbooks available in the resort's shop. The book with the pink cover was filled with dessert recipes. It was the store's most popular item next to the twelve-pack of souvenir postcards.

"So I did. Thank you." Desmond accepted the book with a forced smile. Digging in his pocket, he came up with a crumpled bill, which he pressed into Ned's hand. The moment Ned departed, Desmond lowered himself on the gazebo's built-in bench and stared toward the entrance with a look of desperate anticipation.

Jane's shoulders sagged in relief. Ned wasn't involved. He was merely doing a guest a service. He'd probably been flirting with Sarah and because they were both distracted, neither of them had noticed that Desmond failed to collect all of his purchases. When they finally realized he'd left the cookbook behind, Ned had sprinted after him.

Checking her watch, Jane saw that it was three o'clock on the nose. Beside her, Sinclair raised his binoculars and did a sweep of the area. He then stopped and froze.

Putting his index finger to his lips to signal for quiet, he passed the binoculars to Jane. Taking a moment to absorb the magnified images, Jane looked toward the manor house and nearly shouted in dismay. The twins were home from school early and were pushing Aunt Octavia's wheelchair in their direction. With Ned chasing after the professor, there'd been no one to send the boys to Mrs. Hubbard. And unless they turned right where the path came to a T, they'd either scare off the letter writer or block his or her escape route.

Why are you coming this way? Jane wanted to yell at her aunt, but she clenched her fists and kept still. Sinclair reclaimed the binoculars, pressed the red record button, and stiffened.

Without the slightest noise, not even the merest scuff of a rubber sole against the stone path or the crack of a dry leaf underfoot, a woman dressed in a housekeeper's uniform suddenly appeared at the gazebo's entrance.

Jane's hand flew over her mouth as she tried to force a gasp back down her throat.

"Do you have my book?" Desmond asked.

"Do you have my money?" was the woman's retort.

He touched the bag at his right hip. "Let me see it first."

The woman reached into her apron pocket and pulled out a copy of *Lost Letters*. With blinding swiftness, Desmond grabbed it from her and savagely tore off the dust jacket. A small envelope fluttered onto the floorboards. He scooped it up and gave a little yelp of triumph.

"My money?" the woman persisted.

Ignoring her, Desmond opened the envelope, unfolded a single sheaf of beige paper, and began to read. His mouth curved into a smile and he pumped his fist in the air. "It's true!" he cried. "It does exist! And it's here, in Storyton Hall!"

"Give me my money." The woman's mouth twisted in an ugly snarl.

Desmond was instantly contrite. "My apologies. I am overcome. This discovery will change everything." He offered her the plastic bag. "It's exactly what we agreed upon."

The woman snatched the bag and peered inside. She then sat on the other end of the bench and laid out stacks of twenty-dollar bills. Fanning each stack, she grunted in satisfaction and tossed the money into the bag. "It was nice doing business with you, Professor. Next time you're in the mood for a play, drop by Felix's theater. It'll be coming under new management soon." A wicked grin spread over her face.

"Hi, Lizzie!" a boy shouted from the path. The greeting was echoed by a second boy.

Jane was about to leap forward when Sinclair clamped a hand over her arm. Shaking his head, he mimed someone blowing into a tube. Jane realized that he was trying to warn her that Butterworth had Lizzie in his sights and that she needed to remain still. But the presence of her sons had multiplied the level of the danger and all Jane could think about was putting herself between them and Lizzie.

The boys pushed Aunt Octavia's wheelchair right up to the gazebo's steps and then stopped. With no means of getting her into the structure, they moved to the side of her chair and stood at attention like two soldiers. Throwing their shoulders back and clicking their heels together, they put their hands to their foreheads in salute. "Permission to break for snack, General Octavia?" Hem asked.

"Permission granted." Aunt Octavia returned the salute.

In a flash, a syringe materialized in Lizzie's hand. Though she kept it by her side, her thumb was on the plunger. Jane could see it clearly, but she doubted either her aunt or sons could.

"We're in search of a private spot," Aunt Octavia told Lizzie breezily. On her lap, she had a book and a Tupperware container. She patted the plastic lid and, smiling at Desmond as if including him in her secret, said, "To divvy up the contraband."

"What?" Lizzie asked, her suspicious gaze fixed on Aunt Octavia and the boys.

"Cakes and cookies," Fitz said in a stage whisper and pointed at the food container. "She's not allowed to have them anymore but—"

"We're going to share the ones Mrs. Hubbard gave us," Hem finished his brother's thought. "We got out of school early because our teacher stapled her own leg. It was awesome!"

Jane was in agony. She wished Butterworth would shoot Lizzie already. If that toxin got on either of the twins' skin, there'd be no saving them. Reaching into Sinclair's pocket, she grabbed his phone and texted, *Take her down!*

"The gazebo is yours. I was just leaving," Desmond said and tried to scoot past Lizzie.

Jane had a clear view of Lizzie's face. A moment ago, she'd been composed and calm, but now she had the look of a cornered animal. Her eyes had gone so wide that Jane could see the whites from where she stood. She couldn't keep from lurching forward, instinctively sensing that Lizzie was about to lash out.

Proving Jane right, Lizzie turned to Desmond and raised the syringe. In the same instant, there was a whistling sound and then Lizzie faltered. Dumbfounded, she glanced down to see a dart protruding from the gift shop bag pressed against her hip. Her face wrinkled in fury and her lips pulled back in a terrifying sneer.

"No!" Jane screamed as she saw Lizzie lunge for the twins and Aunt Octavia.

There was another whistle. This time, the dart struck Lizzie in the arm. She shrieked and batted the dart to the ground. As Jane ran toward her sons, she saw Desmond climb over the side of gazebo and break into a run. Sterling jumped out of the woods and leapt onto the professor's back. Jane didn't stop to watch them fall. She was too focused on reaching her boys.

Lizzie was staggering, but if she took another two steps forward, she'd be close enough to fire a stream of toxin onto the twins or Aunt Octavia. Butterworth must have also recognized that the tranquilizer wasn't working fast enough because he vaulted over a fallen log and raced toward the gazebo.

In another second it would be too late.

Jane let out a terrible cry as she realized that she couldn't reach the twins in time.

"Lizzie! You've messed with the wrong family!" Aunt Octavia bellowed and, picking up the book on her lap, hurled it at the enraged housekeeper. A thick, heavy hardback, the book hit Lizzie squarely on the forehead. She dropped like a stone and the syringe rolled down the steps and under the front wheel of Aunt Octavia's wheelchair.

Jane didn't remember closing the distance to her boys. She gathered them in her arms and kissed them until they wriggled from her grasp. "Stop it, Mom!" The twins were confused and vexed. "What's going on?"

And then Hem pulled on Fitz's shirt and pointed up the path. "Look!"

Jane followed his gaze and saw Sheriff Evans and a trio of deputies sprinting in their direction.

"What happened?" the sheriff demanded breathlessly. He gestured first at Desmond Price, who was lying on the grass trussed up like a Thanksgiving turkey, and then at Lizzie's inert form.

"I threw the book at her. Literally!" Aunt Octavia exclaimed. And with a self-satisfied smile, she bit into a Linzer tart.

SEVENTEEN

By the time Jane, the Fins, and Aunt Octavia had given statements to a deputy, it was very late.

The shock over having been betrayed by Lizzie was slowly loosening its hold on Jane. Sipping a hot toddy in her aunt and uncle's living room, Jane was unexpectedly overcome with a mixture of anger and shame.

"How could we have been so blind?" she asked the room at large.

"She used her mother's name and social security number when applying for the housekeeper position," Sinclair said. "She duped us all. I should have screened her more carefully."

Butterworth shook his head. "We checked her references, she came up clean in our criminal database search, and she was most engaging during her job interview. As you said, she duped us all."

Aunt Octavia, who was looking rather wrung out, slapped a throw pillow. "The woman was an actress, for heaven's sake. She played her part with skill and consistency. Not only that, but Mrs. Pimpernel said that Lizzie was one of her best housekeepers. None of you is to blame. I am—" She suddenly stopped. "What is Lizzie's real name?"

"Janet Ingle. Her estranged mother was Elizabeth "Lizzie" Ingle. She was in hospice and passed away just last week." Butterworth handed Aunt Octavia a printout from the Hampden Theater Company in Cambridge, Massachusetts. "This is a list of the theater's staff. Felix Hampden was the general manager, and Janet Ingle served as assistant to the artistic director as well as a regular cast member. Though primarily a member of the chorus, she landed the leading lady role several times as well."

Jane thought back to the moment in which she'd teased Lizzie about joining the Storyton Hall Players. Lizzie had responded by saying that she hated the spotlight. She'd literally cowered at the idea of being onstage.

She was so convincing, Jane thought as she examined an image of Lizzie aka Janet Ingle as Lady Macbeth.

"That explains the *Arcadia* reference," Sinclair said. Our Lizzie knew a great deal about plays. I never thought I'd fail to decipher a literary clue, but I couldn't make the connection between Mrs. Chater and the gazebo." He turned to Jane. "You did that, my dear. By identifying the meeting place, you saved the day."

Aunt Octavia raised her chin and harrumphed.

"And your aim was most impressive, Mrs. Steward," Sinclair hurriedly continued. "The sheriff promised to return your copy of *Trim and Tasty: Cooking for Diabetics* as soon as he's able."

"He can keep it ad infinitum." Aunt Octavia scowled. "The best thing I could have done with that cookbook was use it as a weapon. I read some of the recipes aloud to the twins, and they were gagging all the way to the gazebo."

Jane tried to smother a smile. "Despite your act of heroism, you never got to enjoy those forbidden treats, did you?"

"No, but Mrs. Hubbard was kind enough to prepare

something equally delicious that still adhered to my new diet plan." Aunt Octavia sighed. "Don't you see? I don't mind the modified food. What I dislike is being told what I can or cannot have. I'm too old to change my ways." Suddenly, her eyes filled with tears. "But because of my actions, the twins were put in harm's way. Can you ever forgive me, Jane?"

"Don't be silly, there's nothing to forgive." Jane set down her drink and moved to embrace her aunt. "It'll take time for both of us to adjust to our new lifestyles. For the moment, I'm just trying to figure out what to tell the guests. I've drafted a letter, but coming up with the appropriate language was impossible."

At that point, her uncle returned from checking on Fitz and Hem. He nodded at Jane, indicating that the boys were fast asleep in the spare bedroom. Jane had feared that they'd be upset after watching a guest and a staff member led away in handcuffs, but the twins were more excited than anything. They couldn't wait to go to school the next day and give their classmates a blow-by-blow account. And when the sheriff questioned the boys, he'd barely been able to get a word in edgewise. Basking in the attention, Hem even had the nerve to tell Evans that he'd always felt there was something shady about Lizzie, whereupon Fitz, who was not to be outdone by his brother, added that Lizzie had shifty eyes.

Jane handed the letter to her uncle and he read it quickly, stroking his chin as he did so.

"This is well put," he said, returning the letter to Jane. "After all, we have no precedent on how to inform our guests that a murderer and her accomplice have been removed from our premises and are in custody at the local sheriff's department."

"Will all the guests leave the moment they read this?" Jane stared at the lines she'd typed before joining her aunt and uncle and the Fins for hot toddies and a chance to talk through their dramatic afternoon.

"Stuff and nonsense," Aunt Octavia said. "A few ninnies will demand a refund, but when we refuse to give them a penny, they'll march right off to the dining room and line up for the breakfast buffet."

Sinclair nodded. "I agree. After all, the media is likely to descend upon Storyton Hall tomorrow, and most of the guests will be too enthralled by the drama to depart."

Butterworth gave Jane a wan smile. "In truth, they're more likely to put on their best clothes and promenade before the television cameras. You'll see. The south lawn will look like George Seurat's *A Sunday Afternoon on the Island of La Grande Jatte*."

Jane thought of Seurat's tranquil scene and managed a limp grin. "Thank you. All of you. Our problems are far from over, but at least our guests are safe. And so is our secret." Her eyes widened in sudden alarm. "Or is it? What happened to the letter Desmond Price found inside the dust-cover of *Lost Letters*? Does Sheriff Evans have it?"

Sterling reached into his pocket and retrieved a small envelope. "I liberated this from Professor Price after binding his hands. I also told him that if he discussed its contents with another living soul, I would visit him in prison carrying a vial of poison dart frog toxin."

"Good show," Butterworth said as Jane took the envelope. Gingerly, she removed the letter and read the single paragraph written in tidy cursive on creamy white cardstock.

Dearest P—

Enclosed is the manuscript of Umberto Ferrari's last case. It is unlike anything I've written. And by that I mean that the darkness my little Italian detective has been fighting against throughout his storied career finally overcomes him. He has seen such wickedness and has absorbed the pain and grief of those whose loved ones were taken through acts of violence. I fear that our world is on the brink of darkness as well. Richard believes that war is imminent, and so I am asking you to keep this for me until we are all safe again. Perhaps I will feel more hopeful once the danger has passed. Perhaps I will give Inspector Ferrari a better ending. I suspect we will all have had our fill of death by the time this war is over . . .

Jane swallowed the sob that threatened to bubble up in her throat. Adela Dundee's last line echoed her own feelings. There had been enough death at Storyton Hall. Enough pain and fear. Like Adela, Jane wondered if she had any reason to hold on to hope. She was afraid that not only would her current guests leave, but those planning future visits would cancel their reservations. Eventually, Jane would have to let staff members go and watch in dismay as the manor house and grounds fell into disrepair. It was bad enough now, what with the roof issues, decrepit folly, and overgrown orchard, but Jane knew that things could get much worse.

"Are you all right, my dear?" Her uncle put a hand on her shoulder.

Jane glanced down at the letter. "Adela concludes by telling Percy that she might never reclaim the manuscript and that he should not surrender it to anyone but her. After thanking him for many memorable visits to Storyton Hall, she signs off with her initial.

"Ferrari kills himself," Aunt Octavia said in a leaden voice. "I read the manuscript this afternoon when I was done giving my statement to that nice deputy. Aloysius had to fetch it for me, just like he fetched Storyton Hall's copy of *Lost Letters* for me to read. The book that started all this trouble."

"Both the book containing Adela's letter to Percy Steward *and* her undiscovered manuscript came from up there?" Jane pointed overhead.

"Dear Percy filed the manuscript in the secret library under *D* as expected, but he also wrapped it in butcher paper, bound it with twine, and wrote a note saying that its contents were for Adela Dundee's eyes alone." She threw out her hands in a gesture of helplessness. "I never knew we possessed this jewel. We have so many literary marvels in that library, Jane, that it would take two lifetimes to read them all. Anyway, you know how terribly fond I am of Ferrari, and I just had to know what happened to him in that manuscript." Her gaze turned steely. "I will tell you, but you must never breathe a word of its contents to anyone."

Jane was still reeling from her aunt's opening line. "Ferrari commits suicide?"

Aunt Octavia nodded. "Yes. He returns to his boyhood town, a tiny fishing village on the shores of Adriatic Sea, and begins to drink heavily. He has no family, no friends outside of work, and the woman he's loved his entire life has married another man. So Umberto Ferrari, the character beloved by millions over the world, chases a handful of tranquilizers with a bottle of Chianti and walks into the sea."

"That's completely out of character!" Jane cried. "Ferrari is the quintessential optimist. He's merry and flirtatious and brilliant. He possesses an unflagging spirit and demonstrates unwavering faith in himself and in his fellow man. He always looked for the good in people. Even in those who'd done grievous wrongs. He found something redeeming in everyone. That's why readers devour Adela Dundee's books. They want to see Umberto Ferrari turn chaos into order, and he never let us down." Jane shook her head. "To have him commit suicide? That would have crushed so many people's spirits. Especially with the world at war."

Sinclair nodded. "Would you ever consent to having that book brought to light?"

Jane suddenly realized why some of the items in Storyton Hall's secret collection remained just that: a secret. Turning to her aunt, she said, "I see what you mean now. After the war, Adela Dundee wrote other Umberto Ferrari books. She aged him. Had him retire and work as a consultant. He continued to be the man we loved, but he slowed down. He grew old with dignity and never, not for one second, regretted his calling." She tapped the letter. "But how did this end up inside *Lost Letters*? Why wasn't it kept with the unpublished manuscript?"

Aunt Octavia released a low moan, her hands fluttering in front of her face like startled birds. "Aloysius?" she called. "I need to rest now. Help me to the bedroom."

"Of course, my darling."

Concerned and confused, Jane watched her uncle, Butterworth, and Sterling wrestle her aunt into the wheelchair.

"Good night, Aunt Octavia," Jane said softly. "I hope you feel better in the morning."

Her aunt gazed at her tenderly. "No matter what happens next, don't forget that you succeeded in keeping our secret safe. It was your first test and you passed."

When she was gone, Jane looked at Sinclair. "Aunt Octavia put the letter in the book, didn't she? Why?"

"She made a simple mistake," Sinclair said. "Your aunt wanted the copy of *Lost Letters* she'd purchased from the bookstore to serve as the scavenger hunt prize to remain in pristine condition, so she asked your uncle to see if there was another copy in the secret library she might read. The book was there and Adela Dundee's letter to Percival was tucked between the pages. Percival was a fine man, but he had an acute case of absentmindedness toward the end of his life, so it doesn't surprise me that the letter wasn't properly filed."

Jane stifled a smile. She knew Sinclair disliked disorder more than anything. "Go on," she prompted.

Sinclair inclined his head. "Your aunt took the letter out and, seeing that it was still sealed, laid it on her library table with no intention of opening it. The envelope you're holding was in plain sight and I believe Lizzie entered the apartment while your aunt was dozing on the sofa, saw the envelope, and recognized the handwriting as belonging to Dundee. She must have contacted Felix Hampden immediately." He gestured at Jane's right hand. "Later, your aunt stuck that missive under the dust jacket of Lost Letters, gift-wrapped the wrong copy, and didn't realize her mistake until her collapse in the Jane Austen Parlor. In fact, I suspect she was already feeling unwell when she wrapped the book. Diabetics can be afflicted by a mental fog when they experience extreme fluctuations in their glucose levels."

Jane sagged deeper into her chair. "Now I see. Lizzie opened the letter and knew that there was an undiscovered Adela Dundee manuscript somewhere in Storyton Hall." She paused, thought for a moment, and then frowned. "But the timing doesn't make sense. Lizzie's been working for us for months, so either she or Felix Hampden must have suspected the truth long before the Murder and Mayhem Week. But how could either of them have heard of the manuscript's existence all the way in Boston?"

"We don't have all the answers yet," Sinclair said.

"No wonder Aunt Octavia's health declined so quickly once she heard that Storyton's copy of *Lost Letters* had been given to Felix Hampden," Jane said. "She must have suffered terribly from guilt."

Sinclair got to his feet. "There's been enough suffering under this roof for the time being. We should all get some rest. Tomorrow is sure to be a taxing day."

Jane said good night to her uncle and the Fins and then made her way through the hushed hallways to her office. She knew she wouldn't be able to sleep with so many questions flitting through her mind. There was a connection between Desmond, Felix, and Lizzie and she had to at least attempt to find what it was.

Giving the night clerk a friendly wave, she entered her office and turned on her computer. Next, she searched through the Harvard University website until she found Desmond Price's faculty page. She clicked on the link and then paused when his picture appeared on the top of her screen. She noted the smug tilt of his chin and the look of superiority in his eyes and shook her head. "You could have had a good life. If only you'd poured all that energy into teaching, you'd have been an incredible professor. You could have influenced the next generation. Instead, you became obsessed by a tenuous familial connection to a famous writer."

She clicked on a link listing the classes Desmond had taught over the course of his career and was astounded by the breadth of his expertise. "Nineteenth Century Literature," "Twentieth Century Literature," "Literary Theory," "British Literature," "Romanticism," "Victorian Poetry," "Drama." Jane tapped her lips and stared at the word "Drama."

"Eloise might have been on to something when she said 'The play's the thing'," Jane said, feeling a tingle of exhilaration. "Cambridge isn't far from Boston. Desmond and Felix Hampden could have met at Hampden Theater."

Jane put Desmond's name and the words 'Hampden Theater,' in Google's search box. She was rewarded with a *Boston Magazine* article covering the annual Hampden Theater Benefit. The article was mainly a pictorial piece highlighting the power couples who'd come to support the theater. There were a dozen photographs of silver-haired men in tuxedos and middle-aged women in sparkling gowns. Jane studied a few of the captions and was surprised to find that most of the benefactors were from Cambridge. The article was redolent with quotes from these high-society patrons praising the quality of the theater company's performances.

"You should have stuck to what you did best, Mr. Hampden." Jane wagged a finger at an image of the man who had become the perfect embodiment of Umberto Ferrari. She scrolled to the bottom of the page in order to view the rest of the photographs and when her gaze fell on the second-to-last image, she inhaled sharply. There was Felix Hampden, wearing a top hat and a wide grin, shaking hands with a tall man with an arrogant stare. Desmond Price. The caption clearly identified both men as well as the woman standing at Hampden's elbow. Janet Ingle. "Also known as

Lizzie," Jane said and picked up the phone. "Sheriff?" she said when a male voice came on the line. "It's Jane Steward. I'm sorry to be calling so late, but there's something I think you should know."

By the time Jane left her office, it was quite late. Whispering good night to the front desk clerk, Jane walked through the silent lobby to the back door. When she stepped out onto the terrace, the chill in the air was a shock. But its briskness felt good to Jane. The cold sting against her cheeks and the quickening of her blood reminded her of her own vitality. Drawing in a deep breath, she looked up at the night sky. Thousands of stars throbbed in the velvety blackness, and a high moon shone down on Milton's gardens.

"How beautiful," said a man's voice from behind Jane.

Starting, she swiveled to find Edwin Alcott sitting in a wicker chair. Before she could speak, he got to his feet and held out his hands as if he were approaching a cornered animal. "Forgive me," he whispered. "I didn't mean to frighten you."

"What are you doing here?" Jane asked sharply. The scare had made her angry.

Coming to stand beside her, he placed his coat over her shoulders. "I wanted to make sure you were all right. Eloise was here earlier and was told you were unavailable. I promised her that I'd wait on this porch until you appeared. All night if need be." He quickly averted his gaze and gestured at the wide swath of grass separating the manor house from the cottages and outbuildings. "May I walk you home?"

Touched by his consideration, Jane nodded.

They moved down the stone path in silence. There was a pleasant stillness to the grounds, as if all the trees and plants were slumbering. The insect drone was muted and an owl hooted twice and fell quiet. The somnolent atmosphere should have increased Jane's weariness, but she found Edwin's closeness was both alarming and invigorating.

"I saw you earlier," she whispered. "With Desmond Price."

"Then you saw me showing restraint," Edwin said. "If I'd known what a cad that man was at the ball, I'd have dealt with him then and there. Eloise only told me today."

Jane laughed softly. "And you came rushing to Storyton Hall to defend her honor? Remind me never to make you angry."

"Or me, you. After all, the last time we met, you were filling a straw target with arrows."

Recalling how she'd suspected Edwin of being somehow involved in the murders, Jane felt a rush of shame. When they reached her stoop, she put a hand on his arm. "I haven't been especially welcoming to you since your return to Storyton. I'm sorry."

Edwin took her keys and unlocked the front door. He then stepped back, making it clear that he didn't expect to be asked inside. "I'll accept your apology on one condition."

Jane's heart raced. Was he going to kiss her? Without moving, she studied the planes of his handsome face, noting how the soft moonlight turned his hair a bluish black. She decided that she wouldn't mind being kissed by Edwin Alcott. In fact, she believed she would enjoy it immensely. "What's your condition?" she asked, slightly embarrassed by the huskiness in her voice.

"When things calm down, I'd like to meet you in the ballroom while the band is rehearsing. I'd like you to wear that silver dress. And I'd like to dance with you. Alone."

Jane stared into his eyes, glittering like shards of onyx, and yearned to touch him. She wanted to run her fingers through his wavy hair, trace the line of his jaw, and slide her hands over his shoulders.

You are the guardian of Storyton Hall, she reminded herself sternly. *A murderer in your employ was arrested today, and tomorrow, every guest will wake to find your letter slid under his or her door. This is not the time for romance. Or lust. Or whatever it is.*

Swallowing her desire, Jane handed Edwin his coat. "A dance. With the room to ourselves." She smiled. "I look forward to it. Thank you for coming to check on me, and please tell Eloise that I'll call her in the morning. Tell her not to worry. I can handle whatever tomorrow brings."

"I believe you can, Jane Steward," Edwin said. With his gaze never leaving Jane's face, he grinned and performed a rakish bow. And then he was gone.

EIGHTEEN

The next morning, Jane filled a thermos with dark roast coffee and stood at the reception desk, her spine pole-straight and her shoulders thrown back, awaiting the on-slaught of irate guests. As Aunt Octavia predicted, several people came forward in hopes of a discount. They all cited "the shocking events that occurred during our stay" as cause for tearing up their bill, but Jane produced a regretful smile and told them that while there would be no refunds, the guests were welcome to check out early without penalty.

No one accepted her offer. A wily couple threatened to speak with the media about her lack of contrition, but when the first of the television trucks pulled up behind a line of Storyton Hall Rolls-Royces, the disgruntled guests experienced an immediate change of heart. Like everyone else, they wanted to see what would happen next.

"It's such a thrill!" one woman said to another as they served themselves coffee. "We came here to be immersed in murder and mayhem and here we are! Right smack in the middle of a *real* mystery!"

"They're too interested in the story to leave," Jane said

to Butterworth after he'd issued a statement and then barred the door to yet another reporter.

Butterworth nodded. "I believe Miss Alcott was correct in her prediction." His expression turned grave. "Our guests don't realize that a murder investigation can cast a very long shadow. Lives are ruined. Secrets are laid bare. There is no privacy. No shelter. Not when justice is at stake." He glanced at the people milling around the lobby. "They didn't see what murder did to Mr. Hampden or to Ms. McKee. If they had, they wouldn't be buzzing about like bees. They'd be in their rooms drinking cup after cup of strong tea and trying to read a well-loved book. They'd be looking for comfort."

"Instead, they're asking to reserve rooms for next year's Murder and Mayhem Week," Jane said. "Honestly, I don't know what to feel other than a deep sense of shame. Two people died under this roof. We failed to keep them safe. And yet I can't help but be relieved. For Storyton Hall. For my staff. I was hoping to merely survive this travesty, but now it seems we'll end up profiting from it. That feels wrong to me."

Butterworth regarded her with affection. "I wouldn't have chosen to trade two lives—three, if you include Miss Hart's—for a new roof either, but we must make the best of a tragic situation. That's what you've done since you took over as resort manager. It's why you'll be an excellent guardian. Maybe the best we've ever had."

Jane wished she shared Butterworth's conviction. Though she handled the guests and the members of the media with sincerity, courtesy, and grace, she knew she'd be unable to devote her complete attention to any task until Lizzie and Desmond Price confessed their crimes or were sent to jail to await trial.

That afternoon, after Butterworth had forced the journalists to retreat to the other side of the main gates, Jane drove Sterling's favorite Rolls to the sheriff's station. The majority of her guests were either settled in a reading room, taking an archery class with Sterling, or sampling foods from famous mystery novels with Mrs. Hubbard, so Jane felt she could escape for an hour. She wanted reassurance from the sheriff that the two villains in his holding cells had no chance of obtaining their freedom. After speaking with Evans, she planned to drive the twins home from school. She didn't want anyone from the press talking to her sons about the murders. That was her job.

Jane parked at the Pickled Pig and walked the three blocks to the station. The squat stone building looked more like an English cottage than the village's hub of law enforcement, but Jane strode by the wrought iron garden benches, yellow climbing roses, and wheelbarrow filled with pumpkins and gourds without paying them any mind.

Inside, she found Sheriff Evans speaking to a deputy in low tones. As soon as he saw Jane, he waved for her to follow him back to his office.

"How are you, Ms. Steward?" he asked in a gentle voice, gesturing at a pair of side chairs near the window.

"I'm relieved to know that the killer and her accessory are in custody," she said. "And our guests are taking things in stride. However, I still feel very anxious. I guess I'm looking for confirmation that this nightmare is truly over."

"I do have good news to impart." The sheriff sat opposite Jane and tucked his thumbs into his utility belt. "In the hopes of getting a more lenient sentence, Desmond Price has provided us with a full confession."

Jane felt the air rush out of her lungs. "Thank heavens! Was the article I found on the Hampden Theater benefit helpful?"

"It most certainly was." The sheriff beamed at her. "It tipped the scales in our favor, as a matter of fact. During our previous interviews, Mr. Price denied knowing Mr. Hampden. Repeatedly. This morning, he had a change of tune. When I placed a copy of the photograph from the benefit on the table, he crumpled. Shortly afterward, he told us all we needed to know."

"What happened that night?" Jane was on tenterhooks.

"Mr. Price asked Mr. Hampden if he'd be interested in applying his unique skill set in exchange for fifty thousand dollars." The sheriff shook his head. "According to the professor, everyone in Cambridge viewed Hampden as a crook, but none of them cared because he produced such excellent plays."

Jane raised her brows. "Desmond had that much money to offer as payment? I was under the impression he wasn't exactly flush with cash."

"He raised it by taking a second mortgage and selling anything of value. He gave Mr. Hampden ten thousand up front and Janet Ingle was immediately dispatched to Storyton Hall to apply for a job. I believe she planned to cut out Mr. Hampden from the onset. If she'd found the manuscript the professor was after, I think she would have collected the balance from him and left Mr. Hampden in the lurch." Sherriff Evans smirked. "Ms. Ingle hasn't said much, but she did admit that her lifelong dream has been to open her own theater."

"What manuscript were they looking for?" Jane asked innocently.

"One written by a lady mystery author named Adela Dundee." The sheriff shrugged. "I only read nonfiction, so I don't know her work, but I take it she's quite famous. Mr. Price was under the impression that an undiscovered manuscript was hidden somewhere in Storyton Hall and that if he found it, he'd be compensated by Adela Dundee's descendants. Apparently, he's been trying to win their favor for years."

Jane thought of the small boy on the cover of Desmond Price's much-criticized *Tea with Adela Dundee*. "How sad. But where did he get the notion that this manuscript could be found at Storyton Hall?"

"He cites two sources," Evans said. "The first being a letter in the book edited by Miss Hart, and the second, Miss Hart herself. Mr. Price and Miss Hart had a long conversation at an academic conference they both attended when Miss Hart was still teaching. That same evening, the professor invited Miss Hart to join him at the hotel bar. He bought her several drinks and pumped the rather inebriated young lady for information. Her replies, though cryptic, confirmed his theory that the manuscript existed and had been mailed to Storyton decades ago."

"I wish I knew where it was." Jane managed a dry laugh. "I'm a huge Adela Dundee fan."

Sheriff Evans shrugged. "There's no conclusive proof that it's real, Ms. Steward. Even if it made it to Storyton Hall, who can say what's become of it? It could have been in some attic room being nibbled by mice for the past fifty years."

"We do not have vermin in our resort," Jane chastised the sheriff and then smiled to show that she wasn't truly offended. "I can understand Desmond Price's interest in the manuscript. But what of Moira McKee? How did she fit into this grim picture?"

"According to the professor, Miss McKee was after the same thing. She wanted to auction the manuscript to the highest bidder and use the money to save her school. Janet—"

"Can you please call her Lizzie?" Jane interrupted. "I've come to know her by that name."

"Certainly. To continue, Lizzie decided to eliminate any and all competition. She'd already used the syringe taken from Mr. Collins's medicine kit to kill Mr. Hampden, so she felt confident she could pull off another murder and have it appear as an accidental death. Both Mr. Hampden and Ms. McKee suffered from seasonal allergies, and Lizzie was able to inject the frog toxin into their nasal spray."

Jane instinctively covered her own nose with her hand. "That's awful! And horribly cruel."

"Very cruel," Evans agreed. "And most effective. The toxin shot straight into their nasal cavities. The victims would have experienced its effects almost immediately and been unable to call for help."

Jane fell silent. She tried to block the memory of Moira McKee lying on the bathroom floor, but she remembered the smear of bright red on the toilet as if she were gazing down at it right now. Images of Felix Hampden's twisted limbs and clawlike hands followed and she shuddered. Willing herself back to the present, she said, "Lizzie killed two people for forty thousand dollars?"

"The number may be closer to a hundred grand," the sheriff said. "She admitted knowing the combination to Mr. Hampden's safe. She was confident that he had over fifty thousand in cash, treasury bonds, and stolen jewelry squirreled away."

Jane gave him a baffled look. "How did she know that Kevin's syringe was filled with poison dart frog toxin? How did she even come to find it in the first place?"

Evans sighed. "Astonishing, isn't it? To think that Mr. Collins traveled with something so lethal. Mind you, this is all coming secondhand from Desmond Price, but the story he tells is that Lizzie learned quite a bit about Mr. Collins and his research from Alice Hart. The two ladies became friendly during Miss Hart's visit. The only thing Miss Hart refused to divulge was her real reason for visiting Storyton. Fearing that the girl would leave without sharing what she knew about the Adela Dundee manuscript, Lizzie shot an arrow near the horse Miss Hart was riding. Her intent was to injure the girl—for her to suffer a broken limb or another type of injury that would have her laid up for a few days. Sadly, that was not Miss Hart's fate."

"So it was all happenstance. If Kevin hadn't packed the syringe. If he'd stayed in another hotel. If Lizzie—"

"She would have found another method, Ms. Steward. She was determined to have that money, no matter what the cost."

Jane groaned. "If only we'd never given her a job, but she seemed desperate to support her ailing mother. I am such a fool!"

"No," Evans said. "Kindness isn't foolishness." He got up and walked to the bulletin board hanging above a bank of file cabinets. "This is a poster of the FBI's most-wanted fugitives. These men are here because they made devastatingly terrible choices. They destroyed lives. Including their own. Janet Ingle was motivated by greed. She repaid your generosity by murdering two of your guests. She and Desmond Price are to blame. Not you. In fact, Mr. Butterworth gave me a copy of her employment application and I called the people she listed as references. They were all actors in Janet's company. You wouldn't have known that they lived in Massachusetts because the numbers belonged to disposable cell phones."

"She was clever." Jane felt despondent again. "Clever and devious. I'm going to have to be more careful from now on."

Evan frowned. "Oh, I don't know about that. After all, her plan was foiled by you, a butler, a chauffeur, a librarian, and an octogenarian in a wheelchair. I'd say you've got things well in hand."

The warmth in the sheriff's tone coaxed a smile from Jane. "I need to pick up my boys now, but thank you for filling me in. I hope Lizzie confesses and we can avoid a courtroom trial."

"I have a feeling she just might." The sheriff lowered his voice to a conspiratorial whisper. "You see, I told her that my brother runs the women's prison and that I'd make sure she was given a lifetime of latrine duty should she choose to remain uncooperative. That woman loathed being a housekeeper at Storyton Hall."

Evans escorted Jane to the door and wished her a good afternoon.

Feeling more hopeful than she'd thought possible, Jane stopped in the Pickled Pig to buy the boys old-fashioned candy sticks. She'd barely made it to the bulk candy display before the Hogg brothers and several other locals crowded around her. Jane expected them to ply her for details about the murders, but they didn't. Every last one of them touched her in some way—a pat on the hand or the shoulder—asked if she was all right, and offered to help her in any way. Their thoughtfulness brought tears to her eyes and she could have hugged them all in gratitude, but she had to hurry to reach the twins' school before the final bell.

She arrived just as the children were spilling from the building in a cacophonous burst of shouts and squeals. Fitz and Hem spotted her immediately and ran into her open arms.

"We're famous!" Hem cried. "Everyone was talking about Lizzie today!"

"How she *killed* people!" Fitz added. "And how Aunt Octavia stopped her!"

The twins bounced up and down with every exclamation, and Jane knew that even though they were very young, she had to impress upon them the seriousness of what had happened over the past few days.

Leading them to a nearby bench, she handed them the butterscotch candy sticks and told them that sometimes people could be twisted by their own desires. She explained that Lizzie's greed had grown out of control, making her willing to do horrible things in exchange for money. Jane went on to say that even though TV vans had showed up at Storyton Hall and that the resort was all anyone could talk about, murder was never cause for celebration. It was, she said in a solemn voice, the worst crime one human could commit against another. When the twins' faces lost their animated glow, Jane felt that she'd made her point.

The boys sucked their candy sticks and frowned, trying to process what they'd heard.

"It won't change, will it?" Fitz asked after a long silence.

Jane saw the trepidation in his eyes and picked up his small hand. "What won't change?"

"Home," Hem answered for his brother. "Everything."

Carefully considering her reply, Jane stared at the blue hills rising over the trees. The October sun lit the leaves, and in their autumnal colors Jane saw the burnished copper fixtures in the Jane Austen Parlor, the vermilion cushions in the Ian Fleming Lounge, and the jar of saffron in Mrs. Hubbard's spice cabinet. "Things always change, but as long as we have one another, everything will be all right."

The twins relaxed and nodded. Hem put his hand over Jane's and the three of them sat quietly for a long moment, drawing strength and solace from one another.

Eventually, the twins grew fidgety and told Jane that they were ready to load their bikes into the car. When that was done, they held a brief conference and turned to Jane with solemn expressions.

"Mom," Fitz began. "Since we helped Aunt Octavia stop the bad lady, we decided—"

"That you should double our allowance," Hem said and then added, "for a whole month."

Jane laughed. And that's when she felt the world right itself again. She was Jane Steward. Mother of two. Manager of Storyton Hall. Book club hostess. Avid reader. She was also the guardian of one of the greatest secrets of humankind.

Inhaling a lungful of mountain air, she gazed at the picturesque village spread out before her and smiled. She was ready to face whatever awaited her at Storyton Hall. She was ready to accept the role she'd inherited as a guardian. And when her work was done, she planned to spend the evening with a mug of herbal tea and a good book.

"I think I'll start with *The Mystery of Edwin Drood*," she murmured into the wind. "The Storyton Hall edition. The one with an ending."

EPILOGUE

The first Tuesday after the Murder and Mayhem Week, the Cover Girls gathered in Jane's kitchen to share a meal and discuss Kate Morton's *The Forgotten Garden*.

Because Jane's friends had all brought garden-themed dishes, supper was a selection of sumptuous vegetarian tapas. Jane's favorites were the fried eggplant triangles, sweet potato biscuits, cheese and tomato two-bite pies, and bruschetta with goat cheese, garlic, and capers. By the time Mabel opened the refrigerator to show them the maple pumpkin mousse she'd made, Jane felt ready to burst.

"Let's take a break," she suggested. "I'll brew some decaf and we can chat while we digest a bit."

"I've been saving my best news until after we ate," Mrs. Pratt said as she took a seat on the sofa, primly folded her legs to one side, and smoothed her skirt. Jane tried to picture her with Gavin, the quintessential outdoorsman, and failed.

Violet flopped next to Mrs. Pratt. "Does it have anything to do with Janet Ingle?"

"Yes! She was transferred to a women's correctional facility over the mountain today."

"That's great news," Eloise said, taking her customary spot on the rug. She liked to sit with her back to the bookcase. "Even though she was locked up, it gave me the creeps having her in our village."

Betty nodded. "She's the subject of every conversation at the pub. Our regulars have taken to calling her the Murderous Maid."

Several book club members laughed, but Jane couldn't find any humor in having had two violent deaths occur in her ancestral home. She knew that her friends were being purposely flippant to keep the evening from turning macabre, but she wished they'd change the subject.

"I'm glad she's gone," Anna said. "I almost sent Randall to visit her. He could have lectured her on avoiding the common cold. It's his favorite subject these days. He's been cornering our customers any chance he gets."

Mabel snorted. "Tell me about it! I went to the pharmacy to pick up a bottle of aspirin and that goat's milk lotion I like so much and Randall practically vaulted over the counter to tell me how I could protect myself this winter by purchasing a humidifier. Pretending I had an incoming call on my cell phone, I turned my tail and ran."

This time, Jane joined in the laughter. "No wonder he still lives with his mother. She's the only person who can stand to listen to him."

The women made a few more jokes at Randall's expense before Mrs. Pratt returned to the topic of murder. "We've read every detail in the papers, Jane, but I have unanswered questions. For example, did your aunt get her book back?"

"She did. Minus the dust jacket." Jane described the meeting between Lizzie and Desmond Price, omitting the presence of the Fins and the discovery of the Adela Dundee letter.

"But why was everyone after Aunt Octavia's book? Even if it had been signed by Alice Hart, it wouldn't be worth much," Eloise said. "I love books more than life itself, but I wouldn't kill for one. People don't commit murder over books."

Jane thought of the priceless collection hidden in the uppermost room of Storyton Hall and had to clamp her lips together to keep from disagreeing with her best friend. She knew without a doubt that certain people would do anything to access the items in that library, let alone possess them.

"Sheriff Evans wanted to know the same thing," she said. "He let me look at Aunt Octavia's copy of *Lost Letters*." She shrugged. "It didn't seem remarkable in any way, and though both Desmond and Lizzie claimed there was an important letter tucked between the pages, it was never found. In fact, the book was identical to the one Lizzie had purchased before she started working at Storyton Hall. Lizzie switched her copy with Aunt Octavia's in hopes of discovering a treasure, and she must have been incredibly disappointed." After speaking this untruth, Jane dropped her gaze. Thankfully, none of her friends noticed her discomfort.

"A missing letter? So the mystery is only partially solved!" Phoebe exclaimed.

Betty waved her off. "That bit about the letter must be a lie. Desmond and Lizzie or Janet or whoever she is would have made up anything to save their own skins. It's the same at the pub. Give people who are angry or worried or scared a few drinks and they'll start spinning all sorts of yarns. If I believed half the tall tales I hear, I'd be mad as a March hare."

"Speaking of lunacy, what ever happened to Alice's young man?" Anna asked.

"Kevin Collins? He's finishing his sabbatical at Oxford." Jane walked into the kitchen and started spooning coffee grounds into a paper filter. "I think he's going to be all right. He just—"

"Cracked like an egg." Mabel made a crunching noise.

"I was going to say that his heartbreak morphed into something beyond grief. Something dark and dangerous. But Sheriff Evans told me that the Oxford professor Kevin's working with is mentoring him. He took Kevin to a counselor almost as soon as he got off the plane. When Kevin returns stateside, he'll have to fulfill hours of community service for the unconscionable act of taking frog toxin from his lab."

"To think they plan to make medicine with that stuff." Phoebe gave a dramatic shiver.

"Poisons can be beneficial," Anna said. "Did you know snake venom is being used to treat minor heart attacks?"

Mrs. Pratt grimaced. "I believe I'd prefer the heart attack."

The topic turned to homeopathic remedies, and then someone asked Jane how Aunt Octavia was progressing with her physical therapy and new diet. Jane reported that her aunt had scared off another therapist and that Mrs. Hubbard had caught her in the kitchens at five in the morning.

"She'd somehow gotten herself into her wheelchair, out of her apartment, and into the elevator," Jane said. "There she was, wearing her nightgown and bunny slippers, eating ice cream right out of the carton."

"Speaking of dessert, I'm ready for mine." Mabel joined Jane in the kitchen. She dropped scoops of maple pumpkin mousse into bowls and then added a garnish Jane couldn't identify. Mabel caught her eye and smiled. "Pumpkin seed brittle. You'll love it."

Jane did. Everyone did. The smooth, rich mousse was bursting with fresh pumpkin flavor, and the crunch of the brittle provided the perfect contrast in texture.

When dessert was finished and the coffee cups drained, the women debated over which *F* title to read next. Suggestions included *Faustus*, *For Whom the Bell Tolls*, and "The Fall of the House of Usher," but Eloise dismissed them all.

"For Jane's sake, let's stay away from the morose stuff," she said. "No devils or violent death. How about a sweeping drama instead?"

"I've got it!" Mrs. Pratt snapped her fingers. "*The Forsythe Saga.*"

Several of the book club members shouted their agreement.

"We can rent the miniseries and have our own weekly film festival," Phoebe said.

The women peered at their smart phones or pocket calendars and typed or penciled in a series of dates. After that, they loaded Jane's dishwasher, washed and dried the plates they'd brought to her house, and wished her good night. Except for Eloise, they left en masse.

Jane stood at her kitchen window and watched her friends disappear into the night. The sounds of their bubbly chatter lingered for a moment, only to be whisked away by the wind.

"You seem like you're doing okay," Eloise said, coming to stand beside her.

"I'm getting there." Jane pointed at the wall calendar hanging next to her refrigerator. "I'm going to be so busy from now until January that I won't have time to dwell on the events of the Murder and Mayhem Week." She turned to Eloise. "You were right. Because Storyton Hall has been all over the television and Internet, the reservations have been pouring in. We even increased the rates for the holiday season by twenty-five percent and people kept booking rooms. We only have a few left from now until after New Year's. And I'm already starting to plan the next theme week. A Valentine's theme called Romance in Residence."

"Storyton Hall will be filled with couples in love?" Eloise asked, looking dismayed. "Count me out of the activities. I want to meet single men, remember?"

"It isn't geared toward couples," Jane said. "It's for writers and readers. The American Romance Writers Guild wants to hold their annual conference here. They want to have panels, lectures, fashion shows, contests, wine and chocolate tastings, and a competition of the male cover models."

"Now you're talking! Count me back in, okay?" Eloise took her coat from the back of a kitchen stool and pulled it on. "And no matter how swamped you get, just make sure that you can still spare an hour or two for me and our Cover Girl meetings."

Jane pretended to be offended. "Like anything can hold a candle to my girl time!"

Laughing, Eloise grabbed her car keys from the counter. "Edwin wants to cook for the two of us this weekend. He's trying to decide what to put on his menu. Are you free Saturday for brunch?"

Jane thought of the archery lesson she and the boys had scheduled. After Sterling's lesson, she'd start an intensive course of study with Butterworth on interpreting body language. Despite her new demands as the guardian of Storyton Hall, Jane refused to sacrifice her entire social life. Besides, she wanted to see Edwin again. "I can be at your place by eleven."

"It's a date." Eloise gave Jane a quick hug and left, humming as she stepped onto the path of moonlit stone.

The following night, Jane put the twins to bed and tidied the kitchen. She then poured herself a glass of wine and waited for Sinclair to arrive.

He appeared at ten o'clock on the dot, wearing a quaint bowler hat and carrying a black case in his hand. Directing Jane to a stool, he took off his hat and put the case on the counter. He opened it to reveal a tool that looked like a cross between a gun and a very large hypodermic needle. Jane stared at the ominous tool and chewed her lip.

"It's not so terrible," Sinclair assured her. "This is an ancient art form, and the procedure is perfectly safe." He explained how the needle of his electronic tool would penetrate the dermis layer of her skin and leave a deposit of black ink. Holding up a stack of gauze bandages, he said, "There will be some bleeding. It's perfectly normal so don't be alarmed."

Jane couldn't tear her gaze from the tattoo machine. Finally, she took several gulps of wine, unbuttoned her blouse, and made a hurry-up gesture. "Let's do this before I lose my nerve."

Sinclair laid out a stencil of an owl clutching a scroll in

its talons, an ink cup, latex gloves, alcoholic prep pads, and several other items. Handing her a prep pad, he asked her to clean the area to be tattooed. When she was done, he placed the stencil against the swell of her left breast and transferred the owl design. Picking up the tattoo machine, he raised his brows. "Ready?"

"Ready," she said, steeling herself against the imminent pain.

"Try to refrain from moving." Sinclair said and turned on the machine.

At the first sharp sting, Jane nearly jumped, but she squeezed her eyes shut and managed to stay still.

"See? It's not that bad," Sinclair said.

"No," Jane replied through gritted teeth. "If you don't mind being pricked by a needle over and over again." Jane wanted to talk about something, anything, to keep from focusing on the small stabs of pain. "I've been thinking about *Lost Letters*," she said. "If both Alice Hart and Desmond Price figured out that Adela Dundee sent a manuscript to Percy Steward, then won't others come to the same conclusion?"

Sinclair kept his eyes fixed on his task. "It's very possible, Miss Jane, but nothing to lose sleep over. Such individuals are more than welcome to book rooms, pay for meals, and spend countless days searching for the manuscript. When they try to enter staff-only areas, we'll be watching. When they ask odd questions or make strange requests, we'll be listening. If they cross the line, we'll politely ask them to leave. If not, we'll present them with their bill at the end of their stay and tell them we hope they'll come back soon."

Jane wanted to laugh, but a particularly sharp jab from Sinclair's needle squelched the laughter before it could leave her mouth. "I suppose there are other clues hinting of our secret collection. In other letters, books, or snippets of poetry."

"Indeed," Sinclair said. "After all, the collection has existed for hundreds of years. It was once housed in your ancestral seat in England, but as the house aged, it became harder and harder to guard and several devastating thefts occurred. That's why Walter Egerton Steward had the manor dismantled and rebuilt here. He was able to buy a large tract of land in an isolated valley and add dozens of secret passageways, hidey-holes, and listening nooks to the original design. He did all this to help the Fins and guardians protect the secret collection. And yes, rumors about our treasure trove will continue to circulate, so we must remain ever vigilant."

When Sinclair finished his work, he turned off the machine, rubbed the finished tattoo with ointment, and then affixed nonstick dressing over her skin.

"Don't I get to see your masterpiece?" Jane asked.

Sinclair nodded. "In the morning. You can remove the dressing then. We don't want any bacteria getting in through your wound, because until the skin heals, this is a wound." He smiled. "Your red badge of courage."

"Can I take a shower tomorrow?"

"Certainly. Wash the area with soap and warm water and apply this ointment twice a day for three days. Your skin will probably peel. It will be completely healed in about four weeks."

Jane grinned. "I could do a big reveal during the staff Thanksgiving supper."

Sinclair's eyes twinkled. "That would cause a bigger stir than the time the two bellhops got in a fistfight over the wishbone." He packed up his equipment. "I'd like to review the paperwork on the man Gavin's chosen as his successor— perhaps during afternoon tea. The gentleman's name is Landon Lachlan. He was an Army Ranger until he resigned and began working for a private company. His job was to train other elite members of the military in developing their tracking, scouting, and survival skills. He's also good with animals and volunteered for years at a wildlife rescue center. It won't be difficult to place our trust in Mr. Lachlan, seeing as he's Gavin's relative."

"That's a relief," Jane said. "However, if he decides to join the Storyton Hall staff, he'd better watch out. Mrs. Pratt is very keen on Scottish men."

Sinclair chuckled. "This one's far too young for her. He hasn't even turned forty yet."

Jane was surprised to hear that Landon Lachlan was in his thirties. After all, the rest of the Fins were in their mid-forties and fifties.

"You need a contemporary, Miss Jane," Sinclair said as if reading her mind. "And this one's quite easy on the eyes. Light brown hair. Bright blue eyes. Zero percent body fat. I imagine half the ladies in Storyton will be in love with him by the end of his first week on the job."

"Does he wear kilts?" Jane asked playfully.

Sinclair snapped his case closed. "I can't recall if that detail was in his dossier. I'll rush straight back to my office and reread his file." He winked at Jane, donned his hat, and departed.

On Saturday morning, Jane made the twins her famous smiley face pancakes, in which she created a mouth of sliced bananas, strawberry halves as ears, blueberry eyes, and a whipped cream nose. The twins loved it when she added an unexpected feature to the edible faces, so she gave today's pancakes a bacon mustache. After they devoured their food, she told them to watch cartoons until it was time for their archery lesson.

Jane took a quick shower and dressed in jeans and a camisole. She left her heavy flannel shirt on the bed until her hair was completely dry. Standing in front of her bathroom mirror, she pulled down the top of her camisole and examined her tattoo. It was healing nicely, and Jane could see all the finely drawn details. Sinclair had done an excellent job on the owl's features, and the bird's countenance reflected strength and wisdom.

"Mom!" cried Hem from the doorway. His eyes were as wide as saucers.

Fitz shouldered his brother aside and gaped. "Is that *real*?"

Letting her camisole fall back into place, Jane turned to her sons and scowled. "I thought you were watching cartoons."

"We were, but Fitz changed the channel," Hem said. "And then he put the clicker down his pajama pants."

Making a mental note to spray the remote control with Lysol later, Jane tried to shoo the boys away, but they only came closer. "Is that a real tattoo?" Fitz spoke in an awed whisper.

Hem stared at Jane as if he'd never seen her before. "Is it a secret symbol? Are you like an Avenger or something?"

Fitz drew even closer. "Or one of the X-Men?"

Jane knew she dared tell her sons only certain things about the Steward legacy, and while she wouldn't mention the secret collection, she didn't think she was taking much of a risk in explaining the owl on her chest. "I got this tattoo as a reminder that being a Steward means that it's our job to protect Storyton Hall and everything in it. Uncle Aloysius and Aunt Octavia would like us to help them with this very important task. The three of us are going to train our bodies and our minds so we can be prepared in case we ever have to face someone like Lizzie again. I'm not saying that will happen, but we need to be ready. Butterworth, Sinclair, Sterling, and the new man Gavin hired will train us. Does that sound okay to you both?"

"That's why we're practicing archery and stuff?" Hem asked when she was finished. "Because we're Stewards too?"

Jane nodded.

The twins exchanged looks of wonder and delight.

"That's cool," Fitz said.

"Some of it will be," Jane agreed. "But it'll also be hard. Now we'd better get going. Sterling will be here any minute." Jane ushered the twins out of the bathroom and finished getting dressed.

When she got downstairs, the boys were already clad in

coats, hats, and gloves. They stood at the window, keeping a lookout for Sterling.

"Mom's a superhero," Fitz whispered.

"I know," Hem said in a hushed tone. "And she's *our* mom!"

The twins puffed out their chests with pride.

Jane heard the sound of the Gator's engine outside, and her sons raced to the front door. She stood at the bottom of the stairs for a long moment, smiling widely and touching the tender spot on her chest.

"Their Story is Our Story." As she spoke the motto of Storyton Hall, she thought of all the guests who'd come to the resort in the future. Some would undoubtedly have nefarious purposes, but the majority would be searching for a beautiful and tranquil place where they could read for hours on end. And Jane would be happy to show them to a reading room and to watch their faces light up as they selected one of Storyton Hall's thousands of books.

"As for me?" she murmured, reaching for her coat. "My next chapter has just begun."

Dear Reader,

Thank you for spending time with Jane Steward, her family, the quirky merchants of Storyton village, and the devoted staff of Storyton Hall. Jane and Company will return with the next installment in the Book Retreat Mysteries, Murder in the Paperback Parlor. *When a troupe of romance writers and devoted readers book the resort for their annual conference, Jane believes her biggest difficulties will be keeping her female staff members from swooning during the male cover model contest. Instead, Jane learns that a pretty face and flowery words can mask a wicked heart. And when a body is found in the Jane Austen Parlor, she must solve this literary murder with alacrity if she wants to save the guests, her loved ones, and the treasures hidden within the walls of Storyton Hall from peril.*

Until you're able to visit Storyton Hall again, I'd like to recommend another book-loving, mystery-solving ensemble. Olivia Limoges and her friends, the Bayside Book Writers, live in the quaint, coastal town of Oyster Bay, North Carolina, and are deeply devoted to the written word. In the next installment of the Books by the Bay Mysteries, Lethal Letters, *all is peaceful in their seaside paradise until a time capsule is discovered. When the lid is pried off the battered lead box, a secret escapes—a secret that will change the lives of Oyster Bay's inhabitants forever.* Lethal Letters *is available for purchase.*

For a taste of what's in store for Olivia and the

Bayside Book Writers in Lethal Letters, *please enjoy the first chapter of the novel. And as always, thank you for supporting cozy mysteries.*

Yours,
Ellery Adams

Time will bring to light whatever is hidden; it will cover up and conceal whatever is now shining in splendor.

—HORACE

Olivia Limoges rolled the newest edition of *Bride* magazine into a tight cylinder and brought it down onto the counter with a resounding *thwack!*

"Enough! I don't want to hear another detail about your upcoming nuptials. You've turned into a groomzilla, Michel. Your obsession over the venue and your tux and the guest list is driving everyone in this kitchen insane." She pointed at a sous-chef who'd paused in the act of chopping onions to wipe his eyes with a dishtowel. "That man is weeping, for heaven's sake."

"He always cries when he—" the head chef of the Boot Top Bistro began.

"It started with the tulips, right?" Olivia directed her remark at the sous-chef. "Michel's supposed to be creating the finest cuisine in coastal North Carolina, but his soufflés are falling and his sauces are burning while he frets over whether to have blush-colored tulips, hot-pink tulips, or lavender tulips at his reception." She turned back to Michel. "I will take a meat cleaver to the next tulip you bring into this restaurant, do you hear me?"

Michel opened his arms in a gesture of helplessness. "I want everything to be perfect!"

"Last summer you said that you wanted a simple, intimate affair. But your plans have grown grander and more absurd by the month. I wouldn't be surprised if Shelley were ready to call off the whole thing."

At the mention of his fiancée's name, Michel's petulant look instantly vanished, and he smiled widely. "She told me that I could have all the pomp and circumstance I wanted. Unlike you, she understands that I've waited my whole life for this day and I want—"

"White doves and stretch limos?" Olivia sighed. "This is about you and Shelley. It's a joining of two lives. A chance for the people who love you to share in your happiness. You don't need a chocolate fountain for a wedding to be beautiful. You only need you, the woman you want to spend the rest of your life with, and a few carefully chosen words."

Michel swiveled to face the rest of the kitchen staff. "Have I gone off the deep end?"

They nodded in unison.

"Has my food suffered?"

The line cook exchanged a nervous glance with the sous-chef. Michel had a fiery temper and it was clear that no one wanted to say that his cooking hadn't been up to its usual standards. But Michel caught the furtive glance and instantly hid his face in his hands. "*Mon Dieu!* I have betrayed my art. And for what? Monogrammed napkins? Embossed invitations?"

"And tulips," Olivia added. She put a hand on Michel's forearm and gave it an affectionate squeeze. She was used to his theatrics, but this wasn't a good time for one of his meltdowns. They needed to review the possible menus for the Historical Society benefit dinner before showing them to the president. "You can stop looking around for the perfect venue. The Boot Top is your kingdom, Michel. Its kitchen is your beating heart. Have the reception here. I'm sure your colleagues would be delighted to prepare the food for your wedding feast."

The kitchen staff murmured its agreement.

Michel looked at them and sniffed. "Really? You'd do that for me?"

"Of course we would," Olivia answered on behalf of her staff. "That just leaves the cake."

Michel brightened. "Shelley and I always planned on making our own cake. I'll do the baking and she'll do the decorating. After all, no one can hold a candle to her when it comes to sweet confections."

Olivia thought of the St. Patrick's Day display she'd seen in the display window of Decadence, Shelley's desserterie. Candy coins wrapped in gold foil spilled from a cauldron of solid chocolate. There was a forest of four-leaf-clover lollipops, marshmallow clouds, and a rainbow of jelly-fruit slices. Fondant leprechauns perched atop grasshopper cupcakes or cartwheeled across the frosted surfaces of crème de menthe brownies. "Shelley is truly gifted," Olivia said. "And so are you. Can we talk about the menu for the benefit now?"

"Only if you promise to come with me to the First Presbyterian church before I get started on the dinner service," Michel said. "I promised to swing by with a copy of our program."

"I thought you didn't want a church wedding."

Michel shrugged. "*Maman* does. And since I am her only son, I did what she asked." Straightening, Michel barked out orders to the kitchen staff and they jumped to obey. Scooping the bridal magazine off the counter, he held it aloft as if it were a torch. "I am back, my friends. And I apologize for being so distracted. That's over now. You have my word as a gentleman and a chef. Spring is upon us and we will be busier than ever. We must uphold the reputation of the Boot Top Bistro. We must dazzle every diner!"

Smiling, Olivia grabbed her head chef by the elbow.

"Let's talk in the bar and then we'll stop by the church. Which Saturday did you book?"

"I chose a Monday," Michel said. "The Boot Top is closed on Mondays. You won't lose any business and neither will Shelley. She and I will take Tuesday off and be back in the kitchen on Wednesday."

Olivia poked her head into her office and saw that her standard poodle, Captain Haviland, was fast asleep. She smiled indulgently and then led Michel through the dining room into the bar. "Why rush back to work?" Olivia asked. "What about your honeymoon?"

Michel sank into one of the leather club chairs. "We'll go when the tourist season is over. Mid-October maybe. I want to take Shelley to Paris. We can visit our old haunts from culinary school and then travel to the Riviera, visiting vineyards as we make our way south. It's past time we updated the Boot Top's wine list." Michel gestured at the polished wood bar. "Not that Gabe isn't the finest tender in town, but his palate isn't sophisticated enough to be the restaurant's sommelier."

"Ah, the sacrifices you make for your job," Olivia teased and placed a folder on the small table dividing her chair from Michel's.

Michel reached out and grabbed her hand. He tapped the platinum band embedded with dark sapphires on her ring finger, and said, "I'm not the only person in the room who should be making wedding plans. And yet, I hear nothing of yours. Why not? What are you waiting for, *ma cherie*?"

Pulling her hand free, Olivia straightened the printed menus in the folder. "Mine will be a very quiet affair. Justice of the peace and a champagne toast. That's all. There's not much to organize."

Michel fixed her with an intent stare. "Then why aren't you already married? Are you cohabiting or is the chief still living out of a drawer? I know how much you treasure your independence, Olivia. But when you said yes, you gave up your old life."

Olivia felt her cheeks grow warm. "It's complicated. When he's on duty, the chief needs to be close to town, so he stays at his place. My house is too far out. If there's a police emergency . . ." She shrugged, letting Michel reach his own conclusions. "And I don't like to spend the night in his house. His wife still has a presence there. She picked out the wallpaper and the towels, the dishes and the furniture. It's her home. It's a monument to their life together. Not to mention that it's too far from the water."

"We can't have our resident mermaid living away from the beach. Your scales would dry out." He gazed at her fondly.

Olivia shoved a printed menu under Michel's nose. "Let's focus on these menus now, shall we?"

An hour later, Olivia pulled her Range Rover into a private lot belonging to the First Presbyterian church and opened the car door for Haviland. As he jumped out of the back seat and Michael alighted from the front, Olivia studied the Gothic Revival building, taking in its blocks of somber gray stone, pointed arches, and towering spire. It was one of the most imposing buildings in all of Oyster Bay.

A jarring mechanical noise erupted from inside the church. Michel winced and Haviland started barking.

"Is that a jackhammer?" Michel shouted.

"Maybe they're tuning the organ," Olivia yelled.

Haviland's barking increased in volume, and he retreated several steps. Olivia laid her hand on the poodle's head and tried to calm him, but he was clearly discomfited by the noise.

"I'm putting Haviland back in the car," she told Michel. "Go on. I'll catch up."

As soon as Haviland was safely inside the Range Rover, he stopped barking and stretched across the back seat. Olivia gave him a chew stick, promised she wouldn't be long, and crossed the parking lot. Drawing closer to the church, she noticed several commercial vans and a pickup parked near the building. A man in a hardhat came out of a door in the church's west wall and began rummaging through an aluminum toolbox in the bed of the pickup. After retrieving a pair of safety goggles and a crowbar, he disappeared into the church again.

Olivia found Michel in the sanctuary standing next to a man wearing khakis and a blue dress shirt. Mercifully, the hammering sound had stopped.

Michel introduced her to Pastor Jeffries.

"Please call me Jon," the man said, offering Olivia his hand. His grip was warm and firm. Olivia liked both his handshake and his friendly brown eyes. They reminded her of Haviland's. "I can't believe we haven't met before," the pastor said. "Ours is a small town, but our paths somehow never crossed." He smiled. "I guess I'm surprised because you're very active in community projects. Your name pops up all the time in the paper."

Michel put an arm around Olivia's shoulders. "My boss wrangles money from Oyster Bay's upper crust. You work in the trenches, Pastor. You probably aren't involved with the same charities."

"I suspect you're right," the pastor said amiably. "Until now. Miss Limoges and I are both supporting the upcoming Historical Society benefit. Not only is the Historical Society our next-door neighbor, but the society's founding family, the Drummonds, have been devoted patrons of this church for the past century."

Olivia let her eyes wander up the center aisle to the altar and then over the polished pews to the stained glass windows. The colored glass was cracked in places and coated with a film of grime, making it hard for the light to pass through. Watery yellows and dull oranges spotted the sanctuary's red carpet and Olivia wondered if the windows could withstand the force of the work being done in the room to the left of the vestibule.

Pastor Jeffries followed the direction of her gaze. "I was

just telling Michel that we're in the middle of a minor construction project. At least, it started out as a minor project. The plan was to turn the cloakroom into a comfortable space for prayer and counseling, but as often happens during a renovation, the contractor and his crew encountered problems. Water damage, rotted floorboards, issues with the wiring. They've dug right down to the foundation stone." His eyes slid toward the large brass cross on the altar. "I spent half the morning praying that there wouldn't be any more surprises."

"Pastor Jeffries!" a man called from the doorway dividing the vestibule from the chapel. "You'd better come look at this. We found something buried in the wall."

"And people think the Lord lacks a sense of humor." The pastor winked, told his guests he'd return in a moment, and strode down the center aisle.

Michel sighed. "I hadn't pictured drop cloths and plaster dust as part of my wedding day décor."

"I'm sure the job will be completed by then." Olivia ran her fingers along the back of a polished pew. The sanctuary smelled of beeswax and lilies. Overall, it was a pleasant space. The walls were a soft white, the velvet cushions in a deep cranberry hue covered the pews, and the entire room was illuminated by rows of brass chandeliers suspended from the high ceiling. Olivia swiveled, taking in the second-floor balcony and the gleaming organ pipes. Everything was simple, elegant, and clean. Aside from the Easter lilies grouped around the altar, the only adornment in the entire sanctuary was the windows. "This is the oldest church in Oyster Bay," she told Michel. "Think of all the couples that have walked up this aisle. All the music that's been played. How many secret hopes and fears have been whispered into folded hands. This place is redolent with history."

Sinking into a pew, Michel frowned. "I think it's gloomy, but my mother will love it. It speaks of Old World Europe."

"That's not gloom. It's patina." Olivia wandered over to

the windows on the east wall and studied the biblical scenes. Though she'd only attended a handful of church services throughout her life, she recognized most of them. She didn't tarry too long before Mary and Joseph, the Nativity, or Christ cradling a lamb. After noting more cracked glass and sagging lead in the John the Baptist window, she moved to the west wall. She liked the Daniel in the lions' den window and paused to take in the detailed faces of the slumbering felines. Again, she saw damage to the glass, lead, and putty.

"I'd think these would be more important than the cloakroom renovation," she murmured to herself and walked by a window featuring a young boy holding a harp. In the next scene, she admired how the glass artist had used pieces of green, orange, and red glass to create a burning bush. But she didn't linger, finding that she was inexplicably drawn to the last window.

This one, which was in the worst condition of all, portrayed a woman and child. The child, a girl with an ageless face, gazed forward. Her expression was both hopeful and serene. Most of her body was enfolded in the woman's gown and as Olivia edged closer, she realized that it wasn't a gown but a feathered wing curving protectively around the girl. The angel was in profile, her eye closed and her cheek pressed against the girl's cheek. Olivia could almost hear her whispering words of comfort into the child's ear. The more she stood and stared, the more the angel looked like her mother.

Hesitantly, Olivia placed her fingers against the glass and traced one of the white flowers hanging near the angel's outstretched hand. The girl's small hand rested in the angel's cupped palm and Olivia had the urge to lay her own hand on top of theirs. She wanted to go where they were going, to see what lay beyond the curtain of dogwood blossoms.

"She's a guiding angel," Pastor Jeffries said from behind Olivia, causing her to start. "Sorry. Didn't mean to creep up on you." He flashed her a sheepish smile. "This is my favorite window."

Olivia pointed at the angel. "Her face is completely two-dimensional and yet she reminds me so much of my mother."

The pastor nodded. "Everyone recognizes a special woman in her. A mother, sister, daughter, wife, nurse, teacher."

"Can the windows be restored?"

"At great cost, yes. We'll have to raise more funds, but I have faith that we'll get the money. The capital campaign has been eaten up by all the problems we've run across with our current project, so it's fortunate that we have a devoted bene-factor." Pastor Jeffries didn't seem overly bothered by the setbacks. In fact, he looked quite cheerful. "It seems we were meant to dig deeper than we'd originally intended. The men have just discovered a large lead box buried above the foundation stone."

Olivia was immediately intrigued. "How big is it?"

"About the length of my arm. Let's just hope the first pastor didn't bury his faithful hound inside." With a boyish grin, he waved Michel over and explained what was happening. "The men have asked me to open the box. It could be empty, and I don't want to interrupt the staff unless there's something worth seeing, so I'll grab the digital camera from my office and let them finish Sunday's program. You two are welcome to watch if you'd like."

Michel's eyes were shining. "I'll serve as your photo journalist, but if you unearth a cache of gold, I might have to charge a hefty fee for my services. Weddings are ridiculously expensive."

Pastor Jeffries laughed and then gestured at the stained glass angel and child. "If there's anything of value inside that box, I'll use it to save our real treasures. I'm not supposed to put much stock in worldly goods, but I love these windows. I want to make sure the next generation can enjoy them as much as I do." He rubbed his hands together, looking like a kid on Christmas morning. "Be right back."

Too curious to wait for his return, Olivia and Michel headed for the vestibule. In the cloakroom, two workmen wearing hardhats and gloves stood, hands on hips, staring down at a battered lead box. A third was on his knees, scraping pieces of mortar from the surface of the box with his fingers. The men looked up when Olivia and Michel entered.

"Is it marked anywhere?" Olivia asked the man on the floor.

"I think there's a date stamped into the lid." He turned to one of his coworkers. "Hand me a flathead screwdriver, will you?"

With the tool in hand, he carefully worked its edge under the mortar. It gave way, coming off in large pieces. Brushing a chunk aside, the man maneuvered the screwdriver head until two numbers became clear.

"Looks like a one and a nine so far," the man said. "And the next number looks like a seven. No, it's another one."

At that moment, Pastor Jeffries returned. He crouched down next to the man with the screwdriver and watched, fascinated, as the last digit was revealed. "Nineteen seventeen. Wow."

"The beginning of World War One," another workman said.

"But not the year the church was founded," the pastor said, clearly perplexed. "This box was buried some sixty years after the original church was built." He rubbed his chin, his gaze distant. "There was a fire about that time. A bad one. I wonder if this was placed inside the wall during the reconstruction. I'd have to check with the Historical Society, but if there are relics of our past inside this box, I'll be calling Bellamy Drummond anyway. Let's open it and find out."

Olivia was thrilled that they wouldn't have to postpone the event for Bellamy Drummond. While she certainly approved of the Historical Society president's efforts to preserve Oyster Bay's past, Olivia found Bellamy's punctiliousness a bit overbearing. She was certain to ruin the excitement of the workmen's discovery by lecturing them in her rich, languid drawl on the proper technique for opening an antique lead box.

"May I have the honors?" Pastor Jeffries asked the man with the screwdriver.

The man passed him the crowbar and backed away. "Sure thing. Hold this straight edge under the lid and I'll hit the hooked end with a mallet. You want a pair of gloves? If that bar slips you could get a nasty slice."

The pastor shook his head with impatience. "I'll be fine." Handing Michel the digital camera, he lowered himself to his knees.

Olivia wondered if he felt less manly in his khakis and dress shirt than the workmen. With their tattooed forearms, dirt-encrusted jeans, and weathered faces, these men seemed a different breed than Pastor Jeffries. Next to them, he looked like a naïve and sheltered academic, though Olivia suspected that was far from the truth. Michel had told her that the pastor had been leading his flock for more than twenty years and Olivia could only imagine the things he'd seen and heard during that time.

Baptisms. Confirmations. Marriages, she thought as the workman struck the end of the crowbar with his mallet. *Memorial services and funerals.*

The sound of the mallet striking the metal curve of the crowbar reverberated around the empty room. *Clang, clang, clang.*

"Keep going," Pastor Jeffries said, sounding a little winded. "It's moving!"

The man hit the crowbar again. Without warning, the lid gave way and the sharp edge of the crowbar shot sideways, causing the pastor to cry out in pain. Olivia could see a jagged line of red appear on his palm. He dropped the crowbar and stared at his hand as the blood flowed over his wrist and dripped onto the floor.

Michel pulled a blue bandana from his pocket and offered it to the pastor. Having seen dozens of knife wounds over the years, he was unfazed by the injury. Pastor Jeffries fumbled with the cloth until Michel took it from him, wound it tightly around his palm, and tied it into a knot. "You'll have to disinfect that and you may even need stitches. If not stitches, at least a few butterfly bandages."

"I'll take care of it later. After I see what's inside." Pastor Jeffries glanced up at the man with the mallet. "I should have used the gloves. Right, Kenny?"

Kenny gave a noncommittal shrug and picked up the crowbar again. He inserted the bloodied edge under the lid, pushed down on the opposite end, and gave a satisfied grunt when the box top separated from the base with a low groan.

No one spoke as the pastor raised the lid with his good hand. He reached in and pulled out a sheaf of paper. It had yellowed with age, but otherwise, looked to be in perfect shape.

"It's a time capsule," Pastor Jeffries whispered in awe. "This is an inventory of the contents as well as a list of the contributors." He scanned the document. "Here's the pastor—my grandfather, if you can believe it—and a deacon. Also a physician. The head of the local school. And—" Suddenly, he stopped. "I should get Bell—, ah, Mrs. Drummond." He hurriedly set the letter back into the box and then glanced at the bright drops of blood of the floor.

Olivia was confused by the pastor's abrupt change in demeanor. He'd lost all traces of youthful anticipation. The pleasure and excitement had completely vanished from his face, and had been replaced by an emotion Olivia recognized all too well.

Pastor Jeffries's eyes had gone glassy. His body was rigid. Olivia didn't know why, but the pastor was suddenly, and very obviously, afraid.

And then he blinked. Pressing his injured hand to his chest, he forced his mouth into a tight smile, apologized to Michel for having to cut their visit short, and left the church.